I'M STILL HERE
A NOVEL

JON MILLS

DIRECT RESPONSE PUBLISHING

Published by Direct Response Publishing

ISBN-13: 978-1719528856

ISBN-10: 1719528853

I'M STILL HERE

Also By Jon Mills

Undisclosed
Retribution
Clandestine
The Debt Collector
Debt Collector: Vengeance
Debt Collector: Reborn
Debt Collector: Hard to Kill
Debt Collector: Angel of Death
Debt Collector: Prey
Debt Collector: Narc
Debt Collector: Hard Time
Debt Collector: Her Last Breath
Debt Collector: Trail of the Zodiac
Debt Collector: Fight Game
Debt Collector: Cry Wolf
Debt Collector: Oblivion
Lost Girls
Murder Games
The Promise
True Connection
And many more…

Dedication

For my family.

Part 1

Prologue

Thursday October 31, 1991

Blackmore, Washington State

The stranger took him.

Kara Walker burst out of the dark forest.

Her chest was on fire, her small fourteen-year-old body trembling. A million thoughts bombarded her mind, a chaotic symphony, too loud, too overwhelming. The labored sounds of Bobby, and Sam panting hard as she struggled to keep up only reminded her to quicken her pace. Kara ran faster, knees pumping like pistons.

"Don't look back or he dies!"

The masked abductor's terrifying words still echoed.

I don't want him to die, she told herself.

Kara stumbled forward heading for the glow of lights. Every fiber of her being screamed for help but words failed to escape her lips. *Why? Why did you have to try and impress him?* Tears spilled over, streaking her red cheeks. Her foot caught on an exposed tree root and her knees slammed into the dirt. Scrambling to her feet she pawed at her face smearing the skin with soil.

"Wait!" she shouted to the other two but they didn't

hear. Fear drove them on. Kara picked up her feet, pounding the ground hard. She fished into the single pocket on her torn Halloween outfit and tossed the pack of Marlboro Lights. She wished she hadn't taken them. It was a stupid idea. A bright full moon drooped over Blackmore as kids of all ages went house to house trick-or-treating. As she raced towards the streets full of families, her young fingers clung tightly to the golden Zippo lighter that had started it all.

Chapter 1

Monday, October 24, 2016

Peekskill, New York

Twenty-five years after the abduction, Kara Walker was still running. A habit deeply ingrained from her time in the academy. It gave her structure, routine and made her feel normal. *Normal.* She scoffed, ignoring deep-rooted bitterness. Life had been far from normal. How could it be normal after her brother was snatched from their lives, and his body never found? After the faces of her family had been plastered over newspapers and TV, and her brother had become synonymous with the missing children of America.

Although police eventually incarcerated a man six years later — to this day he'd denied involvement.

A cool October wind ruffled her windbreaker as she jogged through the wooded trails of Blue Mountain Reservation in New York. A gunmetal sky gave way to heavy clouds matching the way she felt. They'd forecast sunshine and blue skies, but once again got it wrong. She surveyed the crystal-clear lake, a picnic pavilion and a few early morning dog walkers. A flock of birds squawked overhead. One year earlier she might have registered the beauty of the morning, but as she fell into a steady pace, her thoughts were too consumed by the future. She'd been out since daybreak. Jogging had become a form of meditation, a means of quieting the mental chatter, and that morning there was more than usual. That's why when the phone in her pocket began buzzing, it was easy to ignore.

Within a period of twenty minutes she received three calls, by the third she slowed her pace and fished into her jacket. As soon as she saw the message, she slipped it back into her pocket. She knew what they wanted, and it was the last thing she needed tacked on to her day. She had enough to deal with without added pressure.

But as she turned the next curve of the trail, passed by an older man feeding ducks, and continued on until she reached the cement pathway that circled the perimeter of the lake, she slowed to catch her breath. Why was he calling again? He rarely called, it was always her mother. She took a sip from the water bottle and checked her watch. There was enough time to phone, and then she'd have to head in for the meeting. After finding a spot on a bench, she took a seat and dialed the number to check her voicemail. She placed the phone against her ear and observed a couple walking their golden Lab.

The voice messaging service's robotic voice kicked in.

"You have three new messages. First message." A few seconds of silence then it beeped once. "End of message." The second was the same. He hadn't bothered to leave a message so she expected the third to be no different. That was when her father's shaky voice came through loud and clear: "Kara, this is your father. Can you pick up?" There was a pause. "Hello?" More dead air. "Look, I know you are busy but it's important

I speak with you. I don't want to leave this as a message." Again more silence though now she heard him struggling to hold back tears. "I… I don't know to say this if you won't return my calls so I'm just going to say it as it is…" Another pause. "I need you to come home. Your mother died. She hung herself. She took her own life."

He hung up.

It beeped. There was no farewell greeting. No details regarding the when, or how, or even the funeral, it was just straight to the point. But that was him to a tee. It was business as usual. Soldier on. As the shock gripped her, she didn't want to believe it. Kara hit replay again and listened to it two more times. The second time was to check she'd heard him correctly, the third time was because it made no sense. Of course to others it would be completely logical. She could hear friends and close relatives already. *Grief can do that. A mother never gets over the loss of her child.* Kara sat there clutching her phone shaking her head in disbelief.

A splash startled her. Farther down the golden Lab had dived into the lake to retrieve a stick and the couple were arguing. In those few moments as the reality of it sank in, the world around her slowed. A bicyclist shot by, two elderly women walked past talking loudly.

Kara immediately phoned her father back. It rang six times before he picked up.

"It's me," she said.

His voice was low and tired. "Glad you could find the time."

She wasn't going to get into it with him, instead she stayed on point.

"What happened?" she asked.

* * *

The Bureau of Criminal Investigation division was located inside State Police Troop K Headquarters, one hour north of Peekskill in Salt Point, New York. A low-slung brown building that crouched at the intersection of Highways 44 and 82 had been like a second home after nine years as a state trooper. Kara felt a twinge in the pit of her stomach upon stepping out of her black SUV that morning. As a senior investigator for a department covering four counties, she wore her usual plainclothes attire as she headed in for the meeting with her BCI lieutenant. A cruiser rolled past her, and several more were parked outside. At the outset Kara already had a strong sense of where the conversation would go but in light of the events that had transpired she could no longer remain at the helm.

Inside the elevator, she tucked a strand of black hair behind one ear and checked her reflection, offering a strained smile to troopers as she stepped out and made her way down to Frank Stephens's office.

The heavy door was ajar, and he was on the phone when she knocked. He waved her in and put up one finger to indicate he'd just be a minute. She took a deep breath and remained composed and calm as she took a seat across from a desk that was immaculate. He, like many of those she worked alongside, was highly organized. She smoothed out her dark navy pants, and adjusted her suit jacket, checking for fluff before gazing around the office.

Stephens twisted in his seat, his jacket hung over the back. He was in his late fifties, with salt and pepper hair, a defined jawline and hard lines around his eyes. His shirts always appeared one size too small for him, making his square face red as if he was being choked.

Years of dealing with some of the worst of society, serial crimes, sexual exploitation, felonies, narcotics and child abuse, could take its toll. Most of the investigators she worked with were skeptical and jaded, and many found humor in the macabre as a sort of coping mechanism — Stephens was no different. He was known for having one hell of a temper. She recalled the first time she'd seen it in its full glory back when she was a brand-new trooper, and he'd been called in to introduce himself. She watched as he tore into a trooper over tardiness. One second he was bellowing and looking like he was one step away from a heart attack, and the next he was calm and joking. No one ever quite knew what they would get with him. Of course over the years as she transitioned from trooper to BCI, she saw a different side to him, or perhaps the years had changed him. Now she considered him a close friend, a colleague as well as her supervisor. One thing was for sure, he was a smart man and understanding.

"Right, I will be in touch. Thank you."

He ended the call and placed the receiver down. There was no greeting. No, how are you this morning? None of that mattered. In front of him was the envelope she'd handed in the day before.

"That was the DA's office," he said before leaning back in his plush leather chair.

"Let me guess, they want me reassigned before you accept my letter of resignation?"

"You know, Walker, they're only trying to do their job."

"So was I, so were the FBI and Putnam County

Sheriff Department. Unfortunately there are too many hands in the jar; there are too many political alliances, egos at stake and differences blocking progress. You and I know this case has been bungled from the start and I refuse to become the scapegoat."

"No one is trying to make you that."

She shook her head in disbelief.

"Have you seen the papers? Caught any of the news lately? It's my name that is out there as the lead detective on this case. We've already had two Putnam County detectives reassigned, another quit and now we have the DA's office preventing us from gathering evidence, simply because they don't want to accept that an affluent member of the community is guilty."

"That's not true, Walker."

"Of course it is. The parents can't get their story straight, they've failed three polygraph tests, and they have intimidated the DA's office at every turn in this investigation," she said.

"I know what you're implying but our job is to follow facts, not a theory."

"And we have for over a year and a half but the district attorney's office continues to mishandle the case. Besides, out of the times that a child has been found dead and the death occurred when the parents were in the vicinity, statistically, how often has it not been the parents?" He didn't respond to that so she continued. "It's been one uphill battle after the next, making it virtually impossible to thoroughly investigate and gather evidence because we've been hamstrung from the get-go. Search warrants have been denied, simple things like obtaining phone or credit card records have been refused. Evidence collected is gathering dust in the lab. They have outright dismissed or ignored evidence presented to them." She shrugged. "So where does that leave us?" She waited for a response but he stared back at her blankly. "I can tell you. It means that anyone who speaks out against the DA's office is quickly silenced. Which explains why others have quit, and false information has been leaked to the media regarding my role in this case."

"Now you're reaching," he said.

"Am I? Because today's papers don't agree." Kara shook her head and blew out her cheeks. "We shouldn't have to plead with the DA's office over basic investigative requests in order to get assistance with determining who was behind this ten-year-old's death. There has been more concern for how this plays out publicly than ensuring that those responsible are brought to justice. Frank, the case is compromised and the DA is compromised and it's because of these reasons and more which I've outlined in my resignation letter that I'm calling it a day."

Stephens leaned forward and clasped his hands together. "I don't get it. You've been one of our best senior investigators. Why not just take a leave of absence? Go spend time with your kid. Go visit family. Think it over."

"And let me guess, in the meantime you'll tell the DA's office that I was reassigned, is that how this works?"

He bobbed his head a few times, and she knew that meant yes. Forget what was right or wrong. It was all about saving face. If she resigned, the media would want to know. The narrative would change and the bureau and the DA's office would fall under heavy scrutiny. The case had already become a running joke on late-night chat shows, and fodder for the tabloids. The high-profile murder case of Adam Swanson had caught the attention of the media from the outset because the Swansons represented the perfect American family — wealthy, community minded, parents with prominent positions in the county, and their only child was set for life. What had begun as a family getaway to their lakefront cottage by Seven Hills Lake had taken a turn for the worse when they reported their child missing. Until the cadaver dogs arrived on scene nine hours later, the preliminary search had yielded nothing. Adam's body was eventually found on the vast property in a heavily wooded area, buried below a shallow layer of leaves. He'd been sexually abused and asphyxiated. What should have been a straightforward investigation spiraled into the convoluted and absurd as countless errors were made by the officers that initially responded. Now it was a circus of lawyers, shot-down requests and debates over what should or shouldn't have been done by deputies, detectives, family members and friends.

"We have to follow protocol," Stephens said.

"Then accept my resignation."

"It's not as easy as that. If it was anyone else, Kara, it would have already been done but I know you will regret it later. You've worked damn hard to get to where you are, and you've been a valuable asset to this department. I don't want you to regret that decision. Take some more time to think it over."

"I've spent enough time."

She squeezed the bridge of her nose. No matter whether they accepted her resignation or not, in a roundabout way he was implying the media would somehow get wind that she'd been reassigned by the department.

"All I'm saying is you are going to be reassigned. Whichever way you want to look at it the powers that be are calling the shots and for the sake of this case —"

She scoffed cutting him off. "The sake of this case? If this case is ever solved and someone is prosecuted, I think we both know it's not going to be one of the parents."

"We'll get to the truth," he added.

"Let's hope that truth doesn't lead you to prosecute an innocent person and the decision is based on evidence presented and not on where they're trying to push the investigation in order to appease the public."

He sighed. "Taking an abductor off the streets would appease them."

"We ruled out that theory," she said.

"That's debatable."

She scoffed. "Like everything else about this case."

He offered a faint smile and leaned forward. Silence stretched between them.

"Accept, decline, to be honest, sir, either way I have to step away from this investigation." She paused and her chin dropped. "My father called to say my mother has died. Suicide."

His eyes widened, and then an expression crossed his face as if he was wondering if her resignation letter had anything to do with that. It hadn't. She'd presented it several days before she received the bad news.

"I'm sorry to hear that, Kara. I gather you'll be heading home?"

"My flight leaves this afternoon."

"Listen, if there is anything I can do. Just..."

"I appreciate that, sir."

He looked down at the envelope in front of him. "Leave this with me. Go home. Be with your family. Think it over. We'll speak again in a week. If you still feel the same I will process your request." He tapped a pen against it. "However, from one friend to another, I think you'd be making a huge mistake. Regarding the investigation, I understand your concerns and I'm not blind to the challenges we've faced working with the family and the DA's office but you know as well as I do, we do everything we can, we gather evidence and try to determine if a person didn't do it, but if they won't confess, we have to place that suspect to one side while we search for more evidence or consider other alternatives, such as the abductor theory, and even then, we might not get it. The fact is, Walker, sometimes the guilty walk away free."

Chapter 2

Three years. That's how long it had been since the divorce. She and Michael had been on relatively good terms since the separation. They shared custody of their thirteen-year-old son, Ethan. He'd have him every other Christmas, on the March break, and every other weekend, as well as nights when she was bogged down in an investigation. Over the past year, he'd spent more time there than at her home. Despite the way their marriage ended, they had always been on the same page over how they raised their son. It was a joint effort and one that Michael took seriously. The SUV bounced up the curb into the driveway of his red-brick, three-bedroom home that he now shared with Laura, his new wife. In the time they'd been together, Ethan had never returned home complaining about her. He liked her, said she was funny and kind. On the few times Kara met her, it was awkward but Laura came across as friendly. Even though there were times she felt a twinge of jealousy that Michael had moved on with his life, she never brought it up and tried to remain polite.

That day she was there to collect Ethan after a long stretch of working the Swanson case. Unfortunately, he was now going to have to stay longer due to the funeral. Kara hadn't told them. Ethan had taken the divorce hard and although he didn't show it, there had been a few times he'd broken down, and blamed both of them. In the first year he'd acted up at school but once he came to terms with it, he just dealt with it the way any other child of divorce did.

With the engine idling she sat there for a minute or two watching them through the thin drapes. She'd often wondered how her ten-year marriage would have gone had she quit the department earlier. Her mother had told her that it wouldn't have mattered, that they would have eventually separated but that didn't stop her from imagining a different outcome.

Then of course there was the aspect of coming home to an empty house. It took her a few years to settle into the new way of living but it wasn't easy. Juggling her career and taking care of her son was hard enough when Michael was living with them, as he had his own career as an EMT, but throw a separation into the fold and it presented some unique challenges.

Even though Ethan and several of her co-workers had encouraged her to start dating again, the desire wasn't there. It hadn't been there in a long time and she wasn't sure why. It wasn't that she didn't like the idea of crawling into bed beside a warm body when she came off a long shift, but she just didn't think it was fair. Her line of work kept her out at all hours of the day and night, and even when she did finish a shift, she never clocked out in her mind. That was part of the reason why her marriage had broken down. She just couldn't switch off, and so it was only a matter of time before Michael started to feel their relationship was being neglected. Still, at thirty-nine she wasn't getting any younger. She figured if she didn't find someone soon, she'd lose whatever spark that had originally attracted Michael.

Kara pushed out of the vehicle, and headed up the snaked pathway to the front door. She pressed the bell and heard Ethan's voice. Michael answered the door. He was thirty-eight, short and stocky with mousy brown hair that was shaved at the sides. One look and he could tell something was not right. Behind him Ethan was crouched, and in the middle of tying his sneakers. He glanced up for a second, flashing a grin.

"Hey darling," Kara said. "You had a good time?"

He nodded but didn't say anything. Since he had turned thirteen, she barely got a nod or a grunt out of him. When he wasn't sitting in front of his computer he was glued to his phone so conversation usually amounted to two words — yes and no.

Michael thumbed over his shoulder. "Yeah, I took him fishing."

She nodded and smiled. Michael had always been good at getting him outdoors and away from technology. In the background Kara saw Laura walk past. She smiled, waved, then disappeared into the living room. She was the perfect trophy wife. Slender, young and apparently an expert chef in the kitchen. What more could a man ask for?

"Ethan, I need a chat with your dad."

He stopped tying and the smile vanished. Whenever she said that he knew what it meant. He pulled off his shoes and before she could explain Michael stepped out and closed the door behind him.

His brow pinched. "What's going on?"

Distracted by her kid's reaction she stepped back and looked across to his neighbor's yard, taking a second to reset. "My mother passed away a few days ago. It was suicide."

He ran a hand over his face and stepped down off the front step.

"Geesh. I'm sorry. I guess you'll be taking him with you to the funeral?"

"Actually I was hoping you could keep him for a few days longer."

He sighed. "Kara. I have work commitments."

"What about Laura?" she asked.

"Both of us work. I was able to get a few days off so we could have a long weekend but…"

"He'll be fine. As long as he has a key to the place."

"You want me to leave him here alone?" he asked.

"You said Laura works until five. I'll give you some more money for after school child care."

"But…"

"Michael, I wouldn't ask if it wasn't important," she added.

"Why don't you just take him with you? I'm sure he'd want to go to his grandmother's funeral."

"Under any other circumstances, yes. But my father isn't in a good state and I know it's going to be down to me to deal with her personal affairs. Besides, I'm…"

She snapped the red elastic band around her wrist. It was used as a form of therapy for anxiety. Ever since her brother had been abducted she'd had trouble focusing, sleeping and dealing with stress. For a while she was able to hide it in order to pass the testing for entry into the State Police but within a matter of years in the field it had returned. She'd now found new ways to cope. The elastic band was one, and the other was taking meds like Zoloft.

Michael glanced at her wrist.

He shifted his weight from one foot to the next and ran a hand through his hair.

"Do you know how it happened?" he asked.

"Details are vague. My father wasn't in the right frame of mind to talk about it over the phone. He said he found her in the basement hanging from the rafters. The funeral is tomorrow. I leave this afternoon."

"How do you feel?" he asked.

He'd been the first person to ask that. And to be honest, she really didn't know. Her relationship with her parents had weakened since Charlie's abduction. Both of them dealt with it in different ways. Although they were distraught for a long time her mother soon funneled all her energy into searching for Charlie while her father struggled to cope, retreating into himself and wanting to move on, with the belief that Charlie was dead.

She shrugged. "Tired."

"I got your message yesterday about you resigning. Did you go through with it?" he asked.

"I handed it in, whether they accept it or not is another matter. Stephens wants me to think about it. He says I haven't given it enough thought."

"Have you?" Michael asked.

"You know I have. Heck, I shouldn't have even got involved in that case to begin with."

She looked off and switched the conversation back to the matter at hand. "So can he stay longer?"

"Of course he can. You know that."

He stepped closer and Kara had a sense that he wanted to give her a hug so she stepped away. "Well I should get home and pack. I have to leave soon."

"Don't you want to see Ethan before you leave?"

Her mind was a whirlwind. She nodded, and he went back inside. A minute later Ethan came out, pulling the door shut behind him. He slumped down on the concrete step and fumbled with his phone. Kara took a seat beside him and they glanced at the neighbor's house. Michael lived on a beautiful street in the heart of Peekskill, called Bleakly Drive. Oak trees lined either side and arched over like fingers joining together. It was an up-and-coming suburb, a new subdivision that had been developed only a few years back. It was safe, which was all that mattered to Kara.

"When are you coming back?" Ethan asked.

She wrapped an arm around his shoulders and pulled him in close.

"In a couple of days."

"That's what you said, a week ago."

She sucked air between her teeth and sighed. "I know."

She never intended for her work to consume her but it had and Michael wasn't the only one who had suffered for it. That's why so many in her department were divorced. It wasn't a job that people could switch off from when they came home. The images, the interviews, the back and forth with lawyers drained her.

"Is it the investigation?"

"No, it's grandma." She took a second to swallow her tears. "She's passed away."

Ethan nodded, his head dropped. He hugged her. "It's gonna be okay, Mom."

She smiled. That was just like him. He was able to see the light in the darkness long before she could. Kara kissed her son on the head and fished into her pocket for some cash. "Here, take this. Make sure you listen to your father. No giving them any problems. I'll phone you each night, okay?"

"You don't have to do that."

"I want to."

She gave him one more hug, and he headed back in. Michael stepped outside.

"Have a safe flight."

"Thank you." She gave a strained smile, headed back to her vehicle and reversed out. Michael stayed on the step with his hands tucked into his pockets, and she was sure she caught Ethan glance out the window as the SUV pulled away.

Chapter 3

On Tuesday, one day after news of her mother's death, Kara arrived in Blackmore on Washington State's Olympic Peninsula. Blackmore was named after its founder, Henry Blackmore, and sandwiched between Forks and Port Angeles in Clallam County. She'd flown into Seattle-Tacoma International Airport, arriving late at night, and stayed in a nearby hotel. Then she rented an SUV the next morning and traveled the two and a half hours' trip into the city. Why they called it a city was unknown as it was more like a small town with only seven thousand citizens. There were even fewer back in 1870 when the town had grown from a remote collection of farms into what it was today — a timber town. As the SUV passed through Port Angeles, memories of taking day trips to the beach with her mother Anna and friends came back. She'd been there through all the highs and lows of growing into a woman; her first period, her first boyfriend, the breakup and the stress of exams. There was something very nostalgic about visiting the places they'd shared.

As she continued on through Olympic National Park, and was swallowed by thousands of acres of dense forest, it brought back the terror of that night. The claustrophobic feeling and fear of a stranger prowling the streets had set the whole county on high alert. It was one of the many reasons why she'd moved across the country as soon she turned twenty. Her mother understood, her father just shook his head with that same look of disappointment.

She thought things would change when they arrested Kyle Harris for the abduction of her brother, but it hadn't. While her father accepted the harsh reality, her mother didn't believe it. She wouldn't accept that he was dead, that her youngest had been taken. Whereas in the years after the abduction she'd thrown herself into campaigning, searching, holding candlelight vigils and being very vocal as an advocate for child safety, that all changed when a jury handed down the sentence of life imprisonment to Harris. Anna retreated and on the few times that Kara was able to pull herself away from her work in New York, she'd noticed a change in her mother. Finding out what had happened to Charlie had become an obsession.

Kara pulled into a truck stop a few miles from the outskirts of Blackmore. As she stepped out, the smells and sights of Olympic National Park overwhelmed her senses. The familiar scent of tall cedars, salty air, and dampness swung her back to her childhood. She groaned. Her head was pounding from a tension headache. She just needed a coffee, some Tylenol, and a few minutes of shut-eye before she continued on. It had been over five years since she'd been back. On the few times she'd managed to pull herself away from her work, she'd taken a vacation with Michael and Ethan. Her mother and father had only seen Ethan a few times over the past thirteen years. Although she wished he could have spent more time with them, her mother just wasn't in the right headspace, and talking to her father was like talking to a wall. Although he acted as if Charlie's abduction hadn't affected him as badly as her mother, that wasn't the truth. It was just different.

"What can I get you, darling?" a waitress said, snapping Kara out of a daze.

"Oh, uh, just coffee, black, and some whole wheat toast."

"Coming right up." She scrawled on her pad, smiled and sauntered away.

Kara fished into her handbag and pulled out some headache medication. She tossed two back with a glass of water then glanced out at the truckers as they came streaming in and filled up on gas. The long eighteen-wheelers were loaded with stacks of thick pine trunks. She'd often wondered if the man who'd abducted Charlie was a trucker. Had he been passing through? At the time, the FBI had created a profile of a white man in his late twenties to early thirties, a loner, someone who worked a low-skill job and probably had a low self-image. She'd never seen his face but his gruff voice had stuck with her. Even as she worked different homicide and abduction cases she'd always paid attention to the voice, wondering if he'd left Blackmore after the abduction, traveled to another state and continued his rampage of terror.

The bell above the door let out a shrill as three large truckers, overweight and in their early fifties, came in. White hair protruded from below dirty baseball caps. All three wore checkered shirts, and smelled like they hadn't taken a bath in several days. That was one thing she'd recalled — the musky cologne he'd worn. It was overpowering. They'd actually smelled it before they even saw him.

One of the truckers glanced at her, tipped his hat and they took a seat on the far side of the café. A composite sketch had been created years later, but that came from a witness who had come forward in the days and weeks after the abduction to say they had seen a suspicious-looking man staring at children in the nearby mall leading up to that night. Two kids had been approached and offered twenty bucks to help a man look for his kid but they'd refused and walked away.

Kara didn't carry around the old composite sketch of the suspect the way her mother had, that was because it was ingrained in her head. Still from time to time she would bring it up on her phone and look at it, but only on the days she was dealing with a suspect that made her do a doubletake. The truth was there was no telling who or where the perpetrator was or even if he looked anything like the sketch now. By now he would have been in his mid-fifties.

By the time the waitress returned with her order, the medication was starting to kick in. She rolled her head around as another wave of tiredness hit her. Two years of going like a bat out of hell had begun to catch up with her. Her thoughts were scattered, unorganized and instead of feeling in control as she had been for many years, she'd found herself bursting into tears for no reason. Of course she did that in private, away from the eyes of her colleagues or son.

Kara's phone started buzzing. She glanced at the caller ID, it was her father.

"Where are you?" he asked.

"About twenty minutes away, having coffee."

"Why?"

She shook her head. "Because I'm tired, Dad. I have a cracking headache."

"But you arrived last night."

"I didn't sleep well."

"Well hurry up because the wake starts in an hour. Burial is at two."

Kara glanced at her wristwatch. She'd been dragging her feet, making sure she arrived a few minutes before the wake because she didn't want to get into it with her father. It was always the same. It didn't matter how many times she phoned, it was never enough and visiting, well that had become a subject she wouldn't even go near. It didn't serve to argue with him as he never heard anyone except his own voice. She wouldn't have minded if he'd showed her some attention but in the few times she'd returned home he'd kept his distance, only coming out of his office when it was dinner. For all her mother's faults, and need to keep talking about what she'd recently discovered in the case, at least she showed an interest in what Kara was doing with her life.

"It's still at the funeral home on Creekside Drive?"

"Of course. I'll see you there."

He hung up.

Some families held the wake the day before the burial while others preferred to have it all in the same day. She had a feeling it would all be done in one fell swoop. She envisioned her father returning to his routine by the next day. To some it might have appeared cold, but that was just him. His life was like most from his generation. He'd learned a trade instead of attending college. He'd gone on to work as a mechanic for a local garage while her mother had been a stay-at-home mom until they were old enough for her to return to her job as a caregiver at a local nursing home. There wasn't a night he didn't come home with grease under his fingernails. She'd got used to the smell of oily blue coveralls, and orange-scented hand cleaner as he washed grime from his hands before taking a seat at the dinner table. They'd always had dinner promptly at six on weekdays, and five on the weekends. The regimen in his life had come from his time in the military. When he wasn't in his work clothes he wore jeans and shirts, always long-sleeved shirts. After dinner he would sit in a chair in the living room, with a cup of cocoa, and listen to the radio and no one was allowed to disturb him. Even after the Internet was found in almost every household in America, he'd still opt to tune into 55.6 FM. That was before Charlie was taken. In the years after the abduction he'd been the first to bounce back, to accept what he felt was inevitable — that Charlie would never return. Her mother on the other hand wouldn't entertain the thought. When she wasn't making flyers, speaking with locals in the neighborhood or canvassing the area for information, she would retreat to the basement and pore over information she'd collected from newspapers and her conversations with the county sheriff department. Some said that if it wasn't for her persistence, they would have never caught Kyle Harris. After the trial, her mother began to have doubts. Her doctor notched it up to stress; locals said it was grief.

"Anything else I can get you?" the peppy waitress asked.

"Just the bill. Thanks."

Kara tossed down a few dollars for a tip and paid up front before heading out. A fine rain started to fall. That was one thing she didn't miss.

* * *

Within ten minutes she was back out on the

highway, and twenty minutes later she was driving into town. The main thoroughfare cutting through Blackmore was lined with rows of small businesses and residential homes. For the most part it was filled with blue-collar workers — hard-working folks who knew the value of a dollar and would bend over backwards to help a neighbor. Several kids rode their bikes down the sidewalk, an elderly man raked brown leaves from his yard, and faded American flags flapped in the breeze outside nearly every porch. She stopped at a stop sign, hung a right and drove past an elementary school with kids chasing each other outside in the playground. As the SUV rolled past homes slowly Kara reminisced. She drove through some of her old stomping grounds and saw the street her best friend lived on, and the neighborhood where her first crush gave her a kiss. Beyond that was a playground that now held nothing more than an aged, rusted frame minus swings. Homes were boarded up; a convenience store she used to visit had been turned into a bicycle shop. So much had changed. Residents lined the sidewalks going about their day. She slammed on her brakes as a young kid darted out after a ball, and then was quickly whisked away by an angry father. A white-haired woman stared at her as she collected letters from her colorful mailbox. As far back as she could remember, she always had a sense that people were gawking and thinking the same thing — there goes Charlie Walker's sister. The missing kid's sibling. The one that got away. How sad. She didn't want their pity, and she quickly grew tired of being asked how her parents were doing. What about her? Didn't anyone want to know if she was okay? After all, she was still alive.

She veered right on to Creekside Drive and eased off the gas as she pulled up outside Franklin Funeral Home. It was a bland-looking one-story structure. The double parking lot was full causing everyone else to park along the street. Kara continued on, and finally found a spot on the opposite side of the road. Gravel crunched beneath the tires as she applied the brakes. She glanced at her face in the side mirror before pushing out and joining the line of people streaming in. Most she didn't recognize. Who were all these people? She couldn't recall her parents having this many friends. The few she did notice glanced at her with curious faces and strained smiles. Two of her cousins, Milly and Trish, approached and gave her a warm hug and offered their condolences. It was very surreal, as she'd only met them a few times at a family reunion. She scanned the faces for her father but couldn't pick him out. No doubt he was in one of the back rooms taking a swig from his steel flask, or arguing with the minister about what words should be said.

Several people were signing a registry book nearby, while others huddled in small groups chatting in low voices. It was her Uncle Rob, from her father's side of the family, that appeared to be in charge of the whole event. He was standing with his wife, Janice, and directing friends and relatives into the chapel where the casket was or towards the bathrooms. He spotted her from across the room and elbowed his way through the crowd. He was a short, pudgy man but with a kind face.

"Kara. My dear, I'm so sorry." He embraced her for what felt like an uncomfortable amount of time before stepping back.

She dipped her head.

Kara expected to hear that at least a few hundred times before the day was out. No one really knew what to say, especially when someone had taken their own life. Rob's approach was to change topic.

His eyes widened. "Wow, you have really grown up. The last time I saw you…"

"I was twenty."

He jabbed his finger. "That's right, at the trial." He shook his head and looked at the crowd before turning back to her. "It's good to have you home."

"Thanks."

"So what have you been up to? Last time I spoke with Anna she said you were an investigator within the New York State Police. Is that right?"

"It is."

"That's good. I caught some of the news about the Swanson case. Terrible. I think they're on the right track with it though. I'm certain it was one of the parents. Do you know if they are going to indict them?"

"Um."

Her mind was elsewhere, far from the case.

Before she could say anything he frowned. "I don't know how you do it."

"Do what?" She asked. Half listening, and half gawking around the room, she noticed someone she hadn't seen since high school — it was Bobby Evans and by the band on his finger, the two kids rushing around his legs and the scolding he was getting from Lisa Brown, it looked as if he was married. Gone was the full head of hair, and the swagger that had once caught her attention. It had now been replaced by a bald head, a goatee, and a dad bod. The years had certainly been unkind to him. To think she'd been into him. They locked eyes for a second, then Rob distracted her.

"You know, you working on those cases after all you've been through..."

She registered what he said and paused for a second before replying. "Someone has to catch these bastards, right?" Kara stared back at him with a deadpan expression.

He snorted, nodded then gripped her gently by the forearm. "Well look, welcome home. We'll catch up after the funeral. Your aunt can't wait to chat. I think your father arranged to have us back at the house for coffee and sandwiches."

Great, that meant even more awkward moments. All she wanted to do was pay her respects to her mother, attend the funeral and retreat from the crowds but that wasn't going to happen, at least not for a few hours.

"How's he been?" she asked.

He pursed his lips and screwed up his face. "Not good. The doctor gave him some meds to help but you know him, he won't take them and it doesn't matter what you tell him, he refuses to listen. Stubborn as a mule. Maybe you'll have some better luck."

"Where is he?"

"Probably out back having a cigarette."

Someone called out to Rob and he excused himself and disappeared into the crowd. After battling through an endless stream of friends and relatives on both sides of the family she eventually made her way into the chapel. Flowers surrounded the closed rosewood casket at the far end; dark drapes hung behind it and either side were two yellow glowing lights. There was no one else in the room. On top of the casket was a beautiful color photo of her mother from better days. The sight of her was overwhelming. Either side of the room were pews. Kara took a deep breath and walked up to the casket. Tears welled up in her eyes and she reached for a tissue to dab the corners. She stood there for several minutes staring at the photo. She was full of questions. Why had it taken this many years for her to give up? Why had she given up? Why didn't she reach out and ask for help? How could this have happened under the same roof as her father? She'd only spoken with her a week prior and there were no signs of depression. Sure, she got choked up over the topic of Charlie but that was to be expected. In fact her mother sounded optimistic, that was something that she hadn't felt in a long time. Kara shook her head trying to come to grips with her death.

There were so many unanswered questions.

She placed her hand on the casket and closed her eyes.

There were so many things she wanted to ask her but it was too late. Kara turned her head slightly at the sound of a shuffle to find her father approaching. He smelled like cheap cologne, as if he'd sprayed it on heavy to mask the stench of the alcohol. He didn't look at her but just stared at the coffin with an absent look in his eyes.

"You think she would have liked the flowers?" he asked.

"I think so."

"I couldn't decide between white carnations or yellow roses, so I went with both."

She nodded. "I'm sure she would have been okay with either." Kara took a deep breath. "How are you?"

There was a moment before he replied. "Well I still

haven't finished building that window seat. And there's a leak coming in somewhere in the basement."

It was typical. Instead of spilling how he really felt he hid behind unfinished projects. Her mother had been pleading for years to have him build a window seat. He'd started but like everything in his life, it fell by the wayside.

She sighed. Silence stretched between them, then he did what he usually would when he felt uncomfortable — he would turn the tables.

"How's things with you?"

Kara shrugged. "Where do I begin?" She explored the depths of the chaos inside her head. It was just a swirling mass of disconnected thoughts tied together by nothing more than a thin veil she called her life. As much as she judged her father for holding back, she was equally guilty of only telling people what she thought they wanted to hear. "I'm still taking the pills if that's what you're asking."

He nodded. "I know someone that can help."

She scoffed and shook her head. Instead of responding to that she took a page out of her father's book and flipped the conversation back to him.

"I'll be here for a couple of days, so I can give you a hand with boxing up mom's things, clothes, and whatnot, if you want?"

"That would be good."

"Yeah?"

"Um. Well. Maybe we should hold off, just for a week or two until I can..." He trailed off and she could tell he was still in the thick of shock. Charlie had been a different case completely. Within a year he wanted his room cleared out, and clothing given to Goodwill. He'd even been the one to try and get her mother to go through his room but she wouldn't. It was too hard. Right up until the day she died, she hung on to the hope that he would return. That's why they hadn't moved to another home, or touched his room.

"Sure. Not a problem," Kara replied.

"Everyone is coming back to our place for a bite to eat. You hungry?"

His questions seemed so off-the-wall but she was used to it.

"A little." She paused. Nothing but silence before she continued. "Well, I should go and see Auntie Janice and see if there's anything I can do to help."

"Help. Right," he muttered.

She turned to leave.

"Mom would be pleased you came. I'm glad you were able to fit it into your busy schedule."

Kara caught the sarcasm but let it slide.

Chapter 4

Later, a light rain fell over the crowd beneath a brooding sky as they gathered in Blackmore Cemetery. The muddy ground had turned into quicksand sludge and caked the bottom of everyone's pant legs and shoes as they made their way to the final resting place of Anna Marie Walker. Kara pulled at her tailored dark raincoat, and held an umbrella as a minister stood at the foot of the rosewood coffin supported by a hydraulic frame rig over a freshly dug grave. She stood beside her father who smelled of bourbon, and Camel cigarettes. Every few seconds he would tug at his shirt collar, and adjust his black suit. Uncle Rob and Janice were across from them with their three kids. To the right of them was her mom and dad's therapist, Lloyd Benson, a middle-aged man who had been their lifeline through the nineties. His chin was dipped, wearing what looked like an expression of failure. To his right was Barbara Stein, late sixties, a large woman that hid her heavy frame below loose-fitting clothes. She'd been her mother's hairdresser and close friend. She would glance over from time to time but avoid eye contact. It was only then, as the minister went through a prayer, that she noticed tears roll down Rob's face. Out the corner of her eye she noticed her father gripping a red stress ball. It was the same one given to him by a friend twenty-five years ago. He scrunched it in his hand and clenched his jaw as if trying his best to contain his emotions. He didn't cry but then again she couldn't recall him being any different after Charlie was taken. Her father had never been one to show his emotions at home, let alone in front of the public. However that could have been the result of descending into a Valium fog. She could hear the steady patter of rain on umbrellas and puddles, the religious words of the minister, and the gentle sobbing from relatives. Although her eyes welled up, no tears fell as Kara had practically drained the well dry the night before at the hotel. Now she looked on, feeling nothing more than a numb ache.

Death was painful in ways words couldn't express. It put a person's existence into perspective and brought all of life's so-called urgent matters to a grinding halt. Having been invited to many funerals over the course of her career by families of the murdered, she'd become accustomed to the finality. Death showed no preference; rich, poor, good, bad, young, old, religious or not. It didn't matter. When it was time it was time, and no amount of griping at how unfair life was changed it one iota.

She scanned the fair-sized crowd of dark suits and tried to put names to the rest of the sincere faces. It was a mixture of friends, neighbors and those who'd worked with her mother over the years; there was even the former sheriff of Clallam County, Robert Smith. He'd assisted in the case along with a number of detectives, FBI agents and special agents from the Washington State Patrol's CID division. He was the only one in attendance from law enforcement.

"Today we say farewell to Anna Marie Walker, beloved wife, mother, sister and cherished friend. We are here today to pay our respects and to show our love and support for the Walker family. Not only have we felt the loss of Anna's passing but also our thoughts are with the family through this challenging time. And let's not forget that we are here to give and receive comfort. Our hearts ache over the death of God's beloved child. It's human nature to want to understand why and maybe one day we will but for now God would have us lean on him and trust that all is as it should be."

He then began quoting passages from scripture. Each one as meaningless as the next, being as her father had given up religion the day he lost his son. It was done for her mother's sake. It was her wish. As he continued to drone on about the Lord's will, the sound of crunching gravel caught her attention as an old, rusted-up blue pickup truck with dark tinted windows pulled up on the rise of the hill overlooking the tombstones. Kara squinted through the downpour. The window moved ever so slightly but not enough to see who was inside. It idled for a minute or two, kicking out a large plume of white exhaust smoke, then drove on. Kara might not have given it much thought if it wasn't for her father eyeing it with a look of death and cursing under his breath.

"Mr. Walker, would you care to give the eulogy?"

Kara wasn't aware that her father would speak at the funeral. She'd barely managed to get two words out of him since arriving. He broke away from the crowd and took a moment to deliver a heartfelt speech about when and where he'd met his wife. He thanked her for keeping him sane through the loss of their youngest, Charlie. However, he didn't mention anyone else; even though Kara had practically taken on the job of a mother after the abduction because her parents weren't able to function. Neither did he mention Uncle Rob or Janice who stepped in to watch over her while they attended therapy sessions, nor her mother's numerous speaking engagements around the country to discuss the dangers for children. It was all about him. Once he was finished he melted back into the crowd. One of the cemetery groundskeepers moved forward.

As the minister wrapped up, he stepped back so the groundskeeper could switch on the hydraulics that would lower the coffin into the ground. Her mother had been adamant that she didn't want to be cremated. Something about fire and what if she wasn't actually dead? Kara couldn't see what the difference was. Being trapped in a box seemed a lot worse. Her father stepped forward and scooped up a handful of soil and released it over the top. Everyone else was invited to the do the same but being as the mud around the grave had turned into a mini landslide of gunk, only family members participated.

Watching the casket disappear beneath the earth brought home the finality of it all and Kara found herself beginning to break. Warm tears spilled over, staining her cheeks, salty and wet. In that moment memories of her mother rose to the surface. She saw birthdays, Thanksgiving, Christmas, trips to the beach, hugs, tears, her mother walking her to school, school plays, after-school baking, meals around the table, game nights, movies and pizza, it all flooded in one after the other along with a heavy dose of guilt. Why hadn't she phoned more? Why did she spend all her time working? Why did she choose to move so far away from Washington State? The whys never stopped even as the crowd thinned and she, her father and Uncle Rob were the only ones remaining.

Silence dominated except for the patter of rain.

As Rob laid a hand on her father's shoulder, in an instant the once-hard exterior that so often took over fell away to reveal the broken man buried beneath.

Thirty-nine years and it was the first time she'd seen her father cry.

* * *

By 1 p.m. that afternoon, everyone reconvened at her

parents' house just off Harmony Crescent. It wasn't one of the well-to-do areas in town, or even a new development. Nestled in thick woodland, and off one of the major throughways, the home was located in a neighborhood that was often used by kids for playing basketball. Occasionally a car would honk its horn and they would move but for the most part, people who lived nearby were considerate. The street was lined on either side with overhanging oak trees that seemed to reach out like gnarled fingers. A fifteen-minute walk from her high school, and only ten minutes from the spot where Charlie was taken, it held many memories, some of which she preferred to forget. It was an average American, two-story red brick home with a wraparound porch and enough room inside to entertain roughly eight dinner guests, any more than that and people would be chewing on elbows and have to spill out into the yard — and that was exactly what happened that afternoon. Fortunately the rain had let up, and a speck of blue sky was trying to peek out from under the belly of a brooding cloud. Aunt Janice took that as a sign of Anna smiling down upon them; everyone just offered thin smiles out of respect. Janice had always been like that — spiritual, that was. She could see Buddha in a piece of toast if someone burned it the right way. Still, she meant well.

Returning home that afternoon was bittersweet for many reasons. Stepping inside she expected to hear her mother's voice, feel the warmth of her hug and a kiss on the cheek. Instead it felt oddly cold, almost like it had in the days after the abduction. Until that night her mother had worked for Lakeview Village Retirement Home. Although her shifts varied, from what Kara could recall from her early years, she was mostly there when they came home from school. She was a woman given to good books, painting, home décor, baking and spending time with friends. But that all changed after the incident. She gave it all up, spending less and less time with friends, allowing the home to fall into disrepair, and instead funneled her energy into doing whatever she could to bring Charlie home. For a time it was like nothing else mattered or existed, including Kara. She was pawned off to her auntie's on the days when it was really bad. Her parents were so distraught and lost in grief they couldn't see they were losing the one child they had left. All Kara wanted was for them to reassure her that it wouldn't happen again. The only time she felt safe was when the police were at their home, it was part of the reason why she turned to a career in law enforcement many years later, that and the desire to feel a sense of control over what had felt so out of control.

Now as she wandered through the home, after six years of being away she noticed how much had changed. Piles of clothes ready for the laundry were still by the washing machine, dishes from previous nights remained in the sink, the trash can was overflowing, and the pride and joy of her mother's home — the yard was overgrown, and the flowerbeds contained only weeds and wildflowers. It was like both of them had given up or had only managed to do the bare minimum. Something about the picture wasn't right. This wasn't like her mother — sure, she had been spending more time looking into the case even after Kyle Harris was in prison, but her conversations on the phone seemed normal — at least she had never let on that there was a problem. And her father, well, he didn't answer the phone so anything she did know was filtered through her mother.

Within twenty minutes, it was a total circus in the house. Flowers were placed in vases and Janice set them down in various spots. Finger foods were handed out on her mother's trays, and the smell of cigarette smoke filled the house. Whatever respect people had for the dead went out the window once Uncle Rob started handing out glasses of scotch instead of cups of coffee. After that it was a burst of interaction. Everyone had something to say, and much of what was said was quickly forgotten. Her mother would have controlled the chaos as people traipsed through rooms pointing to photos and treating the home like a museum. Out-of-place laughter erupted in the kitchen, and before she knew it Aunt Janice had taken Kara by the arm and was guiding her from one group to the next, introducing her to complete strangers.

Then came the horde of relatives, young, old, in a wheelchair, in a baby seat. Chatter swirled around her rising and falling like a party. Relatives on her mother's side of the family would say how much she looked like her mother. Friends would ask how long she was staying. Cousins pushed their kids in front of her yakking about their natural talent of learning. Four people talked simultaneously as one man gave his best wishes through a tracheostomy speaking valve after suffering throat cancer. All around her she saw facial similarities to her mother. Someone held out a photo album and jabbed a photo of her mother from her high school days. And if that wasn't enough, Lloyd Benson slipped a business card into her hand. "It's been a while. My condolences, Kara. I knew your mother well. Your father said you're struggling. Call me. We'll talk."

Before she could reply he melted into the crowd and someone else took his place.

"Hi Kara, Matthew says you're an investigator with the New York Bureau of Investigation. My son is looking to get into that, maybe you can speak with him later," said a woman who she vaguely remembered as the secretary at her father's work. People swirled around her in a dizzying fashion. Too close. Too loud. Smiling. Teary eyed. She witnessed the full gamut of emotions as she bounced from person to person like a pinball. She could feel her heart pounding in her chest. Unable to take it any further, she entered the one area of the home that was off-limits due to it having been the place her mother had taken her life – the basement. As soon as she was behind the door she pressed her back against it and breathed out a relieved sigh. The noise of the home was muted by the thickness of the door. The stairwell was dark as she fumbled around for the cord. One tug and a yellow glow emanated at the bottom of the stairs and partially lit the way. The basement was unfinished. It was one of the many tasks on her father's to-do list that he'd never got around to. Kara swallowed as her heartbeat slowed and she made her way down.

The basement was spacious with concrete floors, exposed wooden beams, steel pillars and a workbench at the far end. Old tattered boxes lined the walls, along with a few pieces of old leather furniture; a couch, two chairs, and a thick mahogany coffee table that doubled as TV stand. In all the years she'd lived in that home, they'd never used it for anything more than storage until October 31, 1991. After, that it became her parents' central hub for keeping boxes of flyers, posters, buttons, T-shirts, folders with news clippings and candles used for vigils. She'd only ever been down there once in twenty-five years and that was when the home was overrun with law enforcement. She recalled finding her mother organizing flyers. There were some nights she didn't emerge from the basement until late in the evening, and even then she would return after having eaten dinner. Kara had come to resent the basement, and so to learn that was where her mother took her final breath made it even more unbearable to be in.

At the bottom of the stairs she stopped and gazed up at the wooden beams. Which one had it been? Had she used a footstool? What did she tie around her throat? Her imagination went there but quickly returned as she closed her eyes and pressed on toward the far end. The basement extended the full length of the home, sections had been divided off with the goal of eventually turning it into a suite for her father's mother but that never happened.

Kara ventured farther in, squeezing between boxes until she rounded a corner and turned on a second light. That's when her jaw dropped.

Chapter 5

Evidence. Theories. Connections. Three walls of corkboard covered in a cluttered mosaic of newspaper cuttings, missing posters, sticky notes, maps, and photographs of young boys and family members, along with a desktop computer, a printer and a laptop resting on a desk. Covering the desk were a couple of empty coffee-stained cups and a French press with dark granules covered in green mold that had formed on the surface. Kara walked into the midst of the room, turning slowly a hundred and eighty degrees. Her eyes soaked in the mishmash of images, handwritten scrawlings, clipboards, folders, stacks of paperwork, numerous colorful push pins, and red string connecting photos, locations and timelines in an intricate web that could have rivaled the investigation wall of the Swanson case. But this wasn't the Swanson case. *What the hell is this?* she thought. Kara was aware of her mother's advocacy in protecting children from abduction and abuse, she knew she was very vocal about the sex offender registry laws and aware she'd given her time as a member of the board of directors for the International Centre for Missing and Exploited Children but that was to be expected — so many parents of missing and murdered children went on to be involved in some form of public speaking but this went beyond that.

Kara heard heavy footsteps behind her. Startled she spun around to find Bobby Evans. Instinctively she placed a hand on her chest. "Damn it, Bobby, you startled me."

"Sorry," he thumbed over his shoulder. "I saw you head into the basement." He raised his eyebrows. "Pretty wild upstairs, isn't it?"

"That's an understatement."

There was a pause as they studied one another for a second or two.

"It's been a long time," he said casually.

She squinted and replied in a soft contemplative tone. "That it has."

"How have you been? You look well."

She breathed in deeply and glanced at the wall again before returning her gaze to him.

"Thank you. So do you."

"Hardly." He ran a hand over his bald head. He ambled forward, his eyes washing over the walls. "I'm sorry about your mother. She was a good woman, always kind to me."

Kara dipped her chin ever so slightly.

"Quite a setup, isn't it?"

"You knew about this?"

He scoffed. "Who didn't?" He continued to speak as he ran his fingers over the table and leaned in to look at the map. "Yep, she was a thorn in the side of the county sheriff department, and there wasn't a damn thing they could do about it." He cleared his throat still examining the map. "Do you know there wasn't a week that went by that I didn't see her out chatting to someone in town? Hell, she phoned me at least once a month, you know, to see how I was doing, but mostly to find out if I could recall anything more about that night. Even offered to pay for a hypnosis session. Can you believe that?" He turned towards her and rolled his bottom lip under his coffee-stained teeth. "I couldn't. Remember, that is. Can you?"

She stared back at him chewing his words. A flash of memories besieged her mind. Laughter. Halloween outfits. Swiping cigarettes. The feel of a Zippo lighter in her pocket. The anticipation of meeting Bobby. Childish attempts at trying to impress him. Then the woods, the darkness, the sick smell of cheap cologne, a flash of a steely knife under the light of the moon, and then a huge masked man followed by a deep booming voice saying to run. Tears and…

Impatient for an answer or just eager to continue, Bobby said, "I can barely remember what happened last month. Hard to think it was twenty-five years ago." He shook his head. "Your mom always thought he was still out there. She refused to believe that Kyle Harris was the man even though your father accepted it, and so did most of the folks in town. But he had a reputation, you know. Harris I mean. Some say the police just wanted to close the case, and he happened to fit the bill. Myself, I don't know. People think that because we heard his voice we should have been able to distinguish if it was him but the guy spoke through gritted teeth, or a scrambler, I think." He inhaled sharply. "Anyway, at least that's the way it sounded to me. What about you?"

"I try not to think about it."

"Yeah, probably for the best. I know I've tried to put it behind me but that night changed me, you know? It's like a part of me was taken that night."

He put into words exactly what she had felt too. That the abductor hadn't just taken her brother, he'd taken much more from them that night — their innocence.

For weeks after the event she didn't sleep in her bed out of fear that he would return and take her. She slept in her parents' room on a blow-up mattress and even then she didn't feel safe. For a long time she felt scared, wondering who would be next. But that wasn't the hardest thing to deal with, it was the guilt. She blamed herself for what happened that night. In many ways she was still out there in the woods, running.

Her thoughts were interrupted by the sound of a female voice calling out at the top of the stairs.

"Bobby, you down there?"

He rolled his eyes. "Oh great, she found me," he said in a low voice with a smirk on his face. "Can't get a moment's peace." He put up a finger and walked to the bottom of the steps. "I'm here, Lisa."

"What are you doing down there?"

"Chatting with Kara. I'll be up in a minute."

That response obviously didn't satisfy her as she trudged down the steps. "Millie has thrown up and I'm all out of baby wipes. I think we should head out now." When she reached the bottom of the steps she turned towards Kara and glared.

Lisa Brown, now known as Lisa Evans, had been one of the girls in school that had earned a reputation of having screwed practically all the guys on the football team. Of course they were all a step up towards getting with Bobby, who at the time had been one of the best on the Blackmore varsity football team. Lisa and Kara had never really liked each other. She had her own circle of friends and after word got out that Bobby had been in the woods on the night of the abduction, it opened up a whole host of questions and accusations. So it was no surprise that Lisa ended up with him.

She'd never really had any aspirations of getting out of their small town, and after Bobby knocked her up at the ripe age of nineteen that sealed the deal. Since then she'd become a baby machine and a stay-at-home mom. She was now in her late thirties; her thick dark locks that once attracted the boys were dyed blond, thinned out and looked like a rat's nest. She was also twice the size but motherhood could do that. The only thing that remained the same was her sense of fashion. She'd always been a brand-name gal. No doubt if Kara asked her what she was wearing she would have reeled off some brand like she was a celebrity on the red carpet.

"Oh, Kara." A look of fake sympathy crossed her face. Kara knew she was only here because of Bobby. Lisa looked her up and down with judgmental eyes, then she caught sight of the crazy boards behind her and her brow pinched. "My condolences on your mother. I never really had a chance to get to know her but Bobby said she was nice. Will you be in town long?"

"A few days. Just to support my father."

"We should get together for a drink, tonight," Bobby blurted out to the horror of his wife. He brought a fist up to his mouth and coughed. "Or tomorrow."

"Bobby!" she said in a reprimanding tone as if he didn't have a life of his own or couldn't meet up with an old friend.

He shrugged and screwed up his face. "What?"

Lisa noticed Kara was waiting for her response. She straightened up. "Kara has more important things to do than waste her time getting drunk with you."

"Actually, that would be nice," Kara said. "I mean having a drink. Not the drunk part." She anticipated her father would be two sheets to the wind by late afternoon and any chance of getting a normal conversation out of him would be next to zero, so going for a drink sounded right up her alley. It would also give her time to clear her head and maybe make sense of what her mother was doing in the days leading up to taking her life.

"See!" he said, his eyes bouncing between the two of them. "For old times' sake."

Lisa shook her head. "For all times' sake," she scoffed and turned toward the stairs. "Let's go, Bobby."

Bobby stood there looking slightly embarrassed. "I'll phone this evening, just in case you change your mind. No pressure."

"Sure," Kara replied.

"Bobby!" Lisa's high-pitched voice echoed.

"I should go. We'll catch up later. Really good to see you, Kara." He flashed a grin, grabbed a hold of the wooden railing and launched himself up three steps with all the zeal of a teenager.

"Yeah, same," she said offering back a warm smile. "Oh Bobby. You wouldn't know if Sam is still in town, would you?"

He ducked his head back down. "He's around. Works in construction. Off and on. He lives in Sunrise Trailer Park. I can dig up his phone number, if you want?" he said pulling out his phone and was just about to do it when Lisa's voice screeched like nails going down a chalkboard.

"Bobby!"

He rolled his eyes.

"It's fine. I'll get it from you later. It's not urgent," she said.

"Sure thing." He winked and smiled and bolted up the stairs. Kara heard Lisa giving him the third degree at the top before the door closed. In the silence of the basement she turned back toward the wall of crazy and sighed. It was one thing to know her mother had been digging into the disappearance of her brother, another to hear that she had been pestering the local sheriff department and locals in town.

* * *

Within an hour, everyone had left except for Rob and Janice. Her father Matthew was slumped in a chair in the sunroom with a glass of bourbon. He hadn't moved from that spot since returning from the funeral.

"Now you listen," Janice said. "We are only a phone call away. If there is anything you need, I expect to get a call, okay?" She gave her a hug and Rob cast a glance towards her father.

"I want you to know, Kara, that after you head home, I will personally keep an eye on him and check in every day. We don't want you to worry about anything."

"I appreciate that."

"And a word of advice. I would probably sneak that bottle away from him. His drinking was heavy before she died, he's liable to drink himself into an early grave if he continues the way he's going," he said.

"Noted," she said giving him a hug.

They were just about to head out when she said, "When did you last speak to my mother?"

Rob turned. "Saturday. We dropped by, Janice brought some of her apple pie for the evening."

"Good apple pie too," she added.

That was three days after Kara had spoken with her.

"And did you notice anything about her that was different?"

"What, like depressed?" Rob asked.

"Yes."

He shrugged. "Nothing. She was her perky self. In fact she seemed—"

"Optimistic?" she interjected cutting him off.

He took a step back. "That's a good way to put it. Very upbeat, and that's saying a lot. Your mother went through some dark times over the past twenty-five years and I think what she was working on gave her some focus, meaning and purpose for each day. Whether she was on to something or not, I don't think it matters. I mean I didn't agree with her questioning people after that monster was put in jail but she just couldn't seem to bring herself to believe that he was responsible. I guess she held out hope that Charlie was still out there, or when they found the man responsible he would confess."

"And Kyle didn't," Kara added.

"No. All these years and he's stuck to the same story of being innocent."

Rob shook his head, she could see the revulsion in his expression.

"Did she ever go see him?" Kara asked.

"I hope not," Rob said. "He deserved what he got. The police might have made some mistakes on that case but I think they eventually got the right man."

"And yet she didn't believe that."

"Nope." He inhaled deeply. "She hassled the department. Questioned the evidence. And got a lot of people's backs up in this town." He frowned. "I would have thought you knew this? Didn't she ever tell you?"

"No. The few times we spoke she was just curious about how I was getting on. She was very-tight lipped after the sentencing."

He sighed. "Probably didn't want to upset you. Bring old memories and whatnot."

She nodded.

"Listen, losing Charlie broke her heart. It broke all of us. But I think all the years of trying to find someone else led her down a path to nowhere. At least that's what I have to tell myself or I would go mad."

Kara looked despondently at a photo of the family on the counter. "I just wish she'd let me in."

"I think there was a lot that she kept from all of us, Kara. So don't be hard on yourself."

Kara ran a hand over her tired face. "At the time of her suicide, do you know who was the first officer on scene?"

"Someone from Blackmore Police Department. Not sure," Rob said. Rob looked at Janice as if looking for support.

Janice touched Kara's arm. "Hon, Anna loved you. Focus on that."

They hugged again and exited. She was quite aware that they were protecting her as much as her mother had been. That had been their role. They were like second parents to her through the time of the abduction until she left for college. Back then she hadn't told them of her aspirations to join the police, only that she was going away to study law. Kara leaned back against the door and stared at her father down the hallway. She walked into the kitchen feeling strangely unraveled. At the sink she filled a glass of water and downed it and tried to comprehend her mother's death and secrecy. Hoping to clear her mind she headed out to her SUV to get her laptop. She wanted to bring up the *Blackmore*

News site and find the first article that was released about her death. That would usually give the name of the officer who had attended the scene. She could have called the department but at this stage she just wanted to get a better understanding of what was said as her father likely wouldn't say, and she didn't want to add to his grief.

She brought in one suitcase and a laptop bag. Kara lugged it up the steps and paused at the top, casting a glance at Charlie's room. Kara placed everything down, and entered his room.

It had remained untouched for twenty-five years. Even after Harris's incarceration, her mother wouldn't let her father touch it. It was like stepping back to 1991. Everything was frozen in time. The bedspread was that of a twelve-year-old. The duvet cover had football players, the walls were covered in film posters from the late '80s, and a Washington State Cougars T-shirt was pinned above his bed. There was an acoustic guitar leaned up against the wall, bookshelves filled with little trinkets, music cassettes and a vintage camera, and it smelled like old gym socks.

A faint smile formed as Charlie's voice came back to her, telling her to get out of his room, and the times he'd borrow her boombox to record his favorite rock tapes.

She was about to walk out, when she saw a framed photo of her and Charlie. She picked it up and blew away a thin layer of surface dust. The shot had been taken at a school track meet where Charlie had come in first place in a two hundred meter race. He had a medal in hand, and Kara had her arm around him. Their mother had taken the shot. She remembered the scent of fresh-cut grass, and the cheers of spectators. It had stuck with her as her father couldn't make it because he was working.

Kara felt an ache in her chest and placed the frame back down before backing out of the room.

Chapter 6

The Dug Out was formerly called Terry's Bar — located just off Main Street, it had been a popular hangout that offered cheap beer and wings until the owner, Terry Manning, got busted for serving dozens of minors. Kara recalled the newspapers the next day after his liquor license was yanked and he was hit with 45 violations including sales to minors, failure to supervise, exceeding the maximum capacity and having locked fire exits. Terry and four of his waiters were arrested and charged with reckless endangerment, unlawful dealings with children, some as young as thirteen, and criminal nuisance. The absurdity of it all was he was still allowed to remain open to serve food, just not booze. It didn't go well after that. He closed up shop and the last anyone heard he was managing a bar somewhere in the Midwest.

Later that evening, Kara pushed open the heavy wooden door that fed into the bar. A wall of alcohol and the aroma of home-cooked fries brought her senses to life. It had changed a lot since the '90s. Gone was the old bar that had locals' names carved into it, the worn-out dartboard, the tacky foosball table, and the sawdust-covered hardwood floors where folks would drop peanut shells as they drank large pitchers of beer. In its place was a modern sports bar with lots of flat-screen TVs, polished floors, a rooftop deck, a fireplace lounge, two brand-new pool tables, and shuffleboard and old-school arcade games in a casual but bustling space.

There were about twenty tables and booths around the exposed-brick, crown-molding interior and down through the middle.

Bobby spotted her and raised a hand. He was seated on a stool at the bar tucked between a young couple and three old-timers. He'd said he would bring Lisa along, and would arrange to have Sam join them, but by the looks of it he was alone.

She squeezed past a group standing in the aisleway, laughing and drinking, and eventually took a seat beside him. She placed her handbag on the bar and looked across to 12 taps and a brightly lit selection of liquor bottles. She didn't recognize the busty brown-haired waitress who had the attention of men pretending to watch sports on the overhead TV.

"Looks different, right?"

"Like night and day," she replied gazing around.

"That flooring. Have a guess where it's from."

"It looks brand-new."

"They stripped it back and polished it up. It comes from the old high school gymnasium."

"Are you serious?"

He nodded, taking a sip of his beer and raising a finger to get the attention of the bartender. "What can I get you?"

"Beer is fine."

He smiled. "Lisa always goes for wine. I like a woman who isn't afraid of a few calories."

"I'm pretty sure it's not that far off."

He didn't respond as he was giving the gal the order. "Thanks, Shelly."

"So, is Lisa in the washroom?"

"No, she decided not to come. Kids and whatnot."

"How many do you have?" she asked.

He took out his wallet and retrieved a few photos of three girls and a baby boy.

"One, four, eleven, and my eldest just turned nineteen. Can you believe that? I mean where does the time go?" He took a swig from his bottle of Budweiser as the barmaid returned and placed a beer mat down, along with a napkin, and set a Corona on it for Kara. Some of the foam from the top dripped down the side creating a circle of condensation around the bottom.

"Can I get you a menu?" Shelly asked.

Bobby looked at Kara and she shook her head. "No, I'm good, thanks."

"Shelly, I'll take some fries," he said as the barmaid ambled away to deal with an unruly crowd down at the far end. "Lisa would kill me. She's always yakking on about me needing to lose some weight. Meanwhile she barely watches what goes in that mouth of hers." He glanced at her. "But you, I see you've managed to keep it off."

Kara nearly spat out her beer. "You always were direct." She set her beer down. "I run a lot."

"Right, with the police and all. I heard you were working on that Swanson case out in New York. Chasing serial killers. I didn't figure you were the type."

"Yeah, go figure."

"So why New York? I would have thought you'd want to be close to family."

She scoffed. "I guess I wanted some space."

Kara had moved to New York when she was twenty and took a law enforcement course at SUNY and majored in criminal justice. She worked a number of part-time jobs in security and by the age of twenty-two took the entrance examination for the New York State Police. The rest was history.

"Well that's certainly far away." He sipped his beer. "So did you ever catch the person responsible for that kid's death?"

"It's still an open investigation. It's tied up in litigation right now. Parents are suing and, eh, it's a mess. I'd rather not talk about it." She cast her eyes down the bar looking at the faces and wondering if she recognized anyone. "So what line of work are you in?"

"I'm assistant editor for the *Peninsula Daily News*."

She raised her eyebrows. "Nice. So you pick and choose what stories run?"

He smiled and took another drink. "Something like that."

"So did you manage to get hold of Sam?"

"No, he didn't pick up. I left a message to let him know you were here and trying to get hold of him." He fished into his jean jacket pocket and pulled out his phone and brought up his number to give it to her. "Try him around noon. He sleeps in a lot, and stays out late."

"Is he married?"

"Sam?" He stifled a laugh. "Shit no, that guy enjoys the single life too much. Though he has got out of his mother's house now. His father Tom passed away a few years back. Cancer. Sad really. Sam will deny it but I don't think he ever recovered from that night. He acts like it doesn't affect him, but it's hard not to, right?"

Sam Young had been Charlie's best friend. They were like two peas in a pod. It was very rare not to see them together. They would have sleepovers at each other's houses, go to the movies together and were even in the same class at school. On the night of the abduction, Charlie was supposed to stay over at their house after they'd gone trick or treating.

"We were only kids," she said gripping the cold beer bottle.

He nodded staring off into space. "I was fifteen. You'd think it wouldn't have affected me as much."

"It's still young."

On that night, Kara had stolen a packet of cigarettes from her father with the intention of meeting Bobby. He was a year older than her. She was trying to impress him, act all grown up and everything.

He nodded. "Do you ever wonder if we hadn't chosen to meet up, how things would have been different? Like, do you think you would have stayed in Blackmore?"

"Maybe." She shrugged. "I think more about what would have happened if I hadn't run than if we hadn't gone to those damn woods."

"Well I can tell you for sure, if we'd stayed he would have killed us."

"You don't know that."

"Of course I do. You saw the knife. He threatened to kill Charlie in front of us and kill us if we didn't run."

Another flash of memory came crashing in. The terror she felt. The look of disbelief and shock on Charlie's face. His final words ringing in her ears. "Kara, don't go." The guilt had eaten away at her like the salty ocean boring into a cliff face and changing its shape.

Kara took another sip of her drink as the barmaid returned with a bowl of fries, and some condiments. He offered her some but she declined.

"Everything changed after that night. I hated the way it made me feel." He took a fry and paused with it a few inches away from his mouth, his mind deep in thought. "There were moments it felt unreal like it wasn't happening to me. You know. It just seemed like a movie playing out on TV, or being part of a nightmare you can't wake up from. I remember how pissed my father would get at the media for camping outside our house just so they could get a soundbite… or the time they took a snapshot of me in the morning in my pajamas and an hour later it showed up on the news. They were savages. No one cared about what we were going through. Everyone had opinions. I so badly wanted to talk to someone about it but both of you were going through the same thing and I didn't feel comfortable chatting with anyone else. I remember being forced to go back to school when I wasn't ready. You weren't there, and Sam, he just stayed away from me. I'm sure somewhere in his mind he blamed me." He looked at Kara. "Do you… Blame me, I mean?"

Her brow furrowed. "No. God, no. We had no idea what would happen."

"But if we hadn't decided to meet…"

"You can't keep thinking like that, Bobby."

"I know but it still haunts me." He nodded taking a bite of his fry and looking ahead. "All the what-ifs." He shook his head and was about to say something else when a female voice from behind them interrupted.

"Well lookie here. I thought it was you. Another Walker staining our streets."

They twisted to face a guy, and two women. All three of them looked to be in their mid forties. Rough. The kind of folks who had hard lines, drank heavily and would slur karaoke lyrics every night of the week. The guy was carrying two pitchers of beer. The one doing all the talking was a beefy gal. It wasn't fat as much as it was her bone structure that made her look more man than woman. She had dark, curly shoulder-length hair, a deep red V-neck T-shirt, stonewashed jeans, and colorful tattoos that extended to her elbow on both arms.

"Excuse me? Do I know you?" Kara asked.

"Do you know me?" She smirked at her blond friend. "No, probably not. You Walkers were never too good at remembering faces. That's why my brother is still locked up doing time."

"Mary, this is not the time or place," Bobby said slipping forward off his stool.

She eyed him with a look of disgust. "Why don't you shut the fuck up? You're not much better than her. Besides, shouldn't you be at home with Lisa? Does she know about this?"

"She's a friend."

"I bet she is, just like that gal last week. You were looking real friendly with her."

Bobby went red in the face.

"Lady, I don't know what issue you have with me but I don't know you."

Kara turned away but kept her eyes fixed on the woman's reflection in the mirror behind the bar. She took another sip of her beer and shot Bobby a sideways glance. Sensing discord the barmaid approached tossing a rag over her shoulder.

"Mary, if you cause trouble, I'm gonna call the police."

"Stay out of it, Shelly," Mary replied. "I'm having a

polite conversation with Walker here." The barmaid shook her head and wandered over to the phone to place the call. Kara figured the woman had a history of outbursts and this wasn't going to end any different than those before.

"Let me guess, you returned for your mother's funeral." She chuckled. "Now that was one crazy bitch."

Kara balled her right hand and clenched her jaw. She was used to having abuse heaped on her as a cop and was trained to remain composed and professional, and not get riled up. Years had taught her to bite her tongue and know that justice would deal with things, however, that was then. She twisted on the stool and Mary took a step back.

"That's it. A little backbone. C'mon. Take a swing."

She knew the game she was playing. Many suspects tried their luck. If they could get a reaction out of the police they could file a civil lawsuit, or at bare minimum get an officer in trouble with their superior and possibly suspended. But that was if she was on duty. She wasn't and she sure as hell wasn't going to let that remark slide. It all came down to who attacked first.

"I don't want to waste my breath," Kara replied.

She knew that would get a reaction out of her. Sure enough, Mary lunged at her with a hook. Kara counter-attacked, slipped sideways off her stool, grabbed her arm and used her forward motion to slam her head against the bar. It struck with such force all the bottles and glasses shook. In an instant Kara had her arm wrapped around and forced up behind her back. Her blond pal looked like she was about to join in but

Bobby hopped off the stool and intervened, and Kara shook her head. "I would think carefully about that if I was you." She kept her left hand pressed against Mary's head and the right applying pressure to her arm. Mary cried out in agony.

"Shelly, did you call the police?" Bobby asked.

"They're on the way."

"Get off me, you psycho bitch!" Mary yelled, struggling to get out from her grasp. Kara leaned in, her lips twisting up.

"Psycho? Now that's a first."

A siren could be heard in the distance. The male friend had placed the pitchers down and seemed to be the only one with a lick of sense. He was trying to keep the blonde back. Meanwhile Mary continued to insult Kara with every curse word in the dictionary. Within minutes, beyond the opaque panes of glass, blue and red strobe lights lit up the night. Things were about to get interesting.

Chapter 7

It could have gone any number of ways. It all depended on the totality of the circumstances. Having been a trooper for many years before joining the BCI division, Kara knew full well that officers had the discretion to handle bar brawls any number of ways. If there was no damage, and no one wanted to press charges, they could handle it informally and send them on their way with a stiff warning. But that relied on a number of factors — who was involved, how the officers' night, week or month was going, and how belligerent those involved were. If that failed, they could file a report and refer the case to the prosecutor and charges would be filed later without a citation, or they could issue citations and force both parties to show up for court at a later date. Alternatively, they could just outright arrest them. In light of how it went down there was a good chance that Mary could still get arrested and hit with an assault 4 charge because she had intentionally taken a swing and tried to harm Kara.

She glanced toward the door as the officers entered looking ready for a brawl themselves. By the expression on their faces as they locked eyes with Mary, Kara figured they'd handle it informally — at least, she hoped so. The last thing Kara needed was for her father to deal with the repercussions of her actions long after she'd left town. Small-town folks with a chip on their shoulder were notorious for handling matters and dishing out their own form of payback, even if the one to get it wasn't directly at fault. It was all about sending a message.

A brawny cop in a dark uniform, six foot four, 245 pounds, bald head, with tanned skin, made the first comment. "Mary Harris, why am I not surprised to see you in the thick of things?" He shook his head. "I thought we had an agreement?"

"I'm not at fault, it's this psycho bitch."

"Always someone else," he said.

His partner eyed Kara, and stepped in to take over. She released Mary and took a few steps back. They separated and the second officer took Mary to the back of the room so he could speak with her. Kara eyed the name on his shirt. Officer Johnson. He pulled out his notepad to take her side of the story. Before he opened his mouth, the barmaid interjected.

"I saw everything, officer. She's not at fault. Mary was mouthing off, took a swing at her, she dodged and held her against the bar to protect herself."

He eyed Kara, and his eyes bounced to Bobby as if looking for confirmation.

"Exactly what she said," he added. "I tried to tell her but she wouldn't listen."

"She never does."

Everyone looked towards Mary who was now acting all sweet like she had done nothing wrong. It was always the same with these idiots unless they were full of liquid courage. Kara wasn't sure what was more disconcerting — that she tried to start a fight with a complete stranger over something that occurred years ago, or that she did it without being intoxicated.

"Any damage?" the cop asked.

Shelly shook her head.

"Alright, well, I'll take that into consideration. You want to give me a name?" he asked.

"Kara Walker."

He looked at her again, his brow pinching. "Any relation to Anna Walker?"

She nodded. "That's my mother."

He took a deep breath, screwed up his face and eyed Mary again before closing his notepad and tucking it back in his breast pocket.

"My condolences. She was a good woman."

"That's what everyone tells me." Kara offered back a strained smiled.

He narrowed his eyes. "You hurt?"

"No."

"Do you wish to press charges?"

She shook her head. "No, it's okay. I know how these things go."

His head cocked to one side. She pulled out her badge from New York.

He tipped his head back. "So you came home for the funeral? How did it go?"

"As good as it could be, I guess."

"Look, hold tight for a minute, I just need to chat with Mary and I think we should be able to get this squared away."

Kara nodded and took a seat at the bar.

"I tell you she is one crazy bitch," Bobby said. "Her and her family."

"Does Kyle have more siblings?"

"One brother. Strangely, he's nothing like her but I wouldn't want to cross him. Your mother had a few run-ins with Mary after the trial. Their property was damaged."

"I remember her saying something about that. You think it was her?"

"Oh without a doubt. The cops weren't able to pin it on her but most in town had a feeling she was behind it. Your mother told me about this one time that Mary approached her at a grocery store and got into a spat with her. Cops had to be called. They know her. Everyone does. If she's not causing trouble in a bar she's up to no good in her business."

"What's she do?"

"She works in the office at some collision and towing service." He picked a few nuts out of a bowl and tossed them into his mouth while glancing over at her. Both cops were speaking with Mary — no doubt, making it clear that she was starting to test their patience and if she didn't get her act together, she'd find herself locked up. When they had wrapped up, one of them escorted Mary and her pals to the door. As they walked past, Mary scowled at Kara.

Officer Johnson came over and adjusted his duty belt, laying the palm of his hand against his service weapon. "Probably best you head home otherwise she'll think we are treating her unfairly."

"You want us to leave?" Bobby asked. "But she was the one who started it."

"I'm not saying you have to go immediately, I'm just suggesting it would make our lives easier. I don't really want to swing back here in half an hour."

"That's fine, I've got a lot to do tomorrow," Kara said, downing the rest of her drink. Bobby grumbled under his breath and drained his beer as Kara thanked Shelly and left a generous tip.

Chapter 8

In the car on the way home, the memories of the night Charlie was abducted came back to Kara in fragments, just as they had many times before over the years. Now, though, instead of chewing over that day's events, from them pleading with their parents to let them go trick or treating without them, through to what followed, her thoughts circled between her mother and Kyle Harris. When she was twenty, six years after that night, she was living in New York, studying at SUNY when she got the call. She remembered her father being adamant that she come home for the trial, which took place a year later. He wanted her there for support and to show a united front. The problem was stepping away from her studies wasn't easy. Of course her explanation didn't hold weight with her parents. Although she couldn't stay for the entire trial, she had caught snippets of it on the news. So much of what they had on Kyle Harris was said to be circumstantial, according to his defense. In the end, having a poor defense, a sexual accusation in his past, and newly submitted evidence found on his farm had worked against him. She hadn't paid much attention to the details as her mind was consumed with the heavy workload they'd piled on her at the university. But now, she was intrigued, especially in light of what she'd discovered in her parents' basement.

Ten minutes after leaving the bar, Kara pulled into the driveway. As her headlights washed over the front of the home, she saw her father carrying two large black trash bags out to the garbage cans beside the house. He slammed them inside with such force that one toppled over. Before she even stepped out of the car he kicked the can then stormed back into the house.

"Dad?" She hurried after him. Stepping inside the home, she could hear him talking loudly. She caught something about it all had to go. Everything. Kara double-timed it up the steps and found him in Charlie's room filling up another black bag. "What are you doing?" she asked.

"What should have been done years ago." He slid his hand across a shelf and a large collection of tapes dropped into the bag.

She placed her hands on her hips and glanced around.

"You're throwing it all out?"

"I want it gone. He's not coming back. I tried to tell your mother but she wouldn't listen. I wanted to move to a new home but she wouldn't do it just in case he returned." He moved at a rapid pace, not stopping even for a second to consider if an item was of sentimental value. He was treating it like trash — nothing more than a collection of painful memories. A few baseball cards scattered on the floor and in a fit of rage he threw the side table lamp at the wall. It shattered, and Kara took a step back before moving in and wrapping her arms around him.

"Enough. I'll do this."

He stank of booze. He wasn't thinking straight.

"I'll do it!" he bellowed.

He shrugged and brushed past her, storming out the door. She stood in the wake of the torrent. Posters had been torn off the walls. The bedding was gone. Charlie's clothes were piled up ready to be taken out. Many of the trinkets lay scattered on the floor, and the… she sighed, bending to pick up the now cracked photo frame of her and Charlie. She picked away the glass and pulled out the photo, placing it in her pocket as her father returned to complete his rampage. He moved through the room like a whirlwind.

"Dad. Please. Stop. You're not thinking clearly."

"I've never been clearer. I've spent twenty-five years walking past this room, unable to go inside and clear it out. I won't do it. He's gone. She's gone. I don't want to be reminded."

Kara reached for his arm and he stopped, like an exhausted runner. He was breathing heavily and his hands were shaking.

"I'm just so tired, Kara."

She pulled him in and he rested his head on her shoulder. Tears began to flow.

"I miss them so much."

"I know you do. So do I." Kara looked around the room, and gripped him tightly. "I'll do this. Come on, you should lie down. Get some rest."

"I want it done tonight."

"It will be," she replied.

"All of it. I want it gone."

She nodded leading him out of the room and into his. There had only been one event in her life that reminded her of the way he must have felt. That was when she lost her Labrador. She'd removed the dog's bed, the blanket, the food bowls, and leash. Seeing them there only caused her pain. But Charlie was different. In the years after he was gone, she had in some ways become like her mother and thought he would return. Whether it was just a fantasy or not, they'd both thought he would one day walk through that door. She'd held fast to that idea until she left home at twenty. Not seeing his room every day made it easier for her but for her father, and mother, it must have been like reliving the nightmare.

Kara pulled back the covers on her father's bed and he took a seat and rolled in. She pulled off his shoes and covered him. "Kara, you think you can get me some water?"

"Sure."

By the heaviness of his eyes and the smell of the booze coming from him, she figured he'd be out like a light within minutes. Sure enough, she went down to get him a glass of water and upon returning he was snoring. He looked so content in the bed. She set the glass down on the table by his lamp and stared at him for a second before glancing across to where her mother slept. She walked over to the open closet and took a handful of material from one of her dresses and brought it to her nose. A flash of memories of being a child, hearing her mother laugh, feeling her scoop her up and give her a hug made her heart ache. She eyed her mother's watch still laying on her side table, and earrings she'd taken off. She felt tightness in her throat. Kara exited the room before crying.

Over the course of the next forty minutes she went through Charlie's room organizing his belongings into different bags. Most of the toys and clothes could go to Goodwill or the Salvation Army. She kept a few items, mostly sentimental things like award certificates he'd received from school, a baseball cap from their time at a summer camp, and the rest went into boxes and bags for the trash. There was no point storing them in the garage, her father would find them and toss them out. It was time.

* * *

An hour later, Kara poured herself a glass of red wine. She was tired and wanted to sleep but her mind was still busy with what Mary Harris had said. Bobby was right. Her mother truly believed Mary's brother was innocent despite the damning evidence the prosecution had presented to the jury. It was so long ago. So much about the way investigations were conducted had changed and been improved. New forms of forensic science had allowed for hundreds of cold cases to be resolved many years after the fact. Touch DNA didn't exist back in 1996, instead they relied on a large blood, saliva or semen sample. Now all they needed was a few cells. Then of course there was what Bobby had mentioned about her mother hassling the police. What had given her reason to believe that Harris wasn't guilty? *What did you find, Mom?* Kara asked as she made her way down into the basement.

She stood in front of the boards, sipping her wine as she tried to sift through the complex mosaic of statements, police reports, phone records, photos, and maps that were used to chart evidence. Where to begin?

Kara set her glass on the table and reached for anything she could find on Kyle Harris. It took her a good ten minutes of opening and closing folders, pulling down newspaper clippings and doing a search on her mother's computer before she was able to make sense of what was before her and organize it in a clear way based on a timeline of events her mother had scrawled on a long piece of paper.

Thursday October 31, 1991: Charlie Abducted

Friday November 1, 1991: Large Scale Search

Saturday November 2, 1991: Special Agent Henry Ellis Joins the Case

Sunday November 3, 1991: Prayer Vigil, Sheriff Robert Smith Weighs In

Monday November 4, 1991: National Broadcast to Generate Tips

Tuesday November 5, 1991: National Guard, State Patrol, Canines and Helicopters Search Hundreds of Square Miles Area

Wednesday November 6, 1991: Flyers Distributed Nationwide

Thursday November 7, 1991: First Suspect Sketch Released After Public Report of Man Acting Suspicious in the Area at the Time

And the list went on with days and days of new items being added until twenty days later when the investigative force started to shrink as many of the FBI and Washington State Bureau of Investigation agents were taken off the case leaving very few remaining. Kara could remember the shift that occurred. How initially they received so much attention from the media, the public and law enforcement until fewer media vans were parked outside their home, and Charlie's became nothing more than another missing kid's face on a flyer.

Her mother and father both reacted differently. Her father got angry, and would often be found on the phone shouting at the county sheriff or FBI agents. Her mind drifted back to the arguments between her father and mother. The constant tension in the home. The days and nights spent at Uncle Rob's home. No one of her age should have gone through that. She was surprised her parents had managed to stay together through it all. Many parents of missing children separated, unable to cope with the loss and stress and upheaval.

Did Charlie's abductor know what he'd done? That one selfish act hadn't just destroyed Charlie's life; it had torn apart their family, their community and made the world seem unsafe. No, they never bothered to think about that. All they cared about was fulfilling their sick and twisted fantasy.

Kara glanced back down and let out a heavy sigh, reaching for her glass again.

From there on, the timeline mentioned persons of interest that were interviewed, and attacks on boys reported in Forks and Blackmore but with no arrests made. She scanned the rest of the timeline, full of dates, places, a long list of suspects' names, those that were ruled out, others arrested then released, all the way through to when Clallam County Sheriff Robert Smith retired six years later, a year after Kyle Harris was arrested and charged with the abduction.

Kyle Harris. She brought out a photo of him, taken at the time of his arrest on August 12, 1996, five years after the abduction. There were similarities to the suspect sketch, which according to the press was one of the reasons why the police took an interest in him. Though if she could remember correctly, there were a lot of people that matched that sketch. Harris was an athletic-looking man, thirty-four years of age. Thinning hair, six foot two. At the time of his arrest, he owned a farm near the abduction site, and ran a martial arts gym part-time in the evenings. Kara pulled up an article taken from the *Peninsula Daily News* on May 3, 1989, two years before the abduction.

Sexual Assault Suspect Leaves Taekwondo Coaching Job

Blackmore Taekwondo co-owner Jake Randal confirmed to the Peninsula Daily News *that the former owner of Elite Taekwondo, Kyle Harris, is no longer teaching classes out of their facility. Harris, 29, of Blackmore faces charges of sexual assault and sexual interference involving a minor. The charges were brought after a recent investigation by Blackmore Police.*

According to Detective Tommy McGee, the offenses took place between February 1987 and March 1988 and involved a student of Elite Taekwondo under the age of 16. McGee said police will not disclose the name or exact age of the victim because of state laws protecting minors, nor will they say how many times it occurred or why it took the victim a year to come forward.

Although the allegations have not been proven, Randal says that Harris felt it was right to step down to avoid any further damage to the business. "The way I see it, until he is proven guilty he is innocent," he added.

Harris declined to comment when contacted at his farm by the Peninsula Daily News. *A court date has been set for May 4.*

Kara pulled up the next one, which was dated April 23, 1991, almost two years later.

Taekwondo Coach Cleared of All Sexual Assault Charges

"A deep sense of relief" was how Kyle Harris described the moment when Judge Hilary Carter found him not guilty of sexual assault. After almost two years of having his name marred, and having locals speak ill of him, the Superior Court finally found the charges to be unsubstantiated. Harris said he can now move forward, leave behind the past and finally clear his name.

"I was born, raised and worked in Blackmore for many years as a taekwondo instructor, and I never once had anyone accuse me of sexual interference. When I learned about the allegations I was devastated. It destroyed me," said Harris from his farm home in Blackmore.

Harris co-owned Elite Taekwondo when he was accused of sexually assaulting one of his students who was under 16 at the time. He was charged with assault and interference with a minor related to the allegations.

After being charged he was forced to step down from teaching taekwondo and his business as a farm owner suffered. Harris said the community shunned him from the moment the media released the news of the charges.

"It has been the worst two years of my life. After I was charged, my vehicle was vandalized, I had people condemning me," said Harris. "It didn't matter that they hadn't heard all the facts, people in the community assumed I was guilty."

When the verdict was announced, Harris broke down as did his sister Mary and brother Brian Harris. Among the supporters were some of his former taekwondo students.

According to Harris's lawyer, Harriet Wesley, the decision to clear him of all charges boiled down to "credibility of the accuser" and that his "version of the incidents could not have occurred."

She was asked if they knew why he was accused. "At this time we don't," said Wesley. She added that her job was to show the inconsistencies in the accuser's allegations. It appeared to have worked as Judge Carter agreed.

"We were able to establish without any doubt that Mr. Harris did not do it," said Wesley. "The judge did not believe the boy's version of events."

A key element in clearing his name involved presenting evidence that showed that the accuser continued to remain a student for over a year after the alleged sexual assault occurred. Blackmore police were able to provide the dates of the said offenses, stating they occurred between February 1987 and March 1988. The accuser didn't come forward until 1989.

"It seems pretty clear that you wouldn't continue to place yourself in the situation if this was occurring," Wesley said. "It's not like he was living at his home."

Currently Harris is trying to pick up the pieces of his life. He is considering a civil lawsuit against the accuser and the Blackmore Police Department to reclaim money lost in clearing his name. Wesley has recommended that this would be the best course of action but would not comment on whether or not she would be involved.

"The travesty in this is no one wins. An innocent man has been accused of a crime he did not commit, and he has faced the backlash of his community and

suffered emotionally, physically and financially because of it," added Wesley.

Even though Harris has been traumatized by the experience, he is relieved at the outcome. He said that he owes a lot of thanks to those who believed in him, including his family, his friends and former students.

Strangely enough, Kara had never heard about the previous accusations against Kyle. When she was between the ages of fourteen and twenty, her parents sheltered her from all matters related to Charlie's case, and that included watching the news or reading newspapers. They tried to give her as best as they could a normal life, even if that was found spending a great deal of time at her uncle's. Even in the year she left home for the university in New York, she didn't follow the updates of the case against Kyle Harris prior to going to trial because she assumed it would be treated like all the suspects that police had already interviewed — nothing ever came of it. Of course when they pulled in people of interest, media whipped everyone into a frenzy — headlines plastered the front page informing the community that someone had been brought in, only to have them released a day later. When they finally felt they had a case against Kyle, and her mother phoned to let her know that he'd been arrested, she fully expected the case to be thrown out. The fact was hardly any "no body" homicide cases went to trial. Without a body it was very hard to charge someone, even though it did happen. However, out of the 480 that had occurred since 1819 in the USA, ninety percent were won and only seven of the accused ended up on death row. And even for those who wound up on death row, they would often get their conviction overturned on appeal or have a death sentence commuted for a lesser penalty. Yep, navigating the justice system was a long and slippery slope that didn't always end up with justice being served.

Kara took another sip of her wine and glanced at the clock. It was getting late. She took a seat on the floor surrounded by folders and photos, and mounds of paperwork. Her mother had certainly gone to a lot of effort. That's what made her death seem so odd. Why? Why go to all the trouble of pursuing answers only to kill yourself? She glanced up at the wooden beams and felt a chill come over her.

Kara fished out the next article dated three years after the abduction, and two years before his arrest. There was a snapshot of Kyle Harris, a few years older than his previous mug shot from the student accusation.

Person of Interest Denies Involvement in Charlie Walker's Abduction

KIRO 7-NEWS recently learned that the person of interest in the Charlie Walker abduction was accused of sexual assault back in 1989 and cleared two years later. We recently spoke with that person, Kyle Harris, a resident and native of Blackmore, about the case.

In October 1991, a masked man kidnapped 12-year-old Charlie Walker in Blackmore. He was taken by force from the Fairground Woods, a location that butts up against Harris's farmland property. According to Blackmore Police, Harris is the only person who has been named a person of interest in the case even though he denies having anything to do with it.

Harris was 29 years old at the time of the abduction. He had previously worked as a taekwondo coach at Elite Taekwondo until allegations were made about him sexually assaulting an under-16 student. It took two years for his lawyer to clear his name. He currently lives on the farm and was home alone at the time of the abduction.

"Look, I understand why the police are looking at me. The previous case against me tainted my name in the community, the parents and locals want answers and I just so happen to live the closest to where the abduction occurred. But I'm innocent and I will fight this as I did the previous allegation."

Harris insists that the only reason police are targeting him is because he filed a civil lawsuit against them and won, and they are now under pressure to solve the case. Still, he vehemently denies being involved.

"My farm is not the only one that is close. There are two other farms. Did the police speak with those owners? No. That's because they have already made up their minds about who they want to pin this on."

When asked what he heard or saw on Halloween in 1991, Harris had this to say.

"I heard the sound of a vehicle, and I saw lights through the trees but that's not uncommon to see. A number of residents are familiar with the farmland road that runs around the perimeter of my property. Teenagers used to use it as a place to make out. I just figured it was another group of kids or an adult taking a shortcut over to Craig Street. I told the police that I was relaxing that night in front of the TV."

Harris says that on the night in question, he

answered the door to a few trick or treaters, then around 8:45 he turned out the light so that everyone else would know that he didn't have any more candy to give out. Before he turned in for the night he saw headlights and watched them disappear at a high rate of speed down the road.

Police arrived within eleven minutes.

No calls were made to 911 by Harris that night.

"Running a farm I have to be up at the crack of dawn so I retired just after nine. I was in the shower when a Blackmore police officer knocked on the door. They are saying that I took too long to get to the door and that when I answered I looked as if I'd been running. But that's not accurate. I got out of a hot shower, threw some clothes on and my hair was still wet. The officer told me there had been an abduction, and I offered to help," says Harris.

According to Harris, officers searched his property.

"At no point did I hide anything from them. I allowed them in my home, allowed them to go through the buildings with farm equipment — all without a warrant, mind you."

The Clallam County Sheriff Department says they don't have the logs from the officers of all the buildings on his property being searched that night. One of which is no longer there. For some reason the officers' notes were lost. However, the department stands behind what their officers said.

"There were a lot of police on the scene. They had a chopper in the air, they had multiple vehicles in my driveway and officers inside my home. To say that they lost these logs and now blame me for it is outrageous. Their job is to document everything. I know I took them

into every building, including the one that isn't there. That's no longer there because there was a fire. Now they are saying that I started that on purpose but you only have to go speak with the fire marshal to see that's a lie."

Investigators say they also visited the two other farms that night and the owners, who didn't wish to be named but gave a quote, say, "Two officers visited and asked if we had seen or heard anything but that was it. No one requested to view our property. If they did they did it without our permission."

Starting a fire on purpose wasn't the only accusation thrown at Harris by the sheriff department. When they asked to enter his home on the night of the abduction, they say he asked about a warrant and acted suspicious. Harris had this to say, "Of course I was nervous. After dealing with the police and having accusations thrown at me from the previous case, you can bet I was nervous. Regarding the request for a warrant, that is bogus. I invited them in willingly. At no point in time did I request a warrant. This is just another attempt at using me as a scapegoat for a bungled investigation. The fact is evidence was not preserved in this case but Blackmore Police Department and the Clallam County Sheriff Department don't want to admit fault."

Within a week of the abduction, Blackmore Police Department performed a search of his property, however, they are still suggesting that Harris had not been forthright and that was made clear when he failed one of three lie detector tests.

"Think about it. If I had abducted this kid, would I really have offered to take a lie detector test? As for the

failure, it was inconclusive. I passed two of their tests but because I didn't pass the third with flying colors they think I'm lying to them. At every turn in this investigation they have attempted to put words in my mouth and get me to confess to something I didn't do. Why are they trying to pin this on me? I'll tell you why. It's payback for the civil lawsuit, and it would certainly make for an easy way to close the case and gain favor in the public eye, would it not? Guy with shady past kidnaps young kid. The media is eating this up. That's why I'm here speaking with you today. I did not take that kid and have no explanation for why the third test was inconclusive. Besides, I have even been asked to be hypnotized but I have refused because I'm nervous about how it would be conducted. I haven't ruled it out but I want to make sure it's performed by a non-biased third party and videoed."

For three years, investigators turned their attention to other leads but the case was broken in 1996 when an anonymous caller gave a tip that led investigators back to the farm of Harris. A search warrant was presented and Blackmore Police, Washington State Bureau of Investigation and FBI were on scene hauling out bags of evidence.

Harris continues to deny involvement.

Anyone with any tips about Charlie Walker's kidnapping, please call the Clallam County Sheriff Department.

Kara moved on to the next article, which was short and straight to the point:

Person of Interest in Charlie Walker Kidnapping

Arrested

A 34-year-old Blackmore man, Kyle Harris, has been arrested on charges related to the abduction and homicide of Charlie Walker even though his body hasn't been found. The arrest was announced on Tuesday at a press conference. The FBI confirmed WIRO7 reports that authorities found vital evidence including a shoe and a pair of jeans that Charlie Walker wore on the night he was taken.

A search warrant was presented a week ago after authorities decided to search for human remains on Harris's farm. The search was performed on August 2.

Charlie Walker was abducted on October 31, 1991, in Fairground Woods close to Harris's property. According to his sister and two friends, they were taking a shortcut home after a night of trick or treating in the neighborhood when they were approached by a masked man who took Charlie at knifepoint.

His parents Anna and Matthew Walker have worked with the police to raise awareness and many people had been investigated and ruled out as suspects before Harris. The Walkers wish to thank the community for helping in the investigation.

The search on the farm was performed one year before Clallam County Sheriff Robert Smith retired and Sheriff Vern Armstrong took over.

She flipped through a few more of the articles that provided some smaller updates before turning her attention to some of the ones related to the trial of Kyle Harris.

No Death Penalty for Charlie Walker Killer: Jury Gives Life Without Parole for Kyle Harris

Six years after Charlie Walker was abducted on his way home on Halloween night, a jury on Friday determined that his killer will spend the remainder of his days behind bars without the possibility of parole. While the Walker family is pleased with the outcome, the result fell short of what prosecutors had wanted — the death penalty for now 35-year-old Kyle Harris.

Although the same jury that had convicted him was involved in Friday's decision, an expert for Washington State said that it's not a surprise since Charlie's body was never found. Harris was originally sentenced last July in Clallam County Superior Court by Judge Richard Davis who was involved in the six-month trial.

It took the jury only four days to find Kyle Harris guilty. Without Charlie's body or the murder weapon, the prosecution had a hard time proving their argument for the death penalty.

When the verdict was announced, Charlie's mother Anna Walker collapsed and had to be taken out. Outside the court, his father Matthew Walker thanked the jury and expressed his sense of disappointment in the outcome.

"My boy doesn't get to come home," he said. "Kyle Harris will get to enjoy the privilege of three square meals a day, he will see his family and we will live with the grief for the rest of our days."

After weeks of deliberation the jury finally convicted Kyle Harris of abducting and killing Charlie Walker.

Harris was previously charged with a sexual assault and interference with a minor two years before

Charlie's abduction but was cleared by the Superior Court. Now a community is left wondering what they could have done. Many are outraged and feel the justice system made a mistake in letting him go.

"If he had been convicted of the sexual assault back in 1989, my boy would still be alive," Matthew Walker said. "It's as simple as that. Yet the courts won't take responsibility."

Defense attorneys for Harris said they plan to file a motion asking for a new trial as they believe in the innocence of Harris, who pleaded not guilty.

Anna Walker pleaded with Harris to reveal the whereabouts of Charlie's remains but he continues to remain steadfast and denies any involvement in the abduction.

Chapter 9

On Wednesday morning, one day after her arrival in Blackmore, Kara's father woke her by shaking her shoulder. Her eyelids fluttered, and light stabbed her eyes. Her throat was dry, and her head throbbing from the alcohol.

"You sleep down here last night?" he asked. She blinked a few times then realized where she was. She was still in the basement, lying on the floor, on top of the photos and paperwork. The computer was still on, a steady hum in the background.

She sat up and pawed her eyes. "I must have passed out."

Her father lifted a half-drunk bottle of wine, and picked up an empty glass from the floor nearby. "Go take a shower. I'll put on some breakfast."

"I'm probably going to go for a run."

"Really?" His eyebrow shot up, a look of astonishment. He gazed around for a second shaking his head and crossing to the stairs. He paused on the bottom step. "Oh, did you throw everything out like I asked?"

Kara nodded then rolled her head around. Her father mumbled something and trudged upstairs. She wiped drool from the side of her jaw and took a few minutes to stretch the ache from her body. A lightning bolt of pain shot through her head and she groaned. She looked down at all the paperwork she'd scoured through the night before and the connections her mother had made in the disappearance of four boys over the last twenty-five years. They weren't from Clallam County but there was a possibility they were linked. What did catch Kara's attention was they all were similar in nature to Charlie's abduction. All occurred on the evening of Halloween and each abduction was spread apart by a period of five years, and if she was reading her mother's notes right, she believed he would take another one on Halloween.

Still eager to read through more of the material but wanting to speak with Sam, and get in her run, she climbed the stairs and got ready to head out. In her old bedroom she pulled back the drapes and took in the sight of the morning. It was gloomy out, the sky was gray, and cumulous clouds rolled in giving her a sense that a storm was coming.

Kara pulled her bag onto the bed and took out her running gear, she slipped into it, donned her windbreaker and tugged on her running sneakers. Then, after going downstairs, she headed out before her father started harping on about clearing out the basement. She knew it was coming. Maybe he wouldn't throw out her mother's clothes but if the expression on his face was anything to go by, the evidence wall would have to go.

* * *

An hour later, after taking a shower, she headed into the kitchen. Her father was sitting at the round table reading through the local paper. Behind him were a number of colorful photographs along the wall that revealed their life before Charlie's abduction. No more family photos were taken after that day. It was as if time stood still and enjoying life had become a guilty pleasure. There were two windows above the sink that looked out to the driveway along the east side of the home. Off to the right was the door that led into the mud room. Hanging over the handle on the stove was her mother's apron. She didn't wear it often. Her father was holding a cup of coffee, wearing his old mechanic overalls and looking as if he was getting ready to head out for work.

"Coffee is in the pot."

She studied him for a second as she crossed the kitchen, her brow pinched. "You haven't worn those in years."

"Well I can't sit around here all day," he said reaching for his cigarettes. He coughed a few times as he lit one. He'd been smoking since she was a kid. Her mother had always been harping on at him to quit but he said it was too late. The damage was done. Fact was he was too old and set in his ways to change. Change was for infomercial junkies and life was for living, he would say. To which her mother would reply, if you keep smoking you won't be living. He would just tut and ignore her.

"But Dad, you don't work anymore?"

She was wondering if he was struggling with his memory.

"I know that. I have to change the oil on the car."

"Today?"

"Of course today. Why wouldn't I?"

"But shouldn't you at least take a few days off?"

"I already have. I can't sit around here all day."

That was just like him. His answer for any of life's problems was to bury himself in distractions and hope it went away. Anna had always been the one that paid the bills, made the doctor's appointments, dealt with problems as they arose.

"Dad."

Without looking at her he answered, "She's gone. I don't want to be sitting here all day thinking about it. At least if I stay busy I can focus on something else."

She gave a nod and poured out a cup. There was no point arguing with him. When he made up his mind no one could change it, including her mother. Kara let the coffee cup warm her hands as she leaned against the counter and contemplated how to ask her father about what he knew, if anything at all. Her mother had always been so tight-lipped; she didn't expect her father to be any different.

"I've been meaning to ask you…" She paused for a second, her fingers drumming against the cup.

"Spit it out, Kara."

"Did mom ever talk to you about what she was doing?"

He looked over the paper, pushed up his round reading glasses. "If you're referring to that mess downstairs, yes. She wouldn't shut up about it. I told her she was wasting her time. They already had that animal locked up inside but she wouldn't listen." He stared off as if recalling a past conversation with her before looking back. "Seeing you down there this morning reminded me of her." He shook his head. "I want it all gone today, Kara. You hear me? I don't want you heading down that path."

"I didn't say I was."

He spoke to her like she was still living under his roof.

"Please, give me some credit. You're like your mother. When you get something stuck in your head, you won't let it go." He took a swig of his coffee and returned to reading the paper. "Anyway, what have you got planned for today?"

She breathed in deeply. "Going to visit Sam."

"Sam Young?"

"Yeah."

He shook his head with a look of disapproval. "You might want to rethink that."

"Why? Something you know I don't?"

"Guy hasn't got the best reputation. Let's just leave it at that."

"He's an old friend."

"Best leave it that way."

Her father rose from the table and set his glasses down, then headed toward the back door. He opened it and paused. "You'll deal with the basement stuff today, right?"

"Later."

He nodded then headed out. She watched him from the kitchen window push up the garage door and disappear inside. Kara pulled out her phone and placed a call to the number Bobby had given her for Sam.

The phone rang several times and she was about to hang up when a male answered, he sounded half asleep.

"Hello?" he croaked.

"Sam?"

"Who is this?"

"It's Kara. Kara Walker."

There was a long pause.

"Right." She heard him scoff. "Kara? Well if you aren't a blast from the past. Who gave you my number?"

"Bobby."

He groaned. "Of course. What can I do for you?"

"I was hoping to catch up with you today. You know, talk. Maybe go for a coffee?"

Again a break.

"Sam?" she said again.

"I'm here. Look I don't think today's a good day."

He coughed, and then she heard him spit.

"When is?"

"I dunno. Um…"

She heard some woman in the background call out to him, Sam must have put the phone to his chest as she heard him tell her to keep it down. When he got back on the line he groaned like it was a huge chore to go and have a coffee with a friend.

"Look, what about lunch time?" she asked. "I'm not in Blackmore long. For old times' sake."

He sighed. "I'm sorry about your mother," he said dodging the question. He sniffed hard. "Alright. You got transportation?"

"Yep."

"Swing by Sunrise Trailers around noon. Mine is number 28."

"Got it."

He hung up before she could say any more. She glanced at her watch, it was a little after eight. She had some time to kill. She tossed the remainder of the bitter coffee in the sink and went back to the basement to continue delving into the files.

* * *

Sunrise Trailer Park was located on the outskirts of Blackmore. It had existed for as long as Kara could remember. Unlike some of the newer mobile home parks that had emerged over the years offering up-to-date facilities, breathtaking views of the harbor and spacious abodes, Sunrise was associated with the working class and impoverished people. She'd known a few people from school who'd grown up there. They were the type of kids that came to school without food in their stomachs and were known troublemakers. Of course that didn't reflect every family that lived there but it only took one bad apple to ruin the bunch. That's what she assumed her father was referring to when she spoke of Sam. Back in her teens she recalled him harping on about police getting called out there at all hours to break up domestics and telling her to stay clear of the place. As she veered onto the vast expanse of green fields and narrow roads, she noticed the one-story office on site looked better than the thirty-two units neatly arranged, twenty-five feet apart and nestled in a dip just on the other side of Coal Creek Road.

The homes didn't look like typical run-down metal trailers, at least not like the ones she remembered. The first batch she saw as she drove in was conventional, prefabricated in various colors, modern as if trying to appeal to new clientele. As she followed the road that curved around, she soon realized it was just a front for what lay behind it. It was as run-down as it could get. Peeling paint on water-stained metal shelters that looked like old fishing boats with a roof. Trash cans were overfilled, and litter blew across the dust-covered ground like tumbleweeds. Most had faded American flags hanging from posts outside their small porches; a few were being used as drapes to keep the light out. Several homeowners sat outside in their folding chairs sipping on beer, observing her as she drove past. Happy hour had started early.

Kara spotted Sam's trailer and parked outside. To find him living in this part of the town was disheartening. He'd come from a good home. They weren't wealthy but then again neither were any of their families. But his parents had held down steady jobs and were considered respectable members of the community, at least until the abduction.

Before she got out of the SUV, the metal door on his trailer swung open and a woman, dressed in cut-off Daisy Duke shorts and a tight white T-shirt, jumped out clutching a bag that was spilling over with clothes.

"Fuck you, Sam."

Kara watched with keen interest as more clothes were thrown over the top of her head and Sam emerged looking weathered by time. He hadn't grown much. He was a short ass even as a kid. Five foot four. His once tidy buzzed hair had been replaced by long dirty-blond locks that were pulled up into a man bun. He was wearing a ratty pair of jeans, yellowed workman boots and a muscle T-shirt. His skin was overly tanned, typical for anyone working in construction. He was also sporting a heavy beard.

"And take this shit with you," he said flinging out a bong that shattered on the ground. The woman hopped into an old beat-up Ford truck, stuck up her finger at him and peeled out at a high rate of speed leaving a plume of dust behind. Sam stood there, one hand on hip, the other against his trailer, then punched the door. Kara got out and leaned against her car.

"I see your taste in women hasn't changed," she said smirking at him.

He glanced over, and squinted through the dust.

"And neither has your timing." He glanced at his

watch then smiled. He made his way over and gave her a hug, then stepped back and took a look at her like a father might do with a long-lost child.

"Damn, you turned out fine. I always told your brother you were a fine bit of ass."

She gave him a slap on the chest, then pointed to his eye which was sporting a shiner. He reached up. "Comes with the territory. Come on in, I'll make you some coffee."

"I thought we could go for lunch?"

He stopped halfway between her car and the trailer, then looked back at his shithole of a place. "You buying?"

She nodded, her lip curling up at the corner.

"Then let me just grab a shirt and my smokes."

He disappeared inside while she gazed up at the gunmetal sky. Her eyes fell upon a neighbor, a young guy sitting outside in a heavy jacket. He was wearing a cowboy hat and was drinking a hot drink. Steam swirled up around his face. He gave a nod and she returned the gesture as Sam came out with one arm in his shirt and a cigarette hanging from his lips.

"I swear this place is going downhill," he said hopping in the passenger side and running his hands over paint-splattered jeans. "Used to be full of respectable, honest, hard-working folks. Now it's just full of young'uns who want to live off welfare."

She fired up the engine.

"How's your mom?"

"Ah, she's doing okay. Getting on in years."

"I heard about Tom. Sorry."

He shrugged. "Yeah, she took it real hard. We all did. Amazing, isn't it? You take your parents for granted when they're alive but after they're gone you would do anything to bring them back, even if it was for just an hour."

Sam dipped his head and sniffed hard as Kara backed out.

"So you working?"

"Off and on. Mostly roofing in the summer. Winters tend to be slower months so I do some painting and construction. But don't get me wrong, when I don't work, it's not because I don't want to work. No. I'm not like all those losers living off the government. I pay my way. Always pay my bills on time. Well lately, it's been a little hard but I just can't seem to land much."

"Bobby said you're in construction?"

"I'm into anything that pays me good money." He cracked the window and blew out smoke. "Sorry, I should have asked."

"That's fine. It's a rental."

He chuckled. "Oh, then they won't mind me doing this," he said placing his dirty boots on the dashboard. He grinned. He still hadn't grown up. Everything was one big joke to him.

"No, but I do. Get them off," she said in a strong tone with a smirk on her face. Kara headed back to town on Carlisle Street. It was one of the main roads that cut through the town, it ran parallel to Main Street. They drove past Westborough, the road that went near Fairground Woods. Sam cast a glance down there.

"You been back there since you've returned?"

"Nope."

"Not at all?"

She shook her head. He nodded and glanced out, taking out sunglasses as the bright noon sun peered out from under the belly of dark clouds.

"I've gone back there a few times. At first it was just to see it again. I guess somewhere in the back of my mind, it didn't feel real. The other times after that were just to reminisce. You know, to try and make sense of it." He sighed. "I still can't, I mean make sense of it. He could have taken any one of us. Why him?" There was a pause as if he was chewing it over or waiting for her to answer. "He would have been my age by now. Probably married with four kids. We would have gone out for drinks a couple times a week. Who knows, right?"

"Yep," Kara said.

"You married?"

"Was. Been separated for three years."

"Kids?"

"One. A boy. Thirteen."

He nodded, an expression of approval.

"You ever worried about him?"

She chuckled. "All the time."

"Where is he now?"

"With his father."

He nodded looking out the window. "So did he sleep with someone else?"

She laughed. "I wish it was that easy. No, I don't have anyone to blame except myself." He looked as if he was waiting for clarification, so she continued. "My work. Keeps me busy."

"Ah right. I hear you're a big-shot detective?"

"First, no. Second, who told you that?"

"Despite my lowly residence, Kara, I can read and I do follow the news."

She chuckled.

"And, well, there was your mother."

Kara looked at him. "You as well?"

He took another hard drag on his cigarette. "I gotta give it to that woman. She was one determined lady. She was sure she was gonna find Charlie's abductor." He shook his head. "Damn pity." He squinted at the road sign. "Where you heading?"

"Rosie's Place."

"No. It's not there anymore."

She shot him a glance. "What?"

"It burned down eight years ago." He frowned. "Seriously, Kara, when was the last time you were back in Blackmore?"

"A long while ago. It was a brief visit."

She didn't want to make him feel bad. She thought back to the few times she'd returned. Initially in the early days, when Ethan was small, she would do the rounds, go visit old friends, but as her work and family life took over she hadn't returned and with the cost of flights, and then the breakup of her marriage — well she didn't exactly want to deal with all the questions. A few of her gal pals had contacted her on Facebook and invited her to a school reunion, and she had considered it but then the thought of looking like a sad sack and having to answer the same question about her marriage didn't appeal to her.

"Here, hang a left on Herald Street. I know a good spot. They do these monster pancakes." He tipped his head back. "You gotta try them."

Chapter 10

The Cliffhouse restaurant had originally been an inn but after a drop in bookings and a string of bad reviews they closed up shop and it was bought by Ginger Rollins, a widow in her early sixties whose late husband had a dream of owning his own diner. She now lived above and worked in the kitchen, cooking up a storm, but only opening a few days a week. All of which were packed due to her home-cooked meals.

The diner was filled with fresh flowers, framed newspaper clippings of historic events from the area, movie photos and knock-off paintings. She greeted everyone by name, and by the looks of it ran a tight ship with only two waitstaff.

"Did you believe her?" Kara asked as she leaned over her cup of coffee. "My mother, I mean."

Sam was getting ready to tuck into a monstrous pile of bacon and syrup-covered pancakes with a side dish of cream and strawberries.

"Oh yeah," he said. He washed down a mouthful with coffee and tucked into the next bite like he hadn't eaten in a week, then continued. "Hell, she even got me looking into it. I should show you some of what I managed to dig up." He paused for a second and jabbed his fork out in front of him. "That guy. Kyle Harris. I don't believe he did it."

"But the papers and cops did."

"Of course. They wanted a scapegoat. He fit the bill. Guy who had already been previously accused of sexual assault, a single man who lives alone, his home butting up against Fairground Woods. He didn't stand a chance in hell of wiggling out of that one. They set him up."

"Who did?"

"Cops. County. FBI. Surely, someone like yourself knows how easy it is for them to bungle a case."

She thought back to the Swanson case. All the people involved, and the contaminated evidence, the family friends traipsing through the house, and the DA's office trying to keep everyone happy. Kara had to admit; she'd become jaded by investigations. Unless a case was clear-cut, or could be swept under the rug and wrapped up in a tidy bow, it often turned into a political game — one which required ensuring people stayed employed and their reputations intact.

He chewed with his mouth open and would occasionally lower his voice and look around the diner like he was sure someone would overhear him.

"He's from around here."

"What?"

"Your mother. She believed he was a local. Someone from Clallam County. She couldn't be sure if he lived in Blackmore, Forks or Port Angeles but she was convinced he was from around these parts."

Kara didn't know about that. Of course she was aware her mother thought it wasn't Kyle Harris but she must have overlooked the part about him being a local.

"And you believed her?"

"Of course. You seen the wall?"

"In the basement."

He nodded, eyeing a truck as it pulled up outside. "She invited me for dinner one night, a few years back. Showed me it. Fuck. Craziest shit I'd ever seen. But she wasn't crazy. Oh no." He shook his head. "That woman had her head screwed on right. But the cops wouldn't listen to her."

"Blackmore or County?"

"Both. Now having said that, she did say she was making some progress with a detective from County. I forget his name."

"Noah Goodman?"

Sam stabbed the air with his fork. "That's it." He nodded. "She said he was the only one that listened to her."

"So he took her seriously?"

He shrugged. "Well let's say he didn't turn her away like the others. You know, I heard what people in this town said about your mother. How she had lost her marbles. The grieving mother. They acted like they cared to her face but spoke behind her back. It wasn't right. But me, I believed she was on to something." He stopped eating and stared at her. "They might not have believed her. But you," he jabbed again. "They'd believe you."

Kara scoffed and leaned back against the red leather seating. "Nah, I'm not getting involved. I'm just home for the funeral, to help my father and I have to return to New York. Whatever ideas my mother had about Charlie are buried with her."

He shook his head. "No, they're not. They're on that wall. She was meticulous about it. Labels, tags, notes, thread. You just need to follow it, Kara."

She pursed her lips and smiled. She snapped the elastic around her wrist a few times and Sam eyed it. "Sammy, I'm not setting aside my life and risking my career to chase someone who may not even exist."

"You do it all the time."

"But that's different."

"How?"

She groaned. "It's been twenty-five years."

His chewing slowed as he studied her. "You believe it was Kyle Harris, don't you? You're just like them. You think your mother was crazy."

"I didn't say that."

"No, you don't need to," he said, before picking up a napkin and wiping his lips. "It's written all over your face."

"Even if I wanted to, I couldn't. I just don't have time."

"How long are you staying?"

She shrugged. "A few days."

"Give it a week. Rattle a few doors. See what you can uncover. Use your position to go through some of the doors that were closed to her."

She scoffed. "Sam. Things like this don't get resolved in a week. You know how long the investigative team worked on this case? It took them five years to even get something on Harris. I can't work miracles."

"You seem to forget all of the cases you've solved."

He had been following her career. In her time with the bureau she'd worked at the helm on a number of high-profile cases, some of which had taken years to crack. But every case was different. They weren't dealing with the same M.O.

"Besides, your mother has already done the hard work for you. You've just got to pick up where she left off."

Kara shook her head and looked over towards the

counter. There were eight older men and women seated there, drinking coffee, eating cake and yakking about ordinary life. People who had lived life, seen it at its worst and best. She'd often wondered what tales she'd have to share when she had grandchildren. Her career had given her so many already and one day she'd look back on it with a sense of pride, or a sense of regret.

"It was the not knowing that bothered her," Sam said before taking a sip of his coffee. "She told me that even if he was dead, at least knowing what had happened would give her some sense of peace. Don't you want to know?" he asked her.

"Of course I do." A pained expression masked her face. There hadn't been a day gone by that she hadn't thought about what Charlie had gone through. Seeing the Swanson boy's lifeless body had brought those questions to the surface. Maybe that's why she walked away from the case. It hit too close to home.

He set his cup of coffee on the table. "Then look into it. Go through what she gathered."

"I already have. Well at least some of it."

"And?" He leaned forward with an eager expression.

"I…"

"Can I get you some more coffee?" A young woman approached cutting her off. She smiled politely and nodded. Sam didn't take his eyes off her even as he pushed his coffee mug to the end of the table to be refilled. He waited until the waitress walked away before he continued.

Sam ran a hand over his jaw. "Look, I'm sorry, I shouldn't have brought it up. I just… I know how much it meant to your mother. I guess I wanted to believe she could find him." Sam tossed down his napkin and Kara asked for the check.

After paying the bill, she took him home. Outside waiting for him was the same woman he'd had an argument with before leaving. Sam groaned and shook his head.

"Here we go again," he said climbing out.

It felt bittersweet as she wasn't sure when she'd see him again. Sam bent down and leaned into the window. A smile danced on his lips and she recognized in his expression the twelve-year-old boy that used to bug the hell out of her when he came around to see Charlie.

"It was good seeing you again, Kara. Next time, I'll buy you lunch."

She nodded. He turned to leave then looked back in again.

"And about what I said. Think about it. Have a little faith in yourself. I know your mother did."

He slapped the top of the vehicle and headed over to his trailer, stopping for a second to wave to a neighbor before disappearing inside. And that was it. All three of their lives had gone in separate directions. Bobby's towards married life, stability, four kids and a suburban home; Sam's on the lower end of the scale, single, rocky, barely scraping by. Each of them swayed and impacted by her mother's refusal to give up on Charlie.

As Kara pulled out of Sunrise Trailer Park and followed the road back to her parents' home, she took a detour and pulled on to Westborough Road. It was just after one in the afternoon as she got closer to the farmland road that ran through Fairground Woods. She pulled into a country lay-by that overlooked the fields which led up to the woods. A shiver washed over her as she got out and looked up and down the road. So much had changed about the landscape; a new housing development had been built on the plot of land that was often used by a traveling fair. Back in 1991 it was nothing but open fields and woodland. Kids would often trek through the fields on their way home from school. Older teenagers would drink and hang out in the woods. Before the abduction, it was notorious for parties. Back in the day, they'd often find the charred remains of wood in fire pits, crushed beer cans and used condoms up there. Carved into tree trunks were initials, confessions of love and the dreams of the hopeful. Before the incident, it represented innocence, coming of age and the young and wild. Now the well-worn trails that were trampled down by teenagers had grown over with long grass, wildflowers and weeds. Everything that it had once represented was forgotten, and plans were in place to clear the woods. Maybe that's what the new development was for.

A cold October wind nipped at Kara's face and she pulled her jacket close peering over a farmyard gate into the field. Her fourteen-year-old voice echoed. She could still see the path they took as they ran. She could still hear her brother's voice pleading, and the man's threats. Changed. Lost. Time was the great divider, shaping, covering and forming the past into something new. For those who would come and live in the new neighborhood, most wouldn't know. But she did. She could never forget. Now it only reminded her of terror.

As much as she wanted to face her fears and walk up the path that led her to the abduction site, she couldn't, not now, not until she knew for sure.

That's what Sam didn't realize. He hadn't asked her that question.

The one that she'd been asking herself ever since they'd locked Kyle Harris up.

Was it him?

Chapter 11

Clallam County Detective Noah Goodman spat the foul-tasting coffee back into the paper cup and tossed it in the garbage by his desk. From outside his office, Sergeant Tremonti burst out laughing and rocked back in his chair. Noah reached for a pastrami sandwich with dollops of mustard and took a huge bite.

"I keep telling you to stop buying that cheap crap," he said before taking a sip of his coffee.

Noah wiped his lips and shook his head. "I refuse to pay $3.40 for a medium Americano. How the hell Starbucks gets away with it is beyond me."

"Supply and demand, my friend, supply and demand."

He fished through the mountain of paperwork in front of him, trying to create some order. Behind him were tons of jam-packed binders lining the shelves. Some days he just felt like a glorified pen pusher. "Bullcrap. They have warped the minds of America, mainly the hipsters, into thinking it's cool to order something that expensive when it only cost them less than 50 cents. It's a sign of the times, Tremonti. People are getting stupid."

That only made him laugh harder. Noah returned to wading through reports related to a domestic incident that ended up as a triple homicide of a mother and her two children. The guy had been on their radar since assaulting his girlfriend, and then a Blackmore police officer about four months ago. After he sobered up, he was all apologetic to law enforcement and his ex who welcomed him back with open arms. It would be a fatal mistake. It happened too often. Victims of abuse would forgive and buy into their promises to never do it again only to suffer a worse fate.

"How's the case coming along?" Tremonti asked.

"His next appearance in court isn't until the end of the month. I can't wait to see them put this asshole away."

"Did you get out of him why he did it?"

"I did," he said gazing down at the report.

Officers finally found him at his residence and arrested him without incident. When interviewed about what had set him off, he said the woman spilled his coffee. They got into an argument and he lost his temper and beat her to death with a statue. The kids were just in the wrong place at the wrong time. They were seventeen and twelve. On top of that, her six-year-old child was with her grandmother at the time. Now she would grow up without her mother.

Noah had been working for the Sheriff Department as a detective for the past four years. Before that he'd been a deputy patrolling the highways until he felt it was time for a change. In the short time he'd been a detective he'd seen it all; arson, sexual assault, theft, homicide, robbery, assault. There were days he felt elated when he managed to get a confession out of a suspect, and the court system did its job, and there were times he second-guessed it all and considered a career change. Sometimes it didn't matter how good they were at dotting their I's and crossing their T's, evidence got contaminated, judges threw out cases, and criminals slipped through their grasp. Contrary to what people believed, police work wasn't bulletproof. It involved a lot of people and if one of them screwed up, it could mean the difference between making or breaking a case.

Jamie, another officer, called out to him. "Goodman, there's a woman here to see you. Says she's related to Anna Walker."

He looked up from his desk and nodded. "I'll be there in a few minutes."

Now there was a woman who'd been a thorn in the department's side. Although he agreed with the rest of the staff that her frequent visits with newfound evidence and tips tended to eat into their duties, he found it difficult to turn her away. Maybe it was her adamant belief that a serial killer was still out there or her belief that County had screwed up the investigation of her son's abduction. Either way, he tried to make time for her, if only to give her a sense that they cared.

As he got up from his desk, he noticed he'd spilled coffee on his white shirt.

"Oh shit."

Of course Tremonti immediately noticed and chuckled. When he wasn't riding some officer's ass he was cracking jokes to lighten the mood in the office. However, not all his gags went over well. Noah headed down to the changing room to get another shirt but there wasn't one as he'd forgotten to do his laundry. He groaned, used a cloth to wipe it clean and glanced at himself in the mirror. At thirty-four he still had a full head of dark hair, it was no longer cropped short like it was when he was a patrol officer. He also no longer missed wearing the uniform. He adjusted his gray suit jacket and tie and headed back up. Five minutes later an officer buzzed him out into the lobby.

The first thing that struck him about the woman was her dark hair. It was short, wavy and unruly. She wore a pair of jeans, a tight light-brown rain jacket that showed off her hourglass figure, and knee-high brown riding boots. She had her back turned and was looking at the cabinet that held numerous thank-you letters, certificates and sponsorship banners that the department had received.

"Can I help you?"

He glanced at her reflection before she turned.

"Kara Walker," she said extending her hand.

He shook it, fixated on her eyes. They were a striking rich blue, the kind of blue seen in wolves, the kind of color that some might have said looked unnatural. "Detective Goodman. Noah."

She got this pained expression on her face. "Um. You've got mustard on your tie."

He glanced down and rolled his eyes. He'd been so focused on the coffee stain that he hadn't seen the blob of mustard. Embarrassment turned his cheeks a bright red and he wanted the ground to open and swallow him whole.

"I was hoping to speak to you about my mother."

He hesitated for a second, still mesmerized by her features. Her eyebrow shot up and he snapped out of it. "Right. Anna. What can I do for you?"

"She passed away a few days ago."

His eyes widened. "I heard. I'm sorry."

"Anyway, I was told she spoke to you on numerous occasions about Charlie."

"Charlie. Right." He clenched his jaw and knew where this was heading. Every time Anna came in it was the same. It didn't matter what workload he had, he was looking at half an hour of his day being eaten up. Phoning in a tip, or leaving evidence with the front desk never sufficed. She always wanted to meet face to face. He figured her daughter would be the same. He looked around then gestured for her to follow him into the office area. He led her past a row of tables. Officers worked away, punching keys, answering phones. A couple glanced at her as he took her into an interview room out back.

"Your mother mentioned you a couple of times. Said you work as a police officer in New York?" he said over his shoulder as he held open the light brown wooden door.

"I work for a division of the State Patrol. The Bureau of Criminal Investigation."

Was she putting that out there to cut through any of the bullcrap he might spew or simply to make it clear that she, like him, wasn't a run-of-the-mill trooper? Kara brushed past him and he caught the scent of perfume. He'd never been one for women wearing strong scents. Most of the time it made him want to gag. Too strong. Too flowery. But not this time. He felt a twinge in his stomach and an urge to ask her what she was wearing but instead opted not to. It would have come across as unprofessional and slightly odd.

"Can I get you a coffee?" he asked with hesitation knowing full well the vending machine sludge tasted even worse than the crap he had earlier.

"Actually, I'm good." She gave a thin smile.

The interview room didn't contain much. A two-way mirror, two chairs and a table, a clock on the wall and a small window that gave them a gloomy shot of the weather outside. Noah took a seat across from her.

"So what would you like to know?"

"What information did my mother share with you?" she asked.

"Mostly tips. She gave us names, persons of interest that she wanted us to look into or bring in to interview."

"And did you?"

He had to refrain from smiling. Most would have assumed they had done their due diligence and followed up on a lead, however, most didn't know her mother.

"Where it made sense, yes. Not all of the leads your mother gave us warranted a follow-up. How do I put this…?" He trailed off trying to be tactful, especially in light of her recent death. "You probably know better than anyone else how cases are treated once they are considered closed. We have limited resources as a department and that's why we rely on a number of outside agencies to assist us when it's required. In your mother's case, it wasn't required. Had it been an open cold case, maybe, but twenty-five years have gone by and someone is already locked up in the pen for that crime."

"So then why did you give her the time of day?"

He leaned forward and clasped his hands together. "She was a grieving mother. What was I supposed to do? Turn her away?"

"And yet you allowed her to continue on down that path."

"Hold on a minute. We didn't allow her to do anything. She had doubts about Kyle Harris. Any grieving parent whose child's body hadn't been found would, regardless of what the evidence showed."

"But you got her hopes up."

He leaned back in his chair unsure of how to respond. He was damned either way. If they had turned her away they would have been considered heartless, if they lent an ear, they were admitting in a roundabout way that perhaps they'd screwed up.

"What do you want me to say?" he asked.

Under any other circumstances he would have nipped this in the bud and told her that he was a very busy man and he didn't have time for accusations but the fact was Anna's concerns had sparked an interest in the old case, and made him consider the possibility that she was on to something.

"Did you believe her?"

He sucked air between his teeth and looked towards the two-way mirror. No one was behind it but it was a habit.

"It doesn't matter."

"It did to her."

"Ms. Walker."

"Kara." She corrected him.

"Kara. You of all people know how abductions and missing cases work. Our focus here is on Clallam County. I don't cover the four counties where those kids went missing. Even if those counties are up against ours, it's outside of our jurisdiction."

"Then tell me this, has the investigative division of the Washington State Patrol linked the disappearance of the four together?"

"You'd have to ask them. We haven't had an abduction here on the scale of your brother's in twenty-five years. How the other law enforcement agencies are handling those four cases is unknown to us."

"You never followed the cases?"

"Did you?" he threw it back to her.

"But they are similar."

"Only based on the day and years spread apart. I read your brother's case. You were there that night when he was taken. In the other four cases, no one else was present. There was no suspect sketch created, or witnesses. Now I understand your mother was looking for some kind of link between them and Charlie's abduction and I'm not saying it doesn't exist but we deal with a lot of cases here every day, and our focus is Clallam County."

"My brother was taken in Clallam County."

"And like I told your mother, the case is closed. I did her the courtesy of passing on the tips to the sheriff's office of each of the four counties but beyond that there wasn't much else I could do with a closed case. Now had there been a recent abduction in Clallam, that might have changed things."

"When was the last time she spoke to you?"

"A week ago. She came in saying that she believed whoever took Charlie was planning on taking another boy from Clallam. She also thought she was getting close." He could tell where she was going with this and Noah was well aware of what Anna believed but his hands were tied until something of significance crossed his table.

"And?" Kara probed deeper.

"And she'd received a few phone calls in the night. I would have thought your father might have told you."

"No." She dipped her head. "Did you check any of the numbers?"

"Yes, the caller had used a VoIP number. However people make prank calls all the time. There were no threats made. You know how these things go. Besides…"

"You thought my mother was just being paranoid?" There was a long pause. "You're aware of how she died?"

"I am and it was cleared as suicide."

"What about the toxicology report?"

"Four to six weeks. Your father wanted to bury her. Unless the ME noticed anything that would have given cause for alarm, they are usually under pressure by family to release the body to loved ones. Besides, your father said your mother was taking medication for anxiety." He glanced at the band on her wrist. She noticed and covered it with her sleeve.

"So they assume grief got the better of her," Kara said.

He nodded.

"Do you believe that?" she asked.

Noah ran a hand over his tired face. He'd only gotten five hours' sleep the night before and was badly in need of a vacation.

"Kara, I believe your mother loved your brother. I go by the facts of a case. I'm not paid to speculate."

She nodded a few times.

"Is that everything?" he asked. She didn't respond. "Look, I have a lot of paperwork to wade through. You know how it is. It never ends." He was trying not to sound rude but it was bound to come across that way.

"Sure, I'll let you get back to it."

As she rose from the table he noticed she didn't have a ring on her finger.

"Your mother said you were married."

"Was."

She didn't expand on it and he didn't wish to pry. Outside in the hallway she turned to him and opened her mouth as if she was about to ask a question.

"Off the record. After going through my brother's case, do you think Kyle Harris was responsible?"

He looked towards the main office and ran a hand around the back of his neck before he added, "Or did they bungle the case?"

She nodded.

He shrugged. "I guess we'll never know. However," he tapped the air with his finger, "I think they did the best job they could under the circumstances. Like the Swanson case." He turned it back on her to put things in perspective. "At the end of the day, that's all we can do, right?"

Her brow pinched and Noah got a sense that perhaps he'd touched a sore point. Now he wished he hadn't said anything. *They did the best job they could?* What was he thinking? Again it was a force of habit to protect the reputation of the investigators involved. He'd followed the Swanson case with interest. It was hard not to, being it was such a high-profile case. Talk shows and the media had eaten it up, made their accusations and turned it into a circus.

Chapter 12

Stonewalled. That's what her mother would have said but that wasn't the case. Kara had already researched the Clallam County Sheriff Department. They operated in a remote area with limited resources. While the county and city departments handled most investigations themselves, special circumstances, such as the abduction of a child under the age of 13, would have required assistance from outside agencies. That's why the state bureau of investigation and FBI were called in when Charlie was abducted. They pooled resources together and while that had its advantages it could lead to problems. Some of which got worse if homicides occurred across county or state lines. It made it harder to connect them, and even more so back in 1991.

As Kara drove away she had this nagging feeling in her gut that told her to leave it be. Too much time had passed, and with all the negative attention she'd got from the Swanson case, it would only make things complicated. Still, call it what you would; survivor's guilt, an investigative mind or simply grief from losing her mother, she couldn't let it go, at least not without speaking to Kyle Harris.

It wasn't a decision she made lightly. This was the man accused and sentenced for taking her brother. Beyond the appearance he made in the courtroom on the day of his sentencing, she hadn't seen him. It wasn't like she was expecting him to confess, or tell her the whereabouts of her brother's body, but she couldn't reject the thought that out of all the people her mother hassled, he wouldn't have been one of them. Harris would have been at the top of her list. Maybe he'd shared something with her that made her question the evidence presented to the jury?

Kara returned home to find her father still working away in the garage. She spent a few minutes making him a cup of coffee and a sandwich before placing the call. To say she was nervous would have been an understatement. She'd dealt with the most abhorrent criminals and being in their presence didn't make her feel close to how she felt now. She glanced out the window making sure her father had returned to working on the car before she ventured into the basement and made the call to Washington State Penitentiary in Walla Walla.

Would he even take the call? What would he say? What would she say?

After being placed on hold for a few minutes while they checked to see if he wanted to speak to her, she glossed over the map in front of her, and the five counties: Clallam, Jefferson, Grays Harbor, Mason and Thurston. Her mother had stuck red pins in the locations where the boys were last seen, then tied them together with red thread. She looked down at the list of names and their ages. All of them were under the age of thirteen. Although Charlie's case was considered closed, the other four were still classed as open investigations as no one had been arrested or charged.

Kara took a sip of her coffee and swallowed hard when she heard him come on the line.

"Hello?" he said.

Kara's voice caught in her throat. That was the thing about the trial. Several people had asked her if he sounded like the masked man in the woods but it was hard to tell. Some part of her thought she would recognize it instantly but she realized that was just wishful thinking. The reality was the man who took Charlie probably didn't sound anything like the way he did that night. People's voices changed when they spoke through gritted teeth, or a voice scrambler. And paying attention to his voice that night was the last thing on her mind.

"Hello?" Kyle said again.

"Mr. Harris. My name is Kara Walker." She let the name hang out there to see how he'd react.

"Anna Walker's daughter?"

"That's right."

There was a pause. "Is Anna okay?"

"Um." She was at a loss for words for a few seconds. "She's dead."

She gripped the phone a little tighter.

"Oh my God." She heard him sigh. "What happened?"

"Mr. Harris."

"Kyle. Call me Kyle please."

"Kyle. First, thank you for taking the call. Did my mother ever speak to you after the trial?"

She got straight down to it. She wasn't comfortable speaking with him and if she didn't stay on track she wasn't sure what she'd say. She heard him inhale deeply. "She visited on two occasions, spoke to me once by way of video and called several times by phone."

"Why?"

It seemed like an obvious question but she wanted to hear it from him.

"She wanted answers about her son. At first it was a confession. She thought I was holding back and she pleaded for me to tell her where Charlie was but like I told her, I couldn't. I wasn't responsible."

Silence stretched between them before he continued. "What happened to her?"

Kara wasn't sure if she should tell him but it didn't seem to matter now. "Suicide."

He sighed deeply. "I'm sorry. I'm really sorry for your loss." It sounded genuine then in the next breath he said, "He got to her, didn't he?"

His answer really threw her off-kilter. She frowned. "What? Why would you say that?"

"The first time your mother visited, she wanted answers. I couldn't give her any but I told her to look into the case. Speak to the original sheriff that was assigned, and the kid that accused me prior to your brother's disappearance. I suggested if she wanted answers she could find them by speaking with those involved in the original case. Hang on a sec." He sounded like he lit a cigarette. The snap of a lighter brought back a memory of that night. As he continued to speak she listened to his voice, trying to place the nuances against those that she'd heard from the masked abductor on that night. "Sorry about that. Anyway, to cut a long story short, she called me back a few months later and said that while she wasn't convinced that I was telling the truth, there were a few discrepancies about the case and she was going to look into it. That was two years after I'd been sentenced. I've been in here nineteen years."

She listened carefully as he continued.

"Ten years after your brother's abduction, there had been two more, one in Jefferson and another in Grays Harbor. The next time I heard from her she believed they were connected and that perhaps I wasn't lying. I told her to watch herself. You know, to be careful and speak to the police. I put her in touch with my attorney who's been handling my appeals with federal and state courts, you know, just in case she came across any evidence that might be useful." He sighed, obviously realizing that whatever hope he'd placed in her mother, it was now gone. A question swirled in her head and she knew she was taking a risk asking it in light of what he'd just told her, but she had to hear it from him.

"Were you in any way involved in the abduction or cover-up?"

Without missing a beat he replied, "No. I want whoever did this just as much as your mother did. Ms. Walker, I've been sitting behind bars for something I never did and for the longest time no one has believed me barring my attorney until your mother."

"Then how did Charlie's jeans and one of his shoes end up on your property?"

"I don't know. I already told them that. Anyone could have planted those. It wasn't like I was a stranger to the community. My name and photo had been plastered across the newspaper."

"Did you have any enemies?"

He scoffed. "Before or after the accusation?"

In the background she could hear doors clanging.

"When did you last speak with her?"

"What day is it?"

"Wednesday."

It was easy for them to lose track of time inside. Days blurred into nights, the same routine made it easy to forget.

"Two weeks ago. She phoned, said that she was on to something. It was a hunch but she would update me as soon as she found out."

"What was it?"

"She didn't say."

"Had she ruled out suspects from the original case?"

"Some, but she still had three people on her radar."

"Do you recall who they were?"

She heard him blow out smoke. "I don't remember the names."

"I would have thought if you were banking on my mother finding whoever was behind this, you would have jotted them down. You know, for your attorney and all."

"Ms. Walker. Do you know how many people she was looking at? Or how many were considered suspects at the time of Charlie's abduction?" he shot back.

Something about the way he said her brother's name got a reaction out of her. It might have seemed strange but Kara wanted to tell him to not use his name. Even though her mother might have been convinced that he had nothing to do with it, she wasn't there, at least not yet.

"So you don't know?"

"Like I said, I'm sorry, but I didn't take notes when I was talking with her. If she found anything of significance she passed it on to my attorney and law enforcement. She said she'd built up quite a rapport with a detective in Clallam County."

Her thoughts drifted to the tall detective. She'd got a

sense that he was holding back, probably not wanting to get sidetracked from his duties, and possibly even relieved that her mother was gone so he'd no longer have to deal with her. She made a mental note to go through the files after the call. She'd barely scratched the surface.

Upstairs she heard the rear door open.

"Kara!"

A shot of fear went through her, the likes of which she hadn't felt since she was sixteen. She'd had a guy over while her parents were out and they'd returned home early. Wiggling out of that one had been tough.

"Look, I have to go. I appreciate you taking the call."

"Again, I'm sorry about your mother. If you have any other questions…'

He didn't finish what he was saying but she knew what he meant.

"Thank you."

She hung up just as her father reached the bottom of the stairs.

"Ah, there you are. I heard you talking. Who was that?"

"Oh just someone from work. What's up?" She tried to act all nonchalant, an act she liked to think she'd mastered over the years.

"I got you booked in with Lloyd Benson tomorrow at one."

Kara's brow pinched. "What?"

"You said you were struggling."

She sighed placing a hand on her head. "Dad, I appreciate the concern but you really shouldn't have done that. Can you call back and cancel?"

"I can but he offered the slot pro bono. I don't want to look ungrateful. Besides, he's been helpful to us over the years. It's only thirty minutes."

She sighed again and waved him off. "Alright."

"Oh and I thought we might order in Chinese tonight."

"But your ulcer?"

"Ah screw my ulcer."

The last thing she needed was to get into an argument with him. He remained there for a minute or two looking over the walls. "You are going to take this down today, right?"

"Yes, Dad, just leave it with me."

"Okay, because I don't want this here anymore."

"I understand."

He trudged back upstairs and she went back to fishing through the files looking for those her mother had considered suspects.

* * *

Later that evening after clocking out, Noah tossed his house keys down on the counter in his empty apartment. He kicked off his shoes and headed straight for the fridge to get a bottle of Budweiser. He yanked at his tie as he gazed inside. For the most part it was empty. The fridge had spaghetti leftovers from two nights ago, and some dishes that were starting to grow something funky on the top. He rarely shopped big. There was only one mouth to feed now. He grabbed up the dishes and scooped the gunk into the trash. Twisting the cap off the bottle he glanced at the photo of Amanda before taking a seat in his La-Z-Boy recliner.

"I know, darling. Time to move on. I wish it was that easy."

It had been three years since he'd lost Amanda in a car accident. Noah had met her when he first moved to Clallam. She worked at PENCOM dispatch center located in Port Angeles Police Department. She had attended a Christmas event for the county. They'd hit it off from the first drink, yet she would have said it was the second. Four years together, six months married when the accident happened. All he could remember was life before her, and then after it was like his world collapsed. He took two months off from work before he couldn't afford to take any more. It hadn't taken long for him to bounce back from it, at least that's what a colleague said when he returned. But what did he know? People made assumptions on appearances. If he wasn't wallowing, he must be healing. The truth was he was hiding more than healing.

He sank into his chair and flicked the TV on to try and unwind. Since taking the position as a detective it had become increasingly hard to switch off. When his mind wasn't on suspects, witnesses or victims, he was thinking about whether he'd remembered to file certain paperwork associated with a case. It was never-ending. For four years he had Amanda to confide in. She understood and had a way of getting his mind off it. But that was then. After surfing through one too many channels he flicked off the TV and got up to get the folder he'd brought home. It was only one of many related to Charlie Walker. Seeing Anna's daughter today, and answering her questions, made him think about the numerous interactions he'd had with her mother. He didn't want to say anything to Kara but he was intrigued by the lengths Anna had gone to in order to uncover who was behind her son's abduction. Every victim was different; few dug as deep as her or left an impact on him. He sat back down and took another swig from the bottle and flipped the file open. He thumbed through tips and leads she'd given him over the years. Her words came back to him as he pored over it. Among the many persons of interest and suspects in the original case there had been three that had stood out:

Ray Owen, a guy with a low IQ who claimed to be psychic, and had contacted the police on a number of occasions back in the '90s to say he knew where the boys were buried. He'd even called Anna a few times.

Seth Leonard, a Catholic deacon and child welfare advocate who resembled the original sketch and had done eight years in state prison for sexual interference, and had been out on a ten-year supervised release at the time of the abduction. He was a local of Blackmore.

Then there was Darryl Clayton, a resident of Forks, an angry individual who worked as a handyman with his son Gregory Clayton. Some of the statements he made around the time of the abduction and his resemblance to the suspect sketch had put him in the crosshairs. However, he was never brought in for questioning.

Anna was convinced that one of them was responsible; unfortunately she didn't have any evidence. *I'm gathering it,* she'd said.

None of them had been brought in and yet they were all residents of Clallam County, all within his jurisdiction. He'd wanted to follow up but sticking his nose out there without solid evidence would have been career suicide, and after all he'd been through with Amanda, he just wasn't sure he was ready to deal with the backlash.

Behind Noah his cell rattled on the counter. He set the file down and answered it. It was the department.

“Goodman. Sarge wants you in. We’ve got an attempted abduction.”

Part 2

Chapter 13

Thursday, October 27, 2016

4 Days Before Halloween

Noah was just about to tuck into his breakfast special of three eggs, bacon, home fries, and rye toast when Kara took a seat across from him in the Blackmore Diner. The *Peninsula Daily News* was tossed in front of him. It was folded open to an article. He caught the headline before he glanced up at her, then turned his head to scan it.

Clallam County Police Investigate Attempted Abduction of 10-Year-Old Boy in Highland Hills

Police are investigating an attempted child abduction in the Highland Hills of Sequim. A man approached a 10-year-old boy on Wednesday evening near Overlook Trail and Stampede Drive and tried to lure him into his vehicle after asking him for directions, according to the Clallam County Sheriff Department. The boy managed to escape his grasp and ran to his nearby home, police said, and the van sped away.

The driver is described as a Caucasian male wearing dark clothing, a black jacket, and had a dark mustache. Police are looking for a white Ford van with tinted windows, a side sliding door, roof racks and a broken rear taillight.

Anyone with information about this incident is asked to contact the Clallam County Sheriff Department.

Noah shook his head. "How did the media get their hands on that story?"

"Uh, I dunno, maybe someone is leaking information or the parents called it in," she replied leaning back and taking in the sight of his breakfast. "You know how many calories that has?"

"Hopefully a lot," he said, cutting some bacon and shoveling it away.

"Ray Owen has a mustache. Has anyone checked to see what kind of vehicle he's driving?" she asked.

His eyebrow shot up. "Have you been stalking him?"

"I might have driven by his residence."

Noah took another bite then washed it down with coffee.

"Ms. Walker. Don't you have something better to do? Look after your father, get home to New York?"

A waitress came over. "Can I get you anything, darling?"

"Just a coffee, thanks," she said without taking her eyes off him. The waitress scrawled on her pad and then ambled away leaving her staring at him waiting for an answer.

"So?" she asked. "You want to fill me in?"

He took a napkin and wiped his lips before taking a second to add a spoonful of sugar to his coffee. He stirred slowly. "We're handling it."

"Four days away. If everything my mother compiled is accurate, she believed he would take another boy four days from now."

He picked at his food. "Then this isn't your guy, so leave it with us."

"Or perhaps this was a warm-up."

He eyed her as he took his cup and sipped it. The waitress returned with a white cup and poured out some coffee. Steam swirled above it.

"Okay, I'll bite. A warm-up?"

"If my mother's notes are correct, in the years leading up to Charlie's abduction, several boys were approached and sexually assaulted. That's how they managed to get a suspect sketch. Now you said the only thing that the four boys who were abducted had in common was the date of abduction — Halloween — and the years they were spread apart. Now I was going over it last night. You know, wondering why he waits five years? Does he keep them alive then once they hit a certain age he disposes of them? Or is there some other significance to the date?"

"Hold on a minute. What are you on about assaults leading up to his abduction?"

"My mother unearthed some additional information, I would have thought she mentioned this to you."

He sighed. "Look, you know how much of my workload involves sexual crimes?"

She knew he was going to tell her so she waited.

"Nearly eighty percent of what crosses my table are sexual crimes."

"But how many are minors, taken by strangers?" Kara added, knowing what BCI dealt with each year.

"Ms. Walker, I was out late last night, and I'm back at it again today. So if you don't mind skipping to the part where you tell me where you are going with this, it would really help."

"I spoke to Kyle Harris."

He took another bite of toast and glanced at someone who walked in the diner. He must have stared a little too long as Kara followed his gaze, then he said, "Let me guess how the conversation went. You asked him if he did it. He said no. The end."

"Not far off. However, he told me that my mother had come across some information that led her to believe that he wasn't involved."

"In Charlie's abduction?"

Without missing a beat she blurted out, "I believe she knew who was behind it."

"Or…" He took a casual sip of his coffee. "After all her searching, knocking on doors and hassling people she reached the unfortunate conclusion that the man who was truly responsible is the same one who is locked up."

"And you think that crushed her and she offed herself out of guilt or sorrow, is that what you're suggesting?"

"You said it, I didn't."

She shook her head. "No, I don't buy it."

He wiped at his lips with the napkin. "Okay, let's go out on a limb for a moment. Let's say your mother did know. Maybe she managed to uncover something that multiple agencies couldn't. Why kill herself? Huh? It doesn't make sense unless she realized that she'd got it wrong."

Kara opened her mouth to state the obvious but he cut her off.

"And don't tell me she was murdered because the ME has already signed the release. There was no evidence to suggest that it was anything more than suicide."

"But you don't have back the toxicology report."

"No we don't but when we do, I'm confident what it's going to say." Noah took another sip of his coffee and leaned forward. "Look, I can't imagine what it must be like to go twenty-five years without knowing what happened to your brother but I'm telling you from one detective to another — leave it. Go spend time with your father, have a drink with old friends and take a trip down memory lane but don't linger. It's not healthy."

She was about to respond when an older gentleman in his late sixties approached.

Goodman groaned. "Now Hal, we've already been through this before. Walk away."

"All I'm asking is you reconsider. She's paid for her—"

"Really? Three years. Is that what you think is fair?"

The old man laid a hand on Noah's shoulder and he shrugged it off. "Walk away now!"

Another man, younger, early forties with short, curly blond hair, came over and tried to guide the old man away. "Leave it, Pops, he'll just arrest us on some bogus claim."

That got a reaction out of Noah. "It was reviewed by a third party. I wasn't involved in the decision and if I had my way she would still be inside. And I aim to make that happen with the appeal."

Hal became all upset, tears streaked his face. "Mr. Goodman, I'm sorry. I really am."

"Don't apologize. It's waste of time," the young man beside him said.

But he couldn't hold the old man back, he lunged

forward and grabbed a hold of Noah by the jacket and started pleading with him. Noah reacted like anyone would if they were grabbed and pulled his arm off. The younger guy snapped. "Get your hands off him!"

Before she knew what was happening, Noah was up and shoved him back into a table, knocking plates and full cups of coffee to the floor.

A woman cried out, "Jesse! No." A dark-haired older woman in a booth farther down stepped out and grabbed a hold of him. She and Noah exchanged an icy glare, though most of the glare came from Noah. He turned and fished into his pocket for some cash and tossed it on the table. Before Kara could say anything he stormed out of the diner leaving behind a room full of stunned patrons. Before the three individuals left, the young guy referred to as Jesse walked over to Kara and said, "Word of advice, choose better company."

They walked back to their booth and after paying, quickly left. Kara sat there wondering what the hell that was all about. She shook her head, drained the remainder of her cup and turned her attention to the paper to zigzag the article again. Was this an attempted abduction by him? She wasn't sure but it was possible. But if it was him, why take the risk of getting caught? Why strike now before Halloween? And if he was responsible for the kidnappings in the surrounding four counties, why had no bodies been found? Disposing of a body was for many serial killers another form of pleasure. Taunting police, media and the families was all about head games and most enjoyed them, but this one was different — none of the boys abducted were ever found. That's why she found it hard to believe this was their guy. In the previous four abductions he'd not been seen. Why was he changing his M.O. now? Or maybe Goodman was right. Perhaps it wasn't him. The waitress came over and handed her the check. She dropped a few dollars for the coffee then sat back and reached into her jacket pocket and pulled out a scrap of paper. It was a list of seventeen names scrawled in black ink with fourteen crossed out in red leaving only three remaining. She'd spent the better part of the previous evening sifting through the many names her mother had obtained from news articles and police incident reports related to the abduction of Charlie. She still had to determine why she had crossed them out and if she had questioned the three remaining. With a head full of questions and a long day ahead of her, she placed a phone call to Bobby to see if he knew anything. If the article had been given the go-ahead by County, it was possible they were selective in what information was released to the public. Often they would hold back key pieces of information that would help them nail a perp.

"I would have thought you'd be on a flight back to New York by now," Bobby said.

"Staying a few extra days."

"It's your mother's wall, isn't it?"

"That and the recent event in the paper."

"Oh that."

"Yeah, about that. What can you tell me?"

"I'm sorry, that was all we got," Bobby said.

"Goodman acted a bit perplexed on how the newspaper got word of it. I told him it was probably the boy's parents."

He scoffed on the other end. "It wasn't the parents who gave us the tip."

"Who was it?"

"Sorry, can't tell you."

"Come on, Bobby. Someone had to have had some interest in the case if they thought it warranted telling the media."

"It would have got out sooner or later."

"Right, but someone gave it a nudge in the right direction. Who?"

He hemmed and hawed, and she heard him muffle the phone. "I'll be right there. Just taking this call." Kara heard him walk a short distance and a door close.

"Look, I could get into a lot of trouble for telling you this. It's a guy named Henry Ellis."

"From ISB?"

ISB was Washington State Patrol Investigative Services Bureau. They had been called in with the FBI at the time of Charlie's abduction.

"That's the one."

She frowned. "But he's retired."

"Officially, yes, but he's still got his ear to the ground. Don't ask me how but he was the one that gave us the tip."

"Huh!" Kara said looking off outside the diner. "Anything else?"

"That's all. Now I need to get back to work. Just do me a favor."

"What's that?"

"If you ever nail this bastard, give me the first scoop."

She chuckled. "Said like a true journalist."

Chapter 14

Kara had to do some digging but she soon unearthed the address for ex-special agent Henry Ellis. He was a resident of Port Angeles, a city located in Clallam County, just northeast of Blackmore. Kara drove out on WA-113, which then merged into WA-112 E. The A-frame home was nestled in a wilderness valley surrounded by lush forest and meadows. It was a short distance from the pristine waters of the East Twin River and was set back on a rise, a hundred feet from the road on twenty acres of quiet river frontage. The house itself was made from pine with dark brown shingles, with an overhanging roof that doubled for the porch, and it sat squarely facing the county highway. The yard looked as if it had fallen into disrepair with weeds growing up through the paving slabs that snaked up to the doorway. Two vehicles were angled at the top of the driveway, a dark blue Impala and a brand-new red Ford 4 x 4.

Off to the left of the home was an old barn and outbuilding, along with a garage and storage shed for yard tools. Down to the right of the house was the glint of a propane tank.

Gravel crunched beneath her tires as she eased off the gas and shut it down. She eyed the front porch where a man was bent over with his hands in the dirt. Beside him was a pile of weeds. He was wearing jean overalls, dark brown boots and a white T-shirt with a red bandanna tied around what was left of his wispy white hair. He'd watched her approach and waited until she got out before he pulled off the bandanna and wiped it across his brow. He had a bit of paunch, and moved like any typical retiree who might have had knee surgery. He wobbled over to the front porch and took a seat on the step.

"Henry Ellis? Special Agent Henry Ellis?"

He smiled. "That would be me. Though I haven't been called that in a long time."

She made her way up and stopped a few feet from him. "My name's—"

He cut her off. "I know who you are. Seen you on TV. Followed some of the cases you worked on."

"Right."

"Guessing you're here about the missing four."

"That and some other things."

"Well let's get out of the sun, or what's left of it. We don't get much sun around these parts but I guess you'd know that." He got up and placed a hand on his knee and let out a groan.

"Knee surgery?"

"Hip. Double. They don't make them like they used to," he said before chuckling and making his way to the storm door. "Take a seat." He motioned to an Adirondack chair. It was at the far end of the porch alongside a porch rocker. "You thirsty? Cause I am," he said before she could reply. He disappeared inside the home. A small hound dog was sleeping at the other end of the porch. He didn't raise his head but lifted a droopy eye as if to find out who was disturbing his rest. Kara took a seat and glanced at a dog-eared book resting on the rocker. On top lay a pair of reading glasses. She took in the fresh air, and could hear the steady churn of the river nearby. Dark clouds tried to blot out what remained of the blue sky. The smell of damp pine lingered in the air.

About five minutes later, when she was beginning to think he'd forgotten about her, the storm door creaked open as he brought out a tray of coffee. He set it down on a table and handed her a cup.

"Help yourself to milk and sugar."

He sighed deeply as he sank back into the rocker and noticed her looking at the book. He smiled and showed her the front cover. *Psychology and the Criminal Mind.*

"Was it hard to hand over the badge at the end of your career?" she asked.

"Thirty-two years. I miss it every day."

"Is that why you tipped off the *Peninsula Daily Times* about the abduction attempt?"

He wagged his finger. "So that's what you're here about."

"Do you have a police scanner?"

"A scanner? Please. When would I have the time to listen to that? I might miss my work but retirement is better. So no."

"So you have someone on the inside who feeds you news?"

He chuckled and eyed her with amusement. "Something like that."

"From Blackmore or County?"

He put on his glasses and eyed her over the top of his coffee. Instead of answering her, he said, "Heard about your mom. Sorry."

She dipped her chin ever so slightly. "Thank you."

"I remember you. You were a lot younger. How do you like being a cop?" he asked.

"It has its moments."

He chuckled. "That it does. You know there was a saying at our department. They took it from the Seals."

"The only easy day was yesterday," she said before he could say it.

"Ah, so I see our east coast friends have embraced it too."

"I think it's doing the rounds," she said smiling before taking a sip of her drink. "Why? Why are you still involved after all this time?"

He shrugged. "I dealt with a lot of cases but there was something about your brother's case that never sat right with me. I was called in to assist assuming we'd find a body in a matter of a week or two. In cases I'd dealt with before they were dead within the first twenty-four hours. When your brother's shoe and jeans showed up on Kyle Harris's property, I put forward that it was possible that whoever had taken him was doing it as a means to draw attention away from himself."

"No one listened?"

"By the time we found that evidence, five years later, they were already knee-deep in a theory that Harris had taken the kid. An army of investigators couldn't have swayed what was going on behind the scenes. Well, you know that… with the Swanson case and all."

She nodded.

"Unfortunately these things get away from us and finding that evidence was like hitting a home run, only problem is back then we didn't have the means to test it the way we could now."

"And so why hasn't anyone done retesting?"

"It's a closed case. They don't want to draw out skeletons from the closet or admit they placed an innocent man in prison. It's bad for business."

"So you believe he is innocent?"

"Of abducting your brother, I do, of what occurred before that, I don't know. But I know it played a huge factor in where they put their efforts. I'm afraid Kyle Harris was just in the wrong place at the wrong time, and with his history with the law and sexual assault accusation — you do the math. Are they going to chase after fourteen other people who were nowhere in the vicinity at the time or build a case around Harris?"

"You said fourteen. There were seventeen people of interest at the time. My mother had scratched out fourteen of them."

"Leaving, three, that's right." He smiled. "Your mother had good things to say about you."

"You met with her?"

"Numerous times. She was a great help after I lost my wife six years ago."

"I'm sorry."

"Ah I knew it was coming. Cancer. Creeps up. She beat it the first time around but fate had other plans." He shook his head and took another sip. "Anyway, she'd bring me these apple pies."

Kara smiled.

"Ah, you know the ones."

"She loved her pie," Kara said.

"Anyway, she never let up. We talked at great length about the case. Her discussions with Kyle Harris and the three men."

"Did she ever speak to them?"

"She had plans to. I think she might have called them. I saw her about two weeks before she passed away."

"Did she ever say who she suspected? Or was there anyone you suspected?"

"I suspected a lot of people, unfortunately I didn't have the time or the resources to dig into their past like I do now and even now I'm limited. But I have my connections."

"In Clallam County? Wouldn't by any chance be Noah Goodman, would it?"

He smiled. He mimicked zipping his lips. "I don't want to get anyone in trouble. Let's just say that I believe he's still out there. Once in a while I did a favor for your mother and got things moving along but for the most part I've remained hands off." He took another sip. "I'm getting too old for this. My wife, Jules, used to remind me when I was veering off track."

"How long were you married?"

He sucked air between his coffee-stained teeth. "A long time. I never forgot an anniversary."

"How did you manage it?"

"What?"

"Staying together. It's rare."

"Jules was rare. Most women would have packed their bags and left."

"Did she work for the department?"

"Nope. She was an attorney. Maybe that worked in her favor as she knew the pressure I was under. We made it work and I guess you could say she wasn't high maintenance."

That got a smile out of Kara.

"Just saying. There's a lot of ladies out there that are very needy. My gal wasn't."

"That she let on."

He laughed. "Ah now you'll have me chewing that

over for the next week."

It was quiet as they drank their coffees.

Kara continued. "She was convinced the cases of the four boys were related and that he was going to take another one."

"That's right. You see, the problem I had was trying to understand the motive. Purely sexual? Did your brother know the individual? Had he been watching him in the previous weeks? I've been through them all."

"And?"

"I think it's something more than sexual gratification, otherwise we would have seen an increase in abduction attempts. As you know, these kinds of offenders can't keep their urges under control. Once they've got away with one and had a cooling-off period, they are right back at it again. Five years is too long. There's something more to this than sex."

She could tell it frustrated him.

"So what can you tell me?"

"Like I told your mother. He's a resident in one of the five counties though my money is on Clallam. Charlie was his first. I'm sure of that. The abduction attempt that occurred prior to Charlie's was…"

"Him warming up."

"Exactly. And every five years the same pattern emerges. A boy is taken on Halloween."

"Washington State Bureau has to have made the connection?"

"They have someone looking into it but you know how it works. There is only so much they can throw at it, and when the leads go cold, so does the case. I wouldn't be surprised if it's sitting on some hard drive just waiting for someone like yourself to crack it open."

"I don't get it," she said. "Okay, in Charlie's case they think they have the individual but no one has been charged with these other four boys. They must have suspects?"

"I can give you the name of the guy who was involved in overseeing it but don't expect miracles. As you know, thousands of kids go missing every year, Kara. There is only so much they can do before they run up against a wall."

"And so what are they waiting for? They want him to take another one?"

He reached for a pack of smokes on a side table and tapped one out.

"Usually. All four of the boys' cases had the FBI and State involved but it dried up. I wish I could say there was more they were able to figure out but they did what they could. All I can tell you is I think our guy lives in Clallam."

"Why Clallam?"

"If Charlie was his first, which I believe he was. They start where they are comfortable, then branch out."

"To avoid detection."

"Exactly."

"And so the bureau has been focusing on the other four counties."

"You got it. With all the circus and bad PR surrounding your brother's case, no one wants to go near it. But like I said to your mother, if they can figure that out, they might just be able to figurc out the other boys."

"And stop him before Monday?"

"That's asking a lot."

Kara finished the rest of her coffee and sat there shaking her head. She thought he'd have answers for her but he didn't know any more than her mother did. She fished into her pocket for a scrap of paper with the three names.

"What about these three: Ray Owen, Seth Leonard, and Darryl Clayton? From what I can tell they were never interviewed but were considered persons of interest. Especially Seth Leonard for his past behavior with minors and Darryl for his likeness to the suspect sketch at the time of Charlie's abduction."

"They weren't brought in for questioning but off the record, I went and spoke with them back in 1991."

"Any connection between the three?"

"None. Ray Owen's mother vouched for him on the night your brother was taken, Seth didn't have an alibi and according to witnesses, people said they saw a dark brown and white station wagon in the area at the time. He was driving one back in those days. It was an '82 Pontiac Bonneville. The problem is Kyle Harris never saw the vehicle, only the headlights through the trees that night."

"And Darryl Clayton?"

"You don't want to go near him. The guy is a loose cannon, liable to shoot you. Anyway his wife, Nancy Clayton, and her brother Edwin Brewer vouched for him."

"But they could have been lying."

"That's what I said." He lit his cigarette and blew out a plume of smoke before coughing. "Welcome to the Charlie Walker case."

Chapter 15

She hated therapists. For the first three years after Charlie was taken Kara was shipped around to various ones like a child that couldn't fit in. It wasn't that the therapists weren't good at the job, or even that they refused to work with her; she was just impossible to work with. She took ownership for that. Opening up as a teenager was hard enough as it was, but discuss the abduction and she clammed up.

On the way back to Blackmore that afternoon, her mind drifted to those days. The sound of a ticking clock. Waiting for them to walk in. The barrage of questions. How does that make you feel? Then repeating her answers back to her. All they wanted to do was get her to talk about her experience. At first she said nothing and would just squirm around in the chair, twisting her long hair between her fingers, waiting for the hour to be up, and when that didn't seem to piss them off — enough to tell her parents that they weren't making progress — she would walk around, picking up items in the office, dropping them and generally acting out. It was usually small things like knocking over their coffee cup, or snapping gum that irritated them, all of them except one — Lloyd Benson. It didn't matter what she did, she could never get a reaction out of him.

He just kept saying the same word over and over again: "Interesting."

Looking back on it now she felt embarrassed by her behavior. But that was her way of dealing with it.

Wherever she went she felt like she was under a microscope. Even the teachers treated her different. "Oh that homework? It's okay. Do it whenever you can."

At first it felt like a dream come true. A few tears and she could be excused from a class. An outburst and she was given a free pass. Why wouldn't she? She was Charlie Walker's sister. That kid has to be screwed up, she'd hear them say.

That's why when her father had booked the appointment to see Benson, she wanted to cancel — the very thought of a million and one questions made her want to gag. Not long after moving to New York she'd stopped going to see therapists, even though her parents encouraged her. Instead, she decided popping pills like Zoloft was easier.

Even though it had been over twenty years since she'd been to his office, she still knew the way. She could have driven with her eyes blindfolded. She knew the exact number of turns, the bump in the road four houses down from his, and the aroma of pine as she made her way closer to the edge of Olympic National Park, to a small community called Elwha. It was located just off U.S. Route 101, not far from Port Angeles.

It was a majestic-looking home that doubled as his place of work. Most of it was made from glass, with stone and iron finishing. The attention to detail was astonishing. She referred to it as "The Glass House." When her parents first took her there back when she was fifteen, she thought she was going to end up in another stuffy room full of encyclopedia-sized books crammed together, and sit across from a sniffling woman peering over her glasses. It was far from that. It often reminded Kara of a secluded resort nestled away at the edge of the National Park. It was located at the end of a road, a good mile from any other neighbor, and had zero drive-by traffic. Outside lush landscaping with year-round colors was spread out over eight acres. The guy even had a stream running through his backyard, three ponds and a manmade waterfall. It offered peace, privacy and tranquility, Lloyd said.

It was strange how places could make her feel like a kid again.

She climbed the stone steps that wound up to his door. She ran her hand over the iron railing and got a flash and a memory of telling her mother to take her home. She didn't want to go through it, not again.

After ringing the bell, she waited, feeling less anxious, more annoyed that her father took it upon himself to push her in a direction when she was old enough to make the decision for herself.

When the thick wooden door opened, she was greeted with a warm hug. His demeanor was always disarming. She glanced at his hair. A full head of thick black hair swept back like someone in their twenties. He was one of the lucky few that managed to hold on to his, even though there were silver flecks now at his temples.

"So good to see you again, Kara. Come on in."

The immediate smell of lemon furniture polish brought back memories of her multiple visits.

"It's been a long while," he said guiding her through to his study. It was spacious with floor to ceiling windows, and blinds that were partially opened to let in warm bands of summer light — except today dark clouds had drifted in blocking out what little sun there was. The hardwood floors were rich in color, a deep red that had come from the redwood forests of California. The gas fireplace was on, tongues of fire flickered behind two single brown leather chairs. Set back from those was a large mahogany table, the same one that had been there since she was a teen. Positioned tidily on the table were a Mac computer, four books, an analog clock and a lamp. The two walls either side of the room were the same. They were jam-packed full of books but they weren't like the type found in the stuffy offices she'd been stuck in prior to meeting Lloyd. These were biographies, non-fiction and the works of the greats, like Charles Dickens, Ernest Hemingway, Mark Twain, William Shakespeare and Oscar Wilde. Often he would quote from them to get a point across, it's what made him stand out from the academics who regurgitated what had been taught to them. In some ways that's what intrigued her about him. He would go off on tangents about life, and the human mind, then in an instant wrap it up with a point that made what she was feeling make sense.

That morning he was wearing grey pants, a dark waistcoat, a white shirt and a burgundy tie. He had a sense of fashion even late into his fifties, and carried himself with an air of confidence that only came from understanding the human psyche.

"You're looking well," he said in his usual upbeat manner.

"Ah, you're too polite." She pointed to her eyes. "Come a bit closer and you'll see I have a few lines around the eyes that weren't there since last time."

He chuckled. "Don't we all."

She took a seat.

"Coffee? Tea?"

"Actually, I'm all caffeinated out for the day. Trying to cut back. Gives me the jitters."

"Right. You don't mind if I do?"

"By all means."

He pivoted and crossed the room to a small cupboard, which he flipped down to reveal a silver espresso machine. She crossed her legs and scanned the shelves absently.

"How's your father?"

"He's back to working on his vehicle."

"Good. It will keep his mind off things."

"That's what he said."

Lloyd glanced at her with a warm smile. "You've been through a lot. All of you. How are you holding up?"

She twisted a necklace around her neck that her mother had bought her when she got married. Her thoughts went to the basement, to the wall, to every conversation she'd had since she'd arrived.

"I'm coping."

"Still taking medication?" he asked as he poured out his drink.

"Zoloft."

"Does it help?"

"It keeps me from losing my mind if that's what you're asking."

He brought his cup over, and took a seat. She fixated on the cup. It was small, the kind used for tiny espressos. It reminded her of those that were used in a kids' tea party. He took a sip and leaned back. For the first ten minutes, the conversation was small talk then it shifted.

"Are you sleeping?"

"Better than I used to, though the last fourteen months have been hard."

"Right. The case of Adam Swanson. What a young life. Are they moving ahead with charges against the family?"

"It's still up in the air."

"And the theory of an intruder?"

"It hasn't been ruled out."

"Interesting."

And there he was back to that again.

"And how about your mother?"

"What about her?"

"Anything you'd like to discuss?"

"Not really."

"Interesting."

"You know, Mr. Benson…"

"Lloyd. I think we've known each other long enough that we can drop formality, right?"

"Sure." She cleared her throat. "Lloyd, I'm curious, in all the times my mother came to you, did she ever discuss our basement?"

"The walls?"

Kara gave a nod.

"She did." He took another sip.

"And?"

"Well that would be breaking client confidentiality, now wouldn't it?"

"I think we are past that now," Kara said.

He breathed in deeply and looked up, closing his eyes for a second. "I'm more interested in knowing, what you thought of it?"

She didn't like the way he turned questions back on her. He might have been different to the others but in that one aspect he was the same. Therapists were masters of manipulating conversation. They would lead you down one road, and if it became uncomfortable and you tried to steer them clear, they would veer you back until you answered their question.

"I thought it was…" she trailed off.

"Disturbing?"

She shook her head. "No. Insightful."

"In what way?"

Kara broke eye contact for a second or two. She really hadn't given it much thought. Of course it was shocking but she wasn't going to say that. It's not like she wasn't aware of her mother's views about how the case went and the verdict but her mother had kept some cards close to her chest and at no point mentioned to her the depths she reached in compiling information.

"In that I wasn't aware of what my mother was capable of."

"Interesting."

If he said it one more time she was going to bat him around the head. Instead, she gritted her teeth and tried to act like it didn't bother her.

"Did she ever talk to you, share her ideas, ask for assistance?"

"No. That's the odd part. She kept me in the dark."

"And how did that make you feel?"

"Look, Mr. Benson—"

"Lloyd."

"Lloyd. I'll be honest with you. The only reason I'm here today is out of courtesy to my father. I really don't wish to discuss the inner workings of my mind. I have

Zoloft for that and it handles it fine."

"But you are curious about your mother?"

"Of course. For someone who never mentioned that she had spoken to Kyle Harris, or seen him in person, or had left behind an intricate web of information that would lead people to believe she thought the man who abducted my brother was still out there. So yeah, I'm curious."

He studied her for a minute or two before finishing his coffee.

"Your mother was deeply troubled. She stopped coming. She stopped the medication prescribed to her. It's not normal but it does happen. Grief can do that to a person. For some they manage to stay afloat and eventually pick up the pieces and move on with life, but for others it can take them over the edge."

"So you're insinuating my mother wasn't in her right mind?"

"I'm saying she was deeply troubled, and rightfully so. As humans we are capable of far more than we give ourselves credit. We are able to weather all forms of tragedy but the loss of a child — it cuts deep, and often the wounds don't heal."

There was a long pause before Kara said, "You asked me what I thought of it. The wall. I wasn't disturbed by it. I was impressed. It didn't speak to me of crazy. It spoke to me of hope. My mother was hopeful that she would eventually find Charlie."

"And you? Do you still hold out hope?"

"Of finding him alive?" she asked.

"Either way."

Kara drew a breath. "He's out there. I know that and we will one day find him."

"And if you don't? Will you be able to let it go?"

She didn't respond to that. After spending hours poring over her mother's notes, reading through the case files of the other abductions, she had begun to notice a change in her mindset. Call it osmosis or the need to know but Kara could feel that spark of hope that had driven her mother on.

"Did you never get married?" she asked, changing the topic.

He looked at his ring finger. "No. I went on a few bad dates but never found someone who was compatible with my taste."

Kara frowned. "Your taste?"

He tapped the side of his temple. "For living, and understanding the mind. Most said I overthink, and analyze everything to death. Maybe they're right. I never switch off."

"Sounds like me."

He smiled.

"When do you return to New York?"

"It was meant to be a short visit but I'm extending it."

"Oh? To help your father?"

"Something like that."

She didn't want to go into it with him. The moment she'd mention the investigation he would draw comparisons to her mother and lead her down another road of questioning that she really didn't want to answer. There was only so much psychobabble she could deal with. Instead she quickly shifted the conversation back to her mother. She wanted to understand her mindset. On one hand she was fairly certain that her mother wasn't crazy but Lloyd had raised a good point. Grief had a way of changing even the sane. And there was a level of obsession involved in her mother's dealings with Charlie's disappearance.

"You said she stopped coming to see you, stopped taking her medication. When?"

"A year ago. She wanted to spend more time on the case. She said the meds were making her foggy and she wanted to stay clear-headed," Lloyd replied.

"And my father?"

"He still sees me every second week of the month."

She nodded. "And what did he say was her mental state leading up to her death?"

Lloyd answered. "Scattered."

"Can you clarify?"

"She was all over the place. Contacting the police, speaking to locals in the town, making accusations. It was sad really. Sad to see such a strong and bright woman spiral down." He glanced at the band around Kara's wrist. "I would hate to see the same thing happen to you, Kara."

She smiled. "Well you don't have anything to worry about there."

She rose from her seat.

"But we still have time left in the session."

"I have a few things I need to attend to. Thank you for your time, Lloyd."

Her mind churned over on the way back to her vehicle. Scattered? And yet that wasn't the impression she got when she was on the phone. It was optimistic, focused and hopeful. Kara left the therapist's more determined than ever to know the truth.

Chapter 16

Around two that afternoon Noah got a call from a Blackmore officer, Raymond Wainright. He'd responded to a call of a breaking and entering at the Walkers' residence. The sheriff's office only responded to calls in the unincorporated area of Clallam County, and the police department in Blackmore handled any calls related to their jurisdiction. That's why it struck him as odd when the call came in.

"He's specifically asked for you. Do you think you have time to swing by?" Wainright asked.

Noah glanced at the paperwork in front of him and groaned internally.

"Sure, give me ten minutes. Oh, Wainright, is his daughter there?"

"No. Just the father."

Noah climbed out of the unmarked car. It was a heap of crap. The department gave him that instead of the Dodge Charger he was hoping for. When he asked why, their response was budget cuts and to avoid being noticed. They didn't want it looking like a regular cop car. It wasn't like he sat in lay-bys clocking people for speeding. His days of doing that were long over.

When he arrived at the Walker residence, one cruiser was out front. He gave a knock on the door before entering. It was the first time he'd stepped foot in their home. Of course Anna had invited him over for dinner, and called him on numerous occasions to discuss the case, but he'd always made a point to keep his distance. It was all about setting boundaries.

He entered the kitchen and found Matthew Walker sitting at the table with a cup of coffee. “Mr. Walker.”

“Who would do this?” he asked.

Wainright pointed to an open basement door. “Go take a look.”

As Noah walked towards the door he noticed several framed photos on the walls. A snapshot of Charlie and another of Kara; both in their preteen days. He headed down into the brightly lit basement. Each step creaked as he went down. When he reached the bottom and turned, he took in the sight of the mess. Papers, photos, a torn map were scattered all over the floor and the word BITCH was sprayed in red paint across the wall. Anna had talked about investigating and having files but he didn’t realize she’d gone to this length. He backed up and made his way upstairs.

“Anything taken?” Noah asked.

“Doesn’t appear to be.”

“Any other damage?”

“Just that,” Wainright said.

Noah looked at Matthew. “You okay?”

“I’m fine,” he replied in a gruff voice.

Noah cast his eyes around the kitchen before asking, “Sir, can you pinpoint when this might have happened?”

“I stepped out to run some errands this morning.”

“At what time?”

“Around eleven, and I got back here just after one. That’s when I noticed the glass at the rear of the house had been smashed. I checked every room and found that message downstairs.”

Noah nodded slowly. “Sir, have you run into any

trouble lately?"

He shook his head.

"What about Kara?"

That's when Wainright chimed in. "Actually I was speaking with one of the other officers — Johnson. He said he was called out to the Dug Out on Tuesday evening to break up a fight between Kara Walker and Mary Harris."

"Kyle Harris's sister?" Noah asked.

Wainright nodded.

"Anyone get in contact with her to find out where she was when this happened?"

"Johnson is trying to track her down as we speak."

He turned his attention back to her father. "Did Kara mention this?"

"No."

He was nursing a cup of coffee, and his hands were shaking a little. He tapped his cigarette ash into an overfilled ashtray.

"Where is Kara?"

He glanced up at the clock. "Probably in a therapy session."

"Therapy?"

"A friend of the family."

Noah nodded and cast his gaze around the room. "Why did you ask me to come out?"

Matthew replied, "Anna used to talk about you. Said you were a good person." He turned his attention to Officer Wainright. "No offense but we've not had the best of luck with Blackmore Police Department."

"Well they're the ones that are going to handle this. We don't cover the city, except under special circumstances," Noah said.

"Typical," Matthew said. Outside, a car could be heard pulling into the driveway. Noah walked over to the window and peered out. It was Kara. He ran a hand over his head and waited.

When she entered her eyes were wild. "Dad. What's happened? You okay?"

She slung her bag on the ground.

"I'm fine. I wish people would stop asking me that."

Kara's eyes darted to the basement door and she made a beeline for it.

"Uh, ma'am," Wainright said.

"Kara," Noah said stepping between Wainright and her. She moved too quickly and was down the stairs in seconds. Noah joined her at the bottom as she looked at the disarray.

"Shit."

He breathed in deeply. "I heard you had a run-in the other night with Mary Harris."

Kara glanced at him. "You think she's behind this?"

"Well, she does have a reputation. Multiple run-ins with the law, and your mother knocked heads with her countless times."

"Does she not know that my mother was also on speaking terms with Kyle?"

"I wouldn't exactly call them speaking terms. Your mother believed someone else was responsible but she hadn't ruled out Kyle."

"That's not the impression I got when I spoke with him."

"Well we all perceive differently depending on where we're sitting."

"But hasn't Mary spoken to her brother since?"

"I wouldn't know. I wasn't involved in the

investigation."

"But surely my mother…"

"Kara. Like I said before. Your mother reached out to me countless times but for the most part I was a listening ear. I wasn't her partner. I certainly wasn't going to get involved in a case that has officially been closed."

"And risk your career. I get it." She shook her head. "Anything stolen?"

"It doesn't look like it but that's where the officer upstairs could use your help. Your father isn't exactly too thrilled to be dealing with Blackmore."

"I wonder why," she said sarcastically, turning and heading back upstairs without touching anything. Upstairs Noah asked to speak with Kara outside while officers went about doing their duty of taking photos, canvassing the neighborhood and waiting for forensics to show up and take prints.

"You want to tell me what the argument with Mary was about?"

"What do you think?" Kara asked shifting her weight from one side to the next and looking across the road to where two neighbors were looking out of a window. "She was hyped up. Passing the blame about her brother."

"Your father said you went to see a therapist today?"

She rolled her eyes. "Out of respect for him. Not because I need it."

Noah nodded and acknowledged the officer as he came out. When he turned back Noah studied her face, his eyes dropping to her mouth. "You haven't been questioning any of the three suspects, have you?"

"No. Why has someone said I have?"

He shook his head.

She smiled. "No. But this morning I went and spoke with Henry Ellis."

"Henry?"

"Oh so you know him. Well that confirms who he's dealing with in your department."

"He's an old friend of my father's. Anyway, what were you doing out there?"

"Does it matter? Speak with him, it sounds like you've built up quite a rapport."

Noah ran a hand over his face. The thought of a mountain of paperwork to plow through for the rest of the afternoon wasn't his idea of fun. He seriously needed a vacation.

"So when are you heading back to New York?"

"Why, you going to grind me if I stay longer?"

He smirked. "No, actually I was going ask if you had plans for supper?"

Her eyebrow shot up. "Detective?"

"Listen, we kind of got off to a bad start. I… bought some extra steaks, a few too many. I hate to see good food go to waste. I just thought if you had any further questions about your mother's interaction with me that maybe we could do it over dinner. And you can tell me what you've uncovered."

"So you are interested?"

"In the case," he replied making sure they were on the same topic.

She smiled. "Sure. What time?"

"How's seven sound?"

"Works for me."

"Right, well, um."

He turned to leave.

"Aren't you going to give me your address?"

"Oh, right, that would be helpful." He nodded and pulled out a pad of paper and scribbled his details down. He tore the page off and handed it to her, then thumbed over his shoulder. "Okay, well I should get back to it."

He headed back into the house and gave his card to her father and told him to call him if he had any further problems. He reassured him that the officers from Blackmore Police Department were more than capable and things had changed down there since 1991. He gave a nod and Noah squeezed past Kara on the way out.

On the way back to the Sheriff Department he thought about Amanda, and wondered what she might have thought about him inviting Kara for dinner. He wasn't looking to start a relationship but he was curious about the investigation wall her mother had created. He knew she had gone to some great trouble to bang on doors and pursue someone that she didn't even know existed, but if she was right, and he was out there — was it possible that she'd found him, or he'd figured out she was on to him in the final days of her life? He got on the phone to the medical examiner to see if they could speed up the toxicology report.

* * *

Back inside the home, long after Kara had gone through the process of checking with Blackmore officers to ensure nothing had been stolen, she was given the go-ahead to start clearing up. As she collected armfuls of papers, her father sat on the bottom step of the basement stairs.

"You know, you can give me a hand," she said.

He waved her off. "Just throw it in the trash."

"Not yet."

He scoffed. "I knew it. I figured this was going to happen. From the moment you said you were staying longer."

"What?"

"That you were going to get tied up in your mother's crazy antics. I had enough of it then, I don't want you to go down that path."

"I'm not, Dad. Just relax."

"I'll relax when this is behind us. You know how badly I wanted to trash this basement when your mother was alive? She wouldn't let me." He shook his head. "And now this."

Kara tried to put her father's fears to rest.

"They'll handle it, Dad."

"I don't want you stirring up trouble. Your mother did enough of that."

"The woman came at me. What do you expect me to do?"

"But you must have antagonized her."

"I was having a drink." She shook her head, scooping up more papers.

"With Bobby Evans. That's another one you should stay clear of."

"He's an old friend, Dad."

Kara looked down at the paperwork and tried to make sense of it all and stack it in an orderly fashion. It was now out of sequence and making heads or tails of it was going to be near impossible. She'd already waded through a lot of it but there was more to get through. Kara thumbed off sheets into different piles. It was going to take hours, probably another day. "Besides, this break-in might not have even been Mary," Kara said.

Her father look perplexed then his eyes widened. "Oh, don't you start that. The man responsible for Charlie is locked away."

"And what if it's not him, Dad?"

He shook his head. "You know what? I'm not listening."

"Is that what you did to mom?"

"Still not listening."

"Geesh. I'm surprised she didn't kick your ass to the curb."

"She tried, I never got further than the couch."

That got a laugh out of her and she was sure he smiled.

She placed handfuls of paperwork on the desk.

"You know she didn't blame you," her father said.

"Certainly seemed that way."

"She was hurting. We all were."

"She ignored me, Dad," Kara said lifting the computer back onto the table. She plugged it in to see if it was still working. The light blinked on, and it whirled up.

"You weren't the only one." He drew a breath. "She just didn't know how to deal with the pain."

"And you did?"

"We had different ways of approaching it." He pulled out his cigarettes and lit one. "I miss Charlie every day but if I dwelt on it, it would have destroyed me."

"Is that why you accepted Kyle Harris as his abductor? You just wanted it to be over?"

He gazed at the wall where there was a collage of photos of their family. Her mother had created it, months after the incident. She thought if she didn't see the family complete, she would lose her mind. That's what drove her on — the belief that one day they'd be reunited.

He father replied, "He couldn't provide a reason for why Charlie's things were on his property."

"Believe me, Dad, after having chased these types of assholes for the better part of sixteen years, I can tell you that there are a lot of innocent people that get dragged into these cases, and if they're lucky they escape with their reputation intact, others wind up fighting for their lives in a courtroom."

He watched her as she tried to piece together the map that had been torn in two. Pin tacks were everywhere. Fortunately, Kara had taken photos of everything with her phone just in case her father took it upon himself to trash it while she was out. It was the photos, paperwork and notes, and the order they were in, that had mattered to her.

"You got a broom?" she asked.

He got up and trudged upstairs, and returned a few minutes later.

"So, I saw the work you did with the cases out in New York."

She eyed him skeptically. "You followed them?"

"Look, just because I didn't get on the phone and talk to you every time, it doesn't mean that I'm not interested in your life."

She scoffed. "You have a funny way of showing it."

He took a hard drag on his cigarette.

"So what did Michael have to say?" he asked.

"About mom's death?"

He nodded.

"He was sympathetic."

Her father sighed. "You know I really liked him."

She smiled as she brushed the tacks into a pile and scooped them up. "I know you did. He still asks about you."

"Does Michael like the woman he's dating? What's her name again?"

"Laura. And yes. He does. In fact they got married. I don't know if that's a good thing or not."

"So what about you?"

"What about me?"

"You going to Goodman's home for dinner tonight."

She stopped sweeping and leaned against the broom and smiled. "Were you listening?"

"It's these newfangled hearing aids."

"You don't wear one."

He laughed then blew out his cheeks before getting a dead-serious expression on his face. "Man, when it rains it pours."

Kara followed his gaze to the graffiti on the wall.

"That's going to take more than elbow grease to get that off," he said.

"Perhaps it's time to repaint," she said. "You were always going on about remodeling the basement."

"Not sure I will. Thinking of selling the house."

"But…"

"The only reason we stayed was because of your brother. Your mom thought if he ever made his way home, he'd know where to find us. But now she's gone." His head dipped. She tried to shift the topic away.

"Actually I was thinking of staying in tonight. Getting some Chinese."

"Please. You'd rather spend time with your old man than Goodman?"

She shrugged. "Not sure I'm interested."

"You're thirty-nine. Guys like that don't come along that often. Besides, I'm going out tonight."

Kara twisted. "To where?"

"The bar."

"C'mon, Dad. I don't want to be called away because you've got into a fight with someone. I think we've tainted the Walker name enough."

He laughed, and headed upstairs. Kara continued clearing up, thinking about the invite from Goodman. He was a good-looking man, certainly would understand her line of work. She shook her head, don't read too much into it, she told herself.

Chapter 17

It had been years since he'd cooked for anyone beside himself. Noah fished out a beer from the fridge, cracked the top off and took a hard swig. He kept eyeing the clock as he darted furiously around the kitchen grabbing ingredients. He wasn't lying about the steaks. The woman at the meat store he went to had misheard him and grabbed four marinated steaks instead of two. He couldn't fault her as he did have a large wad of gum in his mouth at the time, and it was unusually busy that day with a crowd of people putting in their requests. Instead of having her unwrap it all he just bought them all.

Next door the sudden sound of pounding music got a rise out of him.

"No, no, no, not tonight," he said tossing the dish towel over his shoulder and heading to the door that led out into a long hallway on the second floor of the apartment building. After losing Amanda he couldn't handle staying in their old house so he sold it and moved into an upscale apartment block on the west side. It had been touted as catering to those with a taste for the finer things in life. The brochure the real estate agent handed him made it look real good. She tossed out words like hipsters, modern, stylish. Noah figured the kind of people renting there would be similar — he was wrong, so wrong.

"Jamal!" He banged on the door four times before it popped open. An African American with thick dreadlocks and wearing sunglasses opened the door. The aroma of marijuana wafted out, hitting him hard. The first time he'd smelled it he was all ready to bust him, and then he found out he had a medical license, something to do with not sleeping well. It was all bullcrap but he didn't hold it over his head. Many of the states were starting to legalize it. He figured he'd have to get used to the dank smell.

"Mr. Goodman. How are you this evening?" he said in a thick Jamaican accent with a large spliff hanging out the corner of his lips. He was wearing torn jeans, flip flops and a tie-dyed T-shirt. Behind him were two sultry-looking women. He'd invited him to join him one night, said there was plenty to go around, but Noah politely declined. If he wasn't hearing his music, he could hear him getting it on. He hated the nights they came over. The two women howled into the early hours of the morning. He had to buy ear plugs in the end but that made it difficult to hear his radio in the morning.

"I need you to drop the music down a few notches. I've got company."

"Ah?" He leaned out and looked down the hallway as if expecting to see someone. "A few honeys?"

"Look, just lower the music."

"You got it, mon!"

He winked and Noah walked away shaking his head. As he was making his way back, the elevator doors at the far end of the hallway opened and out she came. Great, he wasn't even ready. Fortunately she was looking down at her phone. He darted back into his apartment and shot around the room like the cartoon Tasmanian Devil, grabbing up anything and everything that was out of place, looked dusty, dirty or was liable to raise questions about his hygiene. He dashed into his bedroom and shoved it all in the closet, slamming it shut just as there was a knock at the door. He glanced at himself in the full-length mirror. He'd slipped into a pair of jeans, and a simple white V-neck T-shirt. He ran his tongue around his teeth to make sure they were clean, breathed into his hand and smelled it. *Okay, she's just here for dinner.* He tossed the dish towel behind the door, and scooped up some cologne and splashed some on his neck after the second knock. He cleared his throat and took a deep breath. *Okay, you can do this. You can do this.* He crossed the room and opened the door.

"Hi," she said, offering a smile that made him relax, if only for a few seconds. She was wearing a leather jacket, tight jeans, ankle boots, and a dark brown top that showed off her figure. In her hand was a bottle of red wine.

He waved her in. "Thanks for coming. Glad you could make it." He ducked his head out the door and noticed Jamal was still outside his apartment eyeing him. Jamal gave another wink and a suggestive smile, and Noah rolled his eyes and closed the door.

"I'll take your jacket." He took it and hung it up. He sniffed. *Shoot, I forgot to spray deodorant around.* As he made his way into the kitchen he spotted a single sock sticking out from under the recliner chair. He gave it a shove with his foot. A bead of sweat ran down his back.

"Nice place you have. I don't remember this apartment block being here."

"No, it went up a few years back. Was meant to attract the wealthy but they settled for anyone who would pay their rent."

She chuckled. He smiled. Kara scanned the room like anyone in unfamiliar territory. As he moved past her he caught the smell of her perfume. It was sweet. He liked it. *Focus,* he told himself crossing the room and trying to think about what he was meant to say. He was never good with entertaining. After Amanda's death, he'd got on a diet of microwave dinners and eating out. It was easier. It was only in the last year he'd got back into cooking. Not that he was any good.

"Can I get you a drink?"

"Oh I brought some wine."

She handed it to him and he stared at it like he knew his wines. He had absolutely no idea. Amanda had always gone for that while he opted for beer. "Thanks."

The aroma of the steaks caught his attention and he turned down the temperature.

"You live alone?"

"I do," he replied as he flipped the steaks. They sizzled and he stepped away and looked at her again. She looked relaxed as she walked further into the apartment.

"Nice place. How long you been here?"

"Three years." He jammed a wine opener into the top and popped the cork. He took down a couple of wineglasses and filled them halfway. He glanced at her from the corner of his eye. She was definitely easy on the eyes.

He handed her a glass and she took a sip. "Can I give you a hand?" she asked.

"No. It's fine. Just make yourself at home."

She wandered over to the bookshelf, which was filled with old books, the kind that might be found in a used bookstore. She ran her fingers along the spines and turned her head to the side to read the titles. "You collect?"

"They belonged to my wife. She died three years ago."

Kara turned with a pained expression.

"I'm sorry."

He offered back a thin smile and went back to checking on the food. He emptied out the potatoes into a colander. Steam spiraled up around his face. He flipped the steaks again and watched her browse around his apartment. The place wasn't huge. Two bedrooms. He could have gone for a one-bedroom, but in the event his sister or parents visited, they wouldn't have to suffer with a bad back in the morning. The second room when it wasn't being used he'd turned into a work space for photography. It was the one thing he could get lost in, the one thing that allowed him to get out of his head.

She glanced in the room and looked as if she was teetering on asking him a question.

"Those are mine," he said.

"Beautiful. Do you mind?"

Her waved her on in. "Go ahead."

Kara walked in and he followed with his wine in hand. Hanging up in various frames all over the wall were some of his best. The dense forest of Olympic National Park, waterfalls, the beach, cliffs and sunsets — ones that he'd submitted to magazines and newspapers. If he hadn't gone into policing, photography would have been something he would have liked to pursue.

"If they ever fire you, well, you know—"

He took a sip of wine. "Oh, there's not the need like

there used to be."

"How so?"

"Everyone and his uncle has a camera phone. Why pay an expensive photographer when you can do it yourself?"

"But there's snapping a shot, and snapping a shot," she said.

"I know but it's easier than ever before. I have a friend of mine who's in the photography business. We go out from time to time. He mainly does school shots, weddings and the odd family who wants to update their album but he says it's very much a hand-to-mouth existence."

"Ah, but less stress I imagine."

"Tell him that. He's bald."

She chuckled. "So what got you into it?"

"Well it certainly wasn't taking photos of crime scenes, that's for sure." He smiled leaning against the doorway. The fading light of the day filtered in through a crack in the drapes, casting shadows against the side of Kara's face. "Amanda." He pointed to several photos of sunsets. "Those were hers." He sighed. "I guess I needed an outlet. Well you would know. You remember filling out all those forms when you applied for the police? Them wanting to know what kind of outlet you had because of the stress this job involves? I wrote down photography."

"And were you taking photos then?"

"No. But once Amanda got me into it, it became like a form of meditation for me, you could say. As you can see most are from Olympic National Park. I like to get out there when I can. Lets me clear my head. Sometimes I think about the cases I'm working on but more often than not photography lets me switch off. It replaces the dark images in my mind with something of beauty."

Kara nodded. "Yeah, we do get to see the underbelly of this world a little too often."

"And you?" he asked. "What do you do?"

"Run. I run. Gets the blood pumping." As her eyes scanned the photographs she stopped in front of one and swallowed. It was a shot he'd taken of Fairground Forest. He noted her reaction. A pinched expression appeared on her face

"Have you been back there?" he asked. She never replied as if lost in the past.

"Kara?" He repeated it twice before she seemed to snap out of it.

She shook her head. "Um, what did you say?"

"I said have you been back there?"

"I've been near there but, no, I can't bring myself to go back up there."

He nodded slowly. "Well I think dinner is ready."

Noah quickly changed the subject and wandered back into the kitchen to get everything ready. "I thought we could eat on the balcony. That is if it's not too cold tonight. There is an incredible view of the lake."

She slid the door open and stepped out.

Noah gathered everything and brought out bowls and placed them on the placemats beside the condiments. He returned for the bottle of wine and inwardly prayed that none of it ended up on his white shirt. No sooner had he sat down than the boom of music started up again.

"You've got to be joking!" he said tossing down his napkin. Kara's eyes widened. "Sorry, it's my dopey neighbor. I tell him about it all the time. He forgets. I swear he has a memory like a sieve."

Noah was just about to hammer on the wall with his fist when Kara laughed. "Hey, don't worry. I like reggae."

"You do?"

"Sure."

He cocked his head. "Okay. But if it's too much, just give me the word and I'll…"

"It's fine. Take a seat."

He returned to the meal and over the course of the next thirty minutes, they chatted about what took her out to New York, and her involvement with the State Police. The conversation flowed with ease, like two colleagues; except he couldn't help notice his attraction to her. Soon the conversation circled around to her mother.

"So how did you meet her?"

"Interesting story actually. She showed up wanting to speak with Robert Smith, the sheriff that handled the original case." Noah made a waving motion with his hand. "He's retired, most of them have. Anyway, I'd just wrapped up a big case and was taking some downtime, if you can even call it that, when Lucas our undersheriff thought he would pawn her off to me without telling me the backstory of how she'd been showing up week after week with tips." He took a sip of his wine. "So fast-forward three hours later, I came out of the interview room feeling I'd been interrogated by her. From then on out, she would always ask for me. She refused to give the tips to anyone else."

Kara smiled and stared into her wine.

He continued, "I never knew about the wall of

evidence she'd collected. I knew she was speaking with locals and had even put an ad in the newspaper for people to call her if they had any information."

"An ad?"

He nodded. "Your mother was real proactive. Some folks liked it, others just thought she'd lost her marbles." He got up and asked if she wanted a beer. She declined. He returned with one and twisted around the frosted bottle. "Fortunately there is no law against making enquiries." A circle of condensation formed at the base.

Kara leaned forward. "I'm going to speak to them tomorrow."

"Who?"

"Ray, Seth, Darryl. I figure I'll start with Ray being as he fits the description of the recent attempted abductor."

Noah squirmed in his chair. "I really don't think that's a good idea."

"I've already cleared it away."

"With who?"

"Henry put me in contact with a guy from Washington State Bureau of Investigation. We had a long chat this afternoon about what's being done with the case of the four boys. As I have gained credibility from my work in New York, he was more than willing to have me come in and look over the files."

"Looking over files is one thing, getting involved is another. What's your BCI lieutenant say?"

"I haven't been in contact with him."

Noah closed his eyes and squeezed the bridge of his nose.

Chapter 18

It had been a conversation stopper. Kara could tell he was turned off by the idea of her getting involved but what she couldn't figure out was why. After clearing up, they moved to the living room with their drinks. The music next door hadn't let up and the aroma of weed had managed to seep in through the open patio door so Noah closed it. He turned on some soft music in the background — jazz — and returned to a recliner chair. A large crescent moon illuminated the dimly lit space and for a second, she had a memory of her first few dates with Michael, long before he'd put a ring on her finger and their marriage had spiraled down to become another statistic of failure.

Kara noticed the photo of his late wife on the counter. It was a picture of them both standing on a rocky precipice overlooking the ocean. They looked happy, content, satisfied with their lot in life. She could remember a time like that before the arguments, before the cold shoulder and before the final conversation that made it clear her dream of growing old with someone was just that, a dream.

"Who were those people you got into an argument with in the diner?" she asked.

He took a swig of beer and set his bottle on a table to the right. "It's complicated."

She nodded. "Sorry, I shouldn't have asked."

He smiled. "You have an inquisitive mind."

"Is that a roundabout way of saying I'm nosy?" she

said with a smile before taking a sip of wine. "No, I'm just curious."

"Curiosity can lead you into troubled places."

"Is that why you leaked out information to Henry, to avoid trouble?"

The corner of his lip curled, and he shook his head before picking up the bottle. "The man who approached me, the elderly one. That's Hal Carter. The young guy is Jesse, his son, and the woman is Hal's wife, Sarah."

"So what — you get involved with an older woman?" She chuckled.

"No, she was the drunk driver responsible for the death of my wife."

For a third time that evening she could have heard a pin drop.

"Oh." Kara looked down into her wine. "I'm sorry."

He breathed in deeply. "No need. They're angry because I appealed a decision after she only got three years. She was released two months ago, and was let go."

"Three years, that's all?"

"That's exactly what I said. Currently the law in Washington State for vehicular homicide for first-time offenders is two to three years. Though they have plans to push a new bill through to get it raised to the same level as first-degree manslaughter. That would increase it to eight and a half years."

She nodded. "You think the judge will send her back?"

He sighed. "I don't know." He shook his head. "According to my attorney, the judge claims that she was a model prisoner. She now attends Alcoholics Anonymous meetings."

"And so they want you to drop the appeal?"

He nodded and took another swig of his beer. "I haven't yet filed the appeal as my attorney needs to look into a few things first."

"Damn, that's gotta be hard."

"For them or me?"

"For both of you."

He studied her before he asked, "But am I not right to appeal?"

"You're asking me?" she asked.

He nodded.

She took a deep breath and blew out her cheeks. "Look, I get it. She took a life. How do you put a value on that? The justice system is messed up, that's for sure. Someone deals drugs and they do more time, someone kills someone in a vehicle and they can be out in three." She shook her head trying to wrap her mind around it. It's why she'd thought of quitting. Back when she first had an interest in law enforcement, she thought she could make a difference, and in some ways she had but at the end of the day all of them were slaves to the justice system, and at times it wasn't fair.

"Yeah, especially since in some states the sentence is up to ten years. Even that's a joke."

"How many years did you expect her to get?"

"If I had my way she'd rot in prison."

He got up and went over to the fridge to get another beer.

"For making one bad decision?"

He shot her a sideways glance. "That decision didn't just take her life. It took mine, her family's, hell, there were many in the community that were affected by her death. It was senseless. There was no need for it."

She could feel the atmosphere in the room shift. It no longer felt warm and she was now seeing another side to him, one that was full of pain, one that he probably hid from those around him. Noah tossed a beer bottle into a recycle bin that was already overflowing with bottles.

"You work tomorrow?" she asked.

"I do."

"Then you might want to slow down," she said. He shook his head and took a seat, cracked the top off another beer and downed a large gulp making a point that he listened to no one except himself. Kara remained there for a few more uncomfortable minutes before she said, "Well, I should probably get going."

She got up and placed her half-drained glass of wine on the counter. He rose. "Look, you don't have to leave. I mean, not right away."

"I shouldn't have pried, I'm sorry."

"Stay." He paused. "Please. It's still early."

Kara stood there for a second then picked up her glass again and took a seat.

Over the next hour they talked about their upbringing, parents and what led them to get involved in law enforcement, along with how it was different from the east coast to the west. From there on out the conversation flowed and she shared with him what she'd learned from her mother's files — the different avenues that led to nowhere and some of the tips she'd received from locals who knew the various suspects at the time of Charlie's abduction.

"Listen, I didn't mean to sound like I'm against you talking to them or folks that know them, but whether you agree or not they were cleared in the original case.

You're liable to get some backlash if you go digging up the past. I would hate to see you facing a civil lawsuit," Noah said.

"No, I understand."

"Those three suspects aren't from the four counties where the four boys went missing, and Washington Bureau of Investigation has to be called in to assist with anything related to our county."

"So can't you make it happen?" she asked.

"Me?"

"Well you are the lead detective for Clallam County, are you not?"

"Yes, but like I said, Charlie's case is closed."

"But the attempted abduction isn't," she added.

He stared back at her blankly. Noah scratched his stubble and took another sip of beer. "I'll make a couple of phone calls. I can't promise anything."

"Of course not." She smiled.

"And I would want to be kept abreast of anyone you're going to meet."

"Certainly."

He grumbled. "I have a bad feeling about this."

She smiled. "I guess this makes us partners."

"Well let's not jump the gun." He finished the remainder of his beer before switching the conversation.

Kara downed her drink then crossed the room and scooped up her jacket.

"Where you going?"

She replied as she headed out, "Need to grab something. I'll be right back."

"What?"

She left him with his mouth agape as she headed

home.

* * *

The alcohol was well and thoroughly in his system and he was beginning to doze in his recliner chair when there was a knock at the door. Another knock and he climbed out of his chair and shook his head. “Yeah, yeah, hold on.”

Noah opened the door and Kara brushed past him juggling two large corkboards under her left arm, and another under her right. She tossed them down on the floor looking windswept and exhausted.

“You want to give me a hand? There’s quite a lot of paperwork to bring in.”

“What the hell is this?”

“My mother’s files. You wanted to know what was in them. My father wants them gone. I can’t keep them at the house. Now being as we’ll be working together I thought we could store them here. I’ll of course bring dinner tomorrow night, so you don’t need to worry about that. Although you might want to cut back on the liquid courage.” She made a clucking sound with her lips. “I need you level-headed.”

“Um.”

She brushed past him without batting an eye. “Well come on, let’s go.”

“Kara. Hold on a minute. Wait up!”

Noah lugged the final large box from her car to his apartment and dumped it alongside three others. He collapsed to his knees and exhaled hard. “If I was tipsy earlier, I’m sober now. This is a shitload of paperwork. And I thought my desk was busy.”

Kara tossed her jacket on the back of his recliner and slipped off her shoes. She poured herself a glass of wine. "Right, let's get started."

"What are you on about?" he said looking at her like she was a deranged woman on a mission. She crossed the room and started fishing out papers, and a box of tacks.

"Well, if my mother was right, if Kyle Harris is telling the truth, we have less than four days until another boy is taken, potentially from Clallam County. The question is, where do we start?"

He shook his head. "You've lost me."

"We have four boys that were taken five years apart, three suspects that were originally associated with my brother's case but never questioned, a man in prison telling us to look into the original charges against him. Where to begin?"

She stepped back from the three boards which she'd set up in his living room, leaning them against the wall without even asking him if she could. The middle board held a map that had been torn and taped back together, pins had been stabbed into the locations where each of the boys had been taken. Then there were the suspect photos on each wall, with history about who they were, their age, what they did for a living, where they said they were when the abduction took place.

This woman is out of her damn mind.

"Whoa, whoa, hold up here. When I said I would make a few phone calls, I didn't have this in mind."

She ignored him and tapped a finger against her lips. "Obviously we need to understand why Kyle Harris was focused on as the prime suspect."

"We already know that. Your brother's shoe and jeans were found on his property."

"No, I don't mean that. I mean, back in 1991, Henry

Ellis had suggested to those in charge of the investigation to bring in Ray, Seth and Darryl for questioning but it was shot down. He said that his hands were tied. Any suggestion made unless it was directly related to Kyle Harris, or cleared by Robert Smith, was put on the back burner. And yet we know that at least one of them matched the suspect sketch that was drawn up in the attempted abduction prior to Charlie. So you've got to ask yourself, why?"

"Why what?"

"Why rule them out without due diligence? Why go through the other fourteen but not them?"

"They already had Kyle on their radar."

"Exactly but why?" She took a sip of her wine. "It would have taken less than half a day to bring these guys in and run through a few questions. But all the focus got put on Kyle."

"They had evidence," Noah said.

"Okay but according to Henry, these three were considered people of interest before they searched Kyle's property." She crossed the room and dug into the boxes and fished out a few more sheets of paper and pinned them on the board. "I looked a little deeper into this, you know, going back to the original accusations that were made against Kyle Harris. Besides the obvious flaws in the two-year case — what seemed to be overlooked is what happened after. It was suggested by his lawyer at the time his name was cleared to follow through with a civil lawsuit against his accuser, but more specifically with those involved in the investigation. So I did a little digging. It turns out that he did move ahead with that and one of the names that was brought up in that suit's settlement was Robert

Smith."

"Clallam County sheriff at the time of the investigation," Noah added.

Kara nodded. "He retired one year after Kyle Harris was arrested, charged and went to trial."

"So you think he had a grudge against Harris?"

"I would say so. You build a case against a guy and it falls flat, and then he turns around and sues you and he wins. I know I'd be pissed. So I went back through some of the old reports from the news around that time and it's pretty clear based on the questions posed to him that he didn't consider anyone else a person of interest. At least that's what he was telling the media at the time."

Noah leaned forward in his chair and gazed at the paperwork, then shrugged and tossed it down. "It doesn't matter. What's done is done. He's inside and best of luck trying to prove Smith had some ulterior motive to see it pinned on him."

"Look, I'm not saying the sheriff planted my brother's belongings or that he was in any way involved in the abduction. I'm suggesting that he had a good reason to keep the limelight on Harris and build this picture of a monster living among us. You only have to see the way the community treated him the first time around. Now we have a major event occur and he lives not far from the abduction site. Single guy lives alone, previous shady past, and a sheriff with a grudge against him. It could easily be said that he didn't stand a chance in hell of being ruled out. Meanwhile our actual guy, who we assume is a resident of the area, knows about the case and takes some of the clothing and plants it on his property. The kind of DNA testing back in 1996 wasn't anywhere close to what it is today. Now if we could get some of that retested that would definitely be a step in the right direction."

Noah pulled a face. "That's if it even exists. And best of luck trying to locate it. Evidence retention laws are sketchy at best. The rules for how long they keep evidence vary from state to state. It can be stored until a case is closed or kept in long-term storage if it's a cold case but if you're right and Smith had a grudge against Harris, I would imagine your brother's shoe and jeans would be long gone by now."

"Can you find out?"

He sighed. "I'll make some calls."

* * *

Kara felt hopeful as she returned home that evening. They'd only scratched the surface but the possibility that the one responsible for the attempted abduction could be their man had sparked something new. It was the kind of emotion she felt when she first joined law enforcement. There was a real sense that maybe after all this time they could nail this asshole — if he even existed. As she veered into the driveway, the glow of the SUV's headlights washed over the rear of her father's truck and she spotted a body lying on the ground nearby.

"Dad?"

She slammed the gear into park, pushed out and hurried over to where he was laying. He was sprawled out on the driveway and a portion of grass. The first thing that went through her mind was a heart attack, the second was someone had attacked him — it was neither. As soon as she reached him the smell of alcohol hit her, as did the sound of snoring. The fact that he'd managed to drive back from the bar was a miracle. She cast a glance around. Embarrassed, she tried to wake him by giving him a shake. Nothing. He was three sheets to the wind. She dropped to her knees and slung one of his arms around her neck, clasped on to it and slipped her left arm around his waist and hauled him to his feet. It was like he didn't have bones in his legs. They dangled, and he slurred his speech. She couldn't make sense of it except one word. *Anna.*

"Come on, let's get you inside."

Kara had to drag his limp body a few yards to the side door then lean him up against the wall while she juggled the keys. All the while he was mumbling something under his breath. Please don't vomit, she thought. The last thing she wanted was to end the night coated in his digestive juices.

Once inside, she flipped a light on and carried him into the living room. There was no way in hell she was going to lug a hundred and seventy-five pounds up the stairs. She dropped him onto the couch and went off to find a blanket.

When she returned he mumbled and talked to her like she was her mother.

"Anna. I love you, Anna."

"Alright Dad, quiet down. Go to sleep."

She covered him with the blanket, propped him on his side just in case he vomited and then headed out to the kitchen.

She poured herself a glass of milk and leaned back against the counter. A flood of memories hit her. The sound of her mother's voice. She wanted to smile but all she felt was the loss and pain.

Right then just as she was about to head off to bed

— glass shattered. It was so loud and startling she instinctively dropped to a crouch. Her heart pounded in her chest.

"Dad?" she called out, fearing for his safety.

She hurried down the hallway and entered the living room at the front of the house and then heard a car pull away. Her service weapon was upstairs in her suitcase. The squeal of tires cut into the silence. By the time she reached the window they were gone.

On the ground a few feet from the shattered window was a brick, a scrap of paper was wrapped around it, held together by a piece of twine. She picked it up and read the note.

"GET THE FUCK OUT OF BLACKMORE!"

She peered out but besides a couple of neighbors looking out their windows, the street was once again quiet. She looked at the mess and sighed. Over the next five minutes she used a brush and pan to clear up the shards of glass and then sealed the window with black trash bags and tape.

After the police arrived and grilled her with umpteen questions, it had just turned eleven when she climbed into a recliner chair across from her father. After what had just happened she wasn't going to let him sleep downstairs alone. She placed her service weapon on the table beside her and shut her eyes hoping to get some rest, even if it was just a few hours.

Chapter 19

Friday morning began with an argument. Kara's father wanted to blame her for the window for no other reason than to avoid the conversation about driving home drunk.

"You need to return to New York. It's not safe here," he said, tipping coffee from a French press into a mug.

"You could have killed someone, Dad."

He waved her off like an annoying fly. "I wasn't that drunk."

"Oh no? Then do you want to tell me how you ended up on the couch?" He cast a glance at her but before he could reply she continued. "I carried you in. You were sprawled out in the front yard like a frat boy."

"Arrest me or put a pin in it. I'm tired of listening to this."

He grabbed his coffee and headed out into his garage. That had always been his way even when her mother was alive. Confrontations weren't their strong point. Then again, they weren't hers either. The phone beside her rattled on the table and she glanced at it. The caller ID showed it was Michael. She knew he'd make the call eventually and if it weren't for her son she wouldn't have answered.

Kara took a deep breath then answered. "Michael. I was meaning to phone you."

"Of course you were. Now you told me you would be back by now. Ethan is still here. What's going on?"

"Right, about that."

"Why don't I like the sound of that?"

"I just need a few more days."

"You said you were there for the funeral and that was it, but that's not it, is it?"

She breathed in deeply. "There's been an attempted abduction."

"And?"

"There's a possibility that I might be able to help."

She heard him groan. "I knew it. I knew it. I'm telling you, Kara. You need to get back now. I have a life."

"Yes, you do. Ethan is a part of that."

"Oh don't you try spinning this around. This year I've had him at my place more times than you have."

"And most fathers would be happy about that."

He sighed. "I am except I need my space."

"Is that why you left?"

"I meant we need our space."

"And by we, you mean, you and Laura."

"I'm not doing this. You are not dragging me into an argument and spinning this around to make yourself look like the victim. I have bent over backwards to help you over the past year and a half while you were working the Swanson investigation but there is a limit. You either come home now or I'll be speaking with the lawyers."

"Huh. Really? We already share joint custody."

"We do. Joint means we share the load."

Kara scoffed. "Oh, so Ethan is a load. A real heavy burden, is he?"

"He must be if you keep pawning him off on me."

"You know I can't be there to watch over him every

second of the day."

"You're his mother, for God's sake! Act like one."

She exhaled.

"Tuesday. I'll be back on Tuesday."

"In five more days? Are you kidding me? Laura and I were planning on going away."

"Oh really? Where?" she asked.

"None of your damn business."

"Then take Ethan. I'm sure he'll stay out of your hair."

"You know what, Kara. This is why our marriage fell apart. It was nothing to do with your work. It was to do with you. The choices you make. I tried my hardest. Did everything I could to please you but it was never enough. So if you want to hold a grudge against me actually getting on with my life, I don't want to hear about it. We are done. And if you're not back here by Sunday, I'll be in contact with the lawyers on Monday."

"And what do you hope to gain from that? Sole custody?" She laughed.

"Screw you."

He hung up. She sat there for a second and squeezed the bridge of her nose, then counted to ten under her breath with her eyes closed. She snapped at the elastic around her wrist and headed over to the sink to take her pills. She tossed them back with water and gripped the sides of the sink. Everything inside her wanted to scream but she needed to keep it together. Focus. Put that energy into today.

* * *

A list of seven level 3 sex offenders that lived within a seven-mile radius of where the attempted abduction had taken place was on Noah's desk. There was also one message from a family. They wanted to know when victim services was going to contact them because their son was having a hard time sleeping after a home invasion.

He'd arrived at the office at eight that morning. There was no magic involved in catching someone who did this, just a lot of banging on doors, and hopefully tips from the community. After returning the call, reassuring them he was going to do everything he could to catch those that broke in, Noah gave them a name and the number for victim services. It wasn't much of a gesture but even the smallest offer could give a family a sense that they hadn't been forgotten.

Once he got off the phone, he made a few more calls related to the triple homicide he'd been working on, before scooping up the list of sex offenders and going to speak with the chief about Kara. He was almost sure he would shoot it down because having anyone from State hanging around the department only attracted the media, and that meant answering questions and being held responsible for solving what might end up being a closed investigation. The thought of banging on doors with Kara beside him put his nerves on edge. He was used to working alone or with those he knew. She was a bit of a wild card. Her experience working on high-profile cases was the only thing she had going for her, that and whatever arrangements she'd made with Washington State Patrol's investigative division.

He gave a knock on the door. Sheriff Vernon Armstrong was tapping away on his computer. He dipped his head and peered over his thick rimmed glasses.

"Come in."

He took a seat. "Chief, it's regarding the attempted abduction. I want to bring someone in from Washington State Bureau to assist."

"But we don't have a missing person."

"No, we don't, however, I strongly believe whoever attempted this will try again and with the recent triple homicide, that auto theft last month and the domestic, I'm juggling a number of cases. I think having the expertise of the bureau would greatly speed things up, and it would be good to have someone with a fresh set of eyes look over what we have so far."

"Which is?"

He held up a list of names. "Sex offenders. Level 3. Within 7 miles of Highland Hills. I was going to bang on a few doors today and see what we can dig up."

"And you need State involved?"

"They offered," Noah said.

"So you've already been in contact?"

"Well I think there is a possibility this could be connected to the four missing boys."

Armstrong leaned back in his seat and removed his glasses and tapped the earpiece against his teeth. "Those are cold cases."

"Cold but active."

He scoffed. "Yeah 'active,'" he said, making quote signs with his fingers. It was a running joke that cases that had never been solved were left open but classed active. It gave the families, the media and the higher-ups a sense that something was being done even if it wasn't. "Who's working it?"

"Tim Greer," Noah said.

"Not according to my last conversation with him."

"Well we've had the attempted abduction, that

always sparks leads."

"And what did State suggest?"

He bit his lower lip knowing that eventually it would get back to him who State had sent. "State hasn't suggested anything. The offer is there to get help. I think it's worth taking. I'm not talking about getting the FBI involved but even if we could glean a few insights from them and have them handle questioning a few persons of interest I'd think that's worthwhile."

Armstrong nodded. "I'll speak to Tim."

"Actually, he wouldn't be the one assisting."

"Then who would?"

Oh he knew he'd ask.

"Kara Walker."

He put his glasses down, and chuckled. "Anna Walker's daughter?"

Noah nodded.

"No. It's not happening," he said putting his glasses back on and looking at the screen.

"But you said—"

"If State wants to send Tim, that's fine but I don't want Walker involved. She's not even working for Washington State Patrol." He resumed tapping on his keyboard.

Noah leaned forward. "No but their bureaus do work together across state lines. She's already been in contact with Tim."

"No, I'm not having her involved."

"Chief. You know how many cases she has closed in her short career?"

"I don't care if she holds the world record. People know her family, and her history here in Clallam. It would be a conflict of interest."

"No, it would be ludicrous to pass up the opportunity to work with someone with her track record."

Armstrong peered over his glasses. "From what I can remember, the Swanson case isn't solved. And I believe the media recently said she'd been reassigned."

"Reassigned? She came back for her mother's funeral."

"Not according to the DA's office. I was reading an article online yesterday about the Swanson case. What a screw-up they have made of that. The chance of anyone getting convicted is slim to none. You mark my words, it will be dragged out for another year and then the DA's office will take it to a grand jury and will choose not to prosecute. The whole thing will be swept under the rug, classed an open case but with no active investigation. It's the way they all do it now if they screw up." He leaned forward. "We don't need the bad press, Goodman."

"We won't. I'll take the lead, she'll tag along as and when required."

Chief Armstrong grumbled and rolled his head around. "Listen, if I get one complaint, she is off the case. No exceptions. No second chance. You hear me?"

He got up and shook the paper in his hand. "Don't worry, Chief."

"Yeah, right. Get out of here. Go do some work."

As soon as he got back to his desk he dialed Kara's number.

"Kara? I got it green-lit. Did you square it away with your BCI lieutenant?"

"I had the conversation this morning. He wasn't too happy about it but between that or me resigning he didn't put up much of a fight."

"You have your service weapon?" Noah asked.

"I do."

"Good. You think you can meet me in fifteen minutes in front of the Cliffhouse restaurant?"

At 10:30 a.m. he collected her from the restaurant and they headed to the first of twelve offenders. She was dressed in a dark leather jacket, white blouse, slacks and small heels. Professional but not over the top. She also looked pissed.

"What's up?" he asked.

"Oh not much. Came home to find my dad out cold on the lawn and then some community-minded folks fired a brick through our window as a friendly gesture."

"What?"

"Don't worry, Blackmore is handling it."

He wanted to ask further questions but she tapped the door looking impatient.

As they rolled away his mind shifted back to the men on the list. On numerous occasions he'd had to visit their premises. It was routine if and when there was a sex crime, an attempted abduction or a missing kid. They were the first ones they looked at. He hated dealing with them. They were scum to him. If he had his way they would be locked up for life and the key would be tossed away. Not all of them were the same. They were each assigned a different risk level from 1 to 3 with 2 and 3 being the most at risk of reoffending. Those were the ones that were watched more closely. Anytime someone went missing or an attempt had been made, they would coordinate with the county probation office. Every high-risk offender also had to abide by certain rules, from where they could live and how close they could get to a school or a child-care facility, through abstaining from drinking, giving up their computer, wearing a GPS monitor, taking lie detector tests, telling their future partners about their history, to even getting chemically castrated. That was something the law should have imposed on all of them. Unfortunately only seven states had opted to have a court order this, and it was rarely carried out.

The first guy they saw was a swim teacher by the name of Allan Marshall who had molested a number of underage minors and had ended up doing twenty years inside. On the surface he looked like your ordinary clean-cut guy who held down a steady job, had a girlfriend and drove a sensible car, however, behind all of that lurked a mentally unstable individual who was caught when two of his victims came forward. At first he lawyered up, but when four more came forward they knew they were fighting a losing battle. He now worked as a cook for a nursing home. The irony wasn't wasted.

As soon as they pulled into his driveway he was just about to get into a 4 x 4 truck. He was a thin man that looked ten years older than he was with sunken eyes. He still dressed like any other American in their forties. There was a curvy dark-skinned woman in her late thirties with him. The second he saw Noah he put a hand to his head and said something to her.

"Just let me handle this," Noah said.

"By all means," Kara replied climbing out.

Allan got all theatric raising his arms out wide. "Detective Goodman. What a pleasant surprise."

"Let's go inside, Allan."

"I've not done anything wrong."

Noah walked up to his truck eyeing the new woman. "Didn't say you did." He made a gesture to her. "And who's this pretty little thing?"

She gave a smile.

"Look, I have an appointment."

"Really? With who?"

Allan scratched the side of his face. Noah looked at the woman.

"Do you know he's a registered sex offender?"

Her eyes lit up and darted towards him.

"Oh come on, man."

Kara smirked as Noah made a tutting sound with his lips. "Allan. I would have thought you would have shared that little tidbit with her."

The woman had her door partially open as though she was about to get in the truck, instead she slammed it, gave him the stink eye and trudged away as Allan protested.

"Alliyah, come on. It's a misunderstanding. The cops are always like this."

"Well that has got to be the shortest relationship you've had, although that isn't counting the ones you had with those underage boys, is it?"

Allan threw his hands up. "Fuck's sake."

"Let's go inside."

For ten minutes they searched through his house and peppered him with questions. Noah took down notes, phoned a few numbers to confirm his whereabouts on the night of the attempted abduction and once it was all squared away they left.

Allan stood at the door, a glum look on his face.

"Keep up the good work, Allan. We'll soon turn you into a model citizen."

"Do you always wind them up like that?" Kara asked.

"Hey, I don't get to see them often." He grinned as he got back into the vehicle.

They visited four more before Kara brought up their names.

"So out of the three suspects only Seth Leonard has a rap sheet for sexual offenses," she said.

"Yep, however, rumors have circulated about Ray Owen and Darryl Clayton. I was going to leave Seth until the end but he doesn't live that far from here. Let's take a little ride over to his neck of the woods."

Noah spun the car around and floored the accelerator pedal.

Chapter 20

Parked outside the home of Seth Leonard, both of them stared at the rusted business sign jammed into his neglected lawn. It read: *Exotic Woods.* Wildflowers mixed with weeds, and branches from a tree had snapped and lay on the front lawn begging to be removed. A tan-colored Oldsmobile was parked at the far end of the driveway in front of a one-story home with dark gray shingles and black shutters. There were pine trees to the right and left, and several overgrown hedges that badly needed trimming back.

Leonard had held the position as deacon at the Catholic church in Blackmore until he was charged with molesting two minors back in 1978. He was convicted in 1979 and placed in the Walla Walla pen until 1987 when he was placed on 10 years' supervised release. There were specific conditions that he had to meet, including reporting to his parole officer within 72 hours of his release, no contact with minors, no viewing pornography, attending treatment, and not leaving the limits of his judicial district without written permission. On top of that he had to notify his probation officer within two days if he changed his address, he had to file a report each month, he couldn't violate any law, he couldn't associate with anyone involved in crime, he couldn't be an informant to law enforcement and he had to perform work to the satisfaction of his probation officer. If that wasn't enough, he couldn't drink alcohol in excess, he couldn't use drugs or go where they were sold, he couldn't possess a firearm or ammunition, and he had to submit to drug testing on a regular basis.

Kara listened to Noah reel off the conditions. He also mentioned that in the whole time he'd been released Leonard had met every single one and hadn't been in trouble with the law.

"Some of them just toe the line. Personally I think he's trying to earn brownie points with the big man upstairs," he said as the unmarked cruiser pulled into the driveway. That fact that people like Leonard were able to fit back into society without being killed by anyone was a feat in itself. After pushing out of the car, Noah said that after his release Leonard had moved from Blackmore to Port Angeles in order to avoid public scrutiny. His appearance had changed since he was inside and although he was registered as a sex offender, the families of the victims no longer lived in the area.

"Crazy to think that families trusted this guy with their kids. He was involved with Big Brothers and with his background in the ministry, no one batted an eye when he invited the kids to go along to a church summer camp." He shook his head. "You can't trust anyone."

They made their way up a path to the door and Noah gave the storm door a thump with the back of his hand. There was no answer. Kara noticed the mailbox at the end of the driveway was overflowing and some of it had been placed on the ground against the post itself.

"Mr. Leonard. Detective Goodman from Clallam County Sheriff's Office."

Kara glanced at the windows. All the drapes were closed. That wasn't uncommon for someone who worked night shift, or lived on a street with heavy traffic, but this was a dead-end road, and Leonard operated a craft store from his home. He carved everything and sold it out front. Adirondack chairs, chests, garden arbors, tables, clothes hangers, anything that could be cut, sawed and joined together.

"Haven't seen him in over a week," a voice said from off to their left. "I was thinking of taking in his mail but he has a tendency to lose his temper if I go anywhere near his property."

Kara turned to find an older man, wearing gardening gloves and holding a hoe, looking through two fern trees. He looked to be in his late seventies and was wearing a dress shirt that had several buttons undone, and a pair of cream-colored slacks. It was an odd choice of clothing for someone working in his yard but then again they were from a different generation when men dressed well.

"And you are?" Kara asked.

"His neighbor."

"Well of course," Noah said as they made their way over. "What's your name?"

"Peter Reed."

"So when did you last see him?"

"About a week ago."

"Did he say where he went?" Kara asked.

"No he didn't say anything. He was returning from the grocery store."

"So you talked to him?" Noah asked.

"No, I was in the yard when he was carrying in groceries."

Kara was curious to know a few things and took the opportunity to ask. "You mind me asking how long he's lived here?"

"Well let's see. I've been here since they erected these houses. I was one of the first owners. We had a different family next door until they moved out back in the mid '80s. That's when he moved in. Quiet man. Didn't say much. Kept to himself. But wow could he create some amazing things with wood."

"You ever see him bring anyone in here? Kids, I mean?'

He frowned. "Is that why you're here?"

"It's just a routine check."

He nodded. "No, like I said, he kept to himself. He would say hello if I asked him how he was doing but beyond that he really didn't want to chat like my neighbor on the right here does. Each to their own, though," he said. Kara turned back and looked at his car.

"Did he go away often?" she asked.

"Never. He opened his garage in the morning and closed up around five. He sold wood furniture and carvings." He made a gesture with the hoe. "He would put them out there on his front lawn. All sizes and colors. It was high quality and he got far less than what it must have cost him to make. I told him to raise his prices but he didn't."

"Did he have another vehicle?" Noah asked.

"No, that's it."

"And when he went out he always drove, right?"

The neighbor nodded.

Kara looked at Noah and they knew he hadn't gone away. They thanked the man and then circled around the back of the house. The rear was much like the front. Overgrown, unappreciated and left in a state of disarray. Noah tried the rear exit and called out to him again, banging a little harder on the door and the windows. No answer. As all the doors and windows were locked, Kara opted to use her elbow to break a small pane of glass in the rear door. Noah's mouth opened as if he was about to say something. She reached in and gave the lock a twist and ventured in. From the moment they stepped inside, the smell of death hit them.

Chapter 21

It was a smell that both of them were all too familiar with — a rank and pungent odor that was a mix of rotting meat and cheap perfume. They'd entered the mud room. A dusty closet-sized compartment that hadn't seen a cleaning cloth in years. Hanging up to the left were a variety of jackets, and beneath that a few worn-out shoes and boots in a tray. Off to the right were stacks of old, water-stained newspapers dating back to the '70s. There had to have been over two hundred crammed up against the wall and used as a makeshift table for a vase of dead flowers and a child's rattle. Pressing forward into the kitchen, they were greeted by the sight of a single square table with two sea-green leather chairs and an unfinished plate of spaghetti. In front of that was an open pornographic magazine. There were dirty plates in the sink, and flies buzzing around decaying food. It had obviously been there a while as maggots had begun to form. Kara pulled a handkerchief from her pocket and placed it over the lower half of her face. Noah crossed to the window to open the drapes. Dust lifted and fell as he wrenched it back to bathe the cramped home in daylight.

To the left of the kitchen was the living room. The

TV was on, tuned into some cheesy tabloid talk show where couples would yell at each other, and accuse the other of sleeping with their cousin. The walls were covered in '80s style wallpaper, some of which was peeling in the corners. The single couch and chair were worn to the point that they appeared caved in. The carpeted floors were stained, dated and in one area covered in grime from an overturned ashtray. Below the TV were two old-style VHS recorders. Kara snapped on a pair of blue latex gloves and crouched down eyeing the names he'd scrawled on the sides of the tapes. She hoped to God not to find anything with Charlie's name on it but there was nothing but porn.

"Kara."

She flashed him a sideways glance. Across the room Noah was flipping through what looked like a photo album. When she took a look she immediately diverted her eyes away. It wasn't like she hadn't seen it before but it didn't matter, it still turned her stomach. It was pornographic bondage photos. Noah took one out and felt the material. He flipped it over.

"My guess is he printed it off from the Internet and laminated it. Sicko."

They continued on through into a dining room that wasn't filled with furniture but had a few blow-up beach balls, the kind that might be found in a swimming pool. Though these had slightly deflated, it was certainly a strange sight, only made stranger by young kids' clothing mixed among it. Searching now for the source of the stench they slowly made their way to the rear of the home towards the bedroom. Kara eased open the door with her foot and was hit with a foul smell, three times as bad. She pulled back. "Damn it."

"Aren't you glad you haven't had lunch?" Noah asked with a grin on his face. He brushed past her and without any hesitation crossed to the far side of the room and pulled open the drapes. As soon as the light hit the bed, they had their answer. Below the covers was Seth Leonard. There was no blood. No sign of a crime. Kara approached and pulled back the covers. His skin was dark blue and had green areas over the flesh, his eyes were glazed over as if he had cataracts and they were sunken into the eye sockets. Blood had pooled in the lower region, fungus had begun to form around the mouth and nostrils, and parts of the skin on the body had begun to slip. But that wasn't the worst, it was the maggots squirming around and feeding on the putrid flesh.

Noah immediately got on the phone to get EMTs and a few officers. While he did that, Kara continued to browse through his home. His closets held a minimal amount of clothing, mostly bland colors, the kind of clothing pulled out of a bargain bin. In the spare room, there was a single bed that didn't look as though it had been slept in. There was a brown set of drawers pushed against the wall that were empty. Nothing about it would indicate that it was for a guest or that anyone had been staying there. The closet was empty barring one kid's poster of an old Disney show that was hanging by a single piece of tape.

After exiting Kara headed for the basement. She flipped the light switch and made her way down. It was fully furnished and carpeted. It smelled musty and large spider webs covered windows that were warped. The white paint had turned cream from the sun and was peeling. There was a wooden workbench off to her right, and a couch facing an old-style TV that must have dated back to the '90s as it was clunky and heavy looking. On the bench there were multiple painting canvases, and tubes of paint left open on top of old newspaper. Looking at photos wasn't enough, he had to paint them. She turned her head trying to make sense of what he'd painted of a boy turned upside down in chains.

She turned away and gazed around what other families might have used for storage, or an entertainment room, but he'd turned the place into a macabre space for his inner fantasies.

"Kara?"

"Yes? I'm down here," she replied.

Noah stomped down the steps. "Found human hair in the bathroom. Not sure if it's his. Hope so. The guy also had bondage devices in a bag under his bed. I noticed there were a few hooks in various areas on the ceiling. I figure the guy decided to give in to his inner urges before kicking the bucket. One final hoorah before he went and met his maker." He gave a nod. "What we got down here?"

She made a gesture to the paintings.

"Oh great, our guy considered himself the Picasso of sick porn."

"Take a look at this," Kara said reaching around the back of a chair and pulling out a handful of missing children flyers. There were also news clippings from abductions around the country. She thumbed through them and came across ones related to the four missing boys, and then her eyes locked on to one about Charlie. She stared at it for a second or two.

"Everyone got the newspaper, Kara. It doesn't mean anything. Well, other than he was a very sick individual."

She nodded but didn't say anything. There were multiple boxes pushed into the far corner of the room. She pulled them open and found more kids' clothes, and toys that had the names of missing kids scrawled in black marker pen. They continued searching while they waited for Port Angeles police to arrive. The looks on the faces of officers as EMT carted Leonard's corpse out spoke volumes. How had a man like this managed to hide this from his probation officer? And what had killed him? Not even the EMTs knew.

"We should have the medical examiner's report in about four hours."

Twenty minutes later, Kara stepped outside to get some fresh air. Her mind was in turmoil. What if this man had been responsible for Charlie's abduction? She stood by the car bent over slightly trying to get some air into her stressed-out lungs.

"You okay, Kara?" Noah said walking over.

She nodded. "I just need a moment."

"The EMTs estimate he's been dead for over seventy-two hours, which would rule him out as responsible for the attempted abduction on Wednesday evening."

"But not Charlie. He was out on supervised release before 1991. And if he could get away with all that crap inside and no one knew, makes you wonder what else he got away with."

Chapter 22

Troubled. Disturbed. Strangely satisfied. That best summed up Kara's mind that morning after leaving Seth Leonard's home. With Noah buried beneath the responsibility of filling out a police report, processing the scene and updating his chief, she thought it was best to give him some breathing room. The last thing she wanted was to get in the way and have him change his mind about having her work the case with him.

He dropped her back off so she could pick up her SUV.

"We'll meet back up later."

"Sure."

After he was gone she hit the local café for coffee, and Kara placed a call to her father to check in and keep him abreast of where she was just in case he needed her. After that, she decided to duck into Port Angeles Main Library and see what she could dig up in the archives on the assaults on boys prior to Charlie's abduction. All she had was a sticky note from her mother listing assaults on boys between the years of 1989 and 1991. Somehow she'd tied them to Charlie's case, the question was did it have any merit or was it just coincidence? As there was little more information beyond the names and mentions of assaults, Kara figured it was one of the last things her mother did prior to her death.

She pulled the SUV up in front of the one-story modern structure that crouched at the corner of Peabody

Street and E. Lauridsen Boulevard. A large sign displayed the name NOLS North Olympic Library System. Built back in 1998, its red brick looked fresh, like it had been updated since she'd last been there, but that might have been from the recent downpour of rain which always brought out the color in everything. She thought back to the few times she'd brought Ethan there when he was younger. While the county of Clallam had four libraries, this was the largest and contained far more books than the other three. She remembered seeing Ethan running up and down the aisles with Michael while she browsed. It had always reminded her of a department store with its arched glass interior that let in lots of daylight and the aisles spread out across a carpeted floor.

After chatting briefly at the front desk with a pudgy librarian with a dark bob, she was directed to one of the thirty-two public computers where she could access the NOLS website, database and Internet. For the early afternoon on a Friday there didn't seem to be many people inside. A few teens peered over the tops of their computers while punching at keys. An older lady turned her computer screen ever so slightly as if to prevent her from seeing what she'd pulled up.

According to the librarian, most of the Clallam County newspapers had been discontinued over the years and scanned to PDF but full-text articles from *Peninsula Daily News, Forks Forum* and *Sequim Gazette* could be viewed on microfilm. The only downside to that was it was time consuming and didn't allow for searches. Thankfully she didn't have to go back far in the digital archives and most of it was available through the search feature. She ran a search on the term "assault" in articles across all three papers between 1989 and 1991. Sure enough, it brought up several hits in a 1990 edition of the *Forks Forum* that covered six different attacks on young boys between the ages of 11 and 14. It was featured on the front page with a headline in bold that read: *Local police seek help in sexual assaults in Forks.*

Kara continued reading:

The Forks Police Department is actively seeking help from the public in identifying and apprehending a man who has attacked young boys in the Forks community. There have been six assaults reported.

Sergeant Will Barnett of the Forks Police Department said, "We are appealing to the community to assist us in any way they can. If you have seen anyone acting suspicious please contact us."

According to Sgt. Barnett, the incidents occurred in the previous summer and then there were three more over the winter, two in the spring and another three weeks later.

Parents are worried and the police are taking these attacks so seriously, they are even considering imposing a curfew.

Sgt. Barnett said, "Most of the attacks have been at night with one in the early hours of the morning. In all cases the guy threatens the boy with a knife and forces him into what we believe to be a brown and white Pontiac Bonneville. They are driven to a secluded spot where they are then sexually assaulted. After, he drops them off not far from where he collected them and tells them that if they say anything he will kill their family.

The ages of the young boys range from 11 to 14.

"The kids are extremely scared and the parents are worried," Sgt. Barnett said.

From what the police have said, the assaults are random and there doesn't appear to be any pattern beyond the attacker taking some of their clothing as mementos, how he threatens them and the style of vehicle. One of the assaults occurred near a forest, another in the downtown of Forks, another near a playground, two occurred not far from a school and one close to a video arcade.

The last incident occurred as two friends were walking back from the arcade, and a driver slowed and asked for directions. "It appears that he is watching from a distance before he approaches them which is why we are appealing to the public to be vigilant. If you see anything suspicious, let us know. Tell your kids that if anyone grabs them to scream and run for help," Sgt. Barnett said.

Anyone with any information is asked to contact the Forks Police Department at…

Kara brought up the next article, which came from the *Peninsula Daily News*. Two more incidents were dated a year apart from the others. The request by Blackmore Police was the same but the incidents had not been linked to the attacks in Forks. The only way anyone might have connected them was because of what the man did, and the vehicle was referred to as a Pontiac though no color had been mentioned.

She sat back in her seat and remembered what Henry Ellis had mentioned about Seth Leonard driving a white and brown 1982 Pontiac Bonneville back in 1991. Was it possible that he'd been responsible for these attacks after being let out of prison? Her eyes washed over the room as the library started to get busy with moms and their young kids. She momentarily thought about Ethan and felt an ache.

Kara glanced back at the screen and did a search through online news archives for the other four counties of Jefferson, Grays Harbor, Mason and Thurston in the same time period. A number of articles came up for sexual assaults but none that matched the M.O. reported within Clallam County. It was possible that Seth had graduated up to murder instead of just assault. Her mind was lost in deep thought when a pair of hands grabbed her shoulders from behind. Startled, she nearly fell out of her chair. Laughter erupted as she turned to find Sam curled over. His hair was soaking wet, as were his clothes. He had on a ripped pair of jeans, workman boots, and a North Face black jacket.

"Oh that was priceless."

Placing a hand on her chest, she took in a few deep breaths then said, "Sam. You scared the life out of me. What are you doing here?"

He chuckled as he slipped into a chair beside her and eyed the monitor, drumming his fingers against the table. He had a toothpick sticking out the corner of his mouth. "Got a job working on a roof in town. We got rained out. Suits me fine, we don't have to be back until Monday. I saw you head in here earlier, figured I would see what you're up to." He looked back at the screen. "Sexual assaults. I knew it. You couldn't resist, could you? So what have you managed to find out?" He leaned back and removed the toothpick. She told him about the discovery they'd made that morning at Seth Leonard's house.

"I'm just following up on some assaults that occurred prior to Charlie's abduction. I'm surprised this didn't get mentioned at the time. Did you ever hear or read about it?"

"No, what abductions?"

She brought him up to speed and showed him the article. Once he was done reading it he nodded. "Certainly makes sense. You figure this is the same guy who took Charlie?"

"Not sure. They're processing Seth's home as we speak."

He took the toothpick and tapped it against the screen under the description of the vehicle. "Darryl Clayton had a Bonneville. Same colors too."

"What?"

"My old man knew him back in the day. He'd hired him to help out on a drywalling job. I remember going to his farm as a kid and seeing it in the open barn."

"You remember back that far?"

He nodded. "My dad got into an argument with him over money. Darryl accused him of holding back what was rightfully his. I guess that's why it sticks out in my mind. Things got pretty heated and my dad knocked him on his ass because he took a swing at him. He was younger back then. Cocky. In his late twenties. Fucking guy said he was going to get his gun. We got the hell out of there." Kara looked back at the screen. Maybe that's why the police had focused on him. Though she did recall him matching the suspect sketch at the time.

"Anyway my dad put Clayton's name forward as someone who matches the suspect sketch."

"He thought he could have done it?" she asked.

"Him and others. Look, if anyone could have done

it, it was either him or his brother-in-law. They were both as batshit crazy as each other." He paused.

"You know where they live?" Kara asked.

"Yep." He stuck the toothpick back in his mouth. "But you don't want to go up there. I'm serious, Kara. The guy has issues. So does his son. Well you remember him."

She leaned on the desk. "No."

"Of course you do, he was around our age at the time. Gregory Clayton. C'mon, don't say you don't remember him?"

She shook her head. "He moved from Forks to Clallam because he got expelled for fighting. Caused all manner of trouble. You know, the one who looked a little retarded and used to wear that plaid hat that made him look like Holden from *Catcher in the Rye*." Anyway, I tell you, the apple didn't fall far from the tree when it came to him. Fortunately, he only did a year in our school before Darryl pulled him out and homeschooled him after they accused Darryl of physical abuse." He stared at her. "Man, you really have forgotten a lot."

Kara got up and logged out. "Did you drive here?"

"No, I got a ride. Asshole who was meant to take me back bailed. Said it was too far out of his way. Told me to catch the bus."

She smiled. "So that's why you came in."

"Hey, you've got it all wrong." He smiled. "But sure, I could use a lift home."

They made their way to the exit and looked out at the downpour. That was the thing about Clallam and living by the coast, the weather could change in a heartbeat.

Chapter 23

It was a good hour's drive from Port Angeles to Forks. Highway 101 had turned into a mini stream with the constant battering of rain. The windshield wipers sloshed water back and forth in an almost hypnotic fashion. Kara reached over and switched on the heater as the windows started to fog up. She cracked the window just a little and let in some of the cold, damp air. For most of the journey Sam tried to talk her out of visiting Clayton.

"I'm serious, Kara. The reason they didn't bring him in for further questioning was because no one had the balls to go out there and bring him in. He's mentally unstable."

"Sounds like he fits the profile."

He groaned and ran a hand over his head. "You're just like your mother. No one could get her to see reason. Once she had it in her mind to do something she was like a pit bull," he said. "Even if he's there, you'd have a better chance of speaking to him when he's running errands or out working than showing up on his property. Rumor has it he has brought a rifle out on numerous occasions with his neighbors. Threatens to shoot them. It's nuts."

"Relax, Sam. You can stay in the SUV with the engine running. If things get hot, we'll leave. Okay?"

He didn't look any more satisfied with that answer than those she'd already given. Darryl Clayton's farm was located minutes away from the Quillayute Airport and only ten minutes from Olympic National Park and Rialto Beach. It was everything she expected when she veered into his driveway. The farmland itself was unkempt with fenced pastures, stables and deteriorating storage buildings. The home represented those who might be heavily into fishing and hunting. It was rural, off the beaten path and shrouded by dense pine forest. All the buildings including the barn off to the right had a red tin roof and were made from timber.

"So is he still working as a handyman?"

"His son is, I saw him in Blackmore the other month. Darryl helps him from time to time but apparently makes his money breeding dogs and selling them. Who knows what kind of environment he has them in."

The SUV rumbled up the driveway. As they got closer a woman who looked to be in her early fifties emerged from the barn holding a steel bucket in one hand. She was wearing black boots, jeans and a thick fall jacket. "That's Nancy Clayton. Darryl's wife," Sam said. She put a hand up to her brow and looked over as Kara parked the SUV. She left it idling, checked that her service weapon was loaded and climbed out.

"Hang tight," she said to Sam who had already sunk down into his seat a little. "Hello there," Kara said in a friendly manner as she made her way over. The woman scowled making it clear she wasn't happy with the intrusion. "I'm Kara Walker." She pulled her badge and flashed it but didn't leave it out long enough for her to see. "I'm assisting Clallam County Police Department. I was hoping to speak with Darryl, is he around?" Her gaze bounced between her and the home nearby. She'd always found it best to lead people instead of letting them guide her. She started making her way over to the house when Nancy fell in step.

"What's this all about?" Nancy asked.

"Just a few questions I need to ask him."

"Concerning?"

As they got closer, the front door opened, and a pudgy fella wearing a camouflage baseball cap, a dirty-looking white shirt, and brown pants and slippers pushed open the screen door. It creaked a little but he didn't step out.

"Darryl Clayton?" Kara asked.

"Who's asking?" he replied in a deep voice.

Before she could reply Nancy did the honors. "She's with the pigs."

The guy smirked. "Lady, you better turn around and head out of here if you know what's good for you. I'm tired of you assholes hassling me."

"Just have a few questions to ask and I'll be out of your hair."

He scowled. "Did you not hear me?"

"Mr. Clayton, I was told you own a white and brown Pontiac Bonneville, is that right?"

He didn't reply but thumbed over his shoulder to his wife like he was used to telling her what to do without words. She slipped by him, keeping her distance as if expecting to be swatted. He stepped beyond the screen door and it clattered behind him.

"Who told you that?" His eyes darted to the SUV and he squinted.

"So do you?"

"And what if I do? How's that any of your business?"

There was no other way around it except to come out with it. The whole point of the visit wasn't to get him to confess to anything but to gauge his reaction, get a feel for who he was but more importantly to hear his voice. Even though the man who took Charlie wore a mask, was younger and spoke through gritted teeth, she figured she'd know it when she heard it. Then again there was a chance she could be wrong.

"We're currently investigating assaults that occurred between the years of 1989 and 1991. A vehicle that matches the description of yours was mentioned to us and we would just like to—"

"Get the hell off my property!" he blurted out jabbing his finger in her direction.

"So that would be a no?" Kara asked.

"Lady, I won't ask you again. Get back into your vehicle and…"

As he was saying that Sam stepped out of the SUV and made his way over. "Everything okay here, Kara?"

Darryl scowled and stepped down from his porch. He jabbed his finger. "I know you. Tom Young's boy."

"And I know you too, old man." Sam pulled at Kara's arm. "Let's go."

"Why, we were just getting acquainted," Kara said turning back to him.

"Yeah that bastard is finally where he deserves to be."

Sam balled his fists. "You want to say that again, old man?"

Before things could get out of control, a vehicle could be heard rumbling down the driveway. She turned and saw a van. It splashed through some of the rain puddles and veered in at an angle. A broad-shouldered man in his late thirties, wearing a black T-shirt and dirty jeans tucked into workman boots, stepped out and hurried over.

"These people giving you trouble?"

"They were just leaving."

"And you must be... Gregory? Holy cow. Gregory Clayton. Don't you remember me? Kara Walker."

"Walker?" Darryl blurted out.

"Yeah, you both probably remember my mother Anna, and most certainly Charlie." She let his name linger gauging their reaction, hoping to see anything in their expression that would give her reason to believe they knew more than they were letting on.

"That's it. I'm done with this. I'm getting my gun."

"Hold on, Dad," Gregory said.

"No. Enough is enough."

He slammed the door on the way into his house leaving them outside.

Gregory spun around, a flash of anger. "I would advise you to leave. Now."

"He's right, Kara," Sam said giving a small tug on her coat. She didn't take her eyes off Gregory but then turned away glancing at his blue van with a red decal on the side that read: Clayton Handyman Service. They made it over to the SUV and were just climbing in when Darryl came out of the house with a Winchester rifle in hand. Gregory waved him off and stepped up onto the porch to watch them leave.

"I see what you mean now. Real friendly. Why the animosity, huh?" Kara muttered not taking her eyes off the two of them. Sam didn't answer but just told her to get moving before he took a crack at them.

Beyond the gates of the farm, Sam looked over his

shoulder. "I told you. Insane."

They hadn't made it a few miles down the road when her phone started vibrating. She veered off to the edge of the road and fished into her bag. It was Goodman.

"Go ahead."

"Where you been? I tried phoning a couple of times but got no answer."

She looked over to Sam. "I got caught up running a few errands. Any luck at the house?"

He sighed. "Look, I don't want you to get your hopes up, Kara, but we found video footage of the vigil for Charlie. Seems he was there. There are also a number of articles he kept on the vigils of the other missing boys. We also found a painting of Charlie. Looks as if it's based on the same headshot that was used on the missing flyers. There is a carload of porn here and the team is going to jack-hammer the basement as the cement looks freshly poured. I'll keep you posted."

She was quiet.

"Kara?" he asked.

"I'm here."

"Did you want to come down and take a look around?"

"I looked into those attacks on boys between '89 and '91. Six occurred in Forks, and another two in Blackmore. Do you know if we can get our hands on the original police reports? Find out who the kids were?"

"Best of luck with that. They've probably been destroyed by now."

"Then what about speaking with Sgt. Barnett? As he

was mentioned in the article. Oh, and do you know Clayton was apparently in possession of a brown and white Pontiac Bonneville back then?"

"How do you know that?"

"Sam," she said.

"Please tell me you did not go up to the Claytons'?"

"Afraid so."

He sighed. "Kara. Seriously. If he files a complaint the chief will take you off the case."

"Nothing happened."

"Nothing?"

"Okay so things got a little heated but it was nothing we couldn't handle."

"We?" he asked.

Kara cleared her throat. "Sam."

"Dear Lord. Look, just stay out of trouble for a few hours until I can get this squared away. I have—"

She cut him off. "Noah, you need to get a warrant and speak with Clayton again. I'm serious. Something's not right there. In the meantime I'm going to see if I can speak with the families of the four missing boys. If Seth had a video of Charlie's vigil, maybe he attended the other ones."

"Kara."

"I'll be fine. I promise."

Chapter 24

After dropping Sam off, it was a little after two in the afternoon. Kara sat outside in the SUV thumbing through the case file given to her by Tim Greer. It was a thick, lumpy folder that had faded over time and was jam-packed with papers stuffed into more folders; each one corresponded to the missing boys: Scott Caldwell, Chris Peterson, Dwight Harrington and Richard Beck.

Over the course of the next five minutes she made phone calls in the hope of being able to chat with all the parents. It wasn't to be. The Becks and Harringtons said it wasn't a good time; the Petersons didn't answer so she left a message. The only one that seemed receptive and available was Maureen, Scott's mother.

Before leaving for Jefferson County, she took ten minutes to go through the notes on the family. Scott Caldwell was twelve and the fourth boy to go missing. He went missing on Halloween 2011 while out trick or treating. According to the original police report, his mother had made arrangements for him to go with another family that lived two streets over on Calhoun Street. However she had an unforeseen emergency with her other child and could not take him there. Scott said he'd be fine to walk by himself the five-minute journey over to their home. He was never seen again. No witnesses. No one remembered seeing him on the streets, then again it was dark and most would have assumed a boy walking down the street was just walking ahead of his parents. She ran a hand over her face as memories flooded in of her own fateful night, before setting out on the two-hour journey to the eastern shore.

Port Townsend was the largest city in Jefferson County with just over nine thousand residents. Like Port Angeles, it was often a hot spot for tourists looking to visit the National Forest and take in some of the natural scenery that Washington State had to offer. Its location at the northeast tip of the Olympic Peninsula provided breathtaking views of the bay.

In all the years Kara had lived in Blackmore she'd never ventured into Port Townsend even though the county of Jefferson butted up against Clallam and offered all manner of annual events. The SUV wound through the streets into the heart of the downtown and she took in the sight of Victorian buildings, the federal building, the Rose Theatre, Elks Lodge and various mom-and-pop stores. The water of the bay glistened in the afternoon sun, and waves from the harbor crashed against the shore. Seagulls wheeled over the pier, disappearing behind dockside attractions. A salty smell lingered. The traffic moved ahead of her at a steady pace. The roads around the bay were clearer in October than in the summer when it was ludicrous to attempt to navigate some of the one-way streets in Clallam. After taking a right off Washington Street she eventually found the white clapboard home on the corner of Pierce and Jefferson. It was a one-story abode with brown shingles, white shutters and a picture-perfect landscaped yard.

She parked her SUV outside and made her way to the door. Someone glanced out the window and she heard a thumping, somebody running. A female approached the door as she heard her voice. Kara's hand was reaching for the knocker when the door opened and she was greeted by an auburn-haired woman close to Kara in age.

"Hi, I'm Kara Walker."

"Yes, my mother said you'd be arriving. Come on in, she's just in the kitchen. By the way, I'm Abigail."

Kara gave a nod.

"Should I take my shoes off?"

"No need. My mother got rid of the carpets years ago."

The woman was dressed in a black skirt, and tights with a black sweater and white blouse. She was thin and her clothes seemed to hang off her bones. The aroma of coffee and freshly baked pie carried through from the hallway.

"Mother," Abigail said.

A frail-looking woman in her late sixties was just in the middle of taking a pie out of the oven. She had wiry gray hair that was pulled back into a ponytail, and pasty skin as if she hadn't seen the sun in a long time. It was common to see those who'd lost someone fall to pieces, stop eating, stop socializing and spiral down. Her mother had done it. Maureen was wearing a thin blue sweater, and a blue skirt, along with white flats.

"Hello, come in, take a seat. I hope you like apple pie."

"I hope you didn't bake that just for me," Kara said.

She chuckled. "Don't worry, she does it for everyone, don't you, Mother?" Abigail said. They all took a seat at a round dining table. Kara glanced around. It was a cramped kitchen but big enough for two. The counters were worn, and the backsplash tiles had come away from the wall in the corner of the room. A money plant seated on the windowsill looked wilted. She saw a photo on the counter of Maureen, Abigail, Scott and an older man, big, weathered and with stubble.

"Scott?" Kara asked.

Maureen set down a tray of coffee, and a couple of plates for pie. She nodded. "Taken a year before he was taken."

Her breath smelled like cigarettes.

"Is your husband around?"

"He passed away two years ago."

She wished she hadn't asked. "Oh, God, I'm sorry."

"It was sudden. An aneurysm, though I think it was brought on from all the stress."

"Mom, what did we say?"

"I know. I know. Abigail here doesn't like me to get bogged down in it but it's the truth. These last five years have been like hell."

"I understand."

"Right, you would, of course." She studied Kara's face and smiled sweetly before handing out plates and cutting the pie. "Now be careful, it's really hot." She heaped a scoop onto a plate and asked Abigail to get the ice cream out.

"How many years has it been for you?" Maureen asked.

"Twenty-five," Kara replied.

"That's a long time. But at least you know who was behind it, right? If he hadn't been jailed in '96, I would have thought he was responsible for Scott."

Kara nodded as Maureen took a seat across from her.

"Do you speak with the other families?"

She drew a breath and reached for her cigarettes but her daughter placed a hand on them. She grimaced and looked back at Kara. "Yes, all three of them. In fact we have our annual vigil tomorrow night. At first we were doing them alone but then we decided we might as well do them together being as they all went missing on the same day, just different years." She paused as she put milk into her coffee. "You are welcome to come if you like. It's just a small gathering now. At one time we used to have hundreds show up but as the years have passed that has dwindled."

"Right," Kara said, her eyes darting between the two of them. "So Abigail, you live here or elsewhere?" Kara asked.

"If my mother had her way, it would be here."

"Hey, I just like the company."

Abigail placed a hand on her mother's. "I know you do." She looked back at Kara. "I have three kids, a dog and a husband who doesn't do well with tight spaces."

Kara nodded and smiled looking around the cramped room.

"But I'm down here most days, checking in and making sure she's okay. Isn't that right, Mom?"

"Yep, Abigail is my rock. I wouldn't know what I would do without her."

Kara couldn't help wish that she'd had that closeness with her mother. It was strange how different families responded to tragedy. Some would come together and their bond would grow stronger, and others like hers came apart.

Already familiar with how Scott went missing, Kara didn't want to bring up the events surrounding that night but she was interested in knowing if they had taken any photos or video of the vigils over the years.

"You had mentioned you wanted to discuss the case. Have there been any new leads?" Maureen asked.

"Not exactly, however, we are looking into the recent abduction attempt in Clallam and looking to see if it's somehow linked to Scott and the other boys."

She looked confused. "So how can we help?"

"I was wondering if you captured any video or photos of the vigils over the past four years?"

"Of course." Maureen went to get up but Abigail said she would get it. "But why do you want to see them?"

"Vigils are commonly frequented by offenders. They get off on the misery of others and often enjoy the thrill of being close to the victim's family and the community."

She looked disturbed. "Are you saying that whoever took Scott might have attended?"

"Well that's what I'm here to find out."

Abigail returned with a small album of photos, and a camera in hand. "Some of the footage is on this, I would need to hook it up to the TV. Would you like me to do that?"

"If you wouldn't mind," Kara said.

After being led into a small living room with a brown couch, a throw rug, a coffee table, and an IKEA chair, Kara browsed through the album of photos. It wasn't all dedicated to the vigils. In fact only one-fourth of it contained photos from those events, the rest was of Scott and family prior to his abduction.

When the video began playing on the flat-screen TV, Kara looked up from the album and watched a huge group of people gathered outside Maureen's home.

Candles had been lit and placed on the ground, along with flowers, balloons, letters, paintings and toys. Several people were wearing red football T-shirts.

"Scott always loved watching the Washington State Cougars," Maureen said. It made Kara think of Charlie and his love for the sport. While she continued pointing out things, and discussing the huge amount of support in the early days and the kind letters she received from all over the state, Kara's focus was on the crowd. She scanned somber faces looking for Seth Leonard. Many huddled together holding candles and sobbing. Minutes turned into an hour as they waded through the vigils. The final one was held at a nearby park with all four families.

"Is that where tomorrow's vigil will be?" Kara asked.

"Yes. It's more centralized and with fewer people coming out each year it just feels right to be there to support each other and let them know that we haven't forgotten even if others have." Maureen sighed and looked into her hands. "I understand. People can't dwell on the loss forever. They have to get on with their lives. I just wish I knew what happened to him. If he's dead, I can live with that but it's the not knowing. You know — wondering where he is, what he's thinking and who has him. What have they done to him?" She shook her head and Kara was about to tell her daughter to turn it off because she hadn't seen Seth Leonard when she spotted someone.

She leaned forward. "Hold on. Wait. Pause it and back up a little," Kara said.

Abigail backed it up a bit too far so she asked for the remote and did it herself. When she paused the screen she walked over and touched it. "This guy. Have you seen him before?"

Maureen put her glasses back on and then nodded. "He's a strange fellow, always shows up."

Kara backed up the video and watched him bend down and place what appeared to be a sheet of paper under a candle.

"Shoot. Can you make out what that is? What did he leave?"

Abigail got real close to the TV. "Mom, weren't those the charcoal sketches?"

"Yes," she replied. "Very odd."

"What happens to everything that gets left behind?" Kara asked.

"We gather it up and store it in Scott's room. Do you want to see?" Maureen asked.

She nodded and backed up from the TV keeping her eyes on the face of Ray Owen. He was slightly younger looking but without a doubt that was him. Maureen led her upstairs to a room at the end of the hall. The door was closed and there was a yellow construction sign that read: CAUTION THIS DOOR MUST BE KEPT CLOSED.

Maureen pushed it open and Kara stepped into a room that had been turned into a treasure trove of goodwill items left behind by strangers, family and friends. Cards lined the walls, balloons that were now deflated covered the ground, and toys filled up every inch of space of that young boy's room. She could barely make out the bed beneath the thick layer of jerseys, gifts and artwork.

"Where would it be?" Kara asked.

"Anything that is artwork is in among that stuff."

Maureen pointed and waded through the sea of gifts to assist. She pushed aside items. "I know they are here somewhere. I remember how odd they were. He kept on leaving the same sketch every year."

"Did you consider mentioning it to the cops?"

"Of course. But we've had a lot of strange people approach us offering to help and giving us paintings and well, you name it," Abigail said in defense. "Some people sketch rainbows, others landscapes, though usually they are different each time and colorful. His were always the same. Dark, ominous, weird."

"And you never approached him?"

Abigail sighed. "You know as well as us that these events are heartbreaking. We're really not thinking about why people show up. We just appreciate anyone supporting us, however strange that might seem. Lots of people approached us and gave tips but—"

"Here we go!" Maureen turned and handed over four sheets of cream-colored paper that were covered with black charcoal drawings. It was a sketch of a stone well with a bucket reeled in at the top. All of the images were identical. There was no message on them. No signature. Nothing.

"Do you mind if I take these? I need to show them to someone," Kara asked.

"By all means," Maureen said as Kara walked out of the room lost in thought. She asked her a question on the way down. "Do you think he had something to do with Scott's disappearance?"

"I don't know but I'm going to look into it. You have my word on that." She turned to her daughter. "Can I get the SD card? I'm going to have to bag this as evidence. You'll get it back."

It wasn't hard to see how concerned they were by this. The thought that perhaps the abductor might have been among the community all this time would have been disturbing enough, but to think that he might have been within arm's reach could send anyone over the edge. As she was getting ready to leave, Maureen came over and gave her a warm hug and thanked her.

"It's been a long while since the police have shown any interest in my boy. And to have someone who has been directly affected by a similar situation means a lot to us."

Kara wasn't sure how to respond to that so she simply offered back a thin smile and said she would be there on Saturday for the vigil. After leaving the residence she sat in her SUV for a while looking at the sketches.

Chapter 25

Arriving in Blackmore later that evening, Kara was perplexed to see Lloyd Benson's vehicle parked in the driveway outside her father's home. Inwardly she groaned as she made her way in. The house smelled of chicken soup, the one dish her father was good at cooking. It was a homemade concoction of chicken cuts, with a healthy mixture of veggies. Every time he dished it up, he acted like he was some fancy chef. Her mother used to poke fun at him. As Kara entered the mud room she could hear the faint sound of conversation coming from the kitchen. She peeled off her coat and hung it up, then entered the kitchen to find Lloyd, her father and her Uncle Rob seated around the table with a bottle of wine and a bowl of bread, and dishes with crumpled napkins in them.

"Ah, here she is." Her father twisted in his seat. "I was just telling Lloyd about Ethan, and how much he's grown up." In front of him were a number of photos she'd sent over the years. It felt like an invasion of her privacy. Her father was always in the habit of overstepping his boundaries. Lloyd scrutinized her in his usual fashion. She immediately felt like she was in a session and being picked apart.

"Hey Rob," Kara said acknowledging him alone. He smiled and looked as if he was about to say something when her father chimed in again.

"Have you eaten?"

"No, not yet."

"Well come on, take a seat."

"Actually I had a few things to do."

He turned to Lloyd and spoke about her like she wasn't even there. "See, I told you. She takes after her mother." He said it in a way that sounded almost offensive. Instead of allowing him to get under her skin or make her feel like a fool, she pulled up a chair and began to help herself to some soup.

Lloyd ran a finger around the rim of his glass and it let out a whine sound. He did it in a way to get her attention before scooping it up and taking a sip. There was something about his eyes that bothered her. They were small, sunken, beady. "Your father was telling me you finally got rid of your mother's paperwork in the basement. That's quite an achievement, Kara," Lloyd said it like she was suffering from some inability to move beyond the past.

"Actually I moved it."

"You still have it?" her father asked, his features twisting. "But you said…"

"You wanted it out. It's out. It's not gone," she replied, scooping a few more spoonfuls of soup into her bowl before dipping in a chunk of bread. Her father glanced at Lloyd as if seeking his support or input on a matter that really was none of his business. Meanwhile Uncle Rob sat there observing and withholding judgment.

"Any reason in particular?" Lloyd asked.

Oh great, here he goes again, she thought. He was going to psychoanalyze her reasons. Well she wasn't going to let him. Instead she decided to be clear with them. If they couldn't understand, that was their problem.

"It's of use to the investigation."

"Investigation?" Rob blurted out. "What investigation?" His eyes bounced between them all. Kara had her spoon a few inches from her mouth, she paused for a second then swallowed the soup. Once it was down she leaned back.

"The attempted abduction of a child."

"But what your mother had gathered was related to Charlie," Lloyd said.

Kara eyed him before replying, "And previous attacks on young boys in the days leading up to his abduction. And let's not forget the four that were taken from surrounding counties."

All three of them looked dumbfounded before her uncle said, "She thought they were connected?"

Kara gave a short nod. "It seems so."

"But that's ridiculous," he replied.

"Is it?" she asked breaking off another chunk of bread. Her father straightened up in his chair. She knew what was coming. She'd become accustomed to the way he would react before tossing in his two cents and she figured she was going to hear it whether she wanted to or not. He leaned towards her a little, his hands clasped together.

"You said you were staying for a few days to help me, not get tangled up in your mother's wall of weird and disappearing down that rabbit hole."

"That wall of weird just so happens to have generated a few new leads, and as for disappearing down a rabbit hole, I expected more from you, Dad."

She got up and went over to the sink to fill the jug with more water. In the reflection of the window she saw her father nudge Lloyd.

He drew a breath. "I think your father is just concerned that holding on to the past isn't healthy, Kara."

"Neither are consuming meds and overanalyzing, Lloyd, but we sure seem to do a lot of both," she replied returning to the table. She was surprised her uncle wasn't saying more. She poured out a tall glass of water. There were a few minutes of awkward silence.

"Was that Sam I saw you with today?" Rob asked.

With a mouthful of food she nodded. He and Janice lived in Port Angeles so it wasn't a surprise when he mentioned it. Rob ran a small Italian restaurant just off the main street.

"How is he doing?" Rob probed deeper.

"Fine. In fact he's been very helpful with the investigation."

"And Bobby?"

"Good."

"Bobby was there the night she got into that spat with Mary Harris," her father added, throwing salt on an open wound.

"Oh, really? What spat?" Rob asked hoping that her father might shed some light on the incident.

"Let's not go there, Dad," Kara said.

"Well I think we should, being as she was responsible for the brick through our window."

"Allegedly. We can't go throwing accusations out," she added.

"Why not? She's done her fair share. Someone should toss her in a jail cell with her scummy, child-molesting sicko brother," her father said, reaching for the wine to pour some more. Now it was the alcohol talking. Kara put her hand over his glass.

"I think you've had enough for one evening, don't you think?"

"Don't belittle me."

Rob piped up. "She's right, Matthew."

He huffed and his chair screeched as he got up to take a few plates over to the sink.

"So you mentioned there were a few new leads?" Lloyd asked. "Anything in particular?"

She chewed a piece of chicken and washed it down with water. "Nothing that I should be discussing here."

"Well, we're among friends," her father said. "Besides, I'd be interested to know what is causing my daughter to get involved with the local police department. I gather that's who you're assisting?"

"The Criminal Investigation Division of Washington State Patrol."

"Must be serious if they're involved," Lloyd added, looking at Rob.

Her father turned and leaned against the sink, drying a cup in preparation for making coffee. "It is if she's been filling their head with Anna's theories."

"I've not been filling anyone's head," she replied.

"But you're involved?" Rob asked.

"That's right." She frowned feeling under a microscope. "What is this, twenty questions?"

"We're just curious," her father said.

"So are these new leads related to the attempted abduction?" Lloyd asked.

"Possibly."

"Possibly? You sound unsure," he said.

"It's still in process. Why does it matter to you, Lloyd?"

"Kara," her father said in a correcting tone.

"What? I'm just asking why he's so curious."

"It's okay, Matthew. Kara, it matters to your father and he's my client," he said before quickly adding, "and friend. What affects him is eventually going to be heard by me, and he's concerned for your well-being."

She wanted to snap back at that but instead decided to get them off her back by telling them. "We found a person of interest dead today. His home contained material that could link him to missing cases, even Charlie."

Lloyd studied her. "And Charlie? But his abductor is in prison."

"Alleged."

"Alleged?" Lloyd asked. "No, I think it was proven in court."

"It was," her father added.

She set her spoon down after finishing her meal and sat back. "Well maybe this recent discovery might overturn that sentence."

Again there was another long pause.

"You think Harris is innocent?" Rob asked.

"My mother did and if her files were anything to go by I'm beginning to think she was on to something."

Lloyd looked at her father then shook his head. "Without meaning to sound rude, obviously we can see how that turned out."

She shot him a look of disgust and he must have picked up on it as he was quick to add, "I mean, this isn't healthy, Kara. As someone who has worked with victims, I can assure you that going down this road won't bring back Charlie."

"Victims of abduction have been found before," she said.

"And most are found dead within the first twenty-four hours," Rob said.

"Except his body was never found," she added wiping her lips with a napkin and tossing it into the bowl. There was silence for a second or two. "Anyway, we'll know more once CSI gets through Seth Leonard's home."

"Seth Leonard?" Lloyd asked.

"You know him?"

He nodded and took another gulp of his glass. "I treated him for twelve years after his release from prison." Kara's eyes widened. This was news. "Has he said anything?"

"A little hard. He's dead," she replied.

"Dead?"

"Yep." She took another sip of her wine and studied Lloyd's reaction. "So if you treated him, you must have been aware of what landed him in prison and what was going on in his head. Did he ever say anything?"

Lloyd drained his glass of wine.

"If you're asking if he mentioned Charlie or the other boys, no. But yes, I was aware of his past. He was a very sick individual that really should have been treated at the special commitment center on McNeil Island rather than locking him away for eight years in the state pen." He took a deep breath and continued. "What you have to understand is most of these individuals don't wake up one day and choose to commit an offense. Their actions are birthed out of some tragedy in early childhood — sexual abuse or witnessing it. In Seth's case he was first a victim before he became a perpetrator." He hesitated for a second as if contemplating whether he should say more. He continued, "He was abducted while at a museum with his family. His abductors took him to a nearby forest where he was sodomized and beaten for several hours. Unlike other victims he was released the same day. His abductors were never caught." He looked down into his drink with a blank stare before taking a sip.

"Well on that note, I think I'll call it an evening," Rob said rising to his feet. He leaned over and kissed Kara on top of the head, something he'd done for years since she was a kid. He shook Lloyd's hand before slapping her father on the back. "Good to see you again, Lloyd. And thanks for the dinner, Matthew."

"Anytime."

The door clunked behind him as he let himself out.

They sat there for a few minutes before Kara asked, "So you believed him?"

"He never changed his story," Lloyd said.

Her father snorted. "That sob story still doesn't justify what he did to those kids."

"No it doesn't," Lloyd added. "But it makes you wonder what path he would have taken had it not happened. And let's not forget, he served his time."

"Not enough in my books. They should have castrated him, locked him inside a cell and thrown the key away," her father said.

"But that doesn't cure them, Matthew."

"Neither does letting them out to wander the streets," her father said.

Again more silence.

"Were you aware of his paintings, or kiddie porn?" Kara asked.

"He was a sick man, Kara. These kinds of people need to be treated. He told me he couldn't touch anyone so he painted nudes but he never mentioned anything about pornography. I assumed his probation officer would have been wise to that, if that was going on."

"But you never informed the police about the little you did know?"

"First, it would have broken client confidentiality and second, you can't stop a person from lusting. If painting was therapy to him, then I was all for it. Better that than hurting somebody."

Her father tossed the dish towel over his shoulder and scooped up the remaining bowls on the table. "I think we should call it a night. I'm sure Lloyd doesn't appreciate being grilled like this."

"It's fine, Matthew. Really. I should get going."

He got up and offered to help but her father declined.

"Kara. Matthew. It's been an interesting evening."

Always interesting, she thought. Damn guy never switched off from his work.

* * *

Her father waited until the glow of Lloyd's headlights faded before he unloaded on her. She was in the middle of cleaning the dishes and chewing over what he'd said about Seth's past when he erupted.

"You made me look like a fool tonight."

"Excuse me?" she said, caught off-guard by his accusing tone.

"Lloyd was my guest. I have never felt so humiliated as by the way you spoke with him. Is that how they teach you to speak to people in the academy? Because I know damn well I didn't raise you to speak like that."

"Humiliated? I could say the same thing about you."

"How did I humiliate you?"

"I told you to cancel that appointment with him but

you didn't. I then come home tonight and he's here."

"He's a friend of mine. And..." he jabbed his finger at her. "You told me not to cancel."

She gave a twisted expression.

He scooped up a cup and began drying it while shaking his head. "Just like your mother, expecting me to read minds. I really wish you would just say what you mean instead of being so double-minded."

"Which reminds me. You know, Dad, I'd appreciate it if you wouldn't keep saying that."

"Saying what?"

"That I'm like mom. I wouldn't mind if it was said in a positive light but it's always put in a way that makes me feel like you thought she was crazy."

"She was," he snapped.

Kara stopped washing the dishes and narrowed her eyes at him.

"What?" he asked. He wasn't even aware how out of line his words were. "Kara, you didn't have to live with her. No, while you were out east I was here trying to maintain some semblance of a relationship with a woman who was a shell of the person I married."

"I wonder why, Dad?" she said returning to washing the dishes.

He shook his head and clattered plates together. "I went through it too. I lost a son as well. But you don't see me creating some crazy wall of theories or holding on to my son's belongings. Charlie is gone!" he bellowed. "Your mother wouldn't accept that and it broke apart our marriage. And I refuse to see you head down the same road as her. I won't have it."

Kara shot him a sideways glance. She could feel her emotions welling up inside of her. She removed her hands from the bubble-filled sink and dried them. She scooped up her keys to her SUV and went to head out.

"Where are you going?"

"Out. Before I say something I regret."

She slammed the door and slipped back into her jacket. As she went out she heard her father curse and toss a plate in anger at the floor.

Chapter 26

Kara drove for an hour or so around the county before finding her way to the doorstep of Noah's apartment. When he opened the door, she walked in without even an invitation. Her mind was still lost in the argument with her father. She flung down her bag and slumped into the couch shaking her head. Noah stood at the door with a smile on his face. "Please… come on in," he said in jest before closing the door.

"You think I can sleep here tonight?" she asked.

"Uh… sure." He frowned then thumbed over his shoulder. "But aren't you staying with your father?"

"For a few more days but I would prefer to not go home tonight."

He gave a slow nod as if feeling the tension but still unsure. "You want a drink?"

"Do I ever." She breathed in deeply and exhaled. "Yes. Please."

"Wine okay? I'm out of beer."

"Anything with alcohol is fine."

As Noah clattered around in the kitchen she just blurted it out.

"You know it's been twenty-five years and not once has my father acknowledged or asked how my brother's abduction affected me. And tonight, yet again he brings it back to himself. What he's lost. What he's suffered. No mention about me."

Glasses clinked together and there was a thump as the fridge closed. He returned a moment later and poured her a glass of white wine, handing it off to her before filling his own and curling up at the far end of the sofa.

"Sorry, who?"

"My father." She took several large gulps from her glass, nearly finishing it in one go before reaching for the bottle and filling it back up again. "My mother was the same. After the abduction it was just a whirlwind of activity in our house. I was pushed off to my uncle's and after I returned things were never the same again. My mother blamed me, and my father ignored me. They both did in some ways." She slowed her drinking, taking small sips. "And yet through it all, months after the crowds were gone and the media stopped paying attention, it was like they had forgotten they still had a daughter. I felt invisible to them." She closed her eyes, gripping her glass tightly and thinking back. It was easy to find the emotion. "I just wanted to shout, *I'm still here*." Her eyes opened again. She took a deep breath then looked at him. "Sorry, I really shouldn't be unloading this on you. I can get a hotel room."

She set the glass down and went to get up.

"It's fine. Kara." He said her name louder, getting her attention. "Relax. It's okay."

Kara looked back at him and stood there for a second before taking her seat again.

"I imagine it must have been hard," he said. "I mean I've dealt with victims and I guess in some ways the woman who killed Amanda was an abductor. She took her from me and I never got her back."

"How did she die?" Kara asked. "Like you told me it was a crash but…"

"She was T-boned by a drunk driver on the way

back from her mother's. I'd just got off the phone with her only minutes earlier." He paused for a second. "It was rare that we argued but a few days before that we had this big bust-up. I can't even remember what it was about now. Anyway she took off. I got on the phone and we talked it out and after a couple of days she was making her way home. I'd told her that I'd planned this getaway to Florida. She'd always wanted to go there." He stared off towards a chair across the room. "You think of all the things you wish you could have said, done. You know — the what-ifs."

"You blame yourself?" she asked.

He looked down into his drink and then took a sip. "At times. Obviously I wasn't the driver of the vehicle but if we hadn't had that argument, she wouldn't have gone and well…" He snorted. "I can't believe I just told you that. I haven't ever shared that with anyone else except her parents." He breathed in deeply. There was a long pause before he continued, "But you want to know the worst part? Her parents don't harbor any resentment towards me. Can you believe that?" He drained the remainder of his wine.

The clock in the background ticked quietly.

"What was she like?" Kara asked.

"Amanda?" A smile returned to his face. "A pain in the ass but the good kind. She could give as good as she got. I actually think she's the only one that could have put up with my crap."

Kara smiled. Being married to a cop wasn't easy on the best of days.

He poured some more wine and topped hers off before continuing. "But I loved her. I really did. She was kindhearted and had this way of making you laugh at times when you really shouldn't. You know?" Kara nodded. "Everything could be going wrong but just having her beside me made life easier to endure." He looked off again towards the chair, which by now Kara had gathered was hers.

"I'm sorry that happened to you," she said.

"Ah, it's okay. People lose their lives every day. What does one more light going out matter?"

"It matters," she said.

Her thoughts turned back to the case and she got up and went over to her bag and pulled out the sketches from earlier that afternoon. "Take a look at these. After getting off the phone with you, I visited Maureen Caldwell and asked if she had any photos or video of the candlelight vigils they have each year for Scott. I figured if Seth Leonard had been in attendance at Charlie's vigil that perhaps—"

"He'd been at the others," Noah said cutting her off.

He took them from her and twisted them around. She sat down beside him bringing her one leg up and wrapping her arm over the back of the couch. "Exactly. Anyway, I viewed the video today and while Seth wasn't anywhere to be seen, Ray Owen was. He's left this sketch four times over the last four years."

Noah's brow furrowed as he looked at it. "As well?"

"Four times."

"Why would he do that?" he asked, though it sounded like he was asking himself the question more than her.

She shook her head. "Who knows but here's what I do know. According to Henry Ellis, he approached my mother not long after Charlie was taken offering to help find him. He said he was some kind of psychic. Yet I don't remember any mention of the cops following up on that lead. I figure he was dismissed as a kook. But obviously he raised enough red flags that Ellis wanted to bring him in for questioning."

"And?"

"It never happened. He said the sheriff at the time kept the focus on Kyle Harris."

Noah looked down at the sketches. "I know it's weird but these don't mean anything."

"You have that video of Seth Leonard at one of Charlie's vigils. Maybe Owen is on it. I'm going to attend the vigil tomorrow. It seems the four families hold one together, now that the cases no longer get the attention they once did. I didn't get to speak to the rest of the parents today but I bet you he left something with each of the families." She finished her drink. "And I'm going to find out. Besides, who knows, he might turn up."

"Owen?" Noah asked.

"Well you had him on the list, right?"

"Yeah but with everything that's going on with Leonard's home…"

"Leave it with me," she said.

"Kara."

"I can handle it. I've been at this longer than you."

He got up and smiled. "Let me get you some blankets."

As he went about collecting some, her mind churned over the day's events. "Oh, and I forgot to tell you. Did you know that Lloyd Benson was Seth Leonard's therapist?"

"Get out of here," he said returning with an armful of blankets and a pillow.

"And according to Benson, he was abducted and abused as a child himself."

"Huh." He dumped the blankets on the couch and pointed to them. "You think that's going to be enough?"

She glanced at them. "If it's not I'll let you know."

He blew out his cheeks and cast another glance at the sketches. "If you don't mind I'm going to turn in. I'm exhausted. If you need anything, the fridge is there. Help yourself."

She nodded. "And Noah, thank you."

"Not a problem."

He ambled off into his bedroom and she used the washroom before settling in for the night. Over the course of the next hour she tossed and turned, unable to get Ray Owen's sketches out of her mind. In the darkness of the room, light filtering through the drapes caused shadows to dance against the wall. She closed her eyes and puffed out the pillow and tried again to sleep. No matter how hard she tried she couldn't forget what she'd seen in Leonard's home and the images of missing kids played over in her mind.

Eventually she got up and headed into Noah's room. As she pushed the door open he stirred and looked over his covers. Instead of telling him the truth she said, "It's cold."

He pulled the covers back and jerked his head. She hesitated for a second then crawled in.

Chapter 27

Sam crushed the cigarette beneath his boot, and gazed at the Clayton farm through the dense woodland before trying to call Kara one more time. Nothing. It just went directly to voicemail. He'd left a message asking her to call him back but he wasn't going to wait. He'd left his motorbike near the Quillayute Airport and walked the short distance across farmer's fields and had been crouched in the tree line for close to twenty minutes. The only light came from a crescent moon. The stars were hidden behind rolling dark clouds. It was a little after ten at night.

He looked over his shoulder and second-guessed going in alone. Hours earlier he'd been at home dealing with Mindy's bullshit. After draining three cans of Bud, and getting into another argument, he'd headed out with no destination in mind. It didn't take long for Darryl Clayton's words from earlier to echo in his mind causing rage to swirl. "You're Tom Young's son. That bastard is where he deserves to be."

There was no respect for the dead.

Not long after Charlie's abduction he'd overheard a neighbor talking to his father about Darryl. "Oh yeah, the police showed up here asking questions but they never took him away. He laughed at them. Said they didn't have any proof. When they drove off he felt he was above the law. Acted like the whole abduction was one big joke. Clayton enjoyed the attention."

Sam knew that asshole was hiding something and

after his insult, he was determined to find out if the Bonneville was still there. Oh the look on his face if it turned out that he was involved. He trudged on through the waterlogged field, his boots making a squelching noise. Under the cover of darkness he made his way to the back of the decaying barn. Sam shot a sideways glance either way before sliding around the corner keeping his back pressed to the wood panels. He'd considered bringing a knife or baseball bat as protection, but in the chance he got arrested he didn't want to end up doing time. At least this way if the cops nabbed him he'd only be charged for trespassing.

Under the faint light of the moon, the silhouette of structures loomed before him. He could hear two dogs barking outside, and the faint sound of bluegrass music. Sam ducked and remained still as someone burst out of the back door of the house and yelled at the dogs.

"Shut up, you mangy mutts," the familiar voice said in a slurred fashion.

The yellow glow of an outside door light gave him a clear shot of who it was — Darryl Clayton. He had what appeared to be a bottle of bourbon in hand, and a cigarette hanging out the corner of his mouth. He peered out into the night, grunted and ambled back into the house. The screen door slammed behind him. Sam waited a few more seconds before he continued on to the front of the barn to make his way inside. He glanced over his shoulder before pulling back the door ever so slightly to give him room to squeeze in. The barn stank of chicken shit, and engine oil. He took out his flashlight, and clicked the end. A white beam shot out illuminating the spacious confines. The ground was muddy, covered in a fine layer of hay. There was a John

Deere digger directly ahead of him, and two tiers to the barn. Haystacks were on both sides, and off to his left was a long workbench covered in lots of engine parts, tools and paint cans.

Sam moved through the darkness lifting heavy covers off the first vehicle which turned out to be a battered green 1940 International Harvester truck. Near his feet he heard the sound of rodents scuttling across the ground. He looked back at the main door and continued on to the rear. The next cover he lifted was for an engine that he figured had been taken out of a truck. He dropped the cover and shuffled forward casting the light over the cobweb-filled structure. It looked like it hadn't been cleaned in decades. From what he'd learned from his father, the Clayton family had been residents of Forks for a long time. No doubt the property had been passed down from father to son.

At the back of the barn, he lifted a cover on the next vehicle. Beneath it was a dark black car. He made his way around to the back and saw that the logo for a Bonneville had been removed. At a closer inspection, he could tell that the vehicle had at one time been white. *Bastards! They'd given it a paint job and removed anything that might identify it as being a Bonneville.* He shone the light on the tires and noticed the back one was deflated, the other one was gone and the brake drum was resting on a stack of bricks.

"Gregory?" a voice echoed.

A shot of fear went through Sam and he clicked the light off and ducked down behind the vehicle. His eyes scanned the back of the barn searching for a way out. He'd only seen one entrance, but there was another higher up on the second floor. His heart was slamming in his chest as he waited in the silence. The sound of boots could be heard approaching, puddles splashing and then the door he'd entered opened.

"You in there, boy?"

Sam closed his eyes and willed him to leave. *Don't come in. Don't come in.* The door closed and he heard the sound of heavy boots trudging away. He breathed a sigh of relief as he snuck a peek around the corner of the vehicle. Sam fished into his pocket and brought out his cell phone, pulled back the cover on the vehicle and turned on the video. He spoke in a low, hushed voice.

"Appears to be a 1982 Bonneville. It's had a paint job. A sloppy one but a paint job, nonetheless. The logo emblem has been removed but on closer inspection it's clear to see they used some kind of filler in the holes." Sam scratched away at the body with the keys to his bike and revealed the paint. "As you can see it's white underneath. My bet is another part of the vehicle is brown."

Right then he heard more voices outside — a female, then a louder male voice, possibly Gregory's? "Alright, I'll go check it out."

Shit! He moved fast, holding the small flashlight in his mouth and pulling the covers over the vehicle. He heard the door crack open as he clicked the button and the barn returned to darkness.

"I know you're in there. We saw the light. Now come on out!"

Sam's heart was pounding like a drum. His throat went dry as he shuffled behind the vehicle and tried to remain as quiet as possible. More voices could be heard, a woman and a man arguing. Sam glanced up at the second floor and could see the double barn door. It would be quite a drop but unless Gregory walked away the chances of getting out of the main door were slim to none. He scuttled across the floor, staying low and moving towards a wooden ladder that went up to the loft.

"I've got a gun. You better come out now or I'll set the dogs on you."

Hearing that only strengthened his resolve to get the hell out of there. At the foot of the ladder in the darkness he waited until he saw Gregory go around the far side of the digger before he began climbing. He'd only made it up four steps when he heard him shout. "Hey! Stop."

There was no stopping him. Sam's legs pumped like pistons as he scrambled up the ladder and launched himself into hay and made his way to the back door. Below he could hear Gregory making his way around the digger, yelling at the top of his voice for him to stay where he was. Was this guy out of his mind? Sam kicked the door open and looked down. It had to have been a good ten-foot drop. Crawling over the edge he let himself hang by his fingertips and then dropped to the ground. He landed hard and his ankle twisted. He let out a groan and clamped a hand around it before staggering to his feet. He was going to bolt across the field but before he could, a gun erupted. He saw the muzzle flash and he dashed around the other side of the barn and crossed over to the grain storage. He didn't wait but kept moving, now with the sound of Gregory and Darryl yelling.

"Get the dogs, you idiot!"

He knew he didn't stand a chance of outrunning dogs especially with his ankle, so using the cover of darkness he headed toward the house, hoping to make them think he'd bolted and possibly get the dogs off his scent. Sam limped his way to the rear porch, and saw the dogs barking. One was a hound dog, the other a Rottweiler. Both were up on their hind legs trying to get at him but a thick chain kept them in place.

"Did you see where he went?" the voice of Nancy Clayton hollered.

Sam ducked into the back of the house, groaning in agony. He pushed back against the wall and glanced out seeing Gregory head over to the dogs and release them. The second he did they bolted for the back door and started jumping up at it. Sam didn't wait around, he moved further into the house. It smelled almost as bad as the barn. He slid by the kitchen and saw a mountain of dishes that hadn't been cleaned and a dining table partially peeking out from beneath magazines, and all manner of shit. He was planning on going through the hallway and out the front, hoping they would cross the farm land out the back and he could escape down the main driveway but that wasn't to be.

"What's going on?" another guy's voice bellowed. A large, overweight man stepped into the hallway with his back to Sam and headed for the front door. For a brief second Sam thought it was over. The obese figure grabbed up a rifle by the door and pushed out. It was Edwin Brewer, Nancy Clayton's halfwit brother. Sam twisted around hearing Darryl out back and Edwin out front. He wasn't getting out of there anytime soon. His eyes darted to the stairs and he double-timed it up them. It was dark upstairs. None of the lights were on. It smelled like dirty clothes and piss. He peered into one of the bedrooms and saw what resembled a kid's room.

It was odd for sure. There were posters up and a duvet cover with wrestlers from the WWE. He kept moving still hearing their voices and the dogs barking. Sam slipped into another room and closed the door behind him. His heart was hammering. All he could think about was getting out of there and away but the last thing he wanted was to try and outrun vicious dogs. He walked backwards away from the door and his legs bumped into a king-size bed. Sam glanced over his shoulder and then went over to the window and peered out. He could see Gregory standing just beyond the porch, raking his rifle back and forth.

He fished into his pocket for his phone and dialed Kara's number. "C'mon, pick up. Pick up!" he muttered under his breath while keeping his eyes fixed on Gregory. No answer. Just the voicemail. Shit! He backed away from the window and cast his gaze over the room. His eyes had now adjusted to the darkness and he could make out a few side tables, a rocking chair in the corner and a closet. *Okay, stay calm. You can do this. You'll just wait until they leave and then head out the door or climb out the window.*

The sound of Nancy coming back into the house caught his attention. She was cursing and blaming Darryl. "You are good for nothing. I told you to get rid of them."

More heavy boots entered the house.

"And I will."

"You said that last year and the year before."

"Shut up, woman, I can't hear Gregory," he replied.

It sounded like he was standing in the doorway. "You got anything?"

Gregory replied, "Nothing. Whoever it was is gone."

"Edwin, go around the perimeter. Gregory, check the barn again and leave the dogs off the leashes."

Sam brought a hand up to the bridge of his nose and squeezed it. *Idiot. Why did you have to come here? You should have just left it to her,* he thought as he made his way over to the window and looked out again. Now he had nowhere to go. He scanned the room and cursed multiple times under his breath. The floorboards had creaked when he'd entered but no one was inside at the time. What was he meant to do now? He remained by the window expecting the two of them to eventually give up searching, at which point he would escape but it didn't happen. He glanced at the clock. It was nearly eleven at night. The minutes rolled over and when he heard Nancy say she was heading to bed, he panicked. Sam scanned the room. Her footsteps were getting louder as she reached the top of the stairs. He was about to enter the closet when she headed for the room. He dropped to the ground and slid across the floor, squeezing under the bed frame, a feat that wasn't easy.

Beneath the bed it was thick with dust and there were a single dirty sock, and a used condom wrapper. He grimaced at the thought of them getting it on. *How could anyone fuck that?* The door cracked open and light shined in as Nancy walked in mumbling to herself about how stupid they all were. "I'm telling you, Darryl. I want them gone by the end of the week or I'll get rid of them myself."

He watched from his confined space as she stripped down leaving a pile of clothes on the floor. She padded out of the room into the washroom. The sound of a faucet turning on followed by water rushing was his signal to move it. Sam slipped out and made a beeline for the door only to stop in his tracks at the sight of Darryl coming up the stairs. His eyes widened and he backed up. This time he opted for the closet, slipping inside and pulling the slatted door closed. It was cramped as he pushed back behind mothball-smelling old clothes. Through the slats in the closet door he saw Darryl head over to the window and shift it up. "Get inside, you morons. He's obviously gone."

"At least I know who it was!" Gregory shouted back.

"What?"

"Found a set of keys belonging to one Sam Young."

A cold shiver shot through him as Sam reached for his pocket and patted it. Shit! Sure enough they were gone. He must have dropped them or they fell out of his jacket when he exited the barn. Inwardly he screamed. All he could think about now was the cops showing up at his place and… well, he already had history with them.

"That bastard. Just like his old man. All right, call it a night. We'll deal with it tomorrow." Darryl continued cursing as he shuffled over to the bed and proceeded to peel of his clothes until he was butt naked. His paunch of a belly hung like a sack of potatoes almost covering up his micro sized penis as he hopped up on the bed. *Shit. Shit. Shit!* That's all that went through his mind as he remained still in that stuffy closet, barely able to breathe.

He heard water being shut off and a minute or two later, a haggard-looking Nancy ambled in with a towel wrapped around her. She approached the closet and Sam held his breath expecting her to see him when Darryl piped up.

"C'mon, get over here and service your old man."

"Not tonight."

"What did you say?" he replied in a disgusted fashion.

"I'm tired, Darryl, and not in the mood."

"Woman, you better get your ass over here now before I give you a whipping."

"I'd like to see you try," she snapped back.

He rolled off the bed and made his way over as she fished into a drawer for underpants. Darryl reached around and snatched them out of her hand and tossed them. "You won't be needing those."

"Darryl!"

He pulled her around and led her back to the bed, tearing off the towel and throwing her down before suffocating her beneath his greasy body. She squealed like a stuck pig beneath his grasp. It was hard to know if she was enjoying it or begging for him to stop. All Sam knew was he was trapped there, a spectator to a vomit-worthy sex session that was over before it hardly began. Within minutes he rolled off her like a beached whale and was snoring up a storm. "What about me?" she asked. She slapped him on the belly but it did little to wake him before she gave up and slipped under the covers beside him. There in the silence Sam remained. After an hour he thought Gregory and Edwin would turn in for the night but he could still hear them shuffling around. Swallowed by darkness, and certain both were asleep, he switched on his small flashlight and raked the light over shoes beneath him. He crouched in the closet, cupping a hand over the flashlight to reduce the amount of light. At the far end of the closet he noticed a large brown cardboard box. He might not have given it a second thought if it wasn't for what was sticking out. He squinted. It was a shoe. It was no adult shoe. It looked like the tip of a Converse sneaker. Certainly wasn't the kind that he would imagine they would wear. They were country folks. Farmers rarely wore much else than work boots. Sam slid over and pulled back the cardboard flap and shone the light in. He reached in and pulled out a red and white sneaker. The size was too small for an adult. He gazed inside and found a pair of jeans. Again, too small. They looked like a teen or a young boy might have worn them. He continued fishing out one piece of clothing after another; a jacket, three pairs of underpants, and then there buried beneath them were aged Polaroids like those that came from an old-style camera. Sam grabbed a handful and washed the light over them. What he saw made him drop them. He stumbled back, his heartbeat racing even faster. Darryl stirred and groaned, turning over in bed. Sam was quick to turn the light out.

One, two, three minutes passed before he fished out his phone and turned the light back on and started to record what was in front of him. He couldn't begin to wrap his mind around it. It seemed unreal and yet on the other hand it made sense.

Sometime in the early hours of the morning, Sam crept out of that closet and exited the house armed with everything he needed to bring that sack of shit down.

Chapter 28

Two days before Halloween

Gale force winds howled, and rain beat against the windowpane as Kara stirred that morning. Her eyes fluttered, bordering on the brink of dream state and being awake. She noted the smell of coffee, and vaguely remembered the sound of Noah puttering around the apartment before the clunk of a door snapped her awake.

Kara rolled and breathed deeply feeling relaxed and warm beneath the duvet. She turned on her side and eyed a scrap of yellow-lined paper on the pillow beside her. She shifted up onto her elbows, clasped it in one hand and read it.

Had to get going. Didn't want to wake you. There's a pot of coffee on. Are you aware you snore? (Just joking.) Call me. Noah.

She smiled and rolled onto her back staring up at the bedroom fan. She slipped out of bed and padded into the kitchen. A window was slightly ajar letting in cold air. She went over and closed it and put the heat on, turning it up a few notches. Kara poured herself a cup of coffee and nursed it with both hands as she leaned against the counter eyeing her surroundings. Only the sound of a clock ticking. It was quiet just as Noah said it would be. Fortunately his neighbor only switched on the music at night. She scooped up the sketches from the previous night and took a seat in the recliner and stared at them trying to make sense of it. Her bag and phone were on the coffee table in front of her. Kara scooped it up planning on giving Noah a call when she noticed four messages. She tapped in the code to access them. The first two were from late last night and were straightforward and to the point — call me. The last one was in the early hours of the morning. Sam sounded hyped up but still not clear about why he wanted her to phone — only that he'd stumbled upon something big and to phone him as soon she got the message. She sat back in her seat and dialed his number while looking at the photographs in the spare room across the way. No answer. She left a message and hung up. The last one was from her father asking her where she was but not apologizing. Without giving it another thought she ambled into the bathroom and got ready for the day.

When she emerged twenty minutes later she poured another cup of joe and took the sketches and pinned them to the board alongside the rest of her mother's research.

Kara stepped back and folded an arm across her midsection, resting the other on it, and continued to sip her coffee. Her thoughts shifted to Kyle Harris. If Seth Leonard had been behind the murders of Charlie and the other boys, had he known Harris? Did he have some vendetta against him? She was also keen to find out if his sister had spoken to him about their tussle the other night, and if the brick through the window had been some form of retaliation? She still hadn't heard back from Blackmore Police Department so she assumed they hadn't been able to track down Mary. She still hadn't made up her mind about Harris. Noah might have been right. Perhaps her mother had reached the end of her rope, so to speak, and come to the realization that the murders of the four other boys were the work of someone else. She ran a hand over her tired face. Yesterday felt like she'd made progress but had she? All they had was circumstantial evidence — a home of a known pedophile with images of young boys, and a person of interest seen on a video leaving behind odd sketches.

She wanted to see Harris. Look him in the eyes. She could have used the video system but you had to book 24 hours in advance. And there was very little she could learn from a phone conversation. Ninety-three percent of communication was non-verbal. In all the years of interviewing suspects she had become confident in her abilities to detect liars. It could be found in the facial expression, body language or verbal indicators. Being able to discern required sifting through nervousness, chemical reactions and physical reactions. The best means of determining it relied on observation over a period of time. Seeing the usual reactions, and tics that were characteristic to only that person.

She bit down on her lower lip giving thought to how long it would take and the logistics of it all. She needed to be here for the vigil but the rest of the day was open unless Noah managed to hear back from the medical examiner.

Kara fished out her laptop and did a quick check to see how long it would take to fly down from Port Angeles to Walla Walla airport and what the odds were of getting a same-day flight. A quick browse and she brought it up. It was a quick fifty-five minute flight. *I can do this.* She nodded, snapping the elastic around her wrist. The question though was whether she wanted to do this. If this was him. If this was the man she'd encountered in the woods that night, could she bring herself to face him? She only briefly remembered him walking into the courtroom when she was twenty. It happened so fast and her memory of that day was vague. But to sit across from him? Kara hadn't even considered if he would do it.

Screw it. Just do it, she told herself.

Kara contemplated calling Noah to tell him but decided it was probably best not to, she already knew what he would say — are you out of your mind? It was a question she'd already asked herself and she couldn't answer it. Instead she called ahead to Walla Walla and posed the question. At first he seemed a little caught off-guard, she figured he would. Why visit in person when you can speak by phone? Fortunately instead of turning it down he agreed on one condition, that she pass on a message to his father who hadn't spoken to him since he'd been incarcerated. All attempts at communicating with him through his family had fallen on deaf ears. He figured that his father might listen if it was coming from a cop.

* * *

Just over two hours later, including the journey into Port Angeles, Kara's flight touched down at Walla Walla Regional Airport. On the short ten-minute ride to the state penitentiary she was a bag of nerves. She'd sat with all manner of criminals — many that were guilty of hideous crimes — but nothing came close to how she felt as the taxi brought her through the gates and past multiple barbed wire fences up to the west complex. It was the second largest prison for men in the state after Coyote and surrounded by wheat fields. Over two thousand inmates were crammed into cells, with many on death row, hoping their appeals with the state and federal courts would eventually grant them a commutation.

After being led through multiple barred doors, and hearing the echo of them clanging, and the jeering of inmates, she was eventually led to what was referred to as a no-contact booth. It was a small carpeted room with tiled walls. Basic. Sterile looking. A black phone was set against a steel frame with a large thick window to see the inmate. Either side of her were privacy panels. The room itself had ten chairs; two were in use when she was escorted in. The guard gave her some brief instructions and she took a seat waiting for Kyle to show up. Kara shifted a few times on the burgundy cushioned chair trying to get comfortable. Her throat went dry so she ferreted through her bag for a Fisherman's Friend lozenge to help her breathe better.

She waited for close to ten minutes before a door opened on the other side and in shuffled Kyle Harris. He was wearing the state-issued offender clothing of a white T-shirt, khaki pants, and white sneakers. The years inside hadn't been kind to him. In an instant the memory of him being led into the courtroom came back to her and she felt she was back there gripping her mother's hand. Her pulse sped up a little. His hair was shorter now, buzzed close to the side of his head, and he wore small spectacles. He didn't smile but neither did he look angry. The guard removed the restraints around his wrists and made a comment, and he gave a nod and took a seat beyond the window. Although it had been twenty-five years since Charlie's abduction, it had been nineteen years since she'd last seen him. She wished she could say that she had thought about what this day would be like but she hadn't. After the trial she pushed it from her mind as it was the only way she could deal with the emotions surrounding the loss, the lack of answers and his plea of not guilty. He took a second to tap out a Marlboro Light cigarette and light it before he picked up the phone and stared into her eyes. She figured he had to have been just as nervous. Even though they'd already broken the ice over the phone it was different looking him in the eye.

She took a deep breath, and feigned a weak smile. "This place is noisy."

He snorted. "You get used to it."

She nodded. "I appreciate you allowing this."

He chuckled a little as if finding something amusing in that. "You got your mother's eyes."

She wasn't too sure how to respond to that except to give a short nod and shift the conversation to the reason she was there. She looked down and then back again, then put a hand into her pocket and brought out her phone. A few swipes and she brought up a mug shot of Seth taken back when he was arrested, and one before that when he served the Catholic Church.

"Seth Leonard. Does the name sound familiar?"

He squinted at the phone. "Doesn't ring a bell. No. Who is he?"

"A convicted child molester, previously a Catholic deacon and child welfare advocate."

He scoffed and blew smoke out the corner of his mouth. "The irony."

"I thought you couldn't smoke in here?" she asked.

"And you shouldn't bribe the guards but it happens," he said casting a glance over his shoulder with a smirk. He looked back at her and must have noticed that she was at a loss for words as he said, "Look, I get it. You think I abducted your brother and even if you don't, the thought must be in the back of your mind, right?" Kara cocked her head and he continued after taking another drag of his cigarette. "The fact is I didn't stand a chance in hell. Sheriff Smith had it out for me from day one. It didn't matter that witnesses came forward and told them about suspicious individuals in the area at the time. He had his crosshair fixed on me." He shrugged. "Then when you throw evidence found on my property into the mix, they had what they needed."

"I've put in a request to have them check the DNA on the clothing of my brother," she said.

"You did?" His eyes widened. "And they listened?"

"Goodman is making a few calls. I can't promise anything. There is a possibility that the evidence has been destroyed or lost."

Harris sighed and shook his head. "You know how many times my lawyer put forward to have them retest it but no one listened?" She waited for him to continue but he didn't. Instead he looked down despondently and was quiet, then he said, "Damn justice system. I swear to God that if I'm vindicated I will sue them for everything they have."

"My parents?" Kara asked.

He shook his head. "Your parents were just along for the ride. Nothing more than puppets in the hands of lawyers wanting more money."

Kara nodded. "I met your sister."

He put out his cigarette in a small tin and the guard

stepped forward and removed it. Kyle muttered something to him before looking back at her. "Mary. How is she?"

"I would have thought you knew?" Kara asked.

"Well, let's say that we're not exactly on speaking terms."

"She seemed pretty vocal about you."

He looked intrigued.

"All right, spit it out. What's she done?"

"Our discussion got heated in a bar, the police showed up and since then we've had a break-in at the house and a brick lobbed through the window."

"She's responsible?" he asked.

Kara shrugged. "Who knows? The police are looking into it but they seem convinced that she's behind it after my run-in with her."

He groaned. "I told her to stay out of it and leave your family alone."

Kara stared back at him. "So you are in communication with her?"

He shook his head. "No. This was back when your mother was alive."

Kara studied his face.

"That's why, isn't it? Mary thinks you should be blaming us."

He nodded. "And I did for a time until I met your mother. I realized we had a lot more in common than I thought. All of us have been played by the justice system to cover up for lousy police work and personal agendas."

Silence stretched between them.

"Listen, Kyle, is there anything else you can tell me? Anyone that stands out in your mind who might have had a vendetta against you, barring the sheriff?"

"Did you speak with the kid?"

"The kid?" she asked.

"Ricky Weslo. He had a lot of family that were pissed at me at the time. I received death threats after the case of interfering with him was thrown out. If anyone would have wanted to see me go down, it would have been his kin."

"What about Ray Owen or Darryl Clayton? Any connection to Ricky's family?"

"Who?" he asked.

She didn't have any photos to show of them but it was clear their names didn't strike a chord. "Do you know where he lived?"

"It was a long time ago. But yes. Maybe his parents are still there. Though you want to be careful. If they were behind it they won't take too kindly to someone sticking their nose where it's not wanted."

He told her the address of a street in Blackmore, and also gave her a message to give to his father. It wasn't much, just a few things that he wanted him to know. Just as she was about to thank him for his time, he placed a hand against the window and blurted out, "I'm sorry about your brother, Kara. I really wish I could tell you more but that's all I know."

* * *

Arriving back in Blackmore that afternoon she felt torn. She now understood why her mother believed Harris. He didn't come across as a monster but an ordinary, down-to-earth guy, who may have just happened to be in the wrong place at the wrong time. Although she wouldn't jump the gun and rule him out, she did think that his previous run-in with the law made him a strong suspect. At the bare minimum she wanted to hear Ricky's side of the story. Not much had been released in the media before or after the events due to his age.

The address Harris had given her was for a low, pale-white rambler with a for sale sign in the front yard and an attached garage. A shed and a child's swing set stood behind it, and both looked weathered by time. The garage door was open and the inside was cluttered with all manner of junk. A collection of storage totes was stacked to one side and an elderly woman was sorting through it when Kara pulled into the driveway. The woman glanced back, squinting, and cupped a hand over her eyes. She was tall, thin and had hollow cheeks with oversized glasses. Her hair was gray with a few black strands. She wore a pair of black jeans and a button-up yellow shirt that hung loose.

When Kara pushed out of the SUV the woman piped up, "Can I help you?"

"Mrs. Weslo?"

"Ms. My husband passed away a few years back."

Kara glanced at the sign and flashed her badge as she got close. "I'm working with County and was hoping to speak with your son Ricky."

She put down the bag in her hand and her face screwed up. "Why do you want to speak to him?"

"Just a few questions about the incident with Kyle Harris."

She snorted. "Will it help put him on death row?"

Kara wasn't sure how to respond to that.

"Is he around?"

"Doesn't live here anymore. Moved out when he was eighteen. He's got a place over on Rawlands Drive.

You know it?"

She nodded.

"Can I get the address from you?"

"28. But you won't find him there today. He works for Green Lumber and Millwork in town. Usually knocks off around six." She squinted at her. "Who did you say you were again?"

"I didn't. Sorry. The name's Kara Walker."

"I thought I recognized you. You're Anna's daughter. Sorry to hear about your mother. Poor woman was put through a lot. We were close, her and I. After everything that we'd been through with Ricky's abuse and well, your brother." She stared for a second or two. "That's why I don't get it."

"Get what?" Kara asked.

"The sudden change in your mother's view of him."

"She spoke to you about that?"

She gave a nod. "I told her he was playing mind games. That's how he did it with Ricky. That's how he did it with all those boys."

"All those boys?"

"The ones the cops overlooked. The ones your mother uncovered. The ones that were attacked in Forks."

"You think he was behind those?"

"Damn right he was, and nothing can change my mind." She shook her head and looked off into her garage. "Had they locked him up when my boy told the cops, Charlie would be alive. But that's not how it works. The justice system is crooked. It's all about how much money you have."

She was venting and if there was truth to it, she had every right to be angry.

Kara looked around. "You selling?"

"Have to. Can't afford to keep it. Not on the pension I get."

Kara thanked her for her time and headed back to the SUV. As she was climbing in, Ms. Weslo hollered, "Pass on my regards to your father." Kara nodded.

Chapter 29

Green Lumber and Millwork was a building supply company that served Blackmore and the greater Olympic Peninsula. The A-frame steel facility stood out at the corner of 16th and 17th Streets on the industrial side of the town. Orange forklift trucks carrying large amounts of lumber veered in and out of the storage area that covered building material as Kara was given directions by an employee to where she could find Ricky.

A workman wearing steel-toe boots and a yellow work hat hollered at her as she made her way inside. "Lady, you shouldn't be in here. The pickup area is over there," he said pointing to a space at the front of the store.

"Ricky Weslo around?" she asked.

The guy told another employee to keep it down as he cupped a hand over his ear. "Who?"

"Weslo."

"That's him over there."

He pointed to a large guy driving a forklift. "Ricky!"

Ricky turned off the forklift and twisted in his seat. "What?"

"A lady here to see you."

Someone wolf whistled and Kara shook her head. Ricky stepped out and muttered something to another worker before jogging over. He was a tall, muscular man with a full face, black hair and a beard going slightly gray on the chin. He had on dark pants, and a white T-shirt beneath a thick plaid shirt. If he was under sixteen at the time of the alleged molestation, that would have made him in his early forties. Ricky yanked off a thick pair of yellow workman gloves, and removed his hard hat and wiped sweat from his brow.

"What can I do for yah?" he asked.

"The name's Kara Walker. I'm working with Clallam County Sheriff Department. I need to talk to you about Kyle Harris."

The mention of his name immediately got his back up. "I've already said everything I'm gonna say."

He turned to walk away when Kara blurted out, "Just five minutes of your time. That's all I'm asking for. It might save a kid's life."

He turned and looked back at her for a few seconds as if he was contemplating it. He nodded, then shouted out, "Hey Brian. I'm gonna take that smoke break. Can you cover me?"

"Sure," his buddy replied.

Ricky breezed past her. "Five minutes. That's all you get."

She followed him over to a wooden picnic table that was positioned on a patch of green adjacent to the parking lot. There was a dented paint can full of ash and cigarette stubs, and a small trash can that was overflowing with empty lunch wrappers. Ricky hopped up onto the table, resting his feet where others would sit. He tapped out a cigarette and lit it.

Kara took a seat beside him.

"They've really changed Blackmore, haven't they? This used to be a kids' playground with a splash pad," Kara said looking around.

He scoffed. "Where the hell you been? That was

fifteen years ago."

She smoothed out her navy pants and looked at the other workman hauling in lumber. The high-pitched squeal of a saw, along with hammering and forklifts in operation, could be heard. A dull sky spread out overhead, the remnants of dark clouds faded into blue.

"I don't know how to say this without you taking offense so I'll just come out with it. Was any of your family involved in the abduction of Charlie Walker?"

He shot a sideways glance, a look of surprise more than disgust. Instead of answering he took a hard pull on his cigarette and just shook his head in disbelief.

"Your mother put you up to this?" he asked.

"My mother?"

"She's Anna Walker, right?"

Kara nodded.

"Well then, did she?"

"No. My mother's passed on."

He frowned. "But I only saw her only a few months ago."

"She visited you?"

He snorted. "Four times. Damn woman was persistent, I'll give you that."

"So she asked you about the case against Harris?"

He blew smoke out the corner of his mouth and squinted with one eye. "She wanted details. You know, why did I stay on for another year if he was abusing me?"

"And?"

"I wouldn't answer her. I told her if she came around again I would get a restraining order against her."

"And yet here you are giving me the time of day."

He cast her a sideways glance before looking at his

watch. "Like I told your mother. What happened, happened. He won the case, it's in the past."

"And you aren't pissed?" Kara asked.

"He's behind bars, isn't he?"

He looked away and she nodded.

"Do you think he was guilty of the abduction of my brother?"

He snorted and blew smoke out his nostrils. "It doesn't matter what I think. The jury made the decision and that's it."

"So then why did you stay on that extra year?"

His knee started bouncing and she noticed a few things that changed in his body language. If he was a person of interest in a criminal case and they were having the conversation in an interview room, she'd likely push him harder as he was showing signs that might have given her cause for concern. Still it was hard to tell. Victims didn't always run from their abusers. Most assumed it would eventually stop.

"I had my reasons," he replied.

He hopped off the table and started pacing.

"What do you mean?"

Ricky looked at her. "I'm sorry but that's all I'm going to say."

"Who are you protecting?"

"No one."

"No? Then why won't you tell me? Seems like a pretty normal question to answer unless you have something to hide."

He scowled at her before she continued. "Look, after Charlie, four more boys were abducted and their bodies were never found. Harris was inside when they went missing. They all went missing on Halloween, five years apart. Now either someone out there is copying what the guy did to Charlie or we are dealing with the same person. In which case, he's going to take another one on Monday. This is about a kid's life. Please, Ricky. I need to know."

He sighed and looked back at her before taking a seat on the table again. He stuck his hands into his jacket pockets and gazed down at the ground, kicking a few loose stones out of the dirt.

"At least answer one question. Why weren't any of your family at the trial of Kyle Harris?" Kara asked.

"What was done was done."

"Your mother sounded real pleased to hear that he was inside after escaping justice in your case. Yet none of you came forward and added your two cents. I read the articles, saw videos and was there for the trial. There were a lot of people from the community that showed up and voiced their concerns but strangely enough you and your family were nowhere to be seen."

He shook his head. "Look, it was hard enough going through it the first time. It's in the past, and I would appreciate you not bothering my mother or brother."

Kara's brow furrowed. "Brother? That's right, your brother went to the same dojo, didn't he?"

"Yes. And?" he shot back.

"Did Harris ever touch him inappropriately?"

"What? No. My brother had nothing to do with what I told the police."

"Hold on a second. He had nothing to do with what you told the police?"

He started to look flustered as if he had tripped up over his own words.

"He wasn't involved."

"Involved in what? Is that why you stayed on an extra year? Are you trying to protect your brother? Should I be speaking with him?"

"No. I…" He closed his eyes and exhaled hard.

"This is getting confusing," Kara said running a hand over her head.

"It never happened. It was a lie!" He blurted it out and breathed hard as if a load had been lifted off his shoulders. He put his head in his hands and blew out his cheeks.

Kara's brow pinched. "A lie? What was a lie?"

"The accusation. Everything. It was a mistake."

"A mistake?" she asked.

He groaned and looked off towards his workmates as he if he regretted deciding to speak to her. "It never happened. Kyle Harris never touched me. I made it up."

"Why?"

He shook his head. "I don't want to discuss this."

"I think it's a little too late for that. Please, Ricky."

His jaw clenched. "A few months before the accusation, Caleb was one of the boys that were assaulted in Blackmore."

"But those assaults happened between '89 and '91? The media reported the assault on you between February 1987 and March 1988. That would have placed his assault in late 1986. Are you telling me that there were more than two attacks in Blackmore?"

He nodded. "In December of 1996 we went to the police but there was nothing they could do. They took a statement and said they would look into it but that was it. Nothing ever came of it. It was a joke."

"Did your brother see the face of his attacker?"

"Not clearly. It was late at night. However he

thought he could remember his voice and well my father grilled him over it so badly and wouldn't accept that he couldn't come up with something. So..."

"You pinned it on Kyle," Kara said finishing what he was about to say.

He nodded.

"But why? Why him?"

He tossed up a hand. "Opportunity. Stupidity. We were both young. He was my kid brother. Besides, we'd heard rumors from others saying that Harris was gay. You know, because he was never seen with a woman, and my brother thought his voice sounded similar."

"But he wasn't sure?"

"No, he wasn't." He sighed. "Anyway instead of having my brother deal with it I came up with the idea to accuse him. I just figured if it was him behind my brother's assault he might panic and confess to the police and it would be over." He bit down on the side of his lip. "Look, we were just kids. I didn't expect it to go as far as it did. I didn't know it would ruin his life. I was only fourteen, my brother was eleven."

There was a long moment of silence before Kara spoke. "So you've never told the cops this?"

"I thought about it. Many times. I mean before he was arrested and charged with the abduction of Charlie but no... I guess I just assumed that maybe it was him. You know. Somewhere in my mind I..."

"Hoped it was him?" Kara said.

He nodded. She understood that. Heck, her father would have understood that. It was easier than having to deal with the alternative that a stranger was walking the streets attacking and abducting boys.

"Did Sherriff Smith ever speak with you?"

"No. We dealt with frontline police officers. Listen, for my mother's sake, and my brother, I would really appreciate it if you didn't tell anyone about this."

She couldn't guarantee that. The bombshell he'd just revealed was the smoking gun. Had that been known at the time of the trial it would have no doubt played a key role in determining evidence submitted by Sheriff Smith.

Chapter 30

Lies. Everyone told them. Sometimes it was to protect those closest, other times it was simply a means of surviving how people perceived you. Kara thought long and hard about her conversation with Rick on the journey back. Armed with sketches from Ray Owen, she was keen to speak with him and find out why he kept leaving the same one with the Caldwells, and had he left any others? Her mind was buzzing with activity, trying to connect the dots. It was right there before her but she was still unable to make sense of what she had so far. It could be anyone.

The phone rang and she hit the button on her steering wheel to accept the call.

It was Noah. “Hey, where have you been? I’ve been trying to get hold of you for the past hour.”

“I was busy.”

“Well I’ve got news. There were no bodies buried in Seth’s basement and the team turned over the yard and there are no bones. We also can’t find any DNA or prints that would lead us to believe that he’s had any contact with these boys or Charlie. Despite his home turning up a lot of vile crap, that’s about it. They’ll continue to process what they find but it looks like Seth was just a very sick man.”

“And the autopsy report?”

“Natural death by the looks of it but we’ll have to see what the toxicology report turns up.”

“In four to six weeks.” She sighed.

"Right. Anyway, what have you been up to?"

"I went and spoke to Kyle. Face to face."

"What? You flew to Walla Walla?" Noah asked.

"I had to."

"Had to?"

"I needed to look into his eyes."

"Are you serious?"

"I knew you wouldn't understand."

"I'm not saying I don't, it's just.... Well, what came of it?" Noah asked.

"He didn't know either of the three men, but I followed up with Ricky Weslo. The boy who originally accused him of molestation. Get this... he lied."

"You're joking?"

"He made it all up. Ricky told me everything. But that's not all. His brother was one of the boys that was attacked and assaulted prior to Charlie's abduction."

"Well this just keeps getting better."

She exhaled hard. "Anyway I'm heading over to Ray Owen's place to find out more about these sketches before this evening's vigil."

"Have you eaten today?" Noah asked.

The SUV weaved its way around the streets on the way into Blackmore. "Had a granola bar, and a bottle of water."

"You need to slow down, Kara."

She shook her head. "No, we are down to the wire. By the way, you heard any news from Blackmore Police Department on Mary Harris?"

She heard him groan. "Officer Johnson managed to track her down. She's denying breaking into your father's home or throwing a brick through the window. Though she didn't hide the fact that she doesn't like you."

"I didn't expect she would."

Noah went quiet for a second or two.

"About last night, Noah," Kara began to say before he cut her off.

"It's okay. You don't need to say anything. I get it. It was a mistake."

She scoffed. "Actually that's not what I was going to say but…"

Before she could address the elephant in the room Noah shifted gear. "Look I would come along with you to Ray Owen's place but I have a meeting with my lawyer regarding pushing forward with the appeal in Amanda's case. It's last minute."

"You going through with it?" she asked.

"To be honest I really don't know. I've been so distracted by what's going on with the attempted abduction, I haven't had time to really give a lot of thought to it."

"You sound torn."

"Do I?" He chuckled. "Maybe I am." There was a pause for a second. "Look, I've got another call on the line. Someone's trying to reach me. Did you say you were still planning on going to the vigil tonight?"

"That was the plan."

"Okay, if I manage to squeeze away maybe I'll join you."

* * *

The sun was sliding hard to the west when Kara pulled into the Owens' place. Ora Owen was Ray Owen's mother. Even at the age of forty-five, he still lived with his ailing parent. She was a short, wide woman with red cheeks and curly hair that was almost gray. She wore a low, V-neck flowery dress and sandals, and had one too many beads draped around her neck. Unlike others who were more than willing to talk, the sight of the police badge only got her back up. Instead of inviting Kara in, she stepped out onto her porch and closed the screen door behind her. The instant she folded her arms, Kara knew she wasn't going to get far.

"It's just a few routine questions," Kara said.

She spoke with a Southern twang, which made it clear she wasn't born in Blackmore. "About?"

"Sketches he left at the vigils of the parents whose boys went missing. Look, is he around?"

"He's at work," she replied.

"And where might that be?"

"That's none of your business."

"Then when will he be home?"

"Later tonight."

"Approximately?"

"I don't monitor my boy, how should I know?"

Kara exhaled, putting a hand on her hip and casting a glance across the road to one of the neighbors. It wasn't the best neighborhood in Blackmore but a step up from where Sam was staying. Most of the homes had fallen into disrepair, with crumbling foundations, peeling paint and shingles that needed replacing.

"Look, I'm not sure what your experience has been with the police department but—"

Her face twisted as she cut her off. "They didn't listen to him then and they sure as hell wouldn't listen to him now," she said. "So you're wasting your breath, and you're wasting my time."

"Listen to him?" Kara asked.

"This is about the boys that went missing, right?"

Kara nodded.

"My boy has a gift and he spoke to the police but they wouldn't give him the time of day. I heard what they said about him. Calling him a kook. There were even those who said he was responsible."

She recalled the information her mother had on him, how Owen had approached her in the weeks after Charlie's abduction, and yet she couldn't recall any of his sketches being among the items on the wall. If he had a habit of approaching the parents of the missing, surely he would have left behind sketches. There was a good six years of vigils before Harris was put in jail and the case was closed.

Kara said, "I'm…"

Before she could get any further words out, Ora turned and refused to speak anymore. She closed the door leaving Kara on the porch with more questions than answers. Returning to her vehicle she considered parking a short distance down the street and waiting for him to arrive but with nightfall closing in and the Port Townsend vigil a few hours away, she figured she might stand a better chance of seeing him there than waiting for him outside.

After leaving the Owen residence and making it halfway to Port Townsend her phone rang again. Thinking it was Noah having forgotten something, she tapped accept and said, "Yes, don't worry, I will be staying at my father's place tonight."

"Kara. It's me. Sam!"

"Sam?"

"Didn't you get my messages?"

"I called back and left one of my own."

"Oh the machine is on the blink. I haven't been able to get it to work for weeks. Listen I need to show you something immediately."

"Can't do that, I'm on my way over to a vigil. How about tomorrow?"

"It can't wait. This is important."

"What's important?"

"I went back there."

"What! Where?" Kara asked.

"Clayton's farm."

"Last night? Are you joking?" she said.

"Kara, listen to me. He's got all these kids' clothes in a box in his closet."

"Hold on a second. You were in his closet?"

"Long story. All you need to know is I have evidence. I took photos. Now it might not be there when we go back but I can prove he has it."

"Kids' clothes? Maybe they belonged to his son."

"What, Polaroids of nude kids too?" he asked.

"What?"

"Look, just come over. I'll show you everything."

"I can't, I'm already an hour away. I promised I would be at the vigil, besides, I need to see if Ray Owen shows up."

"Forget Ray Owen. Clayton is the one. It's him."

There was a pause then Kara asked, "Look, where are you now?"

"I'm out but you need to see these."

She sighed. "Sam, are you making this up?"

"Why would I do that?"

"To get back at him for what he said yesterday."

"No. But that's why I went there. I figured I could—
"

Before he finished she said, “Listen, I’m gonna give you the number for Noah Goodman. Tell him what you told me and he’ll…”

“No. I can’t do that. If they find out I’ve been in his house, I’m going to be in a lot of shit. I already have a few black marks against my name. No, this needs to be you. I’ll hand this over to you but I have to stay anonymous in this.”

“Sam.”

“No, Kara.”

She sighed. “Look, I’m nearly in Port Townsend. I’m following up on a lead.”

“Kara!”

“All right. I can be there in about three hours. That’s the best I can do. Otherwise you need to call Goodman.”

Sam cursed then said, “Fine. I’ll be in after nine. Just hurry.”

Before she could say that she couldn’t guarantee she’d make it on time, he’d hung up. She didn’t know what to make of that conversation. He certainly sounded panicked. Kara had already told Goodman to go speak with the Claytons but with him being tied up with a lawyers meeting that likely wasn’t going to happen. However, Sam sounded genuine, and even though she didn’t want him to get into trouble, they were down to the wire and if there was a chance that the Claytons were behind it, it was best Goodman knew about it. She dialed his number.

Chapter 31

It was a touching sign of support. There had to be close to a hundred people gathered together in a park by Pierce Street looking to bring a renewed awareness to the mystery surrounding the disappearance of the four boys. As Kara pushed out of her vehicle and made her way over to the perimeter, she was flooded with memories of Charlie's vigils. So many had turned out that first year but with each passing year the crowds dwindled as did the offers to hand out flyers and posters which were given out to residents and businesses. Seeing the despair in her mother's eyes, and watching her father get choked up, rocked Kara to the core. It was the not knowing that crushed them. Her mother had always held out hope that he would come home. She put on a brave face in front of the media, but behind closed doors it was like living with a ghost.

Her gaze washed over the faces searching for Ray Owen but there was no sign of him. One cameraman from a local news crew was there but that was it. No doubt the coverage would garner nothing more than a two-minute slot on a local channel, and a few hundred words in the paper. Staying on the fringe she observed Scott Caldwell's mother talking with others while her daughter went around lighting candles that were cupped in people's hands. Before them was an area with photos of the boys. Many had already left cards, flowers, balloons and gifts. Kara watched intently looking for anything unusual and out of place. Several cars parked along the sidewalk, and more friends of the family arrived, greeting others with a hug.

Although she was eager to speak to the parents of the other three boys, she chose to wait until the end. Having suffered loss and attended many of the vigils, she knew the mindset the families were in. They heard the same condolences and questions year after year. It was painful, disheartening and soul crushing.

For ten minutes someone led them in song—something to do with "we are not afraid," that was then followed by a couple of hymns before the event was handed over to different speakers who each took a turn to address the crowd on why they were holding the vigil and what it represented to them.

Eventually Maureen took the microphone. She began by reciting Maya Angelou's Poem "I Will Rise," and then there was silence for the four boys that were taken. After she said, "I just want to thank you all for coming out tonight. Every year it gets more and more difficult to hold on to hope but having the support of our community means a lot to us. We want you to know that we are following up on every lead and we are still hoping and praying that we will see justice for Scott, Chris, Dwight and Richard. So please continue to share anything you hear with the police, no matter how trivial it might seem. We are hoping to keep this case in the spotlight until the boys come home or the culprit responsible is brought to justice. Thank you all."

A young minister stepped forward and led the crowd in a prayer before everyone was welcomed to come and speak with the family, leave a gift or get a cup of coffee from a table that had been set up nearby.

Maureen caught Kara's eye and she gave a thin smile before heading over and thanking her for coming.

"I really appreciate you coming out. Have you had any luck with the sketches so far?" she asked.

"It's still early but we are looking into it. That was a lovely poem you shared."

She dipped her chin. "Thank you."

Right then her daughter came over and slipped her arm around her mother's. "Ms. Walker. Thank you for coming. I hope you don't mind but I need to steal my mother away, I have a few people to introduce her to."

Kara waved them on. "By all means."

She watched them walk away before her eyes bounced back to the area where everyone was laying down gifts. She reached into her handbag and pulled out a small bear that she'd picked up earlier that day, along with a card. She wandered over and set it down among the many others.

"Ms. Walker. Kara?"

She turned to find a tall, thin man with hollowed

cheeks and salt and pepper hair at the sides of his temples. "Do I know you?" she asked.

"You left a message on our machine. We were out. I'm Ted Peterson. Chris is my son."

Her mouth widened. "Oh, right. Sorry I didn't recognize you."

He nodded giving a warm smile. "Yes, this getting old business is hard. Twenty years seems like a lifetime now."

"That it does," she replied.

Chris Peterson had gone missing five years after Charlie. It never quite gained the attention that Charlie's abduction had because Chris had got into trouble several times and on two occasions had run away from home, throwing doubt into the minds of investigators and drawing less sympathy from the community. Most assumed he would show up at a friend's but it never happened. Others believed he'd done it simply because he saw the attention that her brother had got from the media. It backfired and besides local media, the gossip surrounding him had caused delays in the investigation.

He fished into a leather bag that he had with him and withdrew a large collection of sketches. "So Maureen said you were interested in any of the charcoal sketches that were left over the years. I took the liberty of gathering the ones that were at ours, and the vigils of the Harrington and Beck families. You'll have to forgive their lack of desire to talk to you but they haven't had a good experience with the police."

"Who has?" she said taking the wad of wrinkled papers and turning them around.

He smiled. "Right. You were the sister of Charlie Walker."

"For a long time, yes. Now, I rarely hear that unless I return here."

He nodded. "Oh I understand. My two other kids struggled after Chris was taken. We had to pull them out of school because… well… kids can be mean."

"How did they turn out?"

"Surprisingly well actually. My youngest is at the university now, and the other is living in Kansas, working as a teacher. He married a real nice girl."

Kara furrowed her brow as she looked over the sketches. While there were duplicates like Maureen's, the sketches were different. One showed a lake, another a mossy tree with a tire hanging from a rope, and the other was of a waterfall.

"Did you ever speak to the person leaving these?"

"I think so, I mean I didn't go out of my way. We speak to a lot of people and we gather up what is left behind at the end of the night but if you want to speak with him, he's over there."

"What?" Kara turned and on the far side of the green walking towards the crowd was Ray Owen. He was holding what appeared to be papers in his hands. At first he looked like he didn't have a care in the world and then he locked eyes with Kara, slowed his pace, then turned and started walking fast in the opposite direction.

She squeezed past Ted, thanking him for the papers. She caught the tail end of something he asked her but by that point she wasn't listening. Ray looked back then broke into a jog. Kara elbowed her way through the crowd and gave pursuit. He had a good hundred yards' head start on her.

"Hey!" Kara yelled. "Ray, hold up!"

He cast another glance over his shoulder and picked up the pace heading for a '90s-style brown Honda Accord. In his haste to avoid her he dropped the papers in his hands and then bolted. Kara scooped them up once she got closer, and then veered off to the right heading for her SUV. Before she'd even reached it, he'd fired up his engine and torn out of the parking lot.

Several people who were making their way back to their vehicles looked on, confused as to what was unfolding. Kara hopped in the SUV and the tires let out a squeal as she slammed the gear into reverse, spun around and took off after him.

There were several vehicles on the road between her car and Ray's. She tried to overtake the one ahead of her but had to swerve back into her lane to avoid an oncoming truck. Farther up the road, the lights changed to red, and she knew she had him. All the vehicles had slowed to a crawl and stopped, and after throwing the gearstick into park, she pushed out and started running towards his Honda.

He must have spotted her in his mirror and got scared as even though the lights were red, Ray smashed the accelerator and took off through the intersection causing two cars to swerve, and a third to nearly hit his vehicle.

All she could do was watch him disappear around a bend.

As she was making her way back to her vehicle, drivers behind her honked and told her to hurry up. "Yeah, yeah, go around if you're in such a hurry!"

Over the next twenty minutes she drove around the streets searching for his vehicle. She circled back to the vigil twice but he wasn't there. In the end she placed a phone call to Ora Owen in the hopes of getting her to tell her boy to call her as soon as he arrived home. She didn't answer and there was no voicemail.

Frustrated but determined to find out why he ran, she made the two-hour journey back to Blackmore. Along the way she glanced several times at the charcoal sketches and tried to make sense of them. Why was he leaving these? What sketches had her own mother been given? And why run? Kara was ten minutes outside of Blackmore when the phone rang. She hit the accept button hoping it was Goodman but the voice she heard made her blood run cold.

Chapter 32

Droplets of rain splattered against the window as the heavens opened. One second she was driving in clear skies, the next powering through a shower, and feeling swallowed by dark clouds. "Hello Kara." Something about the stranger's voice sounded familiar.

"Who is this?" She glanced at the number that came up on the SUV's console. It wasn't a number she recognized. But the voice, that came back to her like a persistent childhood nightmare. It was deep, raspy and…

"You don't remember what I said, do you? Because if you did, you wouldn't have returned to Blackmore."

Her pulse began to race. A shiver ran up her spine, her mind making the connection. A flash of memory. Running. Tears streaking her cheeks. Her body trembling as fear took hold.

"You turn back, he dies. It was very simple. I don't think I could have made it much clearer."

So overcome by the memory of Charlie's abductor, she veered to the hard shoulder. Gravel kicked up, spitting against the side of the vehicle. Kara could hear the blood rushing in her ears. Several motorcycles shot by, as her windshield blurred, and the inside began to fog up. She twisted on the heat to clear it.

"How did you get this number?"

She ransacked her brain trying to remember those she'd given it out to. Of course there were other ways but… before she could form an idea he continued.

"I would have thought the break-in, and brick would have been enough but obviously not. You don't listen. Just like your mother. She didn't listen. Sticking her nose where it didn't belong." He continued rambling about all the ways her mother had got under his skin. All these years, Kara had waited for the moment to talk to this man, played it out in her head what she would say, and how in control she would feel and here she was failing — unable to think clearly.

"So this is your last chance. Back off."

"Where is he?" Kara demanded.

She heard him stifle a laugh. "It doesn't matter. All that matters now is that you stay out of my business. This can get a whole lot worse for you, or Charlie for that matter. I'm sure you would hate to see Charlie punished."

Was he alive or was he taunting her with the idea that he was alive?

"Bullshit. He's not alive."

"Really? Then why am I looking at him right now?"

"Put him on the phone," she said in a calm voice.

He made a tutting noise. "No, no. You don't get to tell me what to do."

“Then how do I know you’re not bluffing?”

“You don’t. But do you want to take that risk?

“Fuck you.”

He snorted. “I kinda guessed you’d go that route.”

Right then she heard him lay the phone down, walk a short distance away. Then there was a thump and an ear-piercing scream echoed over the receiver. “No!” she bellowed.

A few seconds, then he returned and picked up the phone. “Now that I’ve got your attention. Here’s what you’re going to do. You’ll return to your father’s, pack your bags, phone that detective friend of yours and tell him that you have got it all wrong and you’re going home to New York. Then you don’t come back again. Ever.” His breathing sounded labored as if he was out of breath. “And Charlie. He’ll get to live another year. Have I made myself clear?”

Her hand was trembling. She was gripping the steering wheel so tight, that her knuckles went white. “HAVE I MADE MYSELF CLEAR!” he bellowed.

“Yes,” she said not wanting to take the risk of her actions causing Charlie any more pain than what he’d gone through already. If that was him at all.

“Good. Now I must say it’s a pity you’ve spoken to Sam and Bobby. Especially Sam. I was really hoping he’d focus on his pitiful life.” He snorted. “Then again I doubt the police or anyone will miss him when an explosion happens at that shitty trailer park.”

Kara's pulse sped up. "No. No. He hasn't done anything. I haven't told him anything."

"It doesn't matter now."

Click. He hung up.

Fear shot through Kara. She smashed the accelerator and the SUV tore away from the hard shoulder leaving tire tracks in the gravel and mud. She immediately dialed Sam's number. "C'mon, pick up, pick up!"

It rang several times but no one answered.

The forest flashed by in her peripheral vision, just a blur. Kara swerved, nearly losing control of the SUV as she slalomed around vehicles, reaching speeds of ninety miles an hour. Her windshield wipers were on full blast sloshing water. The glow of the town's lights came into view and she tried again to reach Sam.

No one picked up.

She hoped to God that she wasn't too late.

The SUV burst over a rise in the road, and weaved around the narrow roads that led up to Sunrise Trailer Park. Just as it came into view at the far end of the road, the phone was answered. It was Sam's girlfriend.

"Hello?"

"It's Kara. Get Sam out of there."

"What?" she asked.

In the background she could hear Sam asking who it was.

"It's gonna blow," Kara screamed.

"Who are you? And why are you calling here?" She

must have got the wrong end of the stick as she turned and started yelling at Sam. “Is this the bitch you’ve been sleeping with?”

“Mindy, what the hell are you on about?” Sam replied. It sounded as if he got up and approached her and she wouldn’t give him the phone.

“Don’t call back!” Mindy screamed.

“No, don’t hang up,” Kara shouted before the line went dead. Kara sped up and veered into the trailer park. She tried dialing back but there was no answer. Just as she came around the corner and had the trailer in her sights, an enormous explosion erupted. Sam’s trailer disappeared in a cloud of dark smoke and an inferno of flames. Fireballs of debris rained down, large chunks of metal and melted plastic nearly hit the front of Kara’s windshield as she yanked the steering wheel hard to the left. From inside the safety of the vehicle she squinted, looking at the carnage. Flames licked up into the night, a smoldering mess beneath them, nothing but the remains of a frame.

Kara pushed out of the vehicle as neighbors from all over the trailer park emerged to stare. She heard a few screams, and saw several people get on their phones to call the police. Within minutes the park would be swarming with cops.

As she stood there in utter disbelief her father’s face came to mind.

If this man had broken into her parents’ home, what

was to stop him from harming her father? Not giving another thought to the devastation before her she hopped back into her SUV and slammed into reverse and tore out of the park. Her mind was racing. Thoughts of her brother, Sam, Bobby and Goodman, all of them were a target. The SUV powered through the streets of Blackmore until she made it home. The street was empty and the streetlights were circled with glowing halos. She drove up the driveway and was relieved to see her father's vehicle parked outside, and him beyond the window. Satisfied that he was safe, Kara killed the engine and hopped out, and placed a phone call to Bobby. Standing in the driveway she focused on her father, not taking him out of her line of sight for even a second. The call went straight to voicemail.

"Bobby, listen, it's Kara. Sam's dead. The same guy that took Charlie did it. He mentioned you. I think you're next. When you get this message —"

Before she finished she heard a rustle in the bushes behind her and just as she turned to see what it was, a hand clamped over her mouth. She dropped her phone and keys, and was dragged down. She let out a squeal but her attacker was too strong, and the person's hand was clamped so tight over her nose and mouth, her words didn't escape. Within seconds, darkness closed in and everything turned to black.

Part 3

Chapter 33

Freezing cold water splashed against her face. Kara gasped, snapping awake. Daylight stabbed her eyes making her squint. The silhouette of several figures moving before her came into view. It took a few seconds for her eyes to adjust but the world soon came into focus. Before she could make out where she was or who had taken her, a familiar voice was heard off to the right of her.

"Sorry about the water but you had them worried there for a second, they thought you weren't going to wake up. Seems whoever dished out the chloroform went a little overboard."

Kara rolled up into a seated position and squinted. "Henry?"

Henry Ellis sat across from her.

"I told Bill this wasn't necessary, but what can you do? These FBI guys are a law unto themselves." Henry glanced off to his left.

Kara scanned the room and saw two other guys, dressed in blue FBI windbreaker jackets. One of them was talking on a cell phone, the other leaning against a brick-and-mortar wall looking over paperwork. There was lots of light filtering in through dirty windows. It looked like she was in a rough-looking studio apartment. There was a blue couch, a large painting on the wall, a ladder leading up to the roof, hardwood floors, a table and a few home décor items. The steady hum of traffic could be heard outside.

Her brow pinched. "Where the hell am I? And why are you here?"

Her throat was dry, and tension in her head was causing it to throb.

"Right, about that. It's probably best Bill explains," Ellis said.

"Bill? Explains? Did you drug me?"

He put up a hand. "Me? No. The FBI…" He paused looking embarrassed. "Bill should be back in a minute, he just went out for coffee. I figured that might help with the…"

He pointed at her head.

"Nausea? Headache?" she said. Kara rubbed the back of her head. "I don't get it. What's going on?"

"What's going on, Ms. Walker, is that you may have fucked up our investigation."

An African American, broad-shouldered city slicker in a dark navy suit and tie ambled in with a cardboard tray full of coffees. He jerked his head to the two FBI agents waiting near the doorway to indicate for them to wait outside. They left and he strolled over, taking out one of the cups of coffee and handing it off to Henry before making his way over and offering her one. "Wasn't sure if you took milk or sugar so it's black."

He removed his cup and tossed the tray, then pulled up a chair and spun it around the opposite way, plunked down and took a sip of his coffee. "Countless hours of wiretapping, data collection and a year's worth of surveillance, and you may have blown it. Now Henry here tells me that he might have been partially to blame for that so I'm going to give you the benefit of the doubt. I've heard his version, now I want to hear yours. So tell me, what the hell were you thinking?"

Kara squeezed the bridge of her nose and took a hard pull on the drink. "No offense but I usually like to be on a last name basis if we're going to play who's got the bigger dick." She took another hard pull on her drink while he stared back at her with a blank expression.

Henry stifled a laugh.

"Bill Davis, special agent in charge. FBI."

"So tell me, Bill, when did the FBI approve chloroform and kidnapping? Or is that a new policy?"

"You didn't give us much choice. And before you tell us some bogus story about how Washington Bureau of Investigation green-lit your little Clallam County joint effort, let me save you the trouble. You might have been given access to case files but I've already spoken to Tim Greer. He didn't clear your involvement. But let me guess, Detective Goodman isn't aware of that?"

She stared back at him. She could feel the animosity. "You've had five abductions over the last twenty-five years." She glanced at her watch. "And by my calculations you have just over twenty-four hours until he takes another boy. But I'm guessing you already knew that."

"You're damn right we do. What the hell did you think that attempted abduction was for? Your benefit, so you could find a loophole in being able to work with Clallam and interfere with our investigation?"

Kara put her cup down and raised a hand. "Hold on a minute. Back up the truck. You have been doing surveillance for a year. On who?"

"That's none of your business."

"After the shit you just pulled, I think my attorney would beg to differ."

Bill raised his eyebrows and looked at Henry. Kara's gaze bounced between them.

"Are you involved in this?" Kara asked Henry.

He cocked his head but didn't reply.

"Well if you're involved, what about Goodman?" Kara asked.

"No," Henry said.

"But I thought you retired?

"I have. They wanted my input. And let's be clear, for the record I was not aware, and I sure as hell didn't approve of them taking you the way they did." He tossed Bill a look of disgust.

Kara shook her head trying to shake the mental fog. "Okay, so who are we talking about?"

There was hesitation on Bill's part.

Henry spat it out. "Darryl Clayton."

"So let me get this right, you've had him under surveillance for a year and done nothing?"

"These things take time," Bill said.

"Oh don't bullshit me."

"We needed to be sure."

"You mean you wanted him to take a kid?"

"That's not our intention."

"So if you've had him under surveillance, why did you let him get away if he attempted to abduct a kid recently?"

"He didn't," Bill replied.

"Of course he did. It was in the damn newspaper."

"That wasn't him."

"Then who was it?"

They were both reluctant to reply but then Henry spat it out. "The FBI."

"And… there goes what little advantage we had,"

Bill said getting up and walking across to one of the windows.

Kara sat there for a second with a puzzled expression on her face then the penny dropped. She recalled Bill's words. *What the hell did you think that attempted abduction was for?* She looked at him. "Are you're telling me that attempt was made up? That the FBI was behind it?"

Henry nodded.

"I don't get it. Why?" She shook her head. "And how the hell can you get away with doing that?"

Bill turned and folded his arms. He leaned against the window; the sunshine bathed his face leaving half of it shadowed. He took a deep break. "After 9/11, the FBI has turned most of its energy to stopping terror attacks, finding cells and ensuring that no harm comes to citizens. It's a hard job. To do it effectively we have to create new tactics. One of which is running sting operations across America, targeting the Muslim community by luring people into fake terror plots."

"I don't understand," she said.

He returned to his seat and slumped down. "The bureau sends out informants to trawl through Muslim communities, spend time in mosques and community centers, and talk to radical Islamists in order to identify possible targets who are sympathetic. If we identify a high-value target, we will run a sting whereby we create a fake terror plot that involves weapons and targets. Then, before it's carried out we swoop in to make arrests and secure convictions."

"Entrapment?"

"Ah, we don't like to use that word. It tends to get lawyers' backs up and well there is a lot of confusion around its usage. Obviously there is the obvious — where a citizen might see deliberate traps that manipulate unwary people who were unlikely to become a terrorist. Then there is of course where the prosecution has to prove a subject was predisposed to carry out the actions they're accused of — for example, supporting jihad. So we try not to use the word entrapment, even if that is what it is. Ultimately we like to think of what we're doing as preventative."

"So the kid," she said.

"Didn't exist," Bill added.

"And the abductor?"

"Made up."

"I don't get it. What did you hope to achieve?"

Bill glanced at Henry for a second. "We hoped to kill two birds with one stone. If you want to use the word entrapment we figured by creating a false abduction, and drawing attention to it in the media, whoever has been responsible for these abductions would back off with the increased police presence. And then of course there was the fact that if Clayton was behind it, it might push him to do something, you know — dispose of someone."

"You were hoping to buy yourself time?"

"No. We were hoping to save a kid," he replied.

She stared at him for a few seconds then smiled. "You believed my mother, didn't you?"

He chuckled. "Actually, no." He thumbed over his shoulder. "But Henry did, and with his track record that's enough for us."

Kara nodded a few times, reached down and scooped up her coffee and took another sip. "And what about the truth? Does the media know?"

"No and we plan to keep it that way." He paused and said slowly, "We *need* to keep it that way." He sniffed. "We're well aware that someone has been taking a boy every five years in the surrounding counties. What we haven't been able to pinpoint is who, however, with the assistance of your mother, Henry here, and Noah Goodman we've—"

"Noah's in on this?"

He shook his head. "No. He's on a need to know basis. If and when something crosses his table he passes that information on to Henry and…"

"And Henry passes it on to you," Kara said.

Henry spoke up. "We've had to do it this way, Kara. For someone to have managed to elude the police, the FBI and State for this long, we assumed they had to have some connection to the case. Potentially could even be law enforcement."

"So you think it might be a cop?"

"We're not certain but we haven't ruled it out."

There was a long pause as all of them dwelled on that.

"So where does Clayton fall into all of this? I'm guessing you based the fake abductor on Gregory Clayton's description, right?"

"Darryl Clayton was never ruled out as a suspect in your brother's disappearance. If he was involved, it was him. Gregory would have been too young."

"Well of course," she said. "But you think he and Gregory might have been involved in the recent abductions?"

"Let's just say our sources have certainly swayed the investigation in their direction."

She nodded, her brow furrowed. "So why haven't

you've obtained a search warrant?"

"We need probable cause to believe a criminal activity is occurring at the place. Accusations by neighbors and townsfolk might have shone a light on him but that wouldn't fly with a judge and that's who we have to convince. Simply put, no hard evidence." He got up and walked across the room and leaned against thc window looking out, a smidgen of despondence evident.

She nodded for a second then remembered what Sam had said. "What if you had that evidence?"

Henry leaned forward in his seat. "What did you find, Kara?"

"It's not what I found. Sam. Sam Young, he contacted me yesterday." She stumbled over her words trying to take all the jumbled-up thoughts coming at her and make sense of it. "We visited Clayton."

"We know you did," Bill said folding his arms.

"But he went back."

"What?" Bill spun around and listened intently.

"He returned two nights ago. Said he came across a box of kids' clothes, and nude Polaroids in Clayton's home. In the bedroom closet. He said he took video of it and he was going to show everything to me. That's where I was heading last night before…"

"The explosion? Yes, I heard about it. I'm sorry, Kara," Henry said.

Sadness washed over her and all the loss she felt from the night before came back hard and fast. It would have been easy to wallow in it but that's not what Sam would have wanted. She stood up and then had to support herself against one of the pillars in the loft. "We need to…"

"You need to sit down," Henry said.

"No time. We need to find his phone. There's a chance that the forensics lab might still be able to get the data off it even if it's been affected by the fire. If you get that, you get your search warrant," Kara said. Then something dawned on her. "Hold on a minute. If you had him under surveillance, you must have heard my conversation with him last night, right? That's why you took me. You thought he was going to come after me?"

Bill shook his head. "What are you on about?" He looked to Henry to see if he could make any sense of it but both of them seemed clueless.

She ran a hand through her hair. "You said you had Clayton under surveillance. Wiretapping, right? Data collection. Phones and so on. So you must have heard the conversation when he called?"

Henry squinted. "He called you?"

She stared back blankly. She began to pace back and forth. "He must have used a burner phone. You probably didn't know about that, that's one of the reasons why he's managed to stay one step ahead."

"Okay, hold on, Kara. You've lost me." Bill said. "Are you saying Darryl Clayton phoned you last night?"

"Yes. I mean. I assume it was him."

"We didn't hear any conversation, Kara. Our guys were monitoring and had his property under surveillance all night. He didn't leave that property."

"Then you need to update your equipment because I'm telling you that was him. He knew about Sam."

"Are you sure?"

"I'd remember his voice anywhere."

"Darryl?"

"No, the man who took Charlie. I mean, he must have been using some kind of voice scrambler but it was him. I'm certain. He said he wanted me to leave and that if I ever came back he would die. He said Charlie was alive. I heard him."

"Charlie?"

She shook her head, confusion, and panic rising in her chest. "I've got to get back. Bobby. My father."

Bill threw his hands up. "Kara, hold up."

Kara didn't listen. She bolted for the door but before she got a few steps outside into the corridor that led down to the stairwell, she was blocked by the two FBI agents. They had their mouths up their radios. Bill quickly caught up.

"You can't go."

"You can't stop me."

"You said yourself, if you return he'll kill him. We need you to stay out of the picture until Tuesday."

"But Sam. The phone. Clayton."

"We'll deal with it. But I'm gonna need you to stay here," Bill said.

She shook her head. "That's my brother."

Bill took a hold of her. Behind him was Henry, who was also trying to get her to see reason. "Listen to him, Kara."

Bill continued. "You have my word. We'll find that phone, and we can get that information off it. In the meantime I'm gonna need your phone."

"Why? Is keeping me here not good enough?"

He stifled a laugh. "If Clayton called, we'll need to get in contact with your phone company and get the details of the call."

"Best of luck with that," she said. "He's probably running through a voice over IP using a local library."

"Not if he was at the house all night."

She stared back at him then said, "Well, I don't even have it with me. I was on it when your guys grabbed me. I dropped it along with my keys outside my parents' home."

Bill turned to one of his guys and he darted away, obviously to go and check.

"Look, I really need to check on my father."

"We'll take care of that. For now you stay put. I'm sure Henry here will keep you company."

"Great. I get demoted to babysitter," he said.

"Old man, you retired. This is a step up." He scanned Kara like a slave trader. "And not a bad one either." He exited leaving them alone. Henry turned and walked back to his spot on the couch and slumped down. He reached over for a home décor magazine off the table. Pissed off and surprised by how things had turned out, Kara turned and said, "Well you think you can at least tell me where I am?"

Henry replied, "Port Angeles."

Chapter 34

More bad news arrived by way of the phone at nine-thirty that morning. Henry answered and nodded, hemmed and hawed a few times, and then hung up. Kara was sitting cross-legged on a table near the window basking in the warmth of the morning. She squinted looking over. He scooped up a set of keys from the table and jerked his head. “Okay, let’s go.”

“Where?” she asked.

“Blackmore.”

“They found the phone? That was Bill, wasn’t it?”

He didn’t reply but headed straight for the door.

“Henry.”

She hopped off the table and slipped back into her shoes.

“Look, I don’t want to get you worried but the sooner we can get back the better.”

She frowned. “It’s Bobby, isn’t it?”

“No.”

His reply hung in the air as she waited at the door. “My father?”

Henry drew a breath. “He’s had a heart attack. They have him in the hospital at the moment.”

“Wh-aaat?” she stammered rushing over.

“He’s stabilized, Kara.”

“What happened?”

“We don’t know yet but try to remain calm.”

She brushed past him and led the way out onto the bustling street. The day was already in full swing. Store owners were open for business. Pedestrians filled up the sidewalk, and traffic was streaming through the town. For a Sunday it was busy.

* * *

That morning as Henry pulled into the hospital she was mulling over questions and blaming herself for an incident that she had no idea about. She'd grilled Henry on the way over but he'd been given very little information on what occurred, all they knew was that her father had been taken to Blackmore General Hospital. Inside, it was moderately busy. The hectic activity that the hospital was known for on Fridays and Saturdays had been replaced by a slower place. She'd only ever seen the place once and that was when she was eleven and had broken her arm. It had a changed a lot since then.

After making an enquiry with the front desk they were told to stay in the waiting area until someone checked with one of the nurses. Kara remained standing, cradling her chin in hand and tapping a finger nervously against her cheek. Five minutes passed before they were given a room number and the all-clear.

Kara swung the door open and found her father sitting up in bed with the same annoyed look on his face as usual. Although she wanted answers she didn't want to upset him or cause another attack. Instead, Kara said, "Dad," then leaned over and hugged him.

"I'm fine. I don't know what all the fuss is about." Behind her Henry walked in and her father glanced at him with a scowl. "What's he doing here?"

"He brought me. Look, what happened?" she asked.

He shifted his focus back to her, and Henry said he would wait outside in the hallway. He closed the door behind him and her father grumbled. "You know I'm not thrilled by your choice of company."

"Dad, what happened?"

He rolled back the blanket just a little. "I took the trash out last night and found your SUV door open, your keys and phone on the ground and…"

She nodded and took a seat beside his bed. It was clear the strain of losing her mother, the desire to rid the home of anything related to Charlie, and her involvement in the case, along with wondering if she'd been snatched, had finally taken its toll. She knew her father had always been a strong individual, never given to showing too many emotions, but that didn't mean that they weren't hidden below the surface. Kara clutched his hand and gave it a little squeeze. "I'm fine."

"Well I know that now. If it hadn't been for Bobby, chances are I wouldn't be here now."

"Bobby found you?"

"At least that's what the doctor told me."

She remembered phoning him and leaving that panic-stricken message. No doubt the news of Sam's death and the possibility of someone coming after him had freaked him out enough that he headed over. Closing her eyes, a swell of emotions spilled over and she suddenly felt herself wanting to cry. Perhaps like her own father she'd become accustomed to burying it beneath a mask. She'd always had to be strong for others — her parents, Ethan, Michael and… her tumultuous thoughts ran amok until she felt a hand on her shoulder. She hadn't even heard him come in. Kara looked up to find Bobby. She stood up and gave him a hug.

"I heard you were here." He thumbed over his shoulder. "I'd just stepped out to call Lisa."

"You been here long?" she asked.

"All night," he said. "Took me a while to get in contact with Goodman but he managed to speak with one of the FBI agents who showed up this morning. What's going on?"

She sighed, looking back at her father. "Long story. Look, I really appreciate what you did."

"I thought he was gone," Bobby said.

"Unfortunately not," her father added as he reached for a glass of water on the side table.

"I arrived last night and found him on the ground. After getting your call, my first thought was that both of you had been attacked. I called the cops. Ambulance arrived and whisked him away. I decided to follow and stay until they figured out where you'd gone."

"Where were you?" her father asked.

She was just about to respond when Noah walked through the door looking windswept and out of breath. "I came as fast as I could." He hurried over and went to wrap his arm around her when she backed up. Her father and Bobby looked on with puzzled expressions. First off she didn't want to give them the impression there was anything between them and quite frankly she was as mad as heck. Her emotions felt out of control and she was liable to say something she didn't mean. She gestured to the door and they headed out into the hallway. Henry Ellis was sitting in a chair outside with a newspaper in hand. He glanced up and she walked past with Noah in her shadow. She made a beeline for a quiet room, an area of the hospital where she could speak without prying ears. It was cramped and had three vending machines and an icemaker. She walked in, one hand on her hip, the other ran through her hair as she approached the window and looked out. They were on the second story so all she could see was the roof below, steel air vents jutting out and a slice of the parking lot.

"Are you okay?" Noah asked.

"Why didn't you go to Darryl Clayton's when I asked?"

She turned around, her face a picture of anguish.

"What?"

"Clayton."

"I heard you but I'm not understanding what that has got to do with your father."

"It has everything to do with him. Sam is dead."

"I know." He stepped forward, and she took a step back keeping some distance between them. "What is it?" he asked.

"If you'd just questioned him, got a search warrant, we might have been able to stop him from doing this."

His eyebrows shot up and he raised a hand. "Hold on a second. You want to blame me for this?"

She hesitated and looked away.

"Kara, I'm sorry you've lost Sam, and that your father ended up here but I had nothing to do with that. And secondly, why did you lie to me?"

"About?" she asked.

"Please. I've already spoken with Henry, and Tim Greer. You didn't get the green light by Washington State Bureau of Investigation. That little stunt could have cost me my badge."

"A badge is one thing. Someone's life is another."

"Oh no, you are not blaming this on me."

"I asked," she said.

"You've asked a lot. You know I'm still wading through the paperwork related to Seth Leonard, dealing with my lawyer and I've yet to get around to investigating the attempted abduction, and—"

She shook her head. "Don't bother. It was made up."

"What?"

"The attempted abduction. It was a ruse. The FBI was behind it." She looked back at him. "That's where I was last night. Seems they felt I was jeopardizing all the work they've put in over the past year to catch this guy. They've had Clayton in their sights for some time. If they manage to retrieve Sam's phone they should have enough evidence to obtain a search warrant. But by then he probably will have thrown out the box of kids' clothes and nude Polaroids."

Noah shifted his weight from one foot to the next, confusion spreading across his face. "You want to back up and explain? The abduction in Blackmore was set up by the FBI? It never occurred?"

She nodded.

"That's impossible."

"Not according to Special Agent Bill Davis."

Noah looked perplexed. "And what's this about Clayton has kids' clothes and Polaroids?"

"According to Sam. After we visited Clayton, Sam went back that night. He says he found evidence in his bedroom closet that might link him to the disappearance of the four boys."

"How the hell did he get into his closet?"

She shrugged then shook her head gazing back out the window. "I guess we'll never know." The dark clouds that had smothered the sky the day before had now been replaced by a deep blue sky. Several herons heeled overhead.

Chapter 35

Monday, Halloween

The search of Darryl Clayton's property was conducted early Monday morning. Kara remained at the hospital while they continued to keep her father against his wishes under observation for an additional twenty-four hours. After a lengthy and heated conversation with Henry Ellis regarding being used as a pawn in a game, it had taken the better part of a day for the FBI to sift through the debris at Sunrise Trailer Park, locate Sam Young's cell phone and have the data retrieved from it.

Weary but curious to know if Sam's trespassing would amount to anything, Noah joined the FBI and SWAT just as the sun was beginning to rise. Unbeknownst to Clayton's family or his neighbors a team moved in on the place just after 6:15. The raid was fast, and over before Darryl even knew what hit him.

Standing outside, Noah watched as a belligerent Clayton was handcuffed, read his rights and removed from the property along with his son, wife and brother-in-law who would no doubt all be an accessory to what would become one of the most publicized cases since Charlie Walker.

It would take days, weeks, even months before the criminal investigation division would know if any bodies had been buried on the property and if Clayton was linked to Kara's brother. As he watched a cruiser peel away with Darryl's wife, he turned to see them bringing out a box. Noah went over and asked for confirmation. Bill Davis nodded, set the box down in the back of the SWAT wagon and with blue latex gloves on pulled out one piece of clothing after the next and laid them on top of each other. He handed the Polaroids to Noah, and he thumbed through them, although they didn't contain any sexual acts they were nude, and it was enough to turn his stomach.

"I figure he has more boxes like this stashed away. Those kids in there aren't a match to the four or Charlie Walker but with a little digging, I think we should be able to get a confession out of that asshole."

Noah nodded and handed the photos back to him. "Let's hope so."

Bill tapped Noah on the chest with the photos as if none of this fazed him. "At least you don't have to worry about Halloween this year. And you can probably close the case on Seth and anyone else Walker was looking into." With that said he turned to one of his men. "Hey, Danson, you got a cigarette?"

Over the next hour, Noah assisted the FBI in hauling out anything that could potentially be found to contain DNA, or be linked to the crimes. Another van had to be brought in just to carry all the bagged-up evidence. Strangely, unlike Seth Leonard's home, there were no bondage devices, paintings of young boys or pornography that would lead them to believe that the family or even just one of them had an unhealthy obsession with minors. Unless of course they had a room or a storage locker but keeping a box of souvenirs in their closet seemed to contradict that theory. Even the FBI agents on scene were a little surprised. Noah overheard them talking about how it was common to find a secret compartment, a locked room or some kind of dugout created specifically for the purpose of containment and sexual gratification. The separation of normal living quarters and a place to feed the darkest regions of the mind was something they'd come to expect. Whether they found it was to be seen.

* * *

Returning home that morning, Kara tossed the newspaper down. Although a recent car crash, and a small follow-up piece to the explosion from Saturday had been front-page news, it wouldn't compare to the feature they'd run the next day. The raid would most likely attract state and national attention. Kara held the door open as her father walked in. He'd refused to be helped inside, insisting that he was fine and it was nothing more than bad indigestion, perhaps food poisoning. She knew he didn't buy that but to admit the doctors were right would have gone against his stubborn nature. It was easier to make up some absurd reason if only so he could remain argumentative.

"Now you remember what the doctor told you. You need your rest."

"Ah, screw what he said. These doctors think they know everything," he replied.

"No working in the garage, lay off the drink, cut back on those greasy breakfasts and no more late nights."

"Why don't I just die then?"

"Dad, you do love to over-exaggerate." Kara went over and put on a pot of tea. She'd told him that he'd have to cut back on his coffee and switch to something calming like chamomile. Of course that went over like a lead balloon.

"Hippie tea. I don't drink hippie teas. And I certainly am not planning on taking up yoga before you say anything."

She shook her head as she went about filling the kettle with water while her father took a seat at the kitchen table and fished through a pile of bills. "You know, I think I might just put this house on the market."

"You said that."

"Did I?"

His memory wasn't getting any better. As the kettle boiled in the background, the phone rang and Kara headed over. "That's probably Noah with an update on the raid."

Her father wasn't listening or chose not to reply.

"Hello?"

"It's just me," Uncle Rob answered. "Just checking in with the old coot. How's he doing?"

She cast a glance over her shoulder and gave a strained smile. "Ah, you know him. If he isn't complaining about someone, someone is complaining about him."

"I'm not deaf you know," her father said.

"No, you've just got selective hearing," she muttered and Rob chuckled.

"Listen, is there anything you need? Groceries or such?"

She ambled over to the fridge and peered inside. "Nope, I think we're good for a few days."

"Well, you don't have to worry about supper tonight. Janice will bring over some of her homemade shepherd's pie, okay?"

"I appreciate that."

"Any further news?" he asked.

"He has a follow-up with the doctor this week."

"No, I meant with the investigation? Sam's death?"

She sighed. She'd barely had time to process the loss. "No. It's going to take some time, but they have arrested a person of interest so it's in their hands."

"Whose hands?"

"Can't say."

"Right. Man, that's too bad. I'm sorry, Kara. I know you liked him."

"Yeah, well…" She cleared her throat.

"And Bobby?"

"He returned home to get some well-deserved rest. He stayed with dad on Saturday but I was with him last night."

Rob sounded quiet on the phone, mindful even. Losing his sister-in-law was one thing, to nearly lose his brother could have been the straw that broke the camel's back.

"So I guess you'll be heading home today or tomorrow?" he asked.

"Originally, yes but…" She glanced at her father. "I mean, I can't leave him here alone."

"He's not alone, Kara. He has us."

"You're in Port Angeles. That's a lot of running back and forth."

"We were thinking of staying there for a couple of weeks. Janice would keep an eye on him while I'm at the restaurant in the day."

"I dunno."

"Kara. Michael has got to be crawling up the walls by now. You need to head home if only for Ethan's sake. Think about Ethan. We can keep you updated and trust me, Janice won't let your father get away with anything. She rules with an iron fist." They chuckled. He wasn't lying either. She was soft-spoken but definitely not a pushover.

"We'll see how things pan out today," she said.

"Alright, hon, keep us in the loop. And Kara. Get some sleep yourself. I don't want to have to be rushing you off to the hospital."

She exhaled hard. "Oh, no fear of that. I'm about to hit the sack."

After hanging up she made sure her father had everything he needed before she got a few hours. She'd told Noah that she wanted to stay in the loop of the investigation even though Bill had made it clear that she was to no longer interfere. Interfere? If it hadn't been for the tips from her mother and following up with the Claytons, Leonard or… her thoughts shifted back to Ray Owen.

She was beginning to feel bad that she'd pursued him, or caused him grief, and yet at the same time she was still intrigued by the sketches, and curious as to why he would run. She made a mental note to swing by his family home later, if only to apologize. The death or abduction of someone in a community could bring out all manner of people. Just because some were stranger than others — that didn't mean they had anything to do with it.

As she made her way into her old bedroom, she glanced at Charlie's empty room and felt the familiar twinge of loss except now it was mixed with a renewed sense of hope.

Chapter 36

Exhaustion took its toll. What should have been a short nap turned into four hours. When Kara's eyes fluttered open, she found herself staring at the digital clock on the side table. The clock flashed back 3:15. The house was silent. She rolled off the bed and took a second to work out the tension in her neck from having slept awkwardly before checking on her father. He was downstairs, seated in his recliner with a blanket over him. The TV was on, and some daytime show was playing. She left him and went into the kitchen and pulled the blinds up flooding the home with warm light. A quick coffee, and she'd return to the land of the living.

Sitting at the table ten minutes later, she placed a phone call to Bill Davis to see when she could get her cell back and to hear an update on the Claytons.

"Bill. Kara Walker."

"Dear lord, you're like a bad nightmare that doesn't go away."

"You have my cell. I need it."

"See Detective Goodman. I've already given it back. He said he'd give it to you."

"Oh." She nodded. "Any luck with tracing that last call I received?"

"We're working on it. Been in contact with your cell service provider."

"And did you find the box?"

He groaned. "Do you ever stop?"

"My friend gave his life to give you the break you've been waiting a year for. Cut me some slack."

She heard him sigh. "Yes. We found it, and we are in the process of trying to identify the victims."

Her features twisted. "Hold on, they don't match the four boys?"

"No. But our guys are still wading through the property."

In the background she could hear phones ringing, keyboards being tapped and the hum of a busy office. Her mind churned over the findings.

"Bill, do me a favor. See if one of the photos matches a boy by the name of Caleb Weslo."

"Who?"

"Before Charlie was abducted there were a series of attacks in Forks and Blackmore. Although it made headlines nothing ever came of it and none of the attacks were linked to the abductions. One of those boys was Caleb Weslo."

"How would you know that? They don't print the names for minors."

"I spoke with his brother Ricky. The same guy who accused Kyle Harris of abusing him back in 1988. Turns out he never did. It was made up."

"Made up?"

"Yes, like your abduction attempt. A ploy to draw out who was responsible. Except they didn't bank on it going as far as it did. Anyway, look into it and give me a call on my cell once you find out."

He huffed. "Okay, hold on a minute, so now I'm your errand boy?"

She groaned. "Seriously, Bill, you have deep ego issues to work through."

"I'll have you know…"

Before he could finish she hung up. She could envision him standing there dumbfounded, unable to believe that someone had hung up on him. He'd probably never had it happen in his whole career.

After making some lunch for her father, cleaning up the house and doing a quick run into town to give some of her mother's clothes to Goodwill, she got a text back from Goodman to say she could swing by later.

Yes, I have your phone. I'm caught up at the moment. We could have dinner if you like? I should be at my apartment around 5:30. If you want to let yourself in there is a key under a red and brown rock in the yard close to the entrance. I've lost my keys so many damn times; I had to have a backup. Help yourself to a beer.

Kara didn't stay too long in town. Halloween was already in full swing with most of the stores decorated with bats, witches, cobwebs and tombstones outside. Flyers for an evening Halloween Community Party were tacked onto wooden lampposts. Parents were rushing around with their kids taking care of last-minute preparations. The party and costume store that had been there since she was a kid had a giant inflatable pumpkin on top and signs plastered the windows offering twenty percent off everything in the store. People streamed in and out with bags, and the road had several advertising banners strung between the stores. As she sat in her car sipping on coffee watching the world spin around her, she couldn't help think about that night. Halloween was never the same after losing

Charlie. It no longer held the attraction that it once had. Her own son Ethan had suffered for it as well. She'd refused to take him out, which of course had created a point of tension in her marriage with Michael, who kept telling her that she couldn't live in the past and project her fears onto their son. He was right but that didn't make it any easier.

Now that Clayton was behind bars would that all change? She hoped so.

* * *

After letting herself into Noah's apartment she slung her bag down and slid open the doors to the balcony. A cool breeze blew against her cheek as she looked out at the lights of Blackmore. From his apartment she could see right across the town to Olympic National Park. With her father having suffered a heart attack and her career at a standstill she was considering moving back, maybe taking a position with Washington Bureau. Until Charlie's abduction she'd always loved the area. There were few places in the country that brought her close to the evergreen wilderness of the coniferous forest, and the roaring ocean.

Stepping back inside she took out a beer from the fridge and twisted the top off. After, she wandered into the spare room to browse more of the photos that Amanda and Noah had taken. Each one was as striking as the last. Like any curious person, she nosed through a magazine rack by one of the chairs, and pulled open some of the dresser drawers. There inside one of them was a small booklet with the word FAMILY on the front of it. She pulled it out and flipped it open. Inside were photos of them. Some were of their wedding day. Amanda was beautiful. Dark hair, green eyes, petite and slender, the kind of girl any man would have been proud to have brought home to his mother. Noah was beaming. He looked happy, free of worry and the fine lines that now etched his face. Grief had a way of sucking the life out of a person. Kara thumbed through more. There were shots taken in what looked to be Hawaii. They were snorkeling, parasailing and smooching beneath a waterfall. Tucked in among the photos was a snippet from the *Peninsula Daily Times* about the accident. The paper was worn at the edges. A photo displayed the wreckage. Kara sat there reading it, and was engrossed in the article even as a key turned in the front door and Noah let himself in.

Kara got up and walked over to the door with the album still in hand.

"Hey there."

Noah tossed his keys on the table and his eyes shifted from her to the album. Without saying a word he walked over and gently took it out of her hand. "So, I guess you know everything now," he said.

"Sorry. I was just…" Her voiced faded.

He brushed past her and tucked the newspaper clipping she'd set on the dresser back inside and put it all back in the drawer and closed it. He then glanced around the room as if looking to see what else she'd touched — desecrated even.

She thumbed over her shoulder. "You want me to put some dinner on?"

He stood with his back turned and head slightly bowed.

"Actually, I'm… I'm not very hungry."

Kara drummed her fingers against the frame of the door, nodding slowly.

"Your phone is in my bag," he added.

"Right." She went over to collect it. Hoping to shift the mood she thought discussing the case might at least distract his mind. "I spoke with Bill Davis today. Gave him the name of Caleb Weslo. I'm thinking there's a possibility that he might be among the Polaroids."

He came out of the room nodding and walked over to the wall and began to move her mother's boards that were covered in notes and information about the case.

"What are you doing?" she asked.

"It's over," he said without even looking at her.

"What? But they're not done investigating. This is just the tip of the iceberg."

"I meant having this here. I deal with this shit all day, every day and the last thing I need to see when I come home is this staring me in the face. I'm sorry. You'll need to take it with you."

"Is this about…" she jerked her head towards the room.

"No, I just want it out of here. Besides now they have Clayton it looks like they will probably uncover a lot more about this man."

"Right but..."

He folded it up and took some of the paperwork and placed it back in the box.

Again she tried to lighten the mood. "I'm sure they will. In fact I was going to drop by Ray Owen's home and…"

"Enough, Kara."

"What?"

"You're off the case. It's out of your hands now."

"But I was going to..."

"It doesn't matter. You're just going to cause more

trouble, and if they file a complaint…" This time it was him who stopped speaking.

"Cause trouble? You make it sound like that's all I've done since I've got here."

He glanced at her without saying anything as if to indicate that it was true.

She narrowed her eyes. "Just like Bill Davis." She scooped up her bag and walked towards the door but before she left she turned and pointed at him. "You know — maybe I have been sticking my nose in where it's not wanted. I'll admit I stepped over the line and lied to you about having been given the green light by WBI but if it wasn't for the likes of my mother, myself, or Sam, who I might add is dead because he tried to uncover the truth, maybe County and the FBI would still be walking around with their thumbs up their asses. And as for the photo album. I'm sorry but I highly doubt Amanda would have wanted you moping around for years after her death. She'd want…"

He snapped back cutting her off. "You don't know what she'd want. You didn't even know her."

"No I didn't. But I know what it feels like to be left behind and to make the choice to pick up the pieces after losing someone."

With that said, she exited his apartment leaving the door open.

Chapter 37

It was quiet around the table that evening. A somber mood dominated. Unlike all the other homes in the neighborhood, no trick or treaters knocked at their door and it wasn't because the lights were out. Most parents in the community knew to avoid their home. Gossip traveled fast around Blackmore. Years after Charlie's abduction a group of kids had shown up but were quickly shooed away by her father. She figured it had got a reputation and one that had stuck for a long time. Janice reached across for a bun and began buttering it. She had joined them for supper but Rob couldn't because he had to work.

"So you didn't want to help him tonight?"

"No, you don't want to get in his way, especially on Halloween. Anyone would think a full moon was out. He becomes super grouchy," she said, scraping the last of the food from her plate.

"Well, I guess we all have our own reasons for hating the season," Kara said.

As they were wrapping up and Kara was loading dishes into the sink to clean, her cell began vibrating on the counter. A quick glance at the caller ID and she answered.

"You know you hung up on me?" Bill said.

"Took you this long to phone me back?"

He scoffed. "Listen, not that I should be telling you this but I figured being as you gave the lead, you deserved to hear it. Seems you were right. We got a match on one of the kids in the photos. It was Caleb, and he's admitted it."

"And Darryl Clayton?"

"Won't admit to it. Stupid asshole. If he thinks denying everything including the box in his closet is going to work, he's got another thing coming."

"That's good news, right?" Kara asked.

"I'd say so." He went quiet. "Listen, maybe I was a little harsh on you before."

"Davis, no need."

He breathed a sigh of relief. "Whew! I thought you would make me go through with a full apology."

They both chuckled.

"No seriously. I appreciate it," he said.

"You have Sam to thank for that."

"Give yourself some credit. He might not have gone back had you not pushed the issue with Clayton."

"Now you're making it sound like I was to blame. Probably best you stop while you're ahead."

He stifled a laugh. "Anyway. Thanks."

Kara held on to the phone for a few seconds longer after ending the call.

"Any luck?" Janice asked.

Kara turned. "With what?" She was lost in thought.

"The call. Was that Goodman?"

"No. It was…" She trailed off then headed over and scooped up her bag. "Janice, you think you can keep an eye on dad for a while?"

"I'm not a dog," he replied sipping at his tea.

She waved her off. "Of course, go ahead. I think I've got a bone to keep him busy."

Kara gave her father a peck on the head and he grumbled in his usual fashion.

* * *

Under the cover of night, Kara parked two houses down from the Owens' residence. Sitting in her vehicle she observed parents escorting children from door to door collecting bags of candy. The light inside her porch was on, the storm door closed, and the internal one was open. She could just make out the retiree sitting in a chair beyond the door. Every few minutes she would get up with a bowl in hand and fill up the kids' pillowcases with candy. On the surface everything looked normal. The house itself was very old with white clapboard siding, and a brick-and-mortar foundation. It wasn't Ora that was of interest to her but Ray. The driveway was empty, and she hadn't seen the woman talking to anyone besides the dark brown Lab that occasionally pressed its wet nose up against the window and would bark as more kids made their way up the pathway. She knew there was little chance in hell Ora was going to let her inside at least not without causing a scene. The vibe she got from her the last time was one of distrust. Not many people liked having police show up at their door especially if they felt their son had been ridiculed.

While waiting, Kara was tempted to phone Noah and apologize. She had no right to tell him how he should feel. She wasn't exactly a role model of how to deal with grief. Her thoughts soon circled around to Ethan. Had she treated him the same way her mother had treated her? Had she kept him at arm's length, allowing Michael to bear the weight of responsibility just so she could bury herself in work? If she was honest her work really only served to distract her mind from the loss she'd felt as a teen. It had given her a sense of control when so much of her youth had felt out of control.

She thought about what Uncle Rob had said and was tapping in the number for Michael to tell him that she'd be on a flight first thing in the morning when white headlights washed over her car. She squinted — it took a second for her eyes to adjust and when they did, she saw a brown Honda roll into the driveway. Fixed on it, she stuffed her phone back in her jacket pocket and watched as Ray Owen climbed out. He looked around nervously then hurried up to the house. Kara pulled out her service weapon and made sure she had a full magazine before sliding it back into the holster beneath her jacket. Although she didn't anticipate things going south, after the skittish way Ray had acted at the vigil she wasn't taking any chances.

Before exiting her vehicle she noticed his mother twist in her seat and say something over her shoulder. Even though she never saw Ray she assumed Ora was talking with him as she got up and closed the front door and then the light on the porch went out.

Kara slung her bag over her shoulder and glanced up and down the street before dashing across and making her way up to the front door. She pressed the doorbell and stood back keeping her eyes fixed on the Honda just in case Ray attempted to dart out the side door. From inside she heard Ora holler that she was all out of candy. Kara rang the bell again and a light came on. This time she kept the storm door open and waited until Ora opened her door. Ora adjusted her glasses as she peered out, then scowled and said, "This is not a good time."

She went to shut the door and Kara stuck her foot into the frame, placing a hand on the door. "I need to talk to your son about a series of abductions, and sketches he's left."

"I told you he doesn't know anything and even if he did they didn't listen."

Right then she heard the slam of a door out back. Kara turned and jumped down off the porch just in time to see Ray making a dash for his car. She hurried across and cut him off before he reached it. She thrust out both hands. "Stop! You're not in trouble. I just want to talk to you. Please."

Ray bounced from foot to foot looking as if he was contemplating making a run for it. His eyes were wired, and dark like he hadn't slept in days, and he kept scratching at his neck. Under the dim light from the porch she could see it was marked, bloody and in line with his fingers. Kara fished into her bag and pulled out the handful of charcoal sketches he'd left at the vigils over the years. She held them out.

"You left these behind. Why? What do they mean?"

By now Ora had made her way down the pathway and several parents who had seen the light on were about to bring their children up when they saw the commotion and opted to walk on. Ora shook her head. "I'm going to call the cops."

Ora turned and made her way back into the house.

"I am a cop," Kara replied, not taking her eyes off Ray for even a second.

Ray didn't respond except to stare at her.

"Why did you run?" she asked.

"I…" his voice croaked.

She took a step forward, and he stepped back.

"Look. I need to know. Did you leave one of these at my brother's vigil?"

Again no response so she dug into her bag, pulled out her wallet and retrieved a photo of Charlie. She held it up and his eyes widened. "You recognize him?"

Frustration was starting to rise in her chest at the lack of response. She shoved the sketches back into her bag along with the photo. "Why did you leave these sketches?"

He began stuttering. "I… t… tried."

"What?"

Right then her phone began vibrating in her pocket. She put a finger up. "Don't you go anywhere! We are not done." She glanced at the phone and saw a text from Noah. She slid her finger over the surface of the screen to bring it up and that's when she lost it.

Another kid was taken half an hour ago. He's abducted another. Call me. Noah.

How? Her pulse sped up, her heart started pounding in her chest and a sense of panic came over her like the night it all happened. She dropped the phone into her bag and her eyes fixed on Ray. Whether it was a gut feeling, or years of instinct gained from working case after case, she knew that somehow Owen was linked to it but the question was how?

She lunged forward and grabbed a hold of his jacket and he cowered like a teenager under the grasp of an authority figure.

"Where have you been tonight? Huh? Tell me."

Ora came out of the house protesting, holding a cell in one hand. "Let him go."

Kara shoved him towards the rear of the car and glanced through the windows. "Open the trunk. Now!"

He hesitated, and she shoved him up against the side of the car. "I said now. Open it." Ray fished into his pockets for keys while Ora continued to berate her and tell her that she was going to press charges. Kara couldn't have cared less. She was too focused on seeing inside the vehicle. Nervous, Ray dropped the keys.

"Pick 'em up."

He scooped them up and pushed the key into the lock with trembling hands. He popped the lid open, and she moved him to the right. Inside there was a sleeping bag, a flashlight, rope, a couple of empty bottles of water and a spare tire.

"What is this? Where is he? Huh? Where's the boy?"

"I… don't."

She shoved him towards the house. "We're going inside for a talk and you are going to tell me everything." He let out a cry like a child that thought they were about to be punished. Ora attempted to get between them but her feeble hands were no match for Kara who was jacked up on adrenaline, pissed off and determined to get to the truth.

Inside was a narrow hallway. The living room off to the right was larger than it should have been for a home of its size. There were stairs off to the left that went down to a basement, and two bedrooms on the main floor. The first thing that caught her eye as she entered the hallway leading into the living room was that one of the rooms further down had multiple locks on the outside. There were three.

"Whose room is that?"

"That's my son's. Now would you please let go of him!"

She ignored her plea and pushed Ray further down

the corridor. "How about you tell me why you've got so many locks on this door?"

"He's worried. Okay?" Ora pulled Kara around and jabbed her finger at the front door. That's when she saw that it too was covered with locks. Five and two deadbolts.

"Open them. Now!"

Ray took out the same set of keys he'd used for the car and began unlocking each one. When he got to the last one he pushed the door open, and she shoved him in. The light was already on inside. But it was no ordinary light. It was a black light bulb that gave off an almost purple color, giving most of the objects in his room a fluorescent blue glow. If that wasn't strange enough, it was what lined every inch of his wall. Kara stepped inside turning three hundred and sixty degrees to soak in the sight of hundreds of sketches all taped together. She fished into her bag and pulled out the ones left with the families and began to lift one up and match it to those on the walls. Meanwhile Ray stood with his back to the door.

"What the hell is this?" she asked.

Separately the sketches seemed meaningless, but against the backdrop of the rest of what had been drawn it painted a picture of a cabin nestled in a forest with a well, a swing set, a bridge and a cliff, and a nearby lake.

Ray pointed to the cabin. "Thhhh… those. Chhhharlie."

Her eyes darted to him and then back to the wall, looking at the cabin. "Those are the sketches you left at Charlie's vigil?"

He nodded.

She looked back and soaked it all in. Her eyes

dropped to the sketches she had in hand and matched them up with the ones on the wall. Inside his bedroom there really wasn't much, except a simple bed and a table and chairs. There on the table were stacks of papers, most of which were covered in sketches, and to the right of that a tin with charcoal, and what must have been neon pencils. All the ones inside the room had been scrawled with neon color so the whole thing glowed under the light.

"What is this place?" she asked. She turned to him and he just looked petrified like he had seen a ghost. His eyes were wide, and he'd returned to scratching his neck, causing it to bleed.

"Ray!" She hollered even louder, causing him to shake. "What is this place?"

He began stuttering, "Whhwhwheere. Ttththhhe. Chhildren. Aaaare."

Chapter 38

Kara's brow pinched as she looked back at the cabin. Her mind went into overdrive; she brought a hand up to her head trying to get a grasp on reality. She took a few deep breaths and snapped the elastic around her wrist. She reached into her pocket and took out her meds and nearly dropped them trying to shake out a pill.

"Stay right here," she said stepping out into the hallway to place a phone call to Noah. It rang several times before he picked up.

"Hello?"

"I got your message," she said.

Noah didn't waste any time. "The boy's name is Ashton Cole. He's twelve and was taken from the east side of town. Blackmore and County along with family and friends are out searching for him. They said he was with a group but broke off to get another bag for candy. He didn't return and his mother said he hasn't been home."

She walked a short distance down the hallway. "Look, I'm over at the Owens' house."

"What? Didn't you hear what I said?"

"Just listen. I'm going to send a photo to your phone. You've got to see this. Those sketches he drew are part of a bigger portrait with a cabin in a forest and…"

"Kara! Let me just stop you right there. I don't have time for this. Okay? We have a boy missing and…"

"No, you're not listening. When I asked him what this place was, he said it was where the children are kept. I think he knows where they are, Noah. But that's not all, in the back of his trunk he had a flashlight, a rope, several empty bottles of water and…"

"You searched his vehicle without a warrant? Please tell me they invited you in and you didn't just barge your way into the house?"

"Noah. I think he knows," Kara said.

"Well, while you were going off the handle yesterday, I did a little digging into Owen. Seems the guy is a lunatic that was bugging the families, saying he knew where their kids were. His mother told them that he had psychic abilities." He scoffed. "And you know how well that goes over."

"So they didn't do follow-up on his claims?"

"Cops have already spoken to him, Kara. They've already looked into it."

"Who has?"

"County, Jefferson and one of the other departments."

He came across sounding real vague which made her believe he'd only picked up the phone and got the information second-hand. The information was no different from what Ora had said. In fact it confirmed it. While law enforcement did use the help of psychics, it was rare and they didn't allow anyone to toss in their two cents.

"Did they see his room?" she asked.

"Look. I have my hands full here. If you want to help, there is a whole whack of people searching right now. All that matters is finding that boy. And if you want to send me a photo to look at later, by all means but I gotta go. I'll speak to you soon. I just wanted to let you know what was happening." She remained silent for a second or two. "Okay?" he asked before he hung up.

She stood in the hallway, one hand on her hip, the other she ran through her hair. Kara turned and went back into the bedroom where Ora was talking with Ray. Even though he was now in his forties, she still spoke to him like he was a child. The door was partly closed, and she was questioning him as though she hadn't seen any of this herself. How could anyone live in the same home and not know what was going on inside a room across from theirs? Kara squeezed through the gap and turned to see what they were looking at. The only area of the bedroom that she hadn't seen, because the door had been wide open, was behind the door. As she stepped back and looked at the image, it was of a figure. The entire door was taken up with a man dressed in black. The second she saw it her heart skipped a beat. A flashback of that night came to her. The same fear made her mouth go dry. Her hands started trembling.

Like a monster in the closet, that image had been the one thing that had stuck with her over the years — looming and dark, the masked figure that grabbed Charlie.

All of a sudden she was back there in those woods — standing around, waiting for Bobby to show. Sam and Charlie were dressed as skeletons, he'd practically begged their mother to get one of the outfits after watching the 1984 flick The Karate Kid. *She took out the pack of Marlboro Lights, unwrapped the cellophane, dropped it and tapped out a cigarette. She'd wanted to act all grown up and cool. She'd figured it all out in her mind. Bobby would show up and she'd be leaning against the tree with a cigarette dangling out the corner of her mouth, channeling her inner Molly Ringwald.*

"Does mom know you smoke?" Charlie asked.

She took the gold Zippo lighter she'd stolen from her father and lit the end.

"No, and mom isn't going to know because you're not going to tell her," she replied before coughing hard because it was the first time she'd ever inhaled. Kara glanced through the trees, then stared at her watch.

"How long do we have to stay here?" Sam asked.

"Not long," she said.

Within five minutes Bobby arrived and while Sam and Charlie stayed busy chasing one another, counting how many candy bars they had and climbing trees, she and Bobby acted like they were eighteen, smoking a cigarette and wrapping up in each other's arms. It was only when Charlie cried out that they saw him. By then it was too late. She couldn't push the sight of that shiny blade against his throat out of her mind.

Then just like that she was back again.

"Who is that?" she asked Ray.

Ray raised a finger and pointed and stuttered. "Ttthhheee. Catcher."

"The catcher. And who is he, Ray? Huh? Is it you?"

He shook his head and Ora placed a hand around his back. "He sees things. We told you all but you wouldn't listen."

Kara leaned forward. "I'm listening. Didn't you show them this?"

"This wasn't here," Ora said.

"So you knew he'd drawn this?"

"Of course. Not the part on the back of the door and well, it wasn't this complete years ago but then again—"

"Not every kid was missing. He's pieced this together over the years, hasn't he?"

She nodded.

"Where is this place?" Kara asked Ray.

He shrugged.

"Come on, Ray. Think."

He shook his head.

Kara pulled out her phone and started taking

snapshots and then took one panoramic one. After, she attached it with a message for Noah and sent it over. In the meantime she had an idea. It meant returning to the place she hadn't been in twenty-five years but maybe, just maybe it would spark something.

Chapter 39

She had two options: take Ray by force, which was liable to cause Ora to call the cops if she hadn't done so already, or convince her that she believed in her son and that whatever ability he had might be the key to finding the missing Cole boy. Kara opted for the second, and after a lot of back and forth Ora bought it. With Ray riding shotgun the SUV tore away from the home heading for Westborough, the road that went past Fairground Woods.

Veering off to the hard shoulder, near the farmer's gate, she killed the engine and looked out into the darkness. The country roads didn't have any lights, and the only glow came from the nearby housing development. But it didn't matter because even in daylight the location terrified her. It was like she was fourteen all over again. Although the landscape had changed, the way she felt hadn't.

"Come on, pull yourself together," she said pushing down her fears and climbing out of the car. Ray didn't move a muscle. She bent back down. "Ray. Get out of the car." He glanced at her then nervously hopped out the other side.

"Wwwwwhhherre arrre we going?"

"Twenty-five years ago, this is where it all began. I

need you to do whatever it is you do." She walked up to the gate and opened it and beckoned him to follow. He shook his head and remained by the passenger side door. Kara trudged over and grabbed him by the collar and forced him forward. "I don't have time for this crap. Let's go." She gave him a shove, and he stumbled forward. Reluctantly he went with her up the steep grassy incline that she'd once raced down. The wind picked up, blowing her jacket around. She sucked in the bitter cold air while reaching into her pocket to grip the Zippo lighter. It was like an anchor to her past before he was taken, the one thing that kept her from forgetting the past and her role in what should have never happened.

"Now you tell me if you pick up on anything. It doesn't matter what it is."

Ray shook his head slowly and repeatedly like he was suffering from some type of debilitating disease. Every so often he would reach up and scratch his neck and then mumble something under his breath.

As tough as it must have been for him, it was even worse for Kara. Like being taken up into a plane to jump out for the first time. A sense of dread and impending doom weighed down on her heart causing it to beat rapidly. She took slow deep breaths to prevent herself from having a panic attack.

At one point along the journey towards the tree line, Kara had to stop and take a breath. She closed her eyes for a second and inhaled deeply. *You can do this. You can do this. You must do this.* They pressed on until they melted into the forest. Under the cover of night it was hard to tell which way to turn and her memory of where they stood that night had faded over time. Still, she led Ray through the thick undergrowth. She pushed branches out of the way and used her phone to light up the small trail that was barely visible. If it hadn't been for some of the old junk that teens had left behind over the years, she would have walked straight past the spot. There in the darkness were a rear car seat, tires in a circle, and a section of metal from the hood of a car. A shiver came over her as she stepped into the clearing. She slapped away the past. The sound of her brother's cry. Kara breathed in the stench of urine and moss. Her foot kicked several crushed beer cans before turning to find Ray standing at the perimeter of the clearing looking terrified. He shook his head. "Nnnnoooo." Then he turned and bolted. Kara took off after him. He didn't get far before she latched on to his jacket but oh did he struggle.

"I need you to do this," she said.

He shook his head. "I… cccccaaannn't."

"You must," she yelled, her voice cutting into the night.

She had to strong-arm him through the forest and force him out into the clearing. His hands were shaking and he looked as if his legs were about to buckle. The wind howled through the trees, and the sound of critters could be heard nearby. She just wanted to get the hell out of there but not before she got answers.

Seconds turned to minutes.

Ray stood there shaking like a scared animal. His eyes flitted back and forth like he was seeing unseen figures passing by. His teeth chattered, but nothing occurred. She wasn't sure what to expect when he had these visions. Were his eyes meant to roll back? Did he channel the voices of the dead? Then it dawned on her. Paper. Pen. Everything he'd done until now had been sketched out. She fished into her pocket and pulled out a scrap of paper that had a list of persons of interest on it. She flipped it over and took out a pen from her top breast pocket and handed it to him.

"Here."

He stared at it them like they were some kind of foreign objects.

"Ray. Please."

With the wind howling, biting at their ears, he took the paper and pen and walked over to the rusted car hood that was leaning against an old oak tree. He pressed the paper on it and began to sketch. A surge of confidence cut through the fear she felt. It was working. This was it. All he needed was some prompting.

Anything to get him to… Under the glow of her phone she noticed what he was sketching. "No. NO. NO!" she yelled. It was the same image of the cabin in the woods. She waited until he was done and then tore the paper away from him and looked at it. There was nothing new, nothing that would give her any clues as to where the place was. Perhaps the cops were right. Maybe he was just a lunatic looking to steer the investigation in the wrong direction. Maybe she was beginning to unravel like her mother had when she lost herself in the pursuit of answers. For all she knew, Ray might have been behind it and this was some part of a sick game that he was playing. She jerked a finger toward the way out of the forest. "Let's go."

"Wweeee leave?"

"Yeah, we're leaving," she replied.

A look of relief flooded his face as they trudged out of those godforsaken woods leaving behind the memory and fear of that night. The only good thing that had come out of it was she'd confronted her inner fear, the one place that had for so long seemed too overwhelming to visit. Now she saw it for what it was, nothing but a stage to an unfortunate event.

Kara slammed the door shut locking out the wind. She didn't start the engine but instead sat there windswept and despondent while Ray continued to scratch at his neck like a mental patient. She felt so foolish dragging him out there, hoping that he would offer insights, answers, a solution after years of investigative work had failed.

"Home," he said without a stutter. It just rolled off

his lips.

She nodded. "That's right, I'm taking you home."

Kara fired up the engine and had just shifted the gear stick into drive when her phone began vibrating. Keeping her foot on the brake she answered it.

"Kara, I took a look at those photos. Maybe I'm taking a stab in the dark here, and I might be way off, but that bridge and cliff face looks a helluva lot like Devil's Punchbowl out at Crescent Lake, and the waterfall resembles Marymere Falls," Noah said.

"Are you sure?"

"Look, I spent a lot of time in Olympic National Park taking photos. I think I know the area but there's a chance I might be wrong."

"Got it. Thanks."

"Kara, hold up — "

She'd already hung up before he could get another word out.

"Seems like we're going to take a slight diversion, Ray. Strap in, it's going to be a bumpy ride," she said before tearing away from the lay-by heading for Crescent Lake.

Chapter 40

Lake Crescent was located eighteen miles west of Port Angeles. Nestled into the northern foothills of Olympic National Park, it attracted locals and tourists alike to its pristine deep waters for fishing, swimming and camping. It took them close to an hour to arrive near the small community of Piedmont. Based on the various sketches, Kara concluded that if Ray's psychic impressions were real, and not just the concoction of a mind obsessed with the area, pinpointing where the cabin was wouldn't be easy, as the Devil's Punchbowl was on the north side of the lake, and the 90-foot Marymere Falls was on the south. And what about the tire hanging from a mossy tree, or the stream or well? It also didn't help that it was dark. The only light came from a full moon, and a sky full of stars.

Initially, she decided to take the north beach road along the lake and turned down into Spruce Railroad Trail to locate the arching bridge over the Punchbowl. As a kid she'd heard of the place through others but had never visited there herself. Teens were known for climbing the cliff and jumping into the Punchbowl. It was severely dangerous and several teens had lost their lives there back in the early nineties.

Throughout the entire journey, Ray kept scratching

his neck and patting his leg anxiously while shaking his head and telling her to turn around. She'd contemplated dropping him off before she left but at this stage she wasn't sure what role he'd played in the abductions. Her gut told her that he didn't have the mental capacity to pull it off and if Goodman was right about the timeline of the latest kidnapping — unless he dumped the boy's body somewhere locally he wouldn't have been able to make the journey out to Crescent Lake and back before she saw him. Still, she hadn't ruled him out.

Veering into a clearing where vehicles had worn away the grass, Kara told Ray to get out. It was a short walk along a rocky trail that ascended then descended to the infamous bridge that spanned an inlet of the lake known as the Punchbowl. The wind was kicking up the water causing it to splash against the shore. Using nothing more than the light from her phone they made their way down to the bridge and looked out. She was hoping Ray might pick up on something, get an impression, anything that might lead them in the right direction.

"You remember this place?" she asked, pulling up her collar around her ears. There could have only been a few places where a cabin could have been due to the park belonging to the government. She figured it had to have been nearby, maybe off one of the local roads but which? They could be out there all night. She'd taken the sketches along with her in the hope that showing them to him and then pointing might trigger something in him. It didn't. He just shook from nerves or the cold, then turned around wanting to go back to the car.

"Ray."

"Wwwee ssshhouldn't be here."

She caught up with him and grabbed a hold of him. "A young boy is missing! Look, I'm going out on a limb here hoping that you know where they are. You wanted someone to listen, I'm listening. Please. Help me find him."

He kept walking, so she grabbed him and made him stop.

A light rain started to fall, droplets pinged off his jacket, and he stared back at her.

"Please," she said. He nodded but couldn't give her any information on the area. Trying to connect the dots they returned to her vehicle and traveled around the lake on Route 101. Tall pine trees blocked out the view of the landscape while the lake glistened under the night's moon. They passed by a few vehicles on the way, locals, maybe tourists who were heading out from Barnes Point. She headed for the Storm King Ranger Station parking lot and boat launch. It was also the spot that provided tourists with access to the Marymere Falls Trail.

Gravel kicked up, spitting against the side of the SUV as she brought it around into the nearly empty lot.

Off to her left were three other vehicles, two of which were pulling out boats from the lake.

"Stay here."

Kara jumped out and hurried down a steep incline to the boat launch. A large red 4 x 4 pickup truck was hauling a boat out leaving one other boat in the water with a spotlight and fishing gear in the back. Three guys were yakking up a storm as she approached.

"You leaving for the night or doing some night fishing?" she asked.

"What?"

"Leaving or night fishing?"

One of the guys, dressed in a rain jacket, a Nike baseball cap, jeans and yellow work boots, pushed away from the boat which was already on a trailer. It looked as if they were just waiting for their friend to bring the truck down so they could hook it up. He turned and flashed a light in her face. She squinted and lifted her forearm to block the glare.

"About to call it a day," he replied.

"How much to do a loop of the lake's perimeter?" she asked.

"What?"

"The perimeter. How much?"

His two buddies chuckled. "Lady, we're not a tour guide service."

She pulled out her badge and flashed it. "Look, I really need the use of your boat. There is a boy missing.

So I can either commandeer it or pay you some green. What's it gonna be?"

The one guy closest to her looked back at his pals then turned back. "How much you got?"

"How much will it cost?" she asked.

"You just want to go around the perimeter one time, right?"

The rain and wind had begun to pick up, and it was plastering her dark hair to her forehead. She nodded getting chilled by the cold.

"Forty bucks," he said.

"Got yourself a deal." She cast a glance back at her vehicle to make sure Ray was still there then waved him down. She fished out two twenties and was about to hand it over when they caught sight of Ray.

"That's per person."

She frowned. "Are you serious?"

"Lady, does it look like you've got many other options?"

"I could commandeer it."

"And I could file a complaint," he replied. She fished out another forty, and he snatched it out of her hand before she could change her mind.

The weathered-looking man twirled his finger in the air. "Okay boys, let's get her back out." The other two groaned and put the boat back into the water. She and Ray climbed into the eighteen-foot fishing boat and took a seat while the guy she'd been speaking with fired up the motor. Water churned up behind them, turning the pristine water into foam as the boat veered away from the shore.

"You say a boy's gone missing?" he asked, yelling over the roar of the motor. A light mist blew against Kara's face as she made her way up beside him.

"Twelve years old."

"Shit. I'm Reg by the way, and these other fellas are friends of mine."

"Kara Walker."

"So what are we looking for here, Ms. Walker?"

"A cabin."

She pulled out the sketches and was struggling to show him using the light from her phone when he shouted out, "Steve, give this lady your flashlight." His buddy came over and handed over a large Maglite. She shone it on the sketch.

"I know it's not much to go by but it has to be in the area."

He snorted. "Must be some serious cutbacks if that's all they've given you for the investigation." He turned around and yelled for Steve to turn on the spotlight. He moved over to a large LED light attached to side of the boat. A flip of the switch and a bright white light bathed the edge of the shore. The engine continued to roar as they made their way along the south shore.

"Chances are if it's a cabin it will be on the northwest side," Steve hollered. "Closer to Camp David

Junior Road. It's the only area that I know that allows cabins so close to the lake. I've not seen any homes along Olympic Highway. At least not on this side."

She nodded and looked back at Ray who was clinging to the edge of the boat like he was on some kind of roller-coaster ride. The boat bounced over the waves making all of them grab hold of the edge.

They must have been on the water for close to an hour, searching up and down, shining the light on old and new cabins, when Kara spotted it. It wasn't the cabin itself that caught her eye as much as it was the mossy tree that overhung the water and the tire swing hanging off it. She told Steve, and he hollered to Reg.

"Reg! Can you swing it back around?"

She made her way across to Ray and took a seat beside him. She pulled out her phone and tried to get a signal. There were no bars. She got up and held it up. "Come on, you bastard."

"You won't get much out here," Steve yelled. "You need to go further inland."

"Shit."

As Reg brought the boat around and closer to the cabin, she directed the LED spotlight towards it. It was a gorgeous two-story pine cabin with a red steel roof. It was nestled into Olympic National Park on three sides and positioned right on the lake, two miles from the Fairholme General Store, and offered privacy and seclusion. There were double decks and a boathouse with a dock. No interior lights were on in the cabin but there was a fifteen-foot fishing boat bobbing up and down, tied to the dock.

"Can you pull up closer to the dock?" Kara asked.

Reg nodded and brought it in. Kara continued to try and get a signal on her phone but there was nothing. "Listen, do me a favor when you get back to the boat launch, I need you to call Clallam County and ask for Noah Goodman. Tell him where I am. You got that?"

Reg extended an open hand.

"Oh you have got to be kidding me?"

Steve ambled up to the front and slapped it. "Forget money. We'll do it."

"I was just joking," Reg said as she motioned for Ray to climb out of the boat. They hopped on to the rickety wooden dock and it shifted slightly below their feet. She'd considered having Ray go with the three men but with the chance that he might offer some insight into where the boy might be, she opted to keep him close. The rain was now starting to come down harder, splattering against the landscape, blanketing the ground and making the dock slick.

Chapter 41

The smell of pine was heavy in the air as they walked side by side up the dock. Kara looked back at the boat as it kicked up water then disappeared into the night. Further up the slope, an ancient oak spread its low-hanging limbs over the home like an outstretched hand. Their footsteps were lost in the rustle of leaves and the howling wind. The dock turned sharply to the right and led up to the rear of the home. There were four windows that were covered by drapes, and French-style sliding doors.

Kara raised a hand and they crouched a short distance from the windows, waiting. No movement could be heard outside, or even from the house. Farther up, around the house, she could just make out through the trees an SUV, blue, a Ford Explorer. She certainly didn't recognize it. If there was no one out front or around the back, whoever owned it had to be in the cabin. But with all the noise of the boat, why hadn't anyone come out?

Kara reached into her jacket to retrieve her Glock. She did a routine check to make sure the magazine was loaded, and a round was in the chamber, before she turned back to Ray who was shivering. There was little shelter outside except from the overhanging parts of the home, and a few large leafy branches. She shuffled close to Ray. "You picking up on anything? Got any impressions?"

She had no idea how his gifting worked, or even if it was a gifting. For all she knew, he was playing her, and this was all one big act to draw her into some trap. It wouldn't have been the first time criminals had lied to her. Still, something about the way he acted led her to believe he was telling the truth. Ray shook his head, the features of his face twisting in fear. Kara tugged at his arm and indicated where she was heading. He shook his head and cowered back.

"Okay, stay here. Don't move, you understand?" She felt like she was talking to a kid. He still hadn't shown signs that his IQ was anything higher than a child's. Moving forward at a crouch, she scurried to the rear windows of the cabin and peered past the drapes. Noticing there was no movement inside, she pressed on, tiptoeing her way over to the French doors. She pressed her ear to the glass, and strained to hear sounds but heard nothing. No voices, no creaking floorboards, no TV or music.

As soon as she was certain it was all clear she reached up and took hold of the handle and pushed the door. It was unlocked. Perfect.

She glanced back at Ray and gave him the thumbs-up.

Kara kept her service weapon low and entered.

It was dark inside, so dark that she had no other option than to switch on the Maglite. Holding it with her left hand, and her Glock with her right, she scanned the carpeted room that joined to an open kitchen and dining area. To the left of her were several pieces of furniture; a patterned couch, a single armchair, a small table with an old-style boxy TV, some odd-looking artwork on the pine paneled walls, and a fireplace stove in the corner. To the right there was worn vinyl flooring, with a long dining table with six green cushioned chairs, and a kitchen that looked dated. A set of carpeted steps at the far side of the room disappeared up to a second floor. There were also two doors, one that led out to the east side of the home, and one she assumed opened up the front of the cabin. She tried the light switch on the wall but there was no power. As Kara moved inside, a floorboard creaked beneath her feet.

She tried the door ahead of her.

Kara stepped to one side, turned the knob and eased it open. It groaned, its age revealing itself. She was about to step forward when she heard a creak above her. Kara backed up and peered around to the staircase. Her heart was hammering in her chest, her hands sweating and pulse racing. The night she was fourteen played over and over in her mind — the looming figure, the flash of a knife, his gravelly threatening voice. She slapped the past away as she approached the steps and began to climb. Her gun arm was out, just under her line of vision. It swung with her head as she pressed her back to the wall and went up. She'd only made it five steps when the sound of boots pounding the second floor startled her. It was fast. She hurried up just in time to see a large figure head out the sliding doors and jump over the balcony. The word "stop!" came out as a croak before she followed after the figure.

"Kara!" She heard his voice come from behind. It came out like a whisper. Kara swiveled fast, her arms shaking. She had to will her breathing to slow down or she was liable to bring on a panic attack. She peered over the edge of the balcony to see if she could make out Ray. Fortunately he was still there, slightly hidden by low-hanging branches. She could just make out the tip of his boots. Whoever jumped over would have been seen by Ray.

Back inside the house, she heard her name again, this time she was able to get a bead on it. It was coming from the ground level. She hurried down the steps, her mouth dry, eyes darting back and forth, fixating on every shadow.

The beam of the flashlight swept the room picking up the silhouettes of furniture like a lighthouse beam washing over the rocky shore. As she turned into the corridor that led down to where there were bedrooms, she caught a glimpse of him, then he moved. In the darkness all she could make out was his silhouette but it was enough. Enough to know him. Enough to remember that night. Fear shot through her paralyzing her to the spot. Years of training went out the window. In that moment she wasn't a grizzled veteran but a fourteen-year-old, a terrified girl reliving a horrifying event. Seconds felt like minutes as she stood there. Her flight-or-fight instincts kicked in and her mind waged a war. Torn between wanting to flee or instead face her fear, she remained fixed to the spot. It was only the sound of a desperate scream that snapped her out of the trancelike state.

A memory from her time in the academy. A moment when they showed a video of a police officer running into a school while kids were running out after a shooting, and the words of her instructor saying — that will be you. *You go in when others will run out. That's what you've signed up for.*

She swallowed hard, took a deep breath and moved forward making her way to the top of the stairwell. As she turned and shone her flashlight down into the pit of the basement she had to summon every ounce of courage to go down. Her training taught her to call for backup but with zero signal and without having seen a landline phone in the house, she was going to have to hope Reg and his buddies made the call. Right now the life of a kid was hanging in the balance.

Another scream, this time Kara didn't hesitate.

Keeping her gun out in front, angled down, and her

back to the bannister she kept the light washing over the darkness beneath her. Six steps. That's all she'd taken when she felt a jab to the back of one foot. It was so sudden, sharp and painful she lost her footing and tumbled down the steps. The flashlight shot out of her hands but somehow she managed to keep a grip on the Glock. It was the only thing that saved her. Hitting the ground, she saw movement heading towards her. A dark mass appeared out from behind the staircase. Kara fired a round, and the muzzle flash lit up the damp-smelling room.

Boots pounded the ground, darting in between pillars which supported the upper levels. She gasped, her left ribs felt like they were fractured. Every breath was harder than the last. "Ashton Cole!" Kara yelled out. A muffled cry came from her left, further back in the dingy unfinished basement. Kara struggled to get up. Her flashlight was still on, two feet away from her. As she moved to collect it, he ran at her. She turned and fired, and backed up to the wall trying to get a bead on him. The only light came from the moon, and it was barely filtering through the paint-covered windows. Someone had attempted to blot out the light. Kara tried to control her breathing. *Get a grip.* Nervously her eyes whipped from side to side like windshield wipers. Searching. Listening.

A figure flashed past her field of vision, she turned fast but he was gone. She heard him ascend the steps disappearing upstairs. Just about to take off after him, she heard more muffled cries. Kara shone the light to the back of the room. There in the darkness the light washed over a boy tied to a support beam, with his mouth gagged. Kara hurried over, her only thought going through her mind was to get him out. He was sobbing, and he let out a loud muffled cry as she dropped to a knee. His hands were bound with thin rope, and his arms wrapped around a steel beam.

"Ashton?"

He nodded.

"It's okay, you're safe now."

His cries didn't stop, they were so loud as she untied his hands that she didn't hear her attacker approach. A plastic bag went over her face and she was yanked back so fast, the gun slipped out of her hand. Kara reached up, gasping and clawing at the plastic as she was dragged across the concrete basement like a rag doll. Through the blur of plastic, and her breath fogging up the inside, she could just make out her attacker.

It was too dark.

Panic overtook her, sending her into desperation.

Her attacker didn't say anything to her but continued to drag her until he released her, kicking her into a roll across the room. The plastic came off and she gasped for air. Why? Why hadn't he killed her? He had her where he wanted her. He was in full control.

Control.

That's what this was about.

He was taunting her. Dragging it out. Relishing the fear he was instilling in her.

As she lay on the ground trying to catch her breath she saw him scoop up her service weapon. "You know you have more fight in you than your mother did." He scoffed. "Then again she had tetrodotoxin running through her system. It's interesting how the body reacts to it at a high dosage. It paralyzes you, but you can still feel pain. Now I figure they'll find it in the toxicology report, but by then it will be too late. And with your mother's history of depression, I doubt it will make news."

She recognized that voice. It was no longer masked by a voice scrambler or gritted teeth. It was familiar. She squinted into the dark and watched as he removed the magazine from the gun and tossed it near the staircase, then tossed the gun on the ground.

"I never liked guns. Too noisy. Too easy. Too quick." He paused. "Now a knife." He withdrew a large blade from a sheath on the side of his belt, the moon's light filtering through the small window glinted off it. "That's just full of potential."

Chapter 42

"Benson?" The figure stepped into the band of silvery light and pulled back the hood on his jacket. There before her was Lloyd Benson. "I gave you plenty of opportunity but you wouldn't listen. Like mother like daughter." He walked forward stopping a short distance away. "You probably have a lot of questions and I would love to answer them. Damn, I would give anything for one more session with you but if you found me, I'm guessing Goodman isn't that far behind. Of course when they find this place, the kid and me will be long gone. And the cabin? Up in flames. But if they dig through the ash, they'll eventually find the owner, and you of course."

Kara groaned as she crawled up onto her elbows. "Why? That's all I want to know."

He offered back a thin smile. "You don't want to know why. You just want freedom from the guilt and grief." He stared back at her then glanced at his wristwatch. "They all did. It was fascinating to hear in their own words, to meet with them as the years rolled by and to watch their sons."

She stared back, her brow furrowed.

"You gave counseling to all the parents, didn't you?"

He scoffed. "Don't act like you didn't know." He

jabbed the knife in the air. “All these years, all the investigations, all those parents and yet only one of them got close. You know, when your mother started to piece together that I might be behind it, I actually developed an admiration for her. Here was a parent stricken by the same five stages of grief: denial, anger, bargaining, depression and acceptance, and yet she never moved into acceptance. Interesting, really.”

He walked over and crouched down beside her holding the blade close to her face. Kara could see her reflection in it. The look of misery on her face. He had to be getting off on this. “Now Charlie. I had no idea how long I would keep him alive. He was my first, you know. Three wonderful years. That’s how long I kept him alive.” He scoffed and fixed his gaze on her. “I want you to know I never touched him. None of them. Sexually I mean. That didn’t interest me. No, you see, Kara, there is only so much they can teach you about therapy. It’s interesting to hear, but fascinating to see up close. The best teacher is experience. But to heal deep wounds, one must know intimately both sides of the coin. The cause, and symptoms, they’re all the same. But no two people are alike, you see.” He tapped the blade against the side of her cheek, and she felt the cool metal graze her as he pulled it away. “And of course there is no set time on how long grief can last. Four weeks, six months, five years. And even then some will still have unresolved grief. We usually only see one side. But to see both, is marvelous."

"You're sick," she said.

"Am I?" He laughed. "As it seems you are the one still attached to the past, a slave to meds and unable to let go." He glanced at the elastic band around her wrist then back at her. "But I'm going to help you." He tapped his teeth together. "But first, tell me how you knew it was me?"

"I didn't."

"Don't lie," he bellowed, his tone full of venom. "Do you honestly think you're smarter?" He pressed the blade hard against her throat. "Just one small cut to the artery and it's over."

"Ray Owen. He drew sketches of this place."

His brow pinched, a look of disbelief. "Come on. You expect me to believe in that psychic mumbo jumbo?"

Above them a floorboard creaked.

Lloyd's eye flicked up. A momentary distraction was all Kara needed. In one fast, smooth movement, she latched on to his wrist with both hands, twisted and wheeled her leg around over his head, and brought him crashing down. Years of self-defense experience through the academy played out with little thinking involved. Benson collapsed, letting out a lungful of air. She reacted so quickly he didn't know what had hit him until he was lying on his back with her legs wrapped over his throat like an anaconda. She yanked on the knife hand causing him to scream in agony. The elbow popped up, and she continued holding him in an armbar. She had only one intention, and that was to break it. He struggled like a gazelle within her grip, cursing, screaming, and refusing to release his grip on the knife.

But like attempting to fight gravity, it was pointless, within seconds it snapped, and she twisted his arm around into an unnatural position. She shook the hand until the knife flew out, sliding across the ground beneath furniture. Kara rolled off him and stumbled to her feet, tired from attacking him. She glanced over to see him reeling around on the ground like a pitiful fish out of water. She hurried over and tried to reach for the knife but it was too far back. Kara scrambled to her feet and scanned the ground looking for the gun but in the darkness it was hard to see. She looked back at him crying out in agony on his knees, gripping his arm which was flopping around. Was this really the man that had once struck fear into her heart? *Screw you, asshole!* Kara hurried over to Ashton and started to untie the binds around his ankles. They were bound tight. The binding wrapped around his legs multiple times, and the knots were small. She cast a glance at Lloyd still reeling in pain before focusing on getting the knots loose. The last thing to pull away was his mouth gag. Just as she pried it away he yelled.

"Watch out!"

Kara jerked her head in time to see a plank of wood collide with her face sending her sideways. The sting of pain, and the clatter of wood were the last things she remembered. When she came to, she could smell gasoline, and hear it being splashed over the ground. Her eyelids fluttered, the world was sideways then it corrected itself. Lloyd was struggling to empty a large gasoline can under one arm. He dropped it and kicked it letting the rest flood out across the ground. She kept going in and out of consciousness. Each time, Lloyd got further away, and the liquid got closer. He forced the boy up the stairs, his wrists rebound. With another metal canister full of gasoline under one arm he emptied it down the stairs as he backed up. Kara groaned. Her head was throbbing. Painful flashes of light blurred her vision. Before her was her brother, his face, his words. "Get up. Get up!"

"Charlie? Charlie," she muttered.

Her eyes kept closing. It felt like she was caught between the here and after.

Using every ounce of strength she had left she clawed up onto her knees and rose to her feet, staggering like a drunk. She leaned against the pillar trying to see clearly. Blood trickled down from her forehead into her eyes. From where she stood she could just make out the lower half of Lloyd's legs as he backed out while flooding the basement with gasoline. Her eyes scanned the ground watching the gasoline fill every inch of the basement; the fumes stung her nostrils.

Kara stumbled forward and spotted the gun. She scooped it up but it was missing the magazine. He'd tossed it over by the staircase. As she made her way over, Lloyd looked down, a glint of amusement in his face as he saw her searching for the magazine.

"It's too late, Kara. Time to join your mother and brother. Send them my regards."

Lloyd had just reached the top when he turned to head out.

A loud whack, like the sound of something hard hitting something solid, and Lloyd stumbled back, lost his footing and careened down the steps, toppling over until he landed at the bottom, groaning in agony, blood seeping from his head.

Kara looked up to see Ray, holding a solid-looking light stand.

She gave a strained smile.

Unable to find the magazine, Kara stepped over Lloyd and made her way up the steps. When she reached the top, she looked back down to see him crawling up two of the steps. Blood was streaming from the side of his face, covering it in scarlet red.

"I made you who you are!" he said.

Kara glanced down at the gun in her hand without the magazine before dropping it. She fished into her pocket and pulled the Zippo lighter she'd carried with her since that night, she snapped it open, a flame breathed to life. She stared down at him, rage consuming her. Lloyd's eyes widened as she flung his own words back at him. "I never liked guns. Too noisy. Too easy. Too quick."

Before stepping out of the basement she tossed the lighter.

As she closed the door behind her, she heard the whoosh of fire as the gasoline ignited setting fire to everything including Lloyd Benson.

His screams were the last thing she heard.

All three of them hurried out the front of the house and made their way over to the SUV. Within seconds flames crept up turning the once beautiful cabin by the lake into an inferno. Kara had just opened the passenger side door on the truck when Lloyd burst out of the main entrance, his entire body on fire, screaming. Kara's heart leapt into her throat as he rushed forward then collapsed, and fire consumed what remained of his charred flesh.

They stood there for several minutes transfixed as if expecting him to move again. He didn't. The flames from the house licked up into the night, filling the air with smoke and debris. In the distance the sound of a chopper could be heard, and police sirens wailing.

Chapter 43

Seventy-two hours later

After being cleared to leave Blackmore General Hospital, Kara unfolded a copy of the *Peninsula Daily News* left on the chair inside the treatment room. The front page featured a long article by Bobby on the end to a twenty-five year mystery. There was so much to cover it would be the first of many he and many other journalists would write. Social media was buzzing with gossip, rumors, and speculation as television crews from all over the country descended upon Washington State. Lloyd Benson would hog the news for weeks after they sifted through his life. In the short time she'd been in the hospital the media had already begun to unravel Benson's history, starting with his arrival in Clallam County back in the late seventies.

Unlike other mass murderers, his life wasn't filled in with clichéd stories of an abusive upbringing, lonely teenage years or heavy alcoholism. By all accounts he was a stand-out pupil who had come from a well-to-do Midwestern family. He'd excelled and earned a scholarship to Harvard, graduated with honors and had gone on to establish a successful therapy business with a proven track record. He'd written many papers that had earned him the admiration of his peers and even caused him for a short time to give talks around the country. On the surface he led a charmed life, and yet it wasn't enough; deep below he harbored a dark secret.

That's why so many found it hard to believe he was responsible.

Slowly but surely, as news spread, people came out of the woodwork to give statements. Family, friends and neighbors were unable to grasp that he was behind the abductions. Like anyone blindsided by the actions of those close to them, shock and disbelief dominated their response. *He was such a kind gentleman, always helpful. That wasn't the man I knew. He assisted me through troubling times,* they'd said. The community was baffled, outraged and horrified that a monster could live among them — but that was the thing about the depraved and insane. Bundy, Gacy, Dahmer, the worst didn't appear as monsters but just ordinary people, those who could blend in with society, walk the streets without turning heads. They had a natural ability to put a person at ease.

Playing quietly behind Kara on the TV, a national news show tore apart the case, debated and sought the advice of psychologists as they tried to understand how a man could be driven to kill out of a twisted desire to understand the human psyche. With Benson dead, so many questions remained unanswered; as did the belief that the motive wasn't sexual. It was too hard for some to wrap their heads around so tabloids twisted the truth to create their own narrative.

She switched the channel and landed on local news. In the past twenty-four hours the crime team had uncovered the bones of Charlie and the other four boys. They were found at the bottom of a dry well on the property, mixed together with soil, tossed away like they were nothing but trash.

"How you feeling?"

Kara jumped at the sound of a voice behind her.

It was Noah. She smiled and rubbed her forehead. "I've felt better. The doctor said I suffered a mild concussion."

He glanced at the paper in her hand as he handed her a coffee from the vending machine. She took a sip and winced before placing it on the side table.

"Hard to believe it's over, isn't it?" he said.

She jerked her head towards the TV. "I'm not sure it will ever be."

"Ah, give it some time. He'll soon become back-page fodder. They always do."

Noah looked at her with a warm smile and looked as if he was about to say something. Kara quickly said, "I see the Claytons have flown under the radar." She turned the page and tapped a small article. The crime of sexual assaults on young boys dating back to the mid '80s was overshadowed by the recent event.

"It's all about timing, I guess. But don't worry;

they'll be doing some serious time for sure. Darryl Clayton didn't admit to it but the evidence found on his property, witness testimonials and DNA will give his lawyers one hell of a tough job in court." He paused. "Speaking of DNA. It seems your brother's jeans and shoe were still in the evidence archives. It took a while to find them but it looks like Harris might finally see his day in court."

She turned back to the TV and flipped through the channels.

"I would have thought you had enough of hearing about Benson."

"It's not him I'm interested in, it's Kyle Harris."

Noah nodded. "Well even though it's still early days and they have some red tape to cut through, I can tell you through the grapevine that the wheels are in motion to have him exonerated."

"You made the call to his lawyer?"

"The same day you asked."

She smiled and breathed in deeply.

Silence stretched between them as she continued channel surfing.

"Talking about being exonerated, I dropped the appeal."

"Against Sarah Carter?"

He bounced his head from side to side, then shrugged. "I could say she's served her time. But the truth is, I've served mine." He took a deep breath. "You were right, I can't change the past but I can prevent it from holding on to me. Besides, Amanda wouldn't have wanted it."

Kara tapped him lightly on the chest and offered a thin smile.

"So I guess you're heading back to New York?" he asked.

"Yes, this evening. I have a conversation with my kid that is long overdue, and there is a little matter of doing an exit interview."

"Exit interview?"

She nodded. "I decided to leave my position in New York."

His brow pinched. "Really?"

She waited a second before dropping it on him.

"They've accepted me in Washington State."

A smile formed on his face.

"Geez Louise. Does that mean I have to put up with you in my neck of the woods?"

She grinned. "I'm afraid so. But look at it like this, the only time I'll be in your hair is when County calls for assistance from the agency."

"That's the only time?" he asked.

She scratched the side of her face. "Well that and the nights I stay over," she said without looking at him.

She heard him scoff. Right then her father ambled into the room.

He gave a nod to Noah. "So hon, you ready to leave?

We need to be on the road if we're going to make it to the airport in time."

"Sure, I'll be right there. Just give me a minute," she said turning and scooping up her bag. Her father gave a nod then left, leaving Noah and her alone. Kara switched off the TV and placed the remote on the side table and looked at him. "While I'm gone, would you check in on him from time to time?"

"Sure, I'll do that."

She headed for the door, stopped and tapped her fingers against the frame. "Oh, and Noah," she smiled as she pointed. "You know, you've got mustard on your tie."

He glanced down but there was nothing there. When he looked up she winked.

Epilogue

A year later

Sitting around the breakfast table that morning, Noah poured coffee into a silver flask as her teenage son came trudging into the kitchen with a dilemma. Ethan held up two Halloween costumes. “Mom, what do you think? Should I go as the skeleton or Deadpool?”

So much had changed in a year. After she moved back to Clallam County, Noah had moved in with her and the horrors of Lloyd Benson and that night were slowly becoming a distant memory.

“Deadpool, all the way,” Noah said.

His brow pinched. “Really?”

“Oh yeah, it’s way cooler!” Noah said running a hand over his head before leaning down and giving Kara a peck on the cheek. “Catch you guys this evening, okay?”

She twisted in her seat. “Noah, you know where to go?”

“The community center.”

“And the time.”

“Seven.”

“And you’ll remember to wear a costume, right?”

"Of course." He crouched and scratched under their dog Riley's chin before heading off to work. She'd taken the day off from her position as an investigative agent with the Criminal Investigations Division of Washington State Patrol. That year the parents in the community had decided to put on a joint event as a way to keep the spirit of Halloween alive in light of all that happened over the years. Kara had been asked to say a few words. Even though her workload had increased since moving, she'd promised Ethan they'd spend the day together and she was determined to not let anything stand in the way.

"So?" Ethan asked.

"Deadpool," she said not missing a beat.

"Mom, you didn't even look."

"I don't need to. It's a given."

She had no idea what kids were into nowadays but it was easier than ending up in a twenty-minute debate. He muttered something and ambled away. Kara took another sip of her coffee, and jerked her head to Riley. They headed out to the mailbox to collect the mail. A cool October breeze blew leaves across the ground. Kara stuffed a hand into the black box and pulled out a wad of mail. She sifted through the flyers on the way back to the house until she fished out a white envelope. It stood out because the return address was for a lawyer's office in Blackmore. It also had no stamp, leading her to believe someone had dropped it off.

"Come on, boy," she said, calling to her golden Lab. He bounded up the driveway, chasing brown and golden leaves that blew along the ground like tumbleweed. She thumbed it open and pulled out a letter then took a seat in her porch rocker.

Dear Kara,

By the time you read this letter I will have been exonerated and released. I have chosen not to move back to Blackmore for obvious reasons but in some ways a part of me will always remain there. After spending a large portion of my life in prison I am no longer young but I have my health, my family and God willing many years ahead of me. Twenty years locked up inside a cell gives a person a lot of time to think. For so long I was bitter, angry and held a grudge against everyone for what was stolen from me. I pushed away my own family and lost myself in the misery. I think I would have still been there had it not been for your mother. As strange as it might sound I realized after meeting her that I wasn't the only one imprisoned. Whether she believed in my innocence or not, didn't matter, she showed me a kindness that few did, at a time when society had turned its back and for which I'm forever grateful. Her visits meant a lot. I no longer felt alone or without hope.

When you visited me last year, you once again reminded me of that. At that time I forgot to tell you something she had shared a few weeks before her death. She said it wasn't just her son that had been stolen from her but her daughter. Her grief had blinded her to see what she still had, who she still had, and her visits with me had somehow reminded her of that. She said she was proud of you, and who you'd become and had hoped to tell you in person. If she never got around to telling you, I hope at least hearing it now will bring you peace.

Lastly, I wanted to ask if I might send flowers to Anna's grave. If you would rather I didn't, I would understand. Either way, thank you again for all you did.

Kind regards,
Kyle Harris

Kara wiped tears from her cheeks then drew in a deep breath. She glanced up into the morning sky and felt a heaviness she'd been carrying for years leave her shoulders. She wrote him back that day to tell him the plot number in Blackmore Cemetery where Anna was buried next to Charlie.

Later that morning Kara took Ethan to their graves, cleared away the fall leaves, brown and crinkled by the cold, and laid a fresh bouquet of carnations, her mother's favorite. Crouched there in the silence, staring at the tombstones, she thought about Harris's letter.

"I got your message, Mom." A strained smile

formed. “A little late but like you always said, better late than never.”

She wiped a tear. “We did it. I couldn’t have done it without you.”

Then as if Ethan instinctively picked up on her grief, he crouched, wrapped his arm around her shoulder and gave her a squeeze. “It’s okay, Mom,” he said, resting his head against her shoulder. “I’m still here.”

She turned, slowly smiled and said, “Yeah. Yes you are.”

* * *

THANK YOU FOR READING

I’m Still Here.

If you enjoyed this, try Lost Girls

Please take a second to leave a review, it’s really appreciated. Thanks kindly, Jon.

JON MILLS

Jon Mills is originally from England. He currently lives in Ontario, Canada with his family. He is the author of The Debt Collector series, Lost Girls, I'm Still Here, The Promise, True Connection, and the Undisclosed Trilogy. To get more information about upcoming books or if you wish to get in touch with Jon, you can do so using the following contact information:

Twitter: Jon_Mills

Facebook: authorjonmills

Website: www.jonmills.com

Email: contact@jonmills.com

Made in the USA
Monee, IL
20 December 2021

86699445R00236